TANGLED WEB
A NOVEL

By

PAMELA WILLIAMS-GUINN

Mr. House,
Thank you for your
support. Many Blessings to
you from one visionary
to another!!.
Pamela Williams-Guinn

Note from the author: This is a work of fiction. All of the characters, incidents, and dialogue, except for incidental references to public figures, products or services, are a product of the authors imagination and are not intended to refer to any living or dead person.

Printed in the United States by
Morris Publishing • 3212 East Highway 30 • Kearney, NE 68847
1-800-650-7888

i

Acknowledgments

I'd first like to give all praises to God who gave me the wisdom, discipline and good people in my path just as I asked Him at the beginning of this journey.

Thanks to my editor, Maxine E. Thompson, who always referred to the writing process as 'giving birth'. You were right and I couldn't have had this baby without you, girl!

Special thanks to Elton and Associates Publishing who believed in me from day one. I couldn't have made it without my literary sisters, Camille Lyles Akbari (Artist) and Anfra Boyd (Author and Poet). Friends with great minds are hard to come by. Thanks!

Thanks to the people who allowed me to probe into their personal and professional lives for research: Memphis Fire Station #52, Thank you!

My deepest love and gratitude are to my parents, Herman and Gloria Williams. Without them, I would not be who I am.

I love you Shawn, Derek and Pam! Thanks for your patience when I stayed on the computer for hours at a time and didn't cook dinner. I did it for you guys!

Thanks to all of my family in Petersburg, Virginia and all of my friends, long time customers, and everyone at Fairley High School who supported me. Thanks 'L', you always said my imagination was wild enough to write a book.

Many Blessings to you all!

For
Lovette, Shawn, Derek and Pamela
I Love You

And in loving memory of
Brandon Owens-Wallace
(1994 - 2000)

PROLOGUE

"*I*'m warning you, for the final time," Savannah hissed into the receiver, "Stay away from my husband!"

"No. You tell your husband to stay away from me," said Pretty Baby. "Yeah, that's it," she challenged, "See if you can keep your husband away from me. "I was just with him, and he's gone home to see if he can straighten out this confusion with the Langley account.

"I'm tired of you knowing every move my husband makes," Savannah spat. She narrowed her eyes, realizing what had just been said. "And what would someone like **you** know about the Langley account?"

That 'someone like you' comment was not appreciated but it was imperative that Pretty Baby kept her cool and the upper hand in this confrontation. She just calmly replied, "Actually, I don't know a thing about the Langley account." She caught a glimpse of herself in her bedroom mirror. Her usually cool exterior, not looking so cool. In fact, it was startling to know how evilness and hell raising came so easily. "All I know is where he's going, what he's doing and where he's headed afterwards!" Pretty Baby yelled in a take that manner. "Yes, girlfriend, I know what you do know and everything you don't know. I even know what kind of underwear you wear and he doesn't like it." She was on a roll now. "Always shopping for comfort, never to please. You'd think an old broad like yourself would know better." This was becoming humorous, being able to get under this woman's skin.

"You're nothing but a whore. A slut who can't even get her own man," Savannah yelled.

"And maybe if you knew how to please your man you wouldn't have this problem," Pretty Baby rebelled. The confrontation accelerated until the two women could no longer hear each other. "Listen! I did not set out to steal your husband, but he has feelings too. And all during your illness..."

"My illness?" Savannah interrupted. So that's it, you try to build something for yourself out of someone else's misfortune?"

"Of course not," Pretty Baby shook her head profusely, feeling maybe, this would be her only chance to explain. "All during your illness that man stuck by you. Not just for a little while, but for years." She ran her fingers through her hair as her head started to feel like a giant weight on her shoulders that her neck could barely support. "As time went on, he met me....and we fell in love," she let out a breath, "I guess I was what brought him back around. And at the time I needed someone." That victorious feeling was fading fast and a tinge of insecurity came rushing back. "There was a strain on your relationship before your accident, but to show how dedicated he was, he stayed by your side. You've never stopped to think about the length of time he's been alone."

"You don't know what I thought about or what went on here at our house," Savannah screamed. "You... are just a LOW LIFE WHORE!"

"No, no, no, Honey. You've got me and the situation all wrong," Pretty Baby said wickedly. "He's not the kind of man who has an affair or just sleeps around for the hell of it. He's the kind of man that falls in love, and probably any problems you have now didn't start with me and they won't end with me." Her temper was rising again and the vindictiveness reappearing. "I won't take your husband from you," she paused, searching for the right words to make it count, "because no matter what happens, my presence will always exist. So I don't have to take him."

"I'm warning you," Savannah's voice cracked with tears. "He doesn't want you."

"You wish he didn't. Let me tell you something. Keep your tired ass warnings for him and your private investigator. It's you that he doesn't want but he's willing to put his happiness to the side because I guess he feels that he owes you that much. Plus they always say, it's cheaper to keep her." Pretty Baby laughed sarcastically.

Savannah slowly tried to pull all the strength she could find to fight this woman who, to some degree, spoke the truth about her personal life. There was a long silence on the phone. All that she could think was that she was about to slip over the edge... again. Her shoulders heaved uncontrollably because everything was out of her control, including her husband's love. Finally she said, "I didn't come this far in life to let someone like you tear me down. I pray," Savannah managed between mournful sobs, "that all this pain that you two have put on me will come back on you. You may not feel it now, but God will whip you in the worst kind of way, when you least expect it. Take heed to my warning," she said in a barely audible whisper.

Savannah's words were chilling.

Pretty Baby slammed the phone down. "She is one sick woman!" she said out loud, looking around the room wildly. Her hands were still trembling. She sat in disbelief as thoughts ran back and forth through her mind. She had been threatened with a lot of things, but never with God. This brought on a reality check, and a lot of the truth was starting to hurt. Pretty Baby stood, her face streaked with tears, and looked out of her bedroom window. Something so right was turning out to be so wrong. Out of the corner of her eye she could see a spider crawling to the far end of the window. She despised creepy crawly things with their antennas and their unknowing rapid movements. Carefully, she watched as it made its way to the web that had been spun in the other corner. Pretty Baby peered closer at the well-crafted silken strings to see another species of bug fighting for his life in the tangled web. She could suddenly see herself in that same predicament. It reminded her of the old Shakespearean quote: *Oh, what a tangled web we weave, when first we practice to deceive.* Sobs racked her body as she destroyed the web with her slipper in order to save the bug from its predator. Slinging the shoe across the room, she lay on the bed and sobbed. This didn't feel like the victory that was anticipated after all.

Tangled Web

*"The fear of the Lord is the beginning of knowledge:
but fools despise wisdom and instruction."*
Proverbs 1:7

The day before Pretty Baby was scheduled to go to her doctor's appointment, she stood in her Aunt Becky's yard arguing with her Uncle Hubert about something trivial, which was totally unlike herself. She finally went into the house carrying her animosity along where Missy, her cousin and best friend, was about to sample some of Aunt Becky's homemade stew. Pretty Baby immediately started in on Missy about a pair of shoes she hadn't returned.

"I told you I was getting the heel replaced. That's why I hadn't returned the darn shoes," Missy protested.

"That was a month ago." Pretty Baby put her hands on her hips and snapped her head around. "I get sick and tired . . ."

"Now wait one minute!" Aunt Becky said, coming

1

into the kitchen, "Pretty Baby, you not gon' take your problems out on other folks."

"I'm not taking my problems out on other folks. I just want my shoes," she pouted, then turned to leave, in a huff.

Aunt Becky and Missy stared at Pretty Baby's back as she made her way from the kitchen and out the door of the narrow shot gun house.

"She act like she gone crazy or something," Missy sipped her soup with a laugh. "When I pulled up, she was out there arguing with Hubert saying he borrowed her lawn mower and now it ain't running right. That second hand thing ain't never ran right!"

"Ain't nothin' wrong with that gal but pregnant." Aunt Becky shook her head with worry. "I believe it was last Friday she carried me down town, and she was carryin' on so…mad 'bout somethin' with her husband and yellin' at them boys 'til I said, 'ya'll go on, I'll catch the bus back home'. I looked at her good before I got out the car and suspected it then."

"Ugh," Missy rolled her eyes, "I guess I'd go crazy too if I was married to a loser like William."

Aunt Becky shot Missy a 'you not the one to talk' look and went back to her cooking.

The next day Dr. Carter confirmed that Pretty Baby was indeed pregnant. She was depressed beyond belief and ashamed to speak it out loud. Abortion crossed her mind but she couldn't do it, her conscious wouldn't let her.

She didn't tell William at first. Day after day she walked around the track of the University, crying out to the Lord for guidance. Finally, she shared the news with her husband. His voice was filled with love and concern but his actions immediately demonstrated differently. Two months of lies and broken promises had gone by when Pretty Baby got up one morning, careful not to wake William or the children, and went over to the track to get her daily dose of tranquility.

The early morning sun greeted her as she began her walk. That day she didn't cry out, but instead, walked at a steady pace with her heart and her mind open. For many years she had been in denial about the agony of her marriage. It wasn't right. Had never been right and she didn't want to be a part of it any more. Through prayer and tapping into a higher energy on a bona fide quest to seek the truth, she realized that divorce was not the unforgivable sin. It wasn't the best thing, but she knew if she could find it deep in her heart to forgive William's transgressions, she could break free. It would be okay to dissolve the situation and start anew. *Forgiveness was the key,* Aunt Becky's words echoed in her ears.

After her walk, she sat on her car listening to the birds chirp and the rustling of the trees in the wind. She listened with all of her heart then got in her car and drove straight to her Attorneys office.

Three months later after her visit with her attorney, and paying a retainer's fee for the divorce without William's knowledge, Pretty Baby had had enough of him. She pulled into the first available parking space in front of Central Hardware sitting in the car for a moment, feeling sweat trickle down her chest and then over the big hump of a belly that lay in her lap. The heat was suffocating as she took a deep breath realizing how still the hot air was.

3

Pamela Williams-Guinn

It was Mother's Day and she couldn't remember it ever being this hot in May. She squinted her eyes to see the towering digital clock beside the bank. It rotated around, one side blinking 12:18, the other flashing 102 degrees. She wanted to jump right out of her old Electra 225 and run into the air-conditioned store. Pretty Baby ran her hand under the seat in search of the screwdriver that was substituted as the door handle. After an interminable thirty seconds of suffering the heat, pulling out other lost objects and breaking a perfectly manicured nail, she finally had her hands on it. The screwdriver had to be put in just the right position; then giving the door an extra shove with her foot, she climbed out.

The conversation came to a stop between two men standing at the entrance of the store when Pretty Baby walked up. One of them rushed to open the door for her, nodding his head with respect. Even though Pretty Baby was five months pregnant, men still gave her second glances. She had an air of lively intelligence that gave her an aura of confidence. She carried her pregnancy well.

Everything about her was feminine, from her delicately decorated pink toes to her naturally wavy short hair. But underneath that angelic face, no one would ever know how heavy her heart truly was and that she was about to make some changes that would inevitably change her life as well as the lives of her two, almost three, children.

Scanning the middle row, then the top, she finally saw what she came for. "Give me a six foot chain, two combination locks and two dead bolt locks, please," she

4

Tangled Web

said trying to look unconcerned.

The clerk didn't find her request unusual, but the sad look in her eyes was an indication of some type of trouble. "Anything else for you, Ma'am?"

Pretty Baby shook her head, concealing the tear that was about to escape. She paid for her things and went home.

It was Mothers Day, and instead of being fired up over the powerful sermon Pastor Lindley had preached earlier that day and overjoyed at the 'Greatest Mom in the World' T-shirt her sons had given her, her life still seemed incomplete and unfulfilled. On her drive home she couldn't help but beat up on herself about all the years wasted on a bad marriage. But she thanked God for the strength to make such a drastic change at this time in her life. The unexpected pregnancy made her take a long look at the situation.

William was working like always, and it would never have crossed his mind to take off on Mother's Day to spend quality time with his family. His lack of concern hurt like hell, but Pretty Baby had somewhere along the way become immune to William's ignorance. She couldn't remember exactly when or how this change of mindset had come about, but it had, and today would be the finale.

Pretty Baby moved the warm holiday evening along quickly, getting dinner and the boys out of the way. After clearing the dinner dishes, she set out to complete her mission. Her mind traveled back on how a year ago no one could have told her she would be pregnant with her third child and getting a divorce.

Her first mistake was when she met William Casey

5

at one of the popular dance spots. One like those that she had never been allowed to go to while growing up. It was one summer night, after Friday evening prayer meeting. She and Missy told Aunt Becky they were going to a surprise birthday party for a friend of theirs.

William was a really popular guy. All of the women wanted to say they knew him, but his arrogance wouldn't allow him to acknowledge them. However, the night he laid eyes on Pretty Baby, everybody and everything was history.

William walked over to where Pretty Baby stood watching the others dance. "I would be honored to grace the dance floor with a beautiful woman such as yourself," he spoke like a dapper gentleman.

Pretty Baby turned to face the man wearing an intoxicating sweet fragrance that seemed to hang in the air. This guy looked good, smelled good and was very polite. She knew she had been missing out by never going to parties, she thought. With grace, she eased into William's arms as they swayed back and forth to Babyface's "Whip Appeal". They were so engrossed in their slow dance that the song had nearly ended before William said, "What's your name, Baby?"

"Rachel. Rachel Stuart but everybody calls me Pretty Baby," she said shyly.

After their dance, William didn't want to ruin his reputation and give the impression that he was with one particular woman. He moved around the club socializing, while all along his eyes roamed the room in search of Pretty Baby. For a second, he panicked thinking she had left before he could get her number. He couldn't let this one slip away. She had a sexy innocent look and he couldn't remember seeing her out anywhere. Just as he was giving up, he saw her and immediately went over to exchange numbers.

Ordinarily, William wouldn't call a woman until three or four days after meeting them, if at all, because they didn't give him a chance. The very next afternoon he could hardly wait to call Pretty Baby and make plans to see her. She was a real woman, with a lot of class.

The immediate call and his hurry to see her, flattered Pretty Baby. Regardless of her cousin Missy's warnings about his reputation as 'William the Untamable', she secretly accepted the challenge of making a tamed honest man out of him, not knowing what lay ahead.

Within a year, William and Pretty Baby were planning to get married. The family tolerated William, but nobody really could see him as the right husband for Pretty Baby. No one ever commented about it except Aunt Becky, and her truths could really hurt.

Depending on her schedule, Pretty Baby checked on Aunt Becky every morning or every evening to see if she needed anything. This particular morning, she was writing out a small grocery list for her when all of a sudden Aunt Becky blurted out, "Just 'cause you think he's your husband don't mean that's the husband God wants you to have."

Pretty Baby looked over her shoulder, out the corner of her eye. "Aunt Becky, what are you talking about?"

"I'm talkin' bout you," she said, coming away from the ancient gold five-eye gas stove. "You don't really know that man, his background, his history. And love has got

you   so dumbfounded, you ain't even tryin' to find out!"
She shook the dishrag in Pretty Baby's direction. "You
supposed to be friends to start a relationship, first of all,
because that sets a foundation. In the day and a half that
you've known him, I've seen that boy have you all red-eyed
and snotty nosed. Ya'll don't even like each other! Tis' a
shame."
   "Aunt Becky, I'm grown!"
   "Twenty-one don't make you grown or smart! Don't
you know, baby," Aunt Becky said, trying to be
sympathetic, "that what you see is what you get. A zebra
can't change his stripes. Don't you get tired of patching
him up, dragging him along?" She continued before Pretty
Baby could respond. "I just feel like you deserve better.
You can't change and mold a grown man. You can only
change and better yourself. If you would just stop doing
everything yourself and let the Lord handle things, life
would be so much simpler."
   As always, Aunt Becky demonstrated her knack for
cutting anyone to the quick with her honesty. Her words
hurt so badly, because a lot of what she said was true, but
Pretty Baby was determined to go through with the
marriage. She felt like William had two jobs and he loved
her dirty drawers. Anything else he needed to know, she
would help him along once they started their life together.
   Aunt Becky walked over to where Pretty Baby sat
with her tearful eyes focused out the window at nothing in
particular. She sat down and placed her hands on Pretty
Baby's and said, "Now you listen Rachel, Aunt Becky
would never set out to deliberately hurt you. I'm just giving
my honest opinion because I love you. Your Momma and

Tangled Web

Daddy would flip over in their graves if I didn't tell you what I know to be true. Marriage is a serious thing. Young folks take it too lightly. William is a nice young man, but he reminds me of Tarzan, swingin' from vine to vine. Never having a destination in mind. I've seen a lot of men like him in my day. How can he lead if he has no idea where he's going or how he's gon' get there? Every time he has a good thought, and starts on the right track doing something, he never finishes. You know I'm tellin' the truth." She nudged Pretty Baby. "That's a terrible trait for a man to have 'cause it dims his chances of success." ˜ Pretty Baby set mute.

"When two people marry," Aunt Becky paused, going back to the stove to stir her beans, "the love of God alone can't keep them together. They have to be equally yoked in every way. When was the last time, before this wedding, he talked about going to church? Thanking God for his blessings and just trying to have a closer walk with Him in order to lead an abundant and prosperous life? Child, you were brought up in church, you know what God loves."

Aunt Becky could tell by the aggravated look on Pretty Baby's face, she would push her into his arms even quicker if she didn't stop now, so she ended her sermon by saying, "Pray on it, Sweetheart. Ask God to let His will be done, not yours." She gave her niece a big hug with her small round frame that always seemed to carry the scent of lilac and peppermints.

Pretty Baby freed herself from Aunt Becky's embrace and grabbed up the grocery list, heading out the door.

Pamela Williams-Guinn

Aunt Becky has a lot of nerve, thought Pretty Baby. She started getting married at fourteen, had four different husbands and four children. The family joke about her was that she'd get married, get pregnant, raise a family and then the husband would die. One thing they didn't laugh about was that every husband left Aunt Becky either money or land. Her second husband left her both. And that's what really made her the backbone of the family.

Tangled Web

"The heart of him that hath understanding seeketh knowledge: but the mouth of fools feedeth on foolishness."
Pr.15:14

Jason held the dustpan while Chris swept up the debris left from their mom sanding the paint off the old doorknob to the backdoor. The previous tenants had painted all over the door and the doorknob and it was hard to get off but necessary in order for Pretty Baby to install new locks. The front door wasn't as hard, in fact it was quite simple, causing Pretty Baby to wonder why someone would pay a locksmith just to change the locks.

Chris confided in his younger brother, Jason, as they got the last of the paint up, "I'm glad she's putting him out!"

"Me too!" Jason said immediately. He thought about it for a moment then he asked, "Why're you glad, Chris?"

"Because we're probably better off.   He always makes Momma cry. He stays out late, and once," Chris lowered his voice to a whisper, "once, I heard them arguing and Momma said he was ignorant like his own daddy. I peeped through the crack of the door and Momma was holding her face crying." Tears clouded Chris' eyes thinking of that night. "The next morning when we got up, her eyelid looked puffy. Every since then, I wished that 'trick' would stay out and never come back." Chris was almost fifteen-years-old and very wise. He always looked out for his younger brother and was very protective of his mom.

William worked second shift, and as the time drew close for him to get off, Pretty Baby started feeling a little nervous about what she was doing but had come too far to back out now. Ever since the night Pretty Baby and William had argued and he slapped her, something he had never done in all the fights they'd had, she knew the marriage wouldn't survive much longer.

Pretty Baby got her chain and two combination locks and headed out the door. Once William realized he had been put out, he would take the car like he had done so many times before when he got mad or just felt like it. But this time, he would be in for a rude awakening.

She wrapped the chain around the brake and through the steering wheel as many times as it would go. Then she hooked the brake and steering wheel with both locks. He could get in it and start it up, but he couldn't go anywhere.

"Hey woman, what are you doing?" The voice in the dark startled Pretty Baby, but it was only Jesse, her next

Tangled Web

door neighbor.

"Oh, Jesse. You scared me." She continued her task. "Your friend has torn his drawers for the final time with me, and I can't take him any longer." Pretty Baby glanced up at Jesse, a little out of breath from all the back and forth movement.

Jesse always suspected William was a jerk. "What happened this time? I thought you guys were doing better, especially with the new baby on the way," he said leaning on the car with his muscular arms folded, thinking maybe Pretty Baby was over reacting because of the pregnancy.

"Yeah, me too. But you know some things never change and you never know what goes on behind closed doors." She checked the chain again making sure it was secure enough. "Friday night he stayed gone all night long, then called me the next day and said he couldn't get a ride from work so he stayed over at a friends and just went to work from there. He thinks I'm Linda Lunch Meat or some damn body. I told him very calmly, that if he kept that inconsiderate shit up, I had a trick for his ass that would end it all. He said 'O.K., baby, I'll call next time, I'm sorry.' And then," she bent over as if she was in pain, "he did the same thing the very next night. Only he did make it in by 4:30 am," she began to cry. " I'm tired of him, Jesse."

Jesse felt sorry for Pretty Baby but he was secretly happy, because William didn't deserve a woman like her. Too many times Jesse heard Pretty Baby screaming at William for something he did or didn't do. Several times he had to take Jason and Chris to school because William had stayed gone all night with the car. He felt like William needed to be horsewhipped for being such a sorry

13

husband and father, but he wouldn't dare interfere. He just made up his mind to be a true friend to Pretty Baby as he had been for so many years before William.

Jesse and Pretty Baby grew up together from grammar school through high school and their families belonged to the same church. After high school, Jesse joined the Air Force and was gone for several years.

The military did wonders for Jesse because all during school he resembled a weasel with glasses and an afro. After traveling around the world and living over seas, Jesse came back to his hometown, Petersburg, broad shouldered, with a slim waist, contact lenses and a neat faded haircut.

More than just the physical changes, which were very pleasing, but Jesse returned a more focused and mature man. He started working at the post office and before long he bought a new sports car and a two-story brick home which happened to be right next door to where Pretty Baby and William were renting. Jesse was handsome in his own way, though not in the mold of an actor or performer. His was a beauty born of his caring spirit and consistently strong awareness of who he was. His strong facial features held the kindest eyes and the most dazzling smile that complimented his dark brown skin. All the women at church wanted to introduce him to their daughter or nieces because he was one of the few eligible bachelors who really had his life together and his head on straight. Aunt Becky adored him because he was involved in a lot of activities at church. A few times he took Chris and Jason to teen revivals and other functions for the

Tangled Web

youth at church, which was more than William ever did.

Just when Pretty Baby finally dozed off to sleep the continuous ringing of the doorbell awakened her. It was 3:10am, four hours after William had gotten off from work. She came down the steps and went to the front window peeking out. "Go away, William, you don't live here anymore. I'm tired of you and your shit and I'm divorcing you!"

William continued to ring the bell, "Let me in, Pretty Baby. I had to work late." That's what he always said he was doing when he crept in, in the middle of the night, reeking of liquor or some woman's cheap perfume.

"Get away from this door, William, or I'll call the cops," she yelled.

"What are they going to do? This is my house! You my wife!" he shouted.

"Not for long," she said through the window. "I filed for a divorce a few months ago! I kept warning you that you'd be on the outside looking in." She leaned closer to the glass, peeking out. "No pun intended."

"Crazy Bitch!" he yelled and got his keys out of his pocket and went to the car.

The car door slammed so hard, Pretty Baby thought the glass might be shattered. Within minutes the doorbell started ringing again. "Come and get this shit off of my car!" William yelled. His voice sounding distorted and unlike his own.

"I'm keeping the car, William. I'm going to need it with the children. Please, just go away before you wake the boys," she said calmly.

William sat down on the porch and lit a cigarette. Pretty Baby never took her eyes off of him for fear of what he might do because he was so mad.

The doorbell rang one time. "Let me in, Pretty Baby, so we can talk," he whined. "I've been at work. I swear. I know I should've called, Baby. I'm sorry. Just let me in."

Surprisingly, Pretty Baby felt calm. She wasn't upset like she thought she would be and she hadn't shed a tear. She thought about all the times that he said he was working overtime at night, all night, yet he never had anything to show for it. She should've put his lying ass out years ago. She got up to go to the bathroom and when she returned she peeped out of the window, William was gone. At first she panicked for fear that he may try to get in a window or something, but then she saw his broad figure and the glow from his cigarette walking up the street. Going into the kitchen to fix herself something to drink, she breathed a sigh of relief. She went upstairs to check on the boys. They lay peacefully, undisturbed by the chaos at the front door. Chris and Jason had gone through enough because of their Dad's choices and irresponsibility. Pretty Baby pulled the covers up on Jason and kissed his forehead.

She went back downstairs and walked a slow path around the small area and was startled back from her deep thoughts when she heard voices coming from the front yard. She went to the front to see slices of blue lights flickering through her living room. She looked out the window to see William standing in the yard with two police officers. Pretty Baby snapped the blinds shut and swung the front door open securing her robe across the top of her

16

belly. "Is there a problem, Officer?" She spoke from the porch.

The older policeman met her half way in the yard. "We got a call from Mr. Casey." He nodded his head in the direction where William stood with one of his friends who had driven up. "He says there's a domestic problem here that needs to be handled."

Pretty Baby started to speak but the officer raised his hand in silence. "I think maybe you're a little overly sensitive in your condition. So why don't you and your husband call it a night and try to work things out in the morning. At least take the chain off of the car so the man can go and get some rest. How 'bout it?" He gave her a fake smile.

"How about you not thinking so much and concentrate more on getting him off of my property." Her voice was beginning to rise. She turned abruptly and went into the house. She immediately returned with her legal retainer papers she had gotten from her attorney and shoved them toward the officer. He scanned the paper with his flashlight then went over to his partner.

William stood across the street gloating with his friend and a neighbor who had come to observe. He walked over to the two officers who looked confused. "Can I go in my house now or what?" he asked anxiously, looking from one cop to the other.

"Looks like you need to get a room for the night and an attorney in the morning. She's serious about this. These papers indicate she has started divorce proceedings."

William stared at the documents in disbelief, then

started in Pretty Baby's direction. Both officers grabbed him. "Do the right thing, son, and there won't be any trouble," one officer assured him sternly.

William shook his arms free from their hold and walked back to his friend's car. He stooped down to the window, relaying the particulars, as the friend laughed hysterically, slapping five with the neighbor.

William started back across the street. "You're gonna be sorry for this shit." He spoke directly to Pretty Baby.

"The only thing I'm sorry about is that I didn't put your ass out sooner," she yelled.

"You're gonna be sorry," he continued to say.

"Call me in a week and tell me who's sorry, Mr. Homeless. You're just mad because I put you out of what use to be your house and your *boys* are here to witness it." She came closer, laughing in his face.

"Bitch," he sneered through clinched teeth.

"Yeah, I'm a bitch and you're a punk. That's why your boyfriend is here to pick you up." The neighbor observing this confrontation found the remark hilarious along with the two cops. William jumped into the car with his friend and the two sped away.

Pretty Baby told the officers she would be fine and went back into the house. When she got upstairs she checked on her sons one last time, amazed and thankful that they had not been awaken by all of the ruckus out in the street. She climbed into her own bed and lay still, feeling her unborn baby move around. She got her Bible out of her nightstand and turned to Psalms 27.... The Lord

Tangled Web

is my light and my salvation whom shall I fear? The Lord is
the strength of my life; of whom shall I be afraid . . .

"Trust in the Lord with all thine heart;
and lean not unto thine own understanding."
Pr. 3:5

Sitting in his penthouse that over looked Virginia's fabulous beach-front, poring over the annual budget report for this fiscal year and being pleased with the figures, Elliott Banks closed the books with a feeling of pride and victory. For the past eight years, his annual gross sales had exceeded that of each preceding year. As a result of being a magna cum laud graduate of Howard University, Elliott did his internship at the IBM Corporation in DC. Within three years he had worked his way up to a supervisor's position. On the side, he bought lap top computers and word processors wholesale and sold them to individuals. In another two years he moved up to management with the

Tangled Web

company and he started purchasing larger computer equipment and then reselling to small businesses. During this time he met and married Savannah who was eight years his senior. Together they built Banks Incorporated.

When Elliott married Savannah, who was born with a silver spoon in her mouth, she was a divorcee with two teenage sons, Kaleb and Isaiah. At forty-two, having more children was the last thing on Savannah's mind. Even though Elliott didn't have any kids, it was kind of an unspoken agreement that they wouldn't try to have any. At this point, Elliott was so busy nurturing and watching his business grow that that was all the baby he needed. On the other hand, Savannah honestly felt like she had passed her childbearing years. If they had children in the next year or so, she'd be almost sixty years old by the time the child graduated and she really hadn't planned on spending her fifties car pooling and attending school functions. After her previous marriage was a catastrophe and she practically raised the boys single handily, she just wanted to send them on their adult way and throw herself into her career.

Elliott was comfortable with the family arrangement he had. The boys admired and respected him and most importantly, he made their mother happy. Savannah and Elliott always spent time together, setting goals and going on business trips, meeting with other major company heads. The goal of all this networking was to enhance the company's chances for success, but it had the added benefit of bringing them closer together. Savannah held a MBA in marketing and taught evening classes at Richard Bland Community College, making her a great asset to their company. She handled all new contracts and came up with bigger and better marketing strategies all the time.

Life couldn't have been better for the Banks family. The summer before Isaiah went to college, they all vacationed for a month in Hawaii. The next summer, before Kaleb joined his brother at Hampton University, they spent a couple of weeks in Europe which was perfect timing because one of the company's subsidiaries had entered into a merger in the international market and there were some minor details for the couple to wrap up.

Elliott longed for the days before Savannah's accident. His life had been lonely without a real love in his life except for his work. Now, he buried himself in business, cutting himself off from any social events for fear of what they could possibly lead to because of his loneliness. He was a devoted husband who took his marriage very seriously but it had been almost three years since the accident.

Savannah was taking her parents to the airport one cold and rainy night, after a holiday visit, when a drunk driver, in an old pickup, struck them head on. Witnesses say Savannah's BMW hit another car then flipped over and hit a utility post. Her dad, sitting in the back without a seat belt, was thrown from the vehicle and died instantly. Savannah and her mom were wearing seat belts but suffered severe internal injuries. Her mom died two days later. Fortunately, Savannah survived this fatal collision, although, her head hit the windshield causing her brain to swell and she lay in a coma. The doctors didn't expect her to make it. After fifteen days, Savannah opened her eyes. Elliott was right there by her side. God had heard his prayers and answered them. The doctor thought it was best to wait a few days before telling Savannah about her parents, when they did, she took the news so hard she had to be sedated for days at a time. Every time the medication seemed to wear off, she'd go into a hysterical fit saying it was all her fault. Or either she would keep demanding to see her mother. Another three weeks went by and the doctors said her wounds were healing nicely and she could go home, although her mental state was neutral. There were some good days and then some bad ones.

The first two nights at home were peaceful but then nightmares, cold sweats, and migraine headaches prevented her from sleeping. The doctors prescribed hydrocodone and many tranquilizers to help her. A few months went by and her condition started to improve or so it seemed. She eventually went back to work to busy herself. This was a great burden lifted off of Elliott. Working and caring for Savannah were taking their toll on him.

Elliott had gone on a one-day trip upstate to conduct some business. When he arrived back in town, late that evening, he drove past his office building and saw Savannah's new Lexus. Nearly everyone should have gone home by that time except for the cleaning crew and a few others, so he stopped to see what his wife was working on, while she was still suppose to be taking it easy. He eased his big black Mercedes into his reserved parking space beside Savannah's car and entered the building through the back entrance.

"Oh, Mr. Banks, you startled me," said Gracie, Savannah's secretary. Gracie had been her assistant since the early days when she worked as a Marketing Manager at Federal Express. Gracie was a middle aged widowed white woman who proved to be indispensable and Savannah took her with her wherever she went. "I was locking up and just about to leave."

"Where's Mrs. Banks?"

"She left earlier. I didn't see her when I came back from the research room and her door was locked, so I assumed she was already gone."

"Well her car's still outside," Elliott had a look of concern on his face. "You run along, Gracie, I'm just going to go in the office for a second. Maybe she left a note."

"Goodnight, Mr. Banks," she said getting her keys out of her purse.

"See you tomorrow, Gracie."

Elliott used his spare key to Savannah's office. When he opened the door, what he saw horrified him. Savannah slowly raised her head off the desk as she heard the door. Her face had been clawed from top to bottom, leaving her looking as if she'd been in a cat-fight with a real cat. Her beautiful shoulder length hair was now on the floor and all over the desk. Savannah's eyes held a glazed look, like those of an animal caught in the glare of headlights. On the coffee table, beside the sofa, were two teacups and a plate of hors d'oeuvres. It appeared as if she was expecting someone. Elliott approached her cautiously, unsure of what all of this could mean. "What's goin' on baby?" he asked gently.

"Mommy and Daddy were suppose to be here hours ago. I'm afraid they've been in an accident or something," she started to cry.

Tangled Web

"What happened to your face and hair?" Elliott fingered the strands.

"What do you mean?" she cried even harder in a confused state.

Elliott gathered her things, guided her to his car and drove her straight to the hospital. She babbled all the way about her parents being late. He drove in silence holding back his own empathetic tears which were blurring both his vision and his thoughts of concern for what his wife was going through. Savannah's condition did not improve, but it did stabilize with the aid of Mellaril Psychosis, a short-term treatment for moderate to marked depression. It neutralized her agitation, anxiety and depression. At night she took valiums and ativans to cure her sleep disturbances. After five days of observation and treatment there wasn't much more that could be done for her at the hospital. Elliott refused to have her institutionalized, so he brought her home. Because of his hectic schedule, he hired Ms. Savage as a full time nurse. She had extensive experience with cases like Savannah's.

Elliott wished that one day he would come home and he'd have his old Savannah back. But instead he usually would see anything from a once beautiful woman sitting in a catatonic state to a raging self-destructive rag doll throwing tantrums. On several occasions Ms. Savage had been forced to tape mittens or gloves on Savannah's hands to prevent her self inflicted wounds.

Savannah had been diagnosed with severe manic depression. The doctor said only she could bring herself out of this, but she had fallen so deeply he didn't know if she ever would. Elliott tried to pick up the pieces of his life as best he could. He decided to purchase a penthouse in Virginia Beach. It was only a two- hour drive from Richmond, where he lived, and this is where he sought his solitude and came to relax.

The Penthouse rooms were decorated with big bold majestic and museum like furniture. Expensive antiques and the most sublime paintings by artists from all over the world covered the walls. One might expect a velvet rope across the door and there would be a charge for admission. But at the core of all of this elegance, Elliott was lonely.

Tangled Web

"Better is a dinner of herbs where love is,
than a stalled ox and hatred therewith."
Pr. 15:17

Five days had gone by and not a word from William. It seemed like he would've at least called to make sure Pretty Baby hadn't lost the baby or to check on his sons. It wasn't that she wanted him back, but anger, disappointment and embarrassment were setting in. She was angry because he had disappointed her for so many years and it was becoming public knowledge that he was a jerk, which embarrassed her.

On the sixth day, Pretty Baby started to stuff all of William's clothes and personal effects into trash bags. He had a lot of nice clothes, but nothing of any major significance as far as she knew. She went out to the shed in the back, to get more trash bags and ran across the assortment of power tools she was helping him collect over the years. She hoped that he would learn to be handy and   do constructive things around his home, instead of hanging out with his friends. She thought for one half second she would split the things up, but in an instant she changed her mind. He came into her life with little more than the clothes on his back, and he'd be leaving the same way. She didn't care if it was his money that bought the things. It was her idea! And that was how she determined what would go or stay.

Jesse looked out and saw Pretty Baby dragging trash bags out of the house. "Let me give you a hand before you hurt that baby or strain yourself. Where you takin' this stuff?"

"To his sister's house. I started to burn it all, you know, like my girl Bernadine in 'Waiting to Exhale', but I knew he would need something to wear to divorce court or his funeral. Which ever comes first."

Jesse took a double take at his friend. "Your sense of humor is scary."

"But it's real," she said.

Jesse went into the house to retrieve the last two bags. He threw them in the trunk and closed it. When he looked up, tears were streaming down Pretty Baby's face. He tried to comfort her by putting his arms around her. Her body jerked with the inaudible words she spoke. She was so hysterical Jesse couldn't make out why she was crying like that all of a sudden. Feeling bad for her and knowing the situation was all suddenly coming down on her at once, he guided her across the lawn. "Come over to my house and get yourself together. Where're the boys?"

"They stopped around Aunt Becky's after school," she said tearfully.

Pretty Baby exhaled deeply holding the cool rag, Jesse had given her, over her face. She wiped over her face to wash away the anxiety attack that had just come over her. I've gotta get myself together, she thought. Pretty Baby sat on the couch and glanced around Jesse's bachelor pad. It was masculine but very neat. He had black leather furniture with a matching coffee table, a big screen television, stereo system and a large octagon shaped chrome stand he housed all of his athletic awards, military achievements and photos of friends and relatives. Pretty Baby stood to get a closer look at a photo that looked familiar to her. It was a high school picture of Jesse with his arms hanging around Pretty Baby and Missy. Jesse had it blown up and framed. Pretty Baby looked closely at herself in the photo. Life had been so simple then.

Jesse came back in the living room with a tall glass of lemonade. He sat it on the coffee table and then took the washcloth from Pretty Baby's hands and gently wiped her eyes. He had a loving smile on his face. "Now, how are you gonna start bawling like a baby all of a sudden, when you are the baddest of the bad. You don't take no stuff." Jesse boxed at the air as he joked. "Lockin' grown men out their own houses." Pretty Baby managed a laugh and Jesse hugged her. "You can't fall apart now."

"You'd fall apart too, if you were facing what I'm facing!" She sat down on the couch. " Yesterday was the fifteenth and William got paid on both jobs and I have not heard from him. I need the money to pay the bills. He knows the bills we have and he knows I can't pay them on my part-time daycare job. How could he do this?" She started to cry again.

"I guess because you put him out, Rachel." Jesse shrugged. "He probably figures he doesn't have to give you his check."

"No, no, William is just immature like that. He wants me to beg and start callin' around for him." She cried uncontrollably, wiping her nose and eyes. "He's so immature that he would actually neglect the boys just to hurt me. He's a coward!"

Jesse sat back, taking all of this in. He had never realized how selfish William was. A man should never neglect his own children no matter what. It never seemed like their relationship was that bad.

"What am I going to do, Jesse? How will I pay the bills? I need that check!"

"Well, Baby girl, you just have to take it one day at a time. Something will work out. Just stay prayerful."

"I can't pray, I got too much hate in me right now."

"I realize you can't stop the hurt or anger just like that, you've got to let it pass and that will come through time and prayer. And each day you'll feel stronger and stronger"

At that moment Pretty Baby saw Chris and Jason run across the yard to their house. Aunt Becky was trailing behind with, what seemed like, a big tree branch in her hand. Pretty Baby wiped her face one last time, thanked Jesse and went to greet the boys.

"What's with the tree limb, Aunt Becky?" Pretty Baby

Tangled Web

asked half laughing, putting her emotions on the back burner for the sake of the kids.

"Just in case Mr. Jones' dogs were loose, I had some protection for me and the boys."

Pretty Baby laughed to herself at the thought of Aunt Becky defending herself and the boys against the dogs with the stick. She probably would scare the dogs, just by coming down the street in her house-dress, flip flop shoes and her gray hair braided and then pin-curled with bobby pins. She only put her wig on when she was going to church or downtown.

They went into Pretty Baby's house. "What ya'll eating for dinner?" Aunt Becky asked.

"Nothin'. Our cupboard is bare. We're eating with you," Pretty Baby said casually, knowing Aunt Becky wouldn't mind.

"O.K., I just got a head of cabbage out of my garden. Tell the boys to come on. I got a few pieces of fried chicken left over and some yams. That ought to make a decent meal." It sounded delicious to Pretty Baby.

Pretty Baby sat in the tiny kitchen keeping Aunt Becky company while the boys watched cable in the living room. She was trying her hardest to ignore the heat that was smothering her. Aunt Becky really thought her house felt comfortable and cool with that one window air condition unit that was upstairs, around the corner, in the back. Pretty Baby was glad she fixed hot water corn bread instead of turning on the oven.

"You got any Pepsi's, Aunt Becky?"

"No, I just got Cokes."

"It doesn't matter, as long as it's cold and strong. I

need something to make me burp. This indigestion is killing me." Along with the heat in here, Pretty Baby thought.

"That ain't nothin' but a little girl with a head full of hair, sitting up that high," Aunt Becky said believing that old wives tale.

"Momma, it's hot in here," Jason whined, coming into the kitchen.

"If you two would sit down, keep still and shut your mouths you wouldn't be hot. Shut my blinds up too, that's what keeps the house cool," Aunt Becky scolded him.

Please Aunt Becky give me a break, Pretty Baby thought as she gulped her coke.

"Why don't ya'll go outside until dinner's ready. Do somethin' constructive like sweep up the back."

Jason and Chris ran outside where it was probably cooler. They grabbed the broom and the homemade dust mop and proceeded to sweep the back. Aunt Becky's yard didn't have any grass. Everyday, except when it rained, she swept the ground. It was as firm and neat as the concrete on a patio. Separating her yard from the next, she had mattress springs sitting neat and erect as if they were some type of fancy fence. Nobody ever knew why she had all those different mammy-made contraptions around when she could buy almost anything.

"Stay away from my garden!" Aunt Becky yelled, as the wooden screen door slammed shut. The garden, of which she was so proud, consisted of three corn stalks, two cabbage plants and two cotton plants. She didn't care who laughed at her garden because she believed that everyone should have land somewhere to build on for their

Tangled Web

family and grow green and yellow vegetables and cotton in case you need cloth to make clothes. Although she had homes she rented to other people that looked ten times better than hers and she was actually loaded, Aunt Becky never acted any differently. She just enjoyed the simple things in life. Things most people took for granted. The family often wondered why she didn't leave small town Petersburg, and move to New York or D.C. a long time ago. She always said her roots and her family were here and she could be more productive doing the Lord's work right in her own town, with people she knew and loved. Her motto was; When the day came, she didn't want to be remembered for her success in life but for her character and contributions.

"Have you talked to William?" Aunt Becky asked.

"No, but I'm going over to his sister's tomorrow. He got paid yesterday and I need that check to cover my bills," she said with tears stinging her eyes. Every time she thought about not having enough money, it upset her.

Aunt Becky felt sorry for her. She knew this was going to be a long rough ride for her niece. She just wished she would've listened before she made the mistake of marrying William. But it was too late for that now. Poor Pretty Baby. She thought she could make something out of nothing. William hadn't had a stable foundation or any role models when he was growing up. His parents split up when he was young, then his mother, who had been ill for many years, eventually died of cirrhosis of the liver due to alcoholism. William raised himself while his older sister, Ruth, kept a roof over his head. Their father popped in and out of their lives at his own convenience. The truth of the matter was that Pretty Baby and the boys were the only stability he had ever known.

Tangled Web

*"A soft answer turneth away wrath: but
grievous words stir up anger."*
Pr. 15:1

As soon as Pretty Baby got off from work she headed over to Ruth's, where she found out William was staying. She thought she might catch William since this was his day off from his second job.

As she pulled up, there was her dear sister-in-law sitting in her usual spot on the porch, chain smoking cigarettes and nursing a forty-ounce bottle of beer. The house had once been a decent looking home until Mother Casey passed. Then Ruth and her four children took over. The yard had become bald and the poor grass didn't stand a chance due to the litter of cigarette butts and the patter of four sets of feet.

"Well, well, here comes Ms. High and Mighty. William ain't here," Ruth said trying to control her slur. Her face taking the same distorted witchy look Mother Casey had when she was alive. Ruth swore she wasn't an alcoholic like her mother had been because she only drank beer. But she always drank until she was drunk, which made her a beeraholic.

"I didn't come for William," Pretty Baby half lied, "I just came to bring his clothes. Help me with these bags," she said to two of the children standing by.

The long ash from the cigarette that clung to Ruth's dark lips went unnoticed and fell into her lap. "You gon' be sorry you put my brother out! Another woman would love to have a man with two jobs. Humph, while you changin' the locks, somebody else is gon' give him a key, Baby!" Ruth blurted out between loud belches. "It's gon' be tougher than you think raising three kids by yo' self. Take it from me. I know. You need to stop thinking you better than other folks!"

Pretty Baby shot Ruth an angry look because this wasn't about being better than anybody else. This was about her. Her livelihood. Her family and future. Here she was expecting their third child and this was the kind of father image William wanted to portray. Something was definitely wrong with this picture, and she no longer wanted to be featured in it.

Pretty Baby walked closer to where Ruth was sitting. "Your brother asked for what he's getting now. I warned him time and time again," she was trying to control her tears in front of the children, "and as for any other woman," she shook her head in disgust, "she needs to find out why

Tangled Web

his wife didn't want him. Something must be wrong when you get locked out of your own house and car. I really could care less because I'm laughing at them both. But really, Ruth, you're about the only one who wants him around with his two jobs. To help **you** out. Just don't get too comfortable 'cause he's going to support these children one way or the other. "

Ruth glared at Pretty Baby with her head cocked to the side. She snaked her pointer finger in her direction because her words were slow to follow. "Always runnin' to the white man. Get yo' fake ass out my yard," she managed, going deeper into her drunken stupor.

"I'm going, and by the grace of God, I will raise my three kids. In the mean time, you should stop getting drunk and keep your children out of the streets before somebody calls the welfare department on you. Try minding your own business for a change and keep those kids off this bald ass yard. Maybe the grass will grow."

Ruth threw up her hand to dismiss Pretty Baby as she got in her car and left.

Pamela Williams-Guinn

"The just man walketh in his integrity;
his children are blessed after him."
Pr. 20:7

    Pretty Baby couldn't find the screwdriver to open the door when she pulled in her driveway so she just climbed out on the passenger side. Once inside the house she realized the electricity was out. It seemed it had been out for a while the way the heat had taken over the house. She went to the door to see if other homes looked dark. Maybe there had been an accident and someone had struck one of the main poles. She stood on her porch scrutinizing the neighbor's homes.
    "Evenin' Mr. Jones." Pretty Baby returned a wave to Mr. Jones as he let his Rottweilers', off the back of his old

Tangled Web

truck. They ran into the backyard obediently. "Mr. Jones, is your electricity off?"

He came midways across the street wiping the sweat from his brow. "It bet not be! Me, Larry, Curly and Moe," he said referring to the dogs, "been fishing all day." He turned to go back and inspect his home, mumbling, "It sho' bet not be out. 'Tis too hot today."

Pretty Baby went back in the house and called the electric company.

"Virginia Electric, your address please," the voice on the other end said.

"1139 Wilcox street"

"Yes, how may I help you?"

"Is there a problem with my service?" Pretty Baby asked.

"That service was discontinued by Mr. Casey earlier today. He did not give a forwarding address and there is a balance of $236.00."

Pretty Baby began to cry. "That low down punk!" She said out loud but to herself. "What am I gonna do? I have young children."

"I understand that, Ma'am."

"What's the least amount I can pay to get it back on?"

"If you want the service at this same address you must pay the full amount. You can make your payment in the office by 5:00pm or you can get a money order for $236.00 and someone will come out up until 11:00pm," the woman advised her with a mechanical tone.

"I'll call you back."

Pretty Baby hung up. She sat in the dimly lit room fuming with anger. She was motionless thinking about

William's irresponsibility. The tears flowed continuously as she searched her mind with questions she couldn't answer. How could he do this to us? How did the bill get this high? He, obviously, lied about paying it last month. A wave of emotion suddenly overwhelmed her as the hardest realization came to her mind. He really doesn't care.

She shut the front door and walked aimlessly upstairs. Her feet were swollen from the leather loafers she had been wearing all day. She let out a long breath when she got to the top, and out of habit, glanced in the boys' room, which was directly across from hers. Her room was darker than the rest of the house because it sat on the back. Pretty Baby fumbled along her dresser where she thought she had last seen the flashlight. It wasn't there, she went over to the closet straining to see her favorite slide sandals. Her closet, usually neat and organized, somehow looked disheveled. She peered closer to see. 'I couldn't have been rushing that much this morning,' she thought. Some of the clothes were hanging from their hangers. Pretty Baby suddenly had the eerie feeling that someone had been in her house. She stepped into the small hall at the top of the stairs, her senses now heightened. Barely breathing, she listened to every sound around her. She went into the bathroom snatching the shower curtains open then back to her room where she raised the blinds up high for as much light as possible. She glared around the room. Her dresser was not as she had left it earlier that day. She went over to the closet and stared back and forth in disbelief at what she saw. "Twelve, thirteen, fourteen! Bastard! He has taken one of each pair of fourteen shoes! Nobody would do this to me,

Tangled Web

but William," she yelled into the darkness. "And my dresses and suits." She straightened a few of the hanging garments then walked into the boy's room to see if anything looked out of place. The same junk remained intact in there. Tears ran down her face as she slowly descended the stairs. "I can't take much more of this. I can't take it, Lord!" she cried out.

She went downstairs and plopped on the couch straddling her fingers on the sides of her head and slowly massaging her temples. I'm glad I put him out! She winced with a reoccurring anger. I should've listened to Aunt Becky, she was right, as usual. I've got to get some kind of income going. But who'll hire me at five months pregnant? And I sure as hell don't want to have to work two jobs.

"Heavenly Father have mercy on me," Pretty Baby started to pray out loud. "Thank you for your many blessings that we so often take for granted. I'm just asking that you look beyond my faults and give me what I need... Dear Lord, whatever it is about this man, reveal it to me and protect my children and me. Keep us safe from harm...Amen."

She didn't know how much time had passed as she sat sulking and trying to think things through, but she started to feel a calmness come over her. Scooting to the end of the couch as if to will her mind to lift her body, she got up and washed her face then came back to the phone and dialed her attorney's office.

"Jay Russo's office," his secretary answered.

"Is he in?"

"Who may I say is calling?"

"Rachel Casey." The secretary put her on hold and

41

in an instant Jay was on the line.

"My Pretty Baby, what's happnin' momma?"

She hated when Jay tried so hard to act like a brother, but she tolerated him because he had been friends with her family for years. Aunt Becky wouldn't trust anybody but Jay or his dad to handle her property and finances. Last year, Russo Sr. went into corporate law and he turned his private practice over to Jay who had made a very big name for himself all over the state of Virginia.

Pretty Baby went on to tell Jay what had happened from the big put out, to no support, and now, no electricity.

"Wow Rachel, I thought you were just pissed when you came and paid that retainers fee for the divorce a couple of months ago. I never thought the day would come that you would really divorce him after all these years." Jay laughed slyly, "so now you're ready to give a white brother a chance? I knew you'd come around." He turned around in his leather chair, looking out, from his office into the downtown traffic.

"Give me a break, Jay," Pretty Baby said, annoyed.

"O.K.," he said realizing she wasn't in a joking mood. "First of all, you're going to have to get the lights back on and hopefully you'll be reimbursed. I'll draw up the legal separation papers and the temporary support."

"Legal separation? I want a divorce, Jay, and as much money as I can get monthly!"

"We're going to do all of that, Pretty Baby, but no judge is going to grant you a divorce on irreconcilable differences before the baby is born. Just in case you're having some type of hormonal imbalance and you

Tangled Web

suddenly change your mind. You know how you pregnant women do."

Pretty Baby suddenly scribbled on the phone book she was doodling on. "I'm not having any damn hormonal imbalance!" she shouted. "For once in my life I know who I am, what I'm doing and where I'm going. I'm sure about this, Jay. I'm not going to change my mind."

"Okay, okay. I'll be in touch." He paused, making notes on a pad. "Listen, Pretty Baby, when you're feeling up to it, give me a call. I'd like to spend some time with you. I always did like you. You know that. I'd like to spend some time with Jason and Chris too. See," Jay said, changing his tone of voice. "I know what a high maintenance woman like yourself needs and I can give it all to you. Money, love, support... "

"Goodbye Jay," Pretty Baby said abruptly, "I'll call you." And she hung up thinking, 'Jay better keep it strictly business before he finds himself setting out $236.00 and much more.'

Pretty Baby went in the kitchen. She stood in front of the pantry then walked back over to the refrigerator and looked into the darkness then back to the pantry again. "Damn, what am I going to feed my babies? The pickins' are slim." Tears blurred her vision looking at the near bare pantry and refrigerator, but she held back knowing there had to be a silver lining amid the dark, stormy clouds. She was just going to have to tough it out.

Her fingers snapped suddenly in thought. "I got some eggs and pancake mix, we'll eat breakfast food. The kids will like that for a change. But first I gotta get the lights back on." Feeling a little better, she went back into the living room and noticed Jesse's car parked out front. 'Maybe he could loan me a little money. I'm desperate'.

Pretty Baby walked across the yard and rang Jesse's bell. She heard footsteps descending the stairs and then the door flew open, she was not expecting to see a woman. The two eyed each other suspiciously. Pretty Baby, immediately forming her own first impression, took in the full view of the short tank top, daisy dukes and a mane of auburn weave hanging over the woman's shoulders and down her back. Pretty Baby broke the silence, "Is Jesse home?"

At that moment Jesse came downstairs. The woman never said a word. She sashayed her way over to the couch putting her feet up, and started flicking the remote control as if she was at home and really didn't want to be disturbed.

"Could I talk to you for a minute, Jesse... outside?" She asked, stepping out on the porch. "Jesse, I need a huge favor. I wouldn't ask if I had any other choice."

"What's up?"

Pretty Baby explained the whole situation, fighting back tears, still pissed and embarrassed even in front of her old friend.

"Whatever you can spare. I'll get Aunt Becky to lend me the rest. I'm just waiting on her to get back from church."

Jesse shook his head at what he had just heard. William really did have a problem...turning off the electricity not only on his pregnant wife but his two kids, too.

"If Aunt Becky doesn't come home soon I'll try to find Missy, she probably has something she can lend me,"

44

Tangled Web

Pretty Baby thought out loud.

Jesse pulled out his checkbook from his back pocket, "Okay, I'm going to write a check for the whole amount so you can go on and get the lights back on. It's too hot not to have any A/C. I'm *giving* you two hundred dollars. Consider it a gift for the baby. And between you and Aunt Becky, ya'll owe me thirty-six dollars," he laughed tearing the check away from the book. "Don't say I never gave you anything."

She looked at Jesse admiringly. "Jesse, where were you when I was single? Someday, you're going to make some woman very happy."

"You thought I was a wimp and a weasel, remember?" Jesse laughed and then hugged Pretty Baby. "That's what friends are for," he brushed his lips against her hair.

Pretty Baby saw the woman peeking out the window. "Say, Jesse, who's the weave queen?"

"Be nice," he scolded, "that's Charmaine, a lady friend of mine. Now go get your utilities on before the kids get home."

She gave him a questioning look and he gave it right back to her. "Go on now, before I ask you why William would take fourteen women's shoes."

Pretty Baby had to laugh herself. She blew him a kiss and went back across the yard.

Pamela Williams-Guinn

"The light of the righteous rejoiceth:
but the lamp of the wicked shall be put out."
Pr. 13:9

"My Daddy called!" Jason came running to meet his momma, almost knocking her down.

"Slow down, slow down. Help me with the groceries. Is your brother in the house?" Pretty Baby tried to appear calm at this great news flash. It had been two months since she had put the jerk out and they hadn't seen or heard from him. "Chris, come on and help."

"Did you buy squeeze-its?" asked Jason.

"I hate squeeze-its, they're too sweet. I hope she has Capri Suns," said Chris.

"Just bring the groceries in. You can check out the

Tangled Web

goods while you put them away," she said annoyed. "Did William really call, Aunt Becky?"

"The boys talked to him. I could hear Jason telling him he missed him too. Sounded like he was telling them he was gon' come pick them up or something. Chris told him I wanted to speak, and by the time I got the phone, the son-of-a-gun hung up. 'Cause I was gon' give the fool some choice words. I'm gon' pray for him, though, 'cause those boys miss him. Well, Jason does. Chris was a little nonchalant."

"He would call when I'm not home. Coward!"

"Don't worry. You've been doing fine. Just stay prayerful."

"My court date for child support is in two weeks. I know he got his papers. That's why he doesn't want to talk to me."

It bothered Pretty Baby that William had called when she wasn't home. It just seemed like he didn't care what happened to his family. She didn't want him back; she just wanted him to show some remorse. Maybe that was asking too much. She wanted him to show some concern. All she could think about lately was having the baby, getting her figure back and her life on track. That was it, William didn't feel threatened because he figured she'd have a hard time meeting another man and she had three kids. That was just his mentality. He always said that was Ruth's problem all these years. Too many kids. The fact of the matter was that Ruth was a beat up chick and a drunk. That's why she didn't have a man. But her and Ruth were of two different caliber's, and as soon as she got rid of him, she would carefully and patiently find her

47

children another role model and a good man to be by her side. She knew it wouldn't be easy but it surely wasn't impossible because, this time, she knew what she was looking for in a man.

It was funny, the type of hand life often dealt people. But it all depended on how you played it. Everything happened for a reason, and Pretty Baby knew these things would only make her stronger. In fact, her mind actually felt stronger, she hadn't been having too many depressing spells. More than anything, Pretty Baby was praying for strength and guidance and just trying to get along in life.

Every now and then, her mind would go back to different events that happened in her life with William and it seemed like, no matter what, they could never get their lives on steady ground. But she had accepted the failed marriage and, instead of worrying about gossip or that something may be wrong with her, she was ready to move on.

"O.K., all the groceries are put away and you guys can have a Capri sun with your lunch. I've got a doctor's appointment, then I'll be back. Handle it for me, Aunt Becky."

"Oh, you know I will. Is this your monthly check up?" she asked walking Pretty Baby to the door.

"Yeah, and I'm having my first ultra sound today. So when I get back I'll know if it's a boy or girl. I'm excited."

"Aw shoot, only God knows if it's a boy or girl. Them doctors don't know."

"But......" Pretty Baby started to explain that God had given man knowledge for this advanced technology

48

but decided against getting that deep with Aunt Becky or else she'd be late for her appointment. "See ya'll in a little bit."

****

"Oh, that's cold," Pretty Baby said as she squirmed under Dr. Carter's touch.

"This is the gel for the ultra sound so it'll glide easily," the doctor explained, probing further, listening to the sounds and watching the monitor. "You've got yourself a big one. I'd say in the end you'll have about an eight pound baby. Everything looks good. The heartbeat sounds good and strong," Dr. Carter remarked, jotting down comments on Pretty Baby's chart.

"Is it a boy or girl?"

"Oh, did you want to know?" she asked sarcastically.

"Come on, Doc, I'm under enough stress as it is. Tell me," she said anxiously.

"Mrs. Casey, you're having a little or should I say, big.... girl."

Pretty Baby kicked her legs with excitement. "That's exactly what I wanted."

"Keep still now, let me finish my examination." The doctor scolded. Pretty Baby relaxed but she couldn't drop her smile from her face. "Alright, get dressed and meet me in my office."

Pretty Baby looked at all the awards and plaques on the wall. Dr. Carter's cool exterior was strange to her. She had come highly recommended by the doctor's association and was a very well known OBGYN in the city. But Pretty

Baby always wondered why she was always so expressionless. She knew she wasn't married and didn't have any children.

Dr. Carter entered the office looking over her chart. "So I can see that you are elated at the thought of having a little girl. Well, that's good. I'm just concerned about this stress that you're under..."

Pretty Baby interrupted her, "Dr. Carter, now that I know I'm having a daughter, nothing else in the world even matters. I'm so glad I didn't think long about an abortion. This outcome makes all the difference in the world to me."

Dr. Carter raised her brows at this woman she knew to be married. "I see, well, I want you to rest as much as possible and try to slow your weight gain down. Instead of overindulging at every meal as if it were the Last Supper, try having four or five small meals a day. Drink a glass of water with each meal. You're not as young as you were with the last baby and too much weight too quickly could make things hard for you during birth and afterwards."

"Yeah, 'cause I've got to get my figure back." Pretty Baby stated jokingly, but of course Dr. Carter's face didn't budge.

"I'll see you next month Mrs. Casey," she said as she dismissed Pretty Baby.

Tangled Web

"The way of the wicked is as darkness:
they know not at what they stumble."
Pr. 4:19

Pretty Baby pulled into Miller's Gas and Grocery to get a Pepsi. It was such a beautiful day and she was feeling so good just knowing she was going to have a little girl, she decided to drive through the car wash. She hadn't bothered washing the Duce in weeks. It was gray and rusted so you really couldn't tell if it was clean or not. As long as the inside was vacuumed, she didn't care about the outside.

Making sure all the windows were up, except for the back right one, which didn't come down at all, Pretty Baby proceeded to drive through. She gulped her Pepsi half way down by the time she drove through the car wash. The acid fizzed in her ears. It was cold and strong just like she liked it.

Wow! What a difference a car wash could make. That old Duce and a Quarter seemed to even ride better, clean. She decided to take the scenic route home and drive through the park since it hadn't taken as long as she thought at the doctors' office. Besides, she didn't feel like dealing with all of the construction on I-95.

The sound system in the car was its best asset. Pretty Baby popped in a Phyllis Hyman cassette and turned the volume up. Phyllis' smooth voice surrounded her. She felt like she was at a live recording session, it sounded so good. She fast forwarded to one of her favorite songs and sang along. *'When I give my love this time, I'm going to think it through and be for sure...No more mistakes, that's my intentions. Lord knows I've been through so many changes....'*

Pretty Baby cruised the neighborhood, waving at a few people she knew, then through the park, where several people were sitting out on their cars jammin' their music or eating lunch at nearby tables before rushing back to work. She rode absorbing the mood and sound of Phyllis Hyman.

'Yesterday I was somebody's baby, now today I'm a woman on my own.'

She still couldn't believe Phyllis Hyman had committed suicide. She was like one of the family the way Pretty Baby loved her music. Phyllis practically sang her into love and right back out again, through her music. Every time she sang one of those 'baby done me wrong

Tangled Web

songs' in that sultry voice, Pretty Baby felt like they were connected.

She exited the park and headed down Halifax Street toward home thinking, next weekend, if it was nice like this, she would ride down to Hampton and take the boys to the beach. She made a mental note to call Missy when she got home. Her daughter, Monique, was around the same age as Jason and Chris. And maybe even drag Aunt Becky with them. Yeah, that would be perfect. Pack up a lunch and make a day of it. Maybe tomorrow she would run to the mall after work and find a swimsuit. She had seen several maternity fashions that didn't look bad. There were always a lot of good lookin' men on the beach and she wanted to look good too. The thought of having a baby girl gave Pretty Baby a different outlook on this pregnancy. She felt like she was finally glowing.

Pretty Baby suddenly hit the brakes, gripping the steering wheel. Is this bus getting on the road or off? She sat a moment thinking she was going to have to get the seat belt fixed on the driver's side of her car. Finally the bus pulled off. She could see the man that had gotten off walking away. Pretty Baby took a second look. Well, I'll be damned! That's William! Speak of the devil, he would have the bus driver let him off where there was no bus stop. What was he doing on this side of town? She thought about following him but he would surely spot her before he got to his destination. He might even put the duck on her, knowing him. She pulled up beside him, "Hello stranger."

"Hello to you," he said looking a little shocked at the sight of her.

She really wanted to get out and beat him down to

the ground, but she thought about her wonderful news and she wanted to share it with somebody, even if it was William.

"I just came from the doctor. Get in William."

He searched his mind for a quick lie or excuse to no avail, and got in. Pretty Baby cut through the park making small talk. She pulled into the zoo entrance of the park, found a parking spot and they walked over to a picnic table and sat down. They both were kind of at a loss for words. William just sat holding her hand, soaking up the sunshine, and looking like the old handsome William. Jeans creased to perfection, face freshly shaven and the unmistakable fragrance of Cool Water cologne blowing in the breeze. She squinted her eyes in the sunlight at him, inspecting every detail. Now where had he been or better yet, where was he going? I should've followed him.

William looked over at Pretty Baby. He had almost forgotten how beautiful his wife really was. They stood up and she let him kiss her.

"Guess what, Will? I'm...We're having a little girl!" A smile crept across his face and he kissed his wife passionately. She had to admit, it felt good being in his arms. So good, it crossed her mind to let him take her to a nearby motel. It had been a long time and she needed the comfort of a man. Why not him?

They talked about the problems between them. William admitted how wrong he had been and how lonely he was without his family. He also told her how wrong she was for filing for divorce without discussing it with him first. He had been served the papers on his job and after that he just figured there was nothing to say.

54

Tangled Web

She narrowed her eyes at him. So that's why he hadn't come around. COPOUT. They talked for at least an hour before they decided to go in the zoo and walk around for a while.

Pretty Baby had forgotten how she used to love the zoo. She was fascinated with the animals, especially the monkeys and the zebras. Pretty Baby stroked the stout animal. "I love their coats with the big beautiful stripes, don't you, William?"

"Uh, yeah."

"See how the zebras always stay with their mates and are so attentive to their young?" She insisted on him watching their every move. Maybe William could learn something from this African mammal, since I can't seem to teach him anything, she thought. "Oh look at that daddy zebra bending that tree limb down so the mother and baby can eat."

"Uh-huh." William was looking across the park as if he had seen a ghost. "You ready to go, Babe?" He spoke with a certain nervousness Pretty Baby didn't detect.

"O.K., but I want to get a corn dog and a Pepsi first. All this walking has made my little girl hungry," Pretty Baby smiled, rubbing her stomach.

"The concession stand is around the other way. You sure you don't just want to get something on the way home?"

"Nope, I want a corn dog,"

William stood in line for the refreshments and brought them back to where Pretty Baby set. "Mmmmm, the zoo and the fair always have the best corn dogs. All I need now is a funnel cake. Sure you don't want a bite?"

"No, I'm just ready to go so I can see my boys. I've missed them."

"O.K., one last bite. I can take my drink with me."

William put his arm around Pretty Baby lovingly and they headed toward the exit. Two women and a boy about eight or nine-years-old, were standing by the gate. The little boy walked up to William and said, "Hi Daddy."

Pretty Baby stopped dead in her tracks. She thought this kid was approaching them because he was selling something. She couldn't have heard right. Daddy..."What did he say?" A chill ran up her spine. Her feet, face and mind had frozen. Her lips were tightening and there was a big lump in her throat. "Who is this child, William? Why did he call you Daddy?"

William started to shift uncomfortably from one foot to the other, mumbling under his breath.

"Yeah, this his son Jeremy. Jeremy CASEY... " The fatter and uglier woman said.

Pretty Baby felt like she was in the twilight zone. The woman was still talking but Pretty Baby heard nothing. Her ears were burning and she could feel steam coming up her neck. She hauled off and slapped William as hard as she could. Then she threw what was left of her Pepsi in his face. She rared back one last time with her fist balled tightly and cold cocked him right in the eye before running out of the park as fast as she could.

Pretty Baby stared at the shoes in front of her then slowly looked up to whom they belonged.

"Ma'am, are you alright?" An old man asked. He could see she was terribly distraught. She had one leg out of the car door sitting and crying. Her knee was skinned

Tangled Web

"I saw you come tearing outta there like one of the gorillas were loose. I saw you when you fell, but before I could help, you got up and started running again. You want me to follow you home or somewhere? To the hospital maybe?"

Feeling the sting from her knee, Pretty Baby realized this was no dream. The evidence of her husbands infidelity had just manifested before her very eyes. "No, no thank you. I'll be alright." She shut the door, started the car and drove out of the park.

*"The heart of the prudent getteth knowledge; and
the ear of the wise seeketh knowledge."*
Pr. 18:15

"**A**nd you mean to tell me William Casey got another child right here in this small town and this is your first time finding out? I tell you the truth." Aunt Becky moved from one side of the kitchen to the next in disgust. "I ain't surprised, though. How long did that fool think he could hide a whole child? He admitted it, Pretty Baby?"

"Well, I really didn't give him a chance because I tried to knock him out. That's why my hand is swollen."

"Lord have mercy." Aunt Becky held Pretty Baby's hand to the light. "Girl you could've lost that baby. If you would've brought your Uncle Hubert a bottle of wine, him

58

Tangled Web

and his friends would've waited on him outside his job and beat the daylights out of him. Even though that don't solve nothin'. Better them, than you. You sure the woman wasn't lying?"

"No, Aunt Becky, I knew it was his son when I laid eyes on him. He resembled Jason and William a lot. From the big ears, to the eyebrows, that blend all the way across his forehead. It's pathetic...."

"God don't like ugly, 'tis the truth. And that explains a lot of why William could never get his life right. You can't turn your back on your own. I don't care! Everyone will be held accountable for their actions, either now or on judgment day. 'Tis consequences to everything. Some good, some bad."

****

The next day, Pretty Baby worked extra hard with her Pre-k class, trying to escape the confusion that seemed to surround her. "O.K., class, let's recite our ABC's and do our sign language. No singing. I want you to recite it," Pretty Baby emphasized to the class.

"Miss Rachel, I gotta use it," said one of the daycare students in her group of four-year-olds.

"No, Brian, afterwards...can you hold out that long?"

"Yes, Ma'am."

Before she could get started with the kids, she was interrupted. The clicking of the pumps that desperately needed new heels and a hush tap could be heard before the stout Caucasian woman's image appeared. Mrs. Montgomery, the middle aged daycare director, whose greatest achievement in life was having the best husband in the world, after four attempts, appeared in the door. Pretty Baby got up from where she was seated in the semi-circle and walked toward her supervisor who vaguely resembled a poodle the way she styled her hair. "Ms. Rachel, there's a call for you. It's a woman," she whispered. "She said it was important but she didn't want to give her name." Mrs. Montgomery made this comment sound more like a question and she wanted Pretty Baby to say who it was before she could even answer the call. As always, her inquiring mind needed to know.

She turned toward her students. "I'll be right back class. Brian, you can run to the restroom quickly and quietly." She turned quickly, escaping Mrs. Montgomery's nosy gaze.

"You can take it in my office," Ms. Montgomery called after her.

Holding the bottom of her stomach, out of habit, Pretty Baby went into the office and closed the door behind her, wondering who this could be. "Hello."

"Hello. Uh, Rachel, this is Cynthia...I met you at the zoo yesterday. Jeremy's mother?"

Pretty Baby started to hang up but she wanted to know what this woman wanted, calling her on her job. How'd she know where she worked? She had probably been screwing around with William the whole time they were married. "What can I do for you?"

"I didn't mean to upset you," Cynthia said. "Obviously William never told you about Jeremy. He always was a habitual liar," she snickered, "I just wanted you to know I don't want nothing from ya'll. William made it clear, when Jeremy was born, he had a family, so I just

Tangled Web

been makin' it on my own. I told William you never know when you'll need a person 'cause I ended up takin' him to the hospital from the zoo because his eye wouldn't quit bleeding. He got four stitches."

Pretty Baby looked at the big topaz and diamond ring that had been her mothers before she passed. Good for his ass!

"Anyway, since you've met Jeremy, I thought maybe, sometimes, he could come over and get to know his brothers. People should know their kinfolk's," she said as if everything was cool.

Pretty Baby opened her mouth in amazement. This ghetto wench doesn't know who she's talkin' too. "Let me tell you something, Cynthia, I can't change Jeremy's relation to my sons, but I don't keep nobody's kids. Maybe William may want to keep him, but I don't.   Now I'd appreciate it if you never called me, especially on my job, ever again!" Pretty Baby slammed the phone down. Her hands were trembling and she could feel little beads of sweat forming down her back and across her lip.   The nerve of that bitch! She pulled herself together and went back to her class. The day was almost over for her and she had decided, last night when she prayed, she would put this madness behind her. They say you have to be careful what you pray for but she thanked God for that revelation because now she knew for sure that her and her children's lives were headed in another direction. William's loss, not theirs. But she was going to get him and get him good.

"The king's wrath is as the roaring of a lion;
but his favour is as dew upon the grass."
Pr. 19:12

"*C*ome on, Aunt Becky, it'll be fun."

"Girl, I ain't been to the beach, I know, in twenty years."

"That's what Lula said."

"My sister, Lula?"

"Yeah, she's going too. We're going in her new van. Me, my boys, Missy and Monique and Samson." Pretty Baby said, vigorously stirring the potato salad one last time then decorating the top with boiled egg slices and paprika.

"Samson? Oh shoot. I hope his drunk butt ain't driving. I don't know how in the world my sister has managed to stay married to a part-time workin', full-time drunk like him, all these years."

"Samson must talk the right talk to her," Pretty Baby said slyly.

"I can't tell. Every time he opens his mouth, he's either slurring or stuttering." Aunt Becky gave Pretty Baby a knowing look. "You say Missy and Monique going too?"

Pretty Baby nodded. "It'll do Missy good. After everything that's happened, maybe the ocean will kind of clear her head. People handle things in different ways."

Aunt Becky gave a sarcastic grunt. "She needs more than the ocean to clear her head. I just can't understand the logic in the choices that she makes."

Pretty Baby knew this was leading to a conversation that had been discussed a thousands times over again, and nothing could change what had happened.

"So what's the deal, Aunt Becky, are you going to go?"

Aunt Becky looked over all the food Pretty Baby had prepared for the trip. Sure looked good. "Where's the fried chicken?" She asked, lifting lids and sampling along the way.

"I was going to cook some but Chris and Jason want Golden Skillet Chicken so we're going to stop at the chicken house on the way."

"I ain't putting on no bathing suit."

"What you got on is fine. Just get rid of the flip-flops. Put on those sandals you bought downtown the other week. I got a straw hat you can wear to block the sun. Lula will be here any minute. She's picking Missy up first, so hurry. We'll pick you up at your place." Aunt Becky left to go get ready. "Come on, Jason, help me pack this food in the basket. Get the cooler, too, so we can put the drinks on ice. They'll be good and cold by the time we get there."

"They're here," Chris hollered from the front. Then he ran into the kitchen laughing uncontrollably. "Wait until you see Monique. She got on the ugliest bright pink flowered swimsuit and she is dead wrong for that!"

"I'm not going to deal with the arguing cousins this trip, Chris," Pretty Baby said.

Monique, Missy's daughter, bore a striking resemblance to Pretty Baby. At fourteen-years-old, Monique was sassy, bossy and chubby. She was eccentric for her age, wearing bangles, beads and listening to jazz greats like Nancy Wilson and Marlena Shaw. She had been blessed with the voice of an angel and had been on every church program possible since she was four, and they discovered she could lead a choir. Monique stepped into the kitchen sporting her hot pink bathing suit, decorated with beautiful bright satin flowers across the bodice, just as Chris had described. She didn't let her weight get in the way. Pink sandals and sunglasses accessorized her outfit.

"Don't start no mess, Chris, let's go and have a good time. You know Monique can whip you and I don't feel like it today."

"That girl can't whip me!" Chris tried to argue but Pretty Baby just waved her hand for him to shut up.

"Hey Hollywood," Pretty Baby said.

"Hey ya'll." Monique disregarded Chris and his childishness. "Ooh Pretty Baby, you got all the right food for us to get our munch on. I love seafood salad," Monique said, looking over the spread.

64

Tangled Web

"I'm sitting the food by me in the van," Jason said, "so you won't eat it up before we get there, greedy."

Monique stared him down then rolled her eyes. "Shut up child!"

"O.K., let's load up and get going. I want to be on the beach by noon. After making the last minute stops they were on their way.

"Your cassette player work, Aunt Lula?" Chris inquired.

"It better, unless Samson broke it with his Blues tapes."

"I ain't broke nothin'," Samson said coming out of one of his nods.

"Here. Pop this Triple Six Mafia tape in," Chris said, leaning to the front to hand her the tape.

"Oh no you don't," Aunt Becky intercepted it. "I don't want to hear no devil music, Chris"

"It ain't no devil music, Aunt Becky. That's just the name of the group."

"'Tain't nothin' worse than some loud nonsense that you can't understand nothin' they sayin', but the cuss words. Play one of your gospels, Lula."

"Did you bring your Phyllis Hyman?" Missy asked Pretty Baby.

"You know I did," she said.

"Momma, I brought Erykah Badu, Maxwell and Debra Cox," Monique announced.

"Who is Debra Cox, Monique? I never heard of her." Pretty Baby asked.

"She's a black singer from Canada and she is bad! She's been out for a while but not that many people are hip to her. Oh yeah, I brought the Brand New Heavies too."

"You know my baby knows her music," Missy bragged.

"So I guess we gotta listen to these sorry love songs all the way to Hampton?"

"Sit back and take a nap, Chris, and stop complaining," Monique instructed.

"You don't tell me what to do." Chris yelled.

"Alright you two," Pretty Baby warned. "Your headset is in the bag, Chris, so listen to your tape in that."

"Cool," he said reaching in the bag.

"I saw William downtown the other day, lookin' like...." Missy started to say.

Pretty Baby narrowed her eyes at Missy before she could get whatever she was going to say out good. Poor little Jason's ears perked up at the mention of his dad's name. She knew Missy was getting ready to chop him up good and she didn't feel like it right now. Sometimes Missy talked too much at the wrong time. They could bash William and the rest of the 'no good men' later, in private. That's why Monique was so grown, her momma talked about any and everything around her.

Pretty Baby stared reflectively out the window as they rode across the long drawbridge that crossed the James River. It amazed her how Missy was always so eager to dish dirt and give advice but couldn't think her own problems through. Pretty Baby rubbed her hand over her stomach as she glanced over at her cousin who didn't act like a woman who had recently had a baby and given it up for adoption. The family realized she was pregnant right around the time that Missy knew herself, and it was too late to do anything about it. Aunt Becky begged her to turn the baby over to her, but Missy said she knew what she had to do.

"Ten more miles to the beach!" Missy announced. "I'm getting excited like the kids. I hadn't been to the beach in a long time."

"Pretty Baby why didn't you tell me Becky was in a holdup?" Lula suddenly asked.

"A hold up? Turn that music down back here. What are you talkin' about, Aunt Lula?" she said, leaning forward in her seat. "When were you in a holdup?" She turned to Becky. "When was that? You ain't told me nothin'".

"Ain't nobody told me nothin' either," Missy said, going through her beach bag one final time making sure she had all her goods.

"Well, I just didn't say nothin' cause I wasn't hurt and neither was anybody else, praise the Lord."

"So what happened?" Monique and Missy said at the same time.

"Last week my dryer went out. 'Twas so hot I didn't feel like foolin' with the clothesline and besides the clothes shades the sun from my garden so I just went down to the laundromat. I was in the back drying my bedspread in the jumbo dryers and folding my white things when I noticed everybody coming to the back. I asked what was going on but nobody said a word. I made my way to the front and there was a tall young man dressed in a three-piece suit, sunglasses and a hat. I says, 'what's goin' on here?' The fella said, 'get to the back!' I said, 'look son, I got a load here, a load here and a load here,' indicating where my things were. And all of a sudden he pulls out a shiny black gun and said, 'I got a load for you, too, Sister. Now get to the back!' Chile', next thing I know I was lookin' down the barrel of one of them Saturday night specials." Missy kind of snickered at the way Aunt Becky was describing everything. Everyone else was hanging on to her every word. "It was big and black. I was scared to turn around 'cause the fool might shoot me in the back. So I backed up into the crowd then I disappeared through them and straight out the back door. I left my clothes and everything. An hour later, Minsoo, who owns the laundry, called me and said the coast was clear, the police had caught the robber down the street in the process of robbing Pic-way grocery. Come to find out, the robber was Melvina Moore's youngest boy, Bernard."

"No?!?"

"I should've known," Monique said. "He been a crack addict for the longest. He was real desperate robbing the Laundromat. What did he want? A bag of quarters?"

"Aunt Becky, you should've known something was up when you saw that fool dressed in a three piece suit. Don't nobody wear no mess like that no more. Especially, in the middle of the summer. He went to school with me," Missy said, "And he was special, back then. In fact he was a hoodlum then."

"'Tis a shame, Melvina got five boys, and they all have always worried her. Thank God nobody was hurt. That's why I didn't broadcast it, Lula. Melvina's my friend and church member."

"I.....I..would've shot him right between the eye...eye...eyes," Everyone looked over at Samson who

68

Tangled Web

they thought was in a drunken snooze.

    "Every closed eye ain't sleep just like every goodbye ain't gone," Lula said and they all laughed.

    "Well, I'm glad nobody was hurt, Aunt Becky. There's a parking lot up there to the right. Park there so we won't have so far to carry all this stuff."

Pamela Williams-Guinn

"The highway of the upright is to depart from evil:
he that keepeth his way preserveth his soul."
Pr. 16:17

      Basting in the warm sun, Pretty Baby leaned her head back leisurely, with her light golden face pointing upward.   "I forgot how nice and relaxing the beach could be," she said, clawing her toes through the heated sand repeatedly. "The sun feels so good after getting out of that salty water.
    Missy turned to Pretty Baby, her hand shielding her eyes from the sun. "Well, it's baking the hell out of me." She eyed the length of Pretty Baby's legs, then added with a laugh, "But you need it on them pink ass legs of yours. I ain't never seen nobody, no black person, that's brown all

over until you get to the shin. Girl. . . you been wearin' socks all your life?!?" Missy joked.

Laughing at Missy's wise cracks, Pretty Baby scooped sand up in her paper cup and poured it in her lap.

Missy couldn't resist taunting her, "If I was in a bathroom stall next to you, I'd think you was a white woman!"

Pretty Baby, laughing hysterically, scooped up another cup of sand and tried to pour it in Missy's swimsuit. "Girl, you are a real fool."

Aunt Becky walked up to join the two women with a plate of food in her hand, "Look at Lula and Samson under that umbrella like some young honeymooners. I'm too through with Lula and that bathing suit she got on. Couldn't win a brick house contest at a senior citizen home." The girls laughed.

"You should've asked Brother Dickson, from church, to come, Aunt Becky," Missy said.

"That man got better things to do than hang on some beach," Aunt Becky said between bites.

"He might've even put on some swimming trunks and showed off that seventy plus body of his," Missy said.

"Tis one thing about him," Aunt Becky snapped with a chicken leg in her hand, "that man still got a physique on him. Put some of these young men to shame."

"Ah ha, so not only does he eat dinner every second Sunday with you, but you have checked his body out," Pretty Baby joked.

Aunt Becky blushed, "Girl, hush yo' mouth. I just gives credit where credit is due." The girls nodded with understanding. She walked back toward the umbrella where Samson and Lula sat. "I'm gon' get me some more of that seafood salad and fried chicken."

"Aunt Becky, keep an eye out for Chris and Jason. We're going to take a stroll down the beach. Look in some of the shops," Pretty Baby called over the roar of the ocean that was quickly approaching.

"Watch for Monique, too," Missy yelled.

Pretty Baby held her hand out for Missy to give her a pull. "That's one chick who doesn't need watchin'. Hurry up before she spots us and tries to hang. She is grown enough."

"She's still a baby, Rachel."

"Hmm, I can't tell." she said, dusting off her Bob Macke, pink and baby blue maternal, swimwear. It was accented with a light blue trapeze styled swim jacket.

They started walking down the strip. "Now where'd you see William at?" Pretty Baby asked.

"Oh, girl, I saw his ass downtown in front of Lolita's talking to some floozy."

"Lolita's...the tittie bar?"

"Yes ma'am, and he was not looking like his usual suave self. He looked tired in the face and he didn't have a fresh haircut."

"He didn't look like he was smokin' did he."

"No, not like that, I don't guess," she said a little puzzled that Pretty Baby would even ask that. "You know how he was always obsessed with his hair and fashions? Well, he just didn't look fresh. I know he saw me, but I couldn't stop 'cause I was in the car with somebody else. You think he's smokin'?" Missy turned to Pretty Baby.

"No, but he sure doesn't have anything for

72

Tangled Web

somebody who works two jobs. Especially since he's not giving me any money and lives with his sister. What were you doing over in that neck of the woods?"

"Me and Shay Shay were picking up a bag of weed."

"Girl, please! You better be careful over there, especially with Shay Shay's country ass. You better not lose that good job you got. If they pop a drug test on you...I hate to see the day."

"They know us over that way. It's cool. In fact, the guy lives on a dead end and every time we roll through there, it's this old lady who sits on her porch all the time, she waves to us 'cause she knows the car," Missy snickered.

"Your ass is insane. That lady is going to 528-CASH ya'll asses and collect that thousand dollar reward from the police for putting an end to drug trafficking." Pretty Baby had to laugh at the thought of that scene.

"Yeah, but it was worth the risk 'cause it's some one hitter quitter, need a baby-sitter," Missy laughed at her own description. "I got a joint with me if you want to take a toke."

"Girl, I don't fool with that madness, especially while I'm pregnant."

"You used to smoke it."

"That was a long time ago, in high school. Weed ain't like it use to be. I believe they spray it with pesticide or something. That's why folks are always freakin' out. You keep on and your ass *will* need a baby-sitter."

"Oh hell Miss Holy Roller. You are blowing my high." She took one last hit of the joint she had concealed in her hand, then stubbed it out and lit a cigarette. "Let's go in the Daiquiri Factory Sports Bar. It's always some men in here. We can get us something to drink," she said watching the clientele coming out of the door. "A virgin for you, of course, and a 'screamin' orgasm' for me. Or do I want 'Sex on the Beach'?"

"That's the name of the drink?" Pretty Baby asked.

"Yeah, and they're both as good as they sound, honey." Missy winked at Pretty Baby then gave both of their orders to the waitress. "Let's go back on the patio and wait for our drinks. Told you it's always some men in here," she glanced around the room again as they went out.

"So, who was the woman William was talkin' to? One of the dancers?" Pretty Baby asked casually as they sat at the round umbrella table near the door. She leaned forward, so she wouldn't miss a word.

"I don't know. Just some chick with flowing hair that I'm sure was not hers. She looked," Missy searched for the right word, "unkempt, no class at all. I'm not detecting any jealousy, am I?" she said narrowing her eye, giving Pretty Baby a sideways glance.

"Oh, no. Just curious...whoever gets him next, I'm laughing at them because I'm going to hold my foot on his neck so tight he won't be able to afford a woman. She'll have to take care of him."

"That's right, you go to court soon," Missy remembered. "Don't cut that punk no slack, especially for having that other child he conveniently forgot to mention. And that bullshit he pulled when he took one of every pair of earrings you had and your damn shoes. I was mad as hell 'cause he took one of my shoes. Those gold stilettos I got

Tangled Web

from Saks. Remember?" Pretty Baby nodded.

The waitress brought their drinks. Missy sipped her drink, letting the icy liquor float down her throat. "Umm, this 'Sex On The Beach' is just what the doctor ordered, since this looks like this is as close as I'll get to it," she added sarcastically. "If I hit this "J" again, it'll take me on in for the rest of the trip."

"You better not."

"When did you get to be such chicken shit? Relax a little."

Pretty Baby was getting annoyed with Missy and her dope. But that was classic Missy. Some things never change. She had smoked weed and did all types of rebellious things ever since she had come to live with them years ago.

"So what's going on with you and Rodney?" Pretty Baby asked, looking around at all the good looking guys coming and going. Black, white, young, old, vacationers, honeymooners, business men, college students, military men. She was half listening to Missy while sipping her drink down. Everyone seemed to be in their own world, enjoying life. She wondered if anybody here felt as empty as she did at times.

"So Rodney is on his way out. He always has an excuse for not having a job, like other people. All he wants to do is hustle."

"Yeah, that gets tired after a while." Pretty Baby said vaguely, bringing herself back to the conversation.

"But I got to admit, the lovin' is good. I hate to give that up. And when we go out, shiiiit, we throw down. We close the club every time."

"That gets tired too. Don't you want some stability in your life? What kind of example are you setting for Monique? Does Rodney go to church?"

"Yeah, he goes every Sunday," Missy said proudly.

"And sells dope all through the week. See, that ain't gon' get it. You couldn't take his local ass to none of your job functions, especially with that gold across his mouth."

Pretty Baby's criticism was getting on Missy's nerves. "Oh, hell, you want some of this 'Sex On The Beach?'" Missy offered sarcastically. "Anyway," Missy waved her hand, "In the mean time and in between time, when Rodney jumps goofy, I got Virgil on the back burner."

"Now you wrong for that. He should be your main man. So what, he has false teeth. He always takes you and your daughter to nice places. He moved you in that house, and he goes to church."

"Yeah, yeah, yeah," Missy rolled her eyes in her head.

Pretty Baby lowered her voice and spoke sympathetically. "I gotta tell you. I don't know too many men who would have taken care of you while you were pregnant with another man's baby." Missy sighed deeply. Pretty Baby linked her pinky finger with Missy's. She didn't want to argue with her cousin. It was over now. "I'm not gonna mention it ever again. Promise. But I had to bring that to your attention. Look at what I'm going through. It's just hard to come across a man that really cares."

Missy tossed back the last of her drink and changed her mood as if Pretty Baby's last words had never been spoken. "You sound like Aunt Becky. Virgil is sweet and I love him," she shrugged, "but I'm not in love with him. Hell, he's damn near half a century years old."

Tangled Web

"Girl, you *need* a more mature man instead of these young bucks."

"And then when we make love," Missy leaned in closer, "his thing is kind of soft-hard." She looked at Pretty Baby, waiting on a reply.

Pretty Baby burst into laughter. "That can be a problem. Get him some Geritol or some Viagra. Some of that ginseng shit. I don't know." She shrugged her shoulders.

They were both crackin' up when the waitress walked up with another virgin daiquiri and Sex on the Beach. "The gentleman at that corner booth inside sent this over," the waitress announced.

"Oh shit, who?" Missy asked, getting her compact and lipstick out of her pouch, making sure her shoulder-length wrap was in place.

"Thank him for us," Pretty Baby said, taking a sip of her drink wishing it were a Pepsi.

"Come on girl, let's go in and check this secret admirer out. This may be my new man."

Pretty Baby put her arm out to restrain Missy. "That's why you mess up. You're too anxious. Cool out a minute." She hoped whoever sent the drinks didn't see how desperate Missy was acting.

No sooner than she said that, Pretty Baby felt a tap on the shoulder. She expected to see one of the kids.

"I hope you're enjoying your drinks."

"Jay." She said surprised. "What are you doing here?"

"What am I doing here? Were you expecting someone else?"

"No, we didn't know who sent the drinks. That was

sweet of you. So what are you doing here?" She asked again, "Enjoying the sunshine?" Jay was looking red as a beet.

"Yeah," he replied, helping himself to a seat. "And I had to meet with a client for my dad 'cause he's out of town. You know my Dad is in to all kinds of stuff. So I decided to make a weekend of it." He turned to Missy. "What's up, Missy, long time no see. You're lookin' good as always."

"How are you, Jay?" Missy had turned off her colored girl and put on her sophisticated lady act. Slipping her shades on so she could eye Jay without him knowing. She knew he had money. Maybe she could learn to love a white man.

"Over here." Jay waved to the man coming out on the patio. "Come on man, grab a seat."

The man that Jay was waving to stunned Pretty Baby and Missy. He stood about 6'2" with broad muscular shoulders. His silk smooth skin reminded Missy of a strong black pot of coffee. He had on a cut off shirt that said Property of Howard University and cut off jogging shorts. The soft curly black hair on his chest that ran down his six pack into his shorts was visible. His muscular legs were covered with hair too. When he turned to sit down between Pretty Baby and Missy, Missy noticed he had a patch of fine hair at the base of his back. All she could think is that she was going to have 'sex on the beach' after all. She couldn't really guess his age but she knew he wasn't young. He was handsome like a model. The way he wore his hair was a little outdated, but Missy knew that could be easily fixed. His beard and mustache were trimmed so meticulously, with two or three strands of gray that made his lips look enticing.

"Good afternoon, Ladies." His voice was deep and sexy. Missy could smell his masculine cologne blowing in the wind.

"This here's my business associate and friend, Elliott. Elliott Banks," Jay said.

"How do you do?" Missy extended her hand and crossed her leg, "I'm Melissa."

Give me a break, Missy, Pretty Baby thought. Elliott turned and extended his hand to her. "I'm Rachel."

"Oh, go on and tell him they call you Pretty Baby." She blushed as Jay joked with her.

"Pretty Baby? Is that right?" His eyes lingered with Pretty Baby's a little too long and she looked away. "Well Jay and I sure are lucky to be sitting here with the loveliest woman on the beach." Pretty Baby self continuously crossed her arms over her stomach. "If I would've known Jay was sending the drinks to you two, I would've picked up the tab. Would you like something else?"

Missy was just about to make her request when Pretty Baby read her mind and said, "No thank you. We've gotta get back to our kids. Our Aunt's watching them and we're going to be getting back soon before it gets dark."

"Where are you from?" Elliott asked.

"Petersburg." Missy said immediately. "You live here in Virginia Beach, Elliott?"

"No, actually I'm from Richmond, but I come down here quite often during the summer months."

"Are you staying at this hotel?"

Pretty Baby raised her brow. Missy Please....

"No, I have a little beach house about a half mile from

here."

"Oh come on Banks, you've got more than a little beach house. Jeez, so modest," Jay joked.

Missy sat back in her seat and crossed the other leg over. Elliott glanced at Pretty Baby. He was about to say something but instead she said, "It's been a blast, but we've really got to get back. The kids have found us."

Missy looked over her shoulder and saw Chris and Jason running toward them. Monique was trying to catch up but she had to stop and shake sand out of her sandals. Pretty Baby stood up. "Nice meeting you, Elliott."

"Nice meeting you too, Rachel and Melissa."

"Jay, I'll see you soon."

"I want you to call me before then," he said, gently grabbing her elbow. "I want to put a bug in your ear." He gave Pretty Baby a wink.

The children, wanting to get one last swim in, had turned around and started going back when they saw their mothers.

On the way back to their picnic area, Missy was excited. "Ooooh, Chile', that Elliott Banks is the fire! I wonder where he's been hidin'."

"Girl, you're a trip. He said he was from Richmond. He wasn't a local joker. And yes, he was indeed handsome."

"Jay knows he loves him some Pretty Baby. He's got plenty money, why don't you give him a chance?"

"Girl Please! I've been knowing Jay for years and I like him for a friend...but I wouldn't kiss a white man with your desperate lips on." She added sarcastically, "I'm not prejudiced. Some of my best friends are white," she imitated whites she heard use that phrase. "I'm just not

80

Tangled Web

into mixing the races. Besides, I bet his ding-a-ling is pink, just like his ears. And he probably has red pubic hair just like on his head. No ma'am."

"I don't know now, he might be able to pop that pink thing. If nothin' else, it'll match your pink ass legs." Missy started to run down the beach, knowing Pretty Baby couldn't run and catch her.

They got back to the beach site and Aunt Becky, Samson and Aunt Lula were packing up. "Come on here! Ya'll act like ya'll ain't got no children," Aunt Becky complained. "Get them kids out the water, we fixin' to leave."

Missy and Pretty Baby loaded up their kids. It had been a good day so they tuned Aunt Becky's fussing out. Missy climbed in the back feeling no pain at all. By the time they hit the expressway she was knocked out. A combination of the heat, the salt water and those sex on the beach drinks had gotten the best of her. Pretty Baby couldn't tell who snored the loudest, Missy or Samson.

Pamela Williams-Guinn

"A friend loveth at all times, and a brother is born
for adversity"
Pr. 17:17

"This little girl sure has been active today. She keeps balling up in a knot."

"I'd say you were in labor 'cause you keep sayin' that every ten minutes, it seem like, but this is only your 35th week, so it's probably just your nerves and you got that baby up tight too. Relax, girl." Aunt Becky stood in the kitchen doorway, her small frame barely able to see over the swinging door as she talked to Pretty Baby lying on the couch.

"Hand me one of them cold ones, Aunt Becky."

"A cold one. I know you ain't drinkin' no beer. No

82

wonder the baby is ballin' up."

"A Pepsi," Pretty Baby said rolling her eyes.

Aunt Becky opened the refrigerator, the entire bottom shelf was filled with Pepsi's. "My Lawd! Your kidneys gon' come out with the baby. You say you thirsty, drink some water. When was the last time you had some? You know, Pretty Baby, you probably constipated..."

"No I'm not, Aunt Becky, and I had some water earlier today with my lunch," Pretty Baby managed to say as her stomach tightened again.

Aunt Becky filled the ice trays and wiped off the counter top. "Now you need to put your feet up, relax and take advantage of this weekend to yourself. Maybe drink a glass of prune juice and chase it with some water. Chris and Jason will be fine. I finally got in touch with Missy so Monique could come to the shut in at the church with the boys."

"Is she going to the convention in Alexandria with ya'll too?"

"Yeah, but she didn't want to at first. 'Fraid she gon' miss something with her grown tail. I told her it would be plenty of activities for the children."

"You shouldn't have said children."

"I figured that out. But anyway, we're going to leave from the church tomorrow at noon and will be back Monday evening. I want you to pick us up."

Aunt Becky got her purse and kissed Pretty Baby on the forehead. "Get you some rest. You always say you praying for some answers, but the Lord can't get through to you when your mind is racing a mile a minute and you talkin' non-stop." Pretty Baby nodded in agreement.

"You guys have fun, Aunt Becky. Call me when you get back in town." She heard the door close. And then Aunt Becky jiggled the knob a few times to make sure it was locked.

Alone at last...Pretty Baby laid on the couch, gazing around her small house thinking of some changes and enhancements she could make. Maybe the baby would rest even if she couldn't. She kept thinking about what else she had to do to prepare for the baby's arrival. A few weeks ago a friend at work told her about a secondhand baby store. She walked right in and bought a bed that was practically new for little or nothing. No need to try and depend on William because he was useless as always. Pretty Baby was working on a plan on how to make him pay for this in the end anyway. She really hadn't thought much about a baby shower. People don't usually throw one when it's your third go round. She just figured if someone wanted to buy her something, they would.

"I can't take this, I'm not tired, I should be getting something done around here while the coast is clear." She rolled off of the couch and crawled over to the cassette player and turned on Phyllis Hyman. She skipped pass the 'baby done me wrong songs' and played *"When you get right down to it (I'm not in love with him anymore)"*. The upbeat music got her on her feet. She went into the kitchen and fixed herself a big gourmet fried chicken salad with all the trimmings and a cold one on the rocks. She ate and baby girl seemed to have mellowed out. Maybe she was just hungry. Pretty Baby suddenly had a burst of energy and she dug out the nursery rhyme wallpaper border she brought a month ago and started decorating the

Tangled Web

baby bed and her little area. Just when her creative juices had kicked in and she was making progress, the phone rang.

"Hey girl, what's going on?"

"Oh nothing much, Missy. I'm just setting up some things for the baby."

"Your kids are gone, why are you sitting in the house?"

"I told you, I'm getting the baby's things together," Pretty Baby said, going back to her work with the cordless phone. "What are you up to? You got rid of your crumb snatcher too."

"Well I wanted you to come over here. Virgil barbecued."

Pretty Baby thought for a second, she loved Virgils secret sauce. "I just ate, really."

"Girl come on. We're going to play some cards and just chill. A few friends may come by. You got two more days to decorate before the kids come back. I'll pick you up."

"Well O.K., I don't feel like driving my car. The air is out." Pretty Baby thought for a minute. "Give me an hour."

"I'm on my way!" Missy hung up without saying bye. She only lived ten minutes away.

By the time Pretty Baby hopped in and out of the shower, standing in front of the closet contemplating on what to choose from her limited wardrobe, Missy was ringing the doorbell.

Pretty Baby came downstairs and opened the door. "You sure don't give a person much time."

Missy followed Pretty Baby upstairs to her bedroom. "Is this what you're wearing?" Missy said, picking up the beautiful turquoise blue trapeze blouse. "This is cute. I'll knock the wrinkles out for you."

"Thanks." Pretty Baby slipped her white shorts on and her turquoise and gold sandals, then freshened her makeup and hair.

Missy handed her the blouse. "Here you go, now let's roll. I left my macaroni and cheese in the oven."

"Well, you should've picked me up when you were done. I told you to give me an hour," Pretty Baby said, annoyed at Missy's rush. She locked everything up and followed Missy out of the door.

They pulled on Missy's street. "Who else is coming over?"

"I don't know who all Virgil told to come by. Just a few people from his job."

"Are all of these cars at your house?"
"No they're probably at Poochie's house. You know she's always having a cookout or something," Missy said innocently.

"I don't see any cars in her driveway."

Missy climbed out of the sporty Toyota Celica and came around to Pretty Baby's side. "Here, take my purse, the door is open. I gotta get this junk out of the trunk."

Pretty Baby could smell the barbecue. She knew she was going to pig out even though she wasn't hungry. She twisted the door knob and before she could get in good, everyone yelled 'SURPRISE!!!' Pretty Baby was so shocked she started to cry but when she turned to go out the door, there was Missy standing with a beautifully decorated cake with a pink stork on top carrying a little black baby in his mouth. On the baby's diaper it said,

Tangled Web

'Heaven Sent', and on the cake it said, "Welcome to our World, Baby Girl!"

"Oh Missy.......Oh Missy," was all Pretty Baby could manage to say through her tears.

"What are cousins for? I couldn't have pulled it off without Virgil and all of our guest." Pretty Baby greeted everyone in her path to the kitchen.

The shower turned out to be a real party. Pretty Baby had never been to a baby shower with men and women. The guest list included Jesse and Charmaine, two guys and one of the girls from her job and some of Missy's co-workers whom Pretty Baby was acquainted with came. Even Jay made it to the shower. And a whole bunch more.

"Oh my God. . . Nancy and Richard! Now this is definitely a blast from the past. Girl, how've you been? You look so good." Pretty Baby hugged her old high school friend. The two women stood back, admiring one another after embracing. "This is too much of a surprise. How did you know?"

"Well, you know we own a bakery and I recognized Missy when she came to pick up the cake this morning and she invited us. You remember my husband Richard, don't you?" Nancy tugged his arm gently.

"Sure I do." She embraced Richard, trying to make him feel as welcome as possible. Nancy had been a dear friend for years, but Richard looked unsure of himself because he was out of his realm. "Nancy, we've got to exchange numbers so we can catch up."

In spite of the color difference, Nancy and Pretty Baby had become fast friends their sophomore year in high school. Nancy dated a lot of black guys during that time and was sort of an outcast at school. It was a little shocking when they graduated from high school, and she invited Pretty Baby and Aunt Becky to her elaborate wedding and they saw that she had snagged herself a very rich, blond hair, blue eyed white man. He owned his own marketing firm, and he helped Nancy open her bakery.

Pretty Baby found Missy out back with the other guest, "Girl, you got me this time. Everything is wonderful. And I can't get over all the people who came out for me." Pretty Baby hugged Missy.

"You deserve it, cous'. Ready for a cocktail before you eat? I made 'screamin' orgasms'."

"Make mine a moanin' orgasm, I can't handle the scream."

The party was coming alive. More people continued to come, bringing money and gifts. The food and drink never seemed to run out. Pretty Baby was up on the dance floor again. This time leading the electric slide, her and Nancy. Richard had come out of his shell and was at the card table playing spades. Occasionally he checked his wife out, getting her dance on with her black friends. He admired how she could get out there and do all those moves everyone else was doing, 'cause he sure couldn't.

Of course, Jay was in deep conversation with a brother who owned his own auto body shop and towing business. Typical Jay, always trying to either fast talk somebody or pick up a business tip if he could. That kind of attitude contributed to his success. He bought Pretty Baby a beautiful dressing table, picked out by Layloni, his secretary.

The party lasted late into the night. When the last

Tangled Web

guest had gone, Virgil and Missy drove Pretty Baby home. "We packed as many of the gifts as we could in the car, we'll bring the rest tomorrow," Missy said.

"I wish you would've let me help you clean up."

"Don't worry about it," Missy said bringing in the last gift, "Virgil will help."

Pretty Baby looked at Virgil. Poor Virgil. Have to cook and clean to stay in the presence of Mademoiselle Missy.

"Thanks, again, Missy. I'll call you tomorrow. Bye Virgil."

****

"She did what?!? Jesse, why are you just now calling me? I can't believe this! I knew something was up. I've been calling her all morning. I just figured she was out. Let me go so I can get my clothes on and get over there. Lord have mercy! Thanks for everything."

Within an hour Missy was walking into the hospital room. Pretty Baby was feeding the baby. "Girl, I cannot believe you had this baby! She is too pretty. Let me hold her," she spoke loudly reaching for the tiny little girl.

"Wait a minute, let me feed her first," Pretty Baby lowered her voice. "You talkin' too loud. You've been smokin' that shit 'cause I smell it."

"You know I needed something to calm my nerves. Why didn't you call me?"

"Well it all happened so fast. After you and Virgil dropped me off I bumped around in the house for a little while organizing the baby's things then I took a shower and went to bed. I guess it was about 1:30 then. About 2:30, I

89

had a pain that woke me up out of my sleep. I was kind of hurtin' at the shower, but I didn't want to alarm anybody."

"I couldn't tell, the way you were up on that dance floor."

"The pains were coming every three minutes, so I looked out and saw Jesse's light on and I called him. By the time he came over, I had one big contraction and my water broke. Girl, Jesse got me here in record time. I was seven centimeters when the doctor checked me and at about 5:15 she was born," she looked at the baby lovingly.

"You had her naturally?"

"Yes!" Pretty Baby said positioning the baby on her shoulder, "I said I wanted to go that route at first, but those pains were coming so hard I changed my mind. The doctor said I had gone too far. It was too late."

"Better you than me. Let me hold her now," Missy said, taking the baby and cradling her, "You're going to spoil this baby rotten. What did you name her?"

"Ashley. Ashley Lynn," Pretty Baby said, with her face bright as the sunshine. "You like it?"

"Not really, but whatever," Missy joked. "The kids are going to have a fit when they get back. They'll be back tomorrow about 3:00, right? I'll pick them up."

"I get out of here tomorrow, too. As soon as the doctor comes around, I'm free to go. Can you pick us up?"

"No problem, I'll get up early and go by the office. I need to pick up a proposal I need to work on, then I'll pick you up."

Missy caressed the baby's small fingers then looked at Pretty Baby, "I don't mean any harm," she paused for a second, "but where's William? Have you talked to him?"

Tangled Web

Pretty Baby's face started to look as if a storm was approaching at the mention of William's name. She shook her head 'no'. "I'll deal with him when I get home." Detecting the mood swing, Missy changed the subject.

"So Charmaine wasn't at Jesse's when he brought you to the hospital? I'm surprised because she was sticking to him like glue at the shower. Shit, she just don't know we use to boss Jesse around when we were in school and he looked like a weasel."

"Sure did," Pretty Baby laughed. "And ate his lunch."

"I know that chick from somewhere. I just can't place her. She just doesn't seem like his type. She's so common...and country."

"Better not let Jesse hear you say that. He's crazy about that woman." Pretty Baby thought for a moment. "I agree. I see him with somebody a little classier, but that's his choice. She's not from around here. She's from D.C."

Missy sighed. "That's what her mouth says. That girl is probably from Bluefield, West Virginia."

Pretty Baby looked puzzled. "Where is that?"

"I don't know. I just heard of it once and it sounded like way up in the hills." They both laughed.

"I've got to call everybody that was at the shower last night, and tell them you had the baby. Oh, yeah," Missy remembered, "What was the deal with you and Larry Thornton last night? Looked like you were letting him get his mack on. He started working at the agency shortly after me and I'd say he makes a decent salary," she said, mentally checking things off the list. "And he has a sexy body. I think he's about forty and he's divorced. Heyyy." Missy gave her his whole bio all in one breath.

"Girl you're crazy. We were just talking, getting to know each other better. He said he wanted to take me to dinner soon, even with the big stomach. I guess now that I'm the slim goody again, maybe he'll want to take me to dinner and then shopping."

"Now you talkin', girlfriend."

"We'll see what happens."

"I'm going to get out of here and I'll come back this evening and sneak you some leftover barbecue in."

"Oh good, hurry back." She could already taste the brown sugar/hickory smoked ribs and spaghetti.

"Bye Ashley Lynn," Missy said in a southern twang and kissed the little girls' perfectly formed fingers, handing her back to her mother. She shook her head disagreeably, "I bet she'll have them damn pink legs too."

"Get out of here," Pretty Baby laughed.

Tangled Web

*"It is better to dwell in a corner of the house top,
than with a brawling woman in a wide house."*
Pr.21:9

"*M*omma. Monique won't give me my turn holding Ashley," Jason whined.

"Just put her in her seat," Chris said, never taking his eyes off the video game he was playing. "She's sleep anyway."

Four weeks had gone by since Ashley was born and everybody was trying to take their turn spoiling her. One of Aunt Becky's longtime friends and church members, Mother Rogers, was going to be keeping her while Pretty Baby worked. The daycare had decided to open her position up full time and give her a raise since she was being promoted to lead teacher of the pre kindergarten group and had her own little office. Things were working out for her better than she'd expected they would.

Two days after she and Ashley came home from the hospital, William showed up, but instead of being humble and coming peacefully, he came like a mad man from hell, furious because his wage deduction of forty-three percent of his earnings had kicked in and he was pissed! Pretty Baby had warned him, but at the time he thought it was a joke.

"You think you slick with this shit, don't you, Pretty Baby? You're going to be sorry." He shouted, his temper ablaze.

"No, this is only the beginning of you being sorry." She said calmly.

Jay had come through after all. Instead of hurting William by doing bodily harm to him, like she had dreamed of so many times, digging deep into his pockets and not speaking to him unless it was absolutely necessary was even better.

"Look, I know we've had problems, but I'm willing to work it all out," he said, calming down, trying to act sincere. She eyed him suspiciously. That's what they all say once you got a money grip on their asses. "I know about my faults, but I love my family and I want to do the right thing but you won't let me."

"Stop the sob story right there, William." Now Pretty Baby was getting pissed. "During my pregnancy I wish you would've come to me like you're doing now, and admitted your faults and tried to work things out. But noooo, you had too much pride because I locked your ass out. You wouldn't even come by to check on us or see if

94

Tangled Web

we needed anything. You knew we were riding around in an undependable car and your dumb ass, riding the metro with a fucking smile on your face, like a man without a care in the world."

"But you know I didn't have a ride and after you talked about me, my momma, daddy and the rest of the family, I had mixed emotions. I really thought at first, that this wasn't my baby, that's why you put me out." He spoke quietly with his head low.

What did he say that for?   "Oh, motherfucker," Pretty Baby said, coming toward him, "Don't you know I wouldn't put your broke stupid ass off on this child if it wasn't true. I've got enough problems in the world without having to pretend that someone like your sorry ass is her daddy. And as for me talking about your dysfunctional family, I never lied." Pretty Baby's face was flushed and her eyes looked as if they would pop out of her head. "I guess that's where you get your morals and values." Pretty Baby was on a roll now, "And to top it all off you got an illegitimate child running around town you never mentioned and wouldn't have if him and his ugly ass momma wouldn't have popped up at the zoo. You'll fuck a snake if it opens its mouth. You disgust me and I want your sorry ass eliminated from my life!"

William didn't want to touch the subject of his other son. He knew it was the ultimate betrayal. While Pretty Baby went on and on about how ignorant, lowdown, trifling, funky, stinky and shitty he was, he tried to tune her out as he moved closer to the bassinet where innocent Ashley Lynn lay sleeping peacefully through all the commotion. He studied her tiny features for a long moment then bent down and kissed her head saying out loud but to himself, "You'll always be Daddy's girl." This was his only daughter and in his own way he felt proud of her. He snapped back to reality when he heard Pretty Baby saying, "You'll look up one day and these kids will have another Daddy. Treating us the way we deserve to be treated. You are no kind of role model for my boys. Jesse takes more time out with these kids than you do. Hell, he took me to the hospital when I had the baby because you were nowhere around."

"You didn't call me," he said pathetically.

"So damn what! You should've been around just in case!" Pretty Baby started moving toward William with one fist balled up and the other finger pointing in his face. "Get out of my damn house and stay out!" She had backed him out of the house at this point and looked as if she would and could physically harm him if necessary. "I'll see your punk ass in court for the final divorce proceedings, and if I catch you around this house or the kids without my authorization, I'll kill you!" Pretty Baby went in the house and slammed the door. Ashley started to whimper. She patted her back and sat down on the couch literally trembling over what had just happened. If any man could provoke this kind of rage out of her, she surely didn't need him. All of that praying she had been doing for William wasn't working. She was going to start praying for guidance for her and her children. She'd have to learn to pray for her enemies at a later date.

Tangled Web

*"Every wise woman buildeth her house: but
the foolish plucketh it down with her hands."*
Pr. 14:1

*P*retty Baby slipped on her gold Liz Claiborne all-weather coat, securing the belt around her waist. She noticed how she had pulled her figure back together with little to no effort. Working full-time and running with the children was a workout in itself. She still walked in the mornings if she had time before work. Everybody's warnings about how hard it would be to raise three children alone was true. But not hard enough to make her take William back. She took one last look in the full length mirror in the teachers' lounge and placed her cat-eyed Rayban shades on, once again complimenting herself on her small waist and shapely legs. She was back in power and she felt good.

Since she had gotten her promotion, and there were other teachers to stay and have lunch with the children, Pretty Baby was free to go out. Today she was meeting Missy at Aunt Sara's Restaurant.

She stepped out on the parking lot, walking toward her car on this beautiful but cool October day, then decided against fooling with the car. She shook her head. Something was going to have to give on that. Aunt Sara's was only a block away on Washington Street. She would just walk. Missy could drop her back off. Pretty Baby clutched her purse to her side and quickly fell in stride with the rest of the lunchtime walkers.

As soon as the waitress seated Pretty Baby, she saw Missy walk in. Pretty Baby waved to get her attention. "What's up? Girl, that suit is too tough," Missy said, immediately noticing Pretty Baby's attire.

"Thanks, but I keep thinking I didn't have any business buying a suit this expensive. I should've laid it away."

"Girl please! You owe it to yourself. You're always buying for those kids. Momma should be the sharpest in the bunch. Momma's the one working, right? That's how it was when we were little," Missy said, pouring sugar in her tea and stirring, trying to assure Pretty Baby that her philosophy was accurate and to live by. "I don't understand people always buying all this expensive stuff for their kids and they look homeless. As long as you put a roof over their heads, food in their mouths and they're clean, that's all that matters. That'll keep them happy."

"I guess you're right. Monique always looks nice."

Tangled Web

"Yeah, she has some decent things. Thanks to Virgil," she added, "but I bargain hunt for her. Then I treat my self to a little something. I do spend a little more than I'd like to on Miss Monique," she said matter of factly, "'cause she's chubby and can't just wear anything."

The waitress took their orders and collected the menus. "Speaking of buying for the kids," Pretty Baby said between sips of water, "Christmas is right around the corner.

This year has flown by. I'm not going all out this year. My boys are big enough to know the deal. And I'm going to take advantage of Ashley not knowing the deal."

"I know that's right. I love Christmas time," Missy said, with a twinkle in her eye. "I'm going to try to make it to every corporate Christmas party I hear about. Maybe Mr. Do-Right will be there." She went on amusing herself.

"Do you ever think of anything else? You got enough irons in the fire. Maybe if you'd quit looking so hard for Mr. Right, he'd pop up. Maybe Virgil *is* Mr. Right and you don't know it," she laughed.

"You're sounding like Aunt Becky again. You know how she always says 'your husband's lookin' you right in the face and you don't know it'? I don't think so," she said rolling her eyes. "Virgil bores me and I told you, his dick barely gets hard." Missy never cease to amaze Pretty Baby with her bluntness. "I finally had to tell him." The waitress was taking her time putting their food on the table, trying to hear more.

Pretty Baby looked at Missy in shock.

"Don't get me wrong....Virgil is a thorough lover, if you know what I mean, and I was tactful when I told him.

99

He needed to know what the problem was....don't you think, Pretty Baby?" Missy looked innocent and almost childlike when she spoke. Like she really had a conscience about what she said or did to Virgil.

"I guess, Missy. Don't get me started. It feels so good to have a nice leisure lunch break," Pretty Baby said, glancing around the room. "We're going to have to do this more often, at least once a week."

They talked a while longer until the waitress came to clear their dishes and ask if they'd like dessert but they declined.

"Lunch once a week sounds good to me, but I want you to promise me you'll go to at least one Christmas Party with me during the holidays."

Pretty Baby hesitated but then she agreed. Missy dropped her off at work and the rest of the day whizzed by.

Tangled Web

"The king's heart is in the hand of the Lord, as
the rivers of the water: he turneth it whithersoever he will."
Pr.21:1

Pretty Baby raised up out of the bed and glanced over at the brightly lit alarm clock and saw that it was only 4:15a.m. One hour and fifteen minutes since she last woke up. She felt like she had slept for a long time but didn't rest. So much was going through her mind. Today was the Wednesday before Thanksgiving, Missy's birthday and the day her divorce would be final. William couldn't let this go in a civil manner by signing the MDA, (marital dissolution agreement) as Jay had advised him since he didn't have an attorney. Maybe he was dumb enough to think he could represent himself.

"I ain't signing shit! That white boy just want you for himself," William kept saying. It never occurred to him that regardless of who wanted her, she just didn't want him anymore.

Last Wednesday Pretty Baby bragged about her divorce being final in another week. She had even told Missy and Aunt Becky how she was going to kick up her heels and let her hair hang down at Missy's party. She said she might even bring a date. (They knew that was a lie)

Now that the day had arrived, she felt anxious. Kind of jittery like something was going to happen. But through her queasy stomach and fluttering heart, a smile crept across her face because something big was going to happen. She was finally going to be rid of William and she could start a brand new life, her and her babies. The thought of being single was really new to her and a little bit stressful because she really enjoyed being married and had little experience in the dating department. Pretty Baby just thought that when she gave her time and feelings to a man, she wanted to do it to the fullest. Being a woman who enjoyed romancing her man and being good to him if he deserved it and made her happy, she could never live the life that Missy lived, with her collection of men. Almost like she hated to be alone, so she always kept something going, just in case.

Being alone wasn't so bad for Pretty Baby, right now. She realized she needed a cooling off period. Time to think things through. Meditating on how to get her life on track. As for sex...the longer you go, the easier it starts to get. Her days were so full of work and children, that at the end of the day, when she was alone, and the thought of a sexy black man who could love her all through the night, tried to creep into her mind, sleep would take over her worn out body and that would be the end of that.

The sun was starting to rise, a shadow of light casting over Ashley's bed. Pretty Baby could see her small head turning from side to side. She closed her eyes for a silent prayer. "Heavenly Father, giver of every true and perfect gift, thank you for your many blessings. Thank you for all the times you looked beyond my faults and saw my needs. I'm asking now for guidance on closing this chapter of my life and starting another. Lord, I pray that when the time is right, You'll bring a man into my life who is not only nice, but kind, beautiful, smart, prosperous, who doesn't need blow by blow instructions, who can motivate and be motivated, and will love my kids as much as I do. I hope I'm not asking too much but I know You said, I have not because I ask not. Watch over me, Lord. Amen."

Pretty Baby slid her legs over the side of the bed then slowly raised up and drug herself into the bathroom to take a shower before waking the children. Since she had actually been up since 3:00am, she knew this would be an extremely long day.

****

At the courthouse, Pretty Baby paced back and forth on the outdoor terrace. She distinctly remembered Layloni, Jay's secretary, saying her hearing was set for 1:30pm. She looked at the clock in the courtyard. Here it is 1:45, now where was Jay? Or William for that matter.

Wouldn't it be just like him to think if he didn't show up this problem would disappear? Turning around once more to pace in the other direction she realized this was the outdoor smoking lounge and she wished she had a cigarette. She was beginning to be a casual smoker, more and more. A nasty habit she didn't want to pick up, but it really did seem to take the edge off of her stress.

Pretty Baby saw a young woman standing not far away. She looked at the pack of cigarettes in her hand. Looks like a menthol brand. I'll ask her. Oh, no! What am I doing? Bumming from complete strangers. If I don't get a grip now, I'll be getting joints from Missy next. Before she could make a firm decision, she saw William walking hurriedly across the courtyard to the front entrance. Pretty Baby walked back in and sat on one of the benches outside of the courtroom. William tried to look past her as he walked by.

"William," she called out. He never broke his stride but she knew he'd heard her. "William," she said a little louder.

He turned around and looked as if he didn't know her. "What do you want, Rachel?" His eyes looked as if he had cried all night.

"Look. Jay isn't here yet but instead of going before the judge with a lot of back and forth crap, why don't you just sign the papers and it can be over." She looked at him pleadingly, making one last attempt at being civil.

"That's what I was going to do anyway. You don't want to be happy with our family and try to work things out." He looked pitiful.

As always, he was lying and trying to hide his true

Tangled Web

feelings by putting the blame on her. Pretty Baby didn't even bother to comment. She walked back to the smoking area and stopped the blond just as she was leaving. "Could I bother you for a cigarette?" She asked. It really didn't matter what brand at this point. The woman gave her a book of matches to go with the cigarette. Pretty Baby took a long satisfying drag and exhaled deeply trying to clear her head as she saw Jay coming up the front steps, taking them two at a time.

****

The drive home from the courthouse seemed longer than usual. Pretty Baby had been living for this day but all of a sudden she felt depressed. She drove down her street but didn't see anyone out so she decided to keep riding for a while before she picked up the children. She pulled into Miller's Gas and Grocery. With her trusty screwdriver, she popped the door open and went in the store.

"How's it going, Miller?" she said to her old friend, trying to put a smile on her face and in her voice.

"I do just fine, Pretty Baby. What about you and the children?"

"We're doing fine. Let me have five unleaded and....." she scanned the shelf with the cigarettes. "Let me have a pack of Virginia Slims menthol."

Miller took a second look at her. "I thought you looked a little funny in the face, but I know something's wrong if you smokin'. You don't smoke! Let me get this other customer. Hold on." He motioned for the customer to step up.

Pretty Baby stepped to the side for the customer

who happened to be Terry Moore, one of Miss Melvina's boys. She should've known it was him before she looked up because she could smell the funk steaming off his body and clothes. The neighborhood called him Stank and he answered. He had been in Vietnam and came back crazy as hell. He was a crack head but pretty much harmless.

Terry was considered handsome in his day, but now he could be seen walking around the neighborhood, with his neck crooked, one raggedy tennis shoe on the left foot and a cut out orthopedic shoe on the other foot. He wore the same clothes continuously and always wanted to bum a cigarette. Aunt Becky said she saw him down at the church from time to time, asking for a handout or just waiting to get some left over scraps from the meals. She asked Pastor Lindley to give him a little job cleaning up but he refused knowing his history as a crack addict.

"What's up, Pretty Baby?" He spoke slowly, revealing his rotten teeth.

"Hey Stank," she said, taking shallow breaths trying to avoid the funk. Stank paid for his can of beer and went out the door.

"Come 'round here and step in the office," Miller said. Pretty Baby walked around the counter and sat down in the tiny room that was Miller's office. He squeezed his big belly around the desk and sat down with a thud. "Tell me what's troublin' you. Got you smokin'. You havin' a hard time with the children? I heard you and Casey split up."

Miller had always been known for being nosey. He knew everybody's business and he was about to know Pretty Baby's because she was definitely depressed and

106

Tangled Web

desperate to unload on somebody, anybody....maybe even Stank if he would've asked.

"No, it's not the children. I mean it's hard, but I'm surviving." She could feel the emotion building in her throat and the tears coming to her eyes. "My divorce was final today," she finally said.

"Aaw, girl. You said you was makin' it, so keep on doin' what you doin'. If you and him is meant to be you can start dating again."

"I don't want to date him!" Pretty Baby shouted.

"Well why you cryin'?" He asked, stunned at her reply. Miller handed Pretty Baby the tissue after he found it on his junky desk. She wiped her eyes and regained her composure. "I think I know what it is," he said after a while, "It's the finality of it all coming down on you. And it's Okay to cry. Get it off your chest. 'Tis more room on the outside than it is on the inside. You fool around and go crazy tryin' to hold it all in. Look at Ol' Stank. He should've got some kind of counseling when he came back from the war but he just kept all that horror trapped in his mind and look at him now....he's a crack head and don't even know how funky he is." Pretty Baby laughed. "You too pretty to be walkin' around crazy and funky." Miller laughed then turned serious and hesitated a moment, "I knew William's daddy, long time ago, and he wasn't what you call a family man so I guess that's where William gets it." Miller eyed Pretty Baby cautiously, "I knew your Daddy too. The whole town grieved when he was accidentally shot on that hunting trip. Your Daddy was a good man." Miller reflected for a moment then clapped his hands going back. "Yeah, I never thought William was the right pick for you. You from good

107

stock." Pretty Baby gave him a quizzical look. "Yeah," he assured her, "you ever seen a champion thoroughbred in the stall with a jackass? Never!" Miller sat back, agreeing with his own logic. "But I tries to mind my own business when it comes to people's personal affairs."

Pretty Baby stood and smoothed her dress, turning to check her face in the cracked mirror that hung on the wall. "Everybody knew he wasn't right for me but me. Not until now…three children later."

Miller grunted. "You knew. You just wasn't ready to face it until now. You still young, life has just begun for you. Shoot, you in your prime now. How old are you, Gal? Thirty-five? six? Yep. I remember when you was born. Got a little wisdom under your belt." Miller's fat belly shook as he chuckled.

Pretty Baby dried her eyes and blew her nose. "But my main words of advice to you is, in these hard times…is pray…and when things are going so good you can't believe it….pray mighty," he advised sternly.

"Alright, Miller, you got a customer out here." She came back around to the front of the counter and waited her turn. "Now give me my five unleaded and my Virginia Slims." She smiled. "And thanks, Miller." Pretty Baby walked out the door but was stopped by Stank, standing against the building.

"Hey, Pretty Baby, let me get one of them squares." Pretty Baby hesitated then she said, "Come on and pump my gas. Nothing in life is free." She smiled at the broke down man. He pumped the gas and she gave him half of the pack.

Tangled Web

*"He that tilleth his land shall have plenty of bread: but
he that followeth after vain persons shall have poverty
enough."*
Pr. 28:19

*T*oday is the first day of the rest of my life. Pretty
Baby squinted her eyes at the sun that was in the midst of
rising high. Now, what author said that? I don't know but
I'm taking it today as my motto. Pretty Baby stood on the
University track getting ready for her early morning walk.
She snapped her Phyllis Hyman tape in on side two, she
was ready. The morning air was a little cooler than she
expected. Good thing she opted for the sweat shirt instead
of the big T-shirt with her stretch pants. Looked like it may
be an early winter after all. She thought Chris and Jason
needed new coats. Before Christmas! Ashley was the

least of her worries. That girl has plenty of stuff. And the car.....Oh God, the car! What am I going to do this winter? A thousand thoughts were whisping through Pretty Baby's mind.   She picked up her pace a little, controlling her breathing against the wind. That car has gotta last at least until next spring. Then I'll be in more of a position to afford one. She focused on the other dedicated early morning walkers. Trying to keep up her pace as Phyllis played in the background of her thoughts. Coming around the track for the third time, she could see people jogging up and down the stadium steps. One brother she could see in a fluorescent sweatshirt, had been at it when she started her walk. Those steps were tough but Pretty Baby made up her mind she was going to graduate to them soon. That would keep her hips firm and her waist slim. She thought about the car again. But to get a car, I really need another job. Ugh, I sure don't want to do that, but I will. I just have to cut corners where I can. I wouldn't have any of these problems if it weren't for William.   Pretty Baby smiled to herself, I gotta give myself credit, at least I'm not walking around this track boo-hooing like I use to do.

The sun was getting brighter and warming up. More people were getting on the track taking in an extensive workout, jogging or just leisurely walking with a partner. Today really was the first day of the rest of her life and she was not going to worry about a man or anything that could bring her down.

Jesse really is a sweetheart, she thought. He is the one person who really is concerned about somebody else's feelings besides his own. She couldn't help thinking about how concerned he was about her at Missy's party wondering how she was feeling and if she needed to talk about the divorce. Everyone else was acting as if it was a grand celebration. The words were in her mind. They could be seen clearly. But she could not begin to explain what she was feeling at that moment. Jesse's smooth voice and his perceptive small talk were a comfort, letting her know someone was sensitive about the issue.

She brought her mind back to her walking, trying to really feel this last lap. The fluorescent sweat shirt caught her attention as the man jogged a steady trot toward her. She looked at him. He sure is handsome.

With his mind focused on his workout, he nodded his head good morning and kept on by. He kinda looked familiar. "To hell with men!" Pretty Baby said out loud as she picked up speed into a full jog the last quarter of the way right on to the car.

****

"Good Afternoon, Simmons and Burns Advertising (I can't deal with you right now, she wanted to say) this is Melissa, how may I help you?" she said enthusiastically.

"Hi, Missy. Don't you sound refreshed this morning?"

"Oh, hey Pretty Baby," she said with frustration in her voice.

"Now that's a mood swing if I ever heard one. What's wrong?"

"I'm just trying to pull this information together for Mr. Burns, he wants it on his secretary's desk ASAP. That's why I couldn't meet you for lunch. And that's why I

111

sounded the way I did in case it was her. That bat is a big time snitch and she's sneaky."

"Well, I won't keep you. I'm just sitting here snackin' on a salad."

"Oh no, I needed to take a little break. This system is moving at a snail's pace. Maybe it'll pick up if I take a break." She rolled her chair away from her computer and stood to take a stretch. "So what's going on?" Missy sounded like her old perky self.

"Nothin' much, I just hadn't talked to you much since Thanksgiving and the party."

"The party was the bomb!! All my men came through for me."

"Yes, I know, and I'm sure Virgil noticed too. Girl, you are something else. What was Poochie's story? She didn't have no business with that little bitty outfit on, dirty dancing like that all over the place, with her fat butt."

Missy couldn't help but laugh, "Honey, you left too soon. She got even looser and drunker. Her boyfriend had to walk her back across the street to her house. I saw you and Jesse standing outside talking then he came back in and told me you had gone home."

"Well, you know, I had had a full day, and I was tired."

Missy, suddenly recalling the divorce as she filed down a broken nail said, "You never did tell me what happened in court."

Pretty Baby took a deep breath, "Nothing really. William signed the papers, so we didn't have to go in front of the judge. I don't know, Missy, it just seems that I was married to a complete stranger." She closed her salad, suddenly losing her appetite. "William acts like he just doesn't care about the kids or anything. And I don't know what he does with his money. Living at Ruth's house, it seems like he should be able to get his self together...."

Missy stopped her before she could go any further. "Rachel you need to stop obsessing yourself with William. He's history."

"But he's my kids' daddy."

"Right, and if he doesn't know what he's suppose to do to maintain a relationship with them, that's his problem. The way that he acts has nothing to do with your kids. William is caught up in some vicious cycle that makes him deny all of his children. But you need to quit worrying about what he's doing. William is just mad because you have taken control of your life and pulled all the plugs on his ass. As long as you get those checks every month, you shouldn't care. You think he's worrying about you? NO."

"I guess you're right."

"I know I'm right. Now listen," Missy said, going back to her computer to see if it had completed her job. "You told me you were going to a Christmas party with me and I'm holding you to it. You know that mall where Nancys' bakery is? Dunivan Plaza? Her husband's business is over there too. Well, I saw her last week and she told me that that whole plaza is having one big Christmas party at the New Millennium. You know that movie studio that Tim and Daphne Reid opened?. Yes, baby, the NEW MILLENNIUM," she said, enunciating every syllable. "You gotta go girl. So plan for a baby sitter now. It's in two weeks."

"That sounds like fun," Pretty Baby said, throwing

away the remains of her lunch. "O.K., I gotta get something sharp to wear. It's going to be all kinds of people there." The thought of the festivities improved her mood. "Yeah, Missy, that sounds like a winner." She looked in the mirror thinking she needed to make a beauty shop appointment. This was going to be her coming out affair. "My break is almost up so let me get off this phone. I'll talk to you soon. I forgot to tell you," Pretty Baby laughed to her self, "I have a date next weekend. Bye."

"A what? With who? Uh-uh, Ms. Thang, don't you hang up."

"Toodle-loo." Pretty Baby hung up. She put her hand over her mouth in a snicker. That ought to keep her on ice for a minute. Wait until she finds out with who.

Tangled Web

"The glory of young men is their strength: and
the beauty of old men is the gray head."
Pr.20:29

Elliott drove down the long narrow street that led to the back-side of the airport. It was a clear and sunny day even though the air was a little brisk at about 62 degrees, it was a perfect day for flying. Instead of the usual Saturday afternoon of golf or shooting basketball, which he usually did on his off day to exert a little energy, he decided to go out to the airport and fly.

He felt a liberation he couldn't explain when flying as he played his Phil Collins and Rod Stewart tapes thinking back to when he and his college roommate, a crazy white guy named John Brown, first met Lt. Wallace Newman. John was a pre-med student at the University and one of the coolest guys you ever wanted to meet. One day, as they were sitting in a coffee shop on campus, shooting the breeze with some of the other guys, John began to brag about how fast his '71 Impala was, because he and his old man had put some big engine in it. He road a Suzuki Motorcycle around campus like a bat out of hell, so everyone knew he was a speed demon or either a damn fool. John was making bets with an older gentleman, at the opposite table, that his Impala could outrun the man's '57 Chevy that had an engine he had rebuilt himself. This went on for a while until another man sitting at a nearby table spoke up and said, "I got something faster than either one of your vehicles put together."

"I don't think so, Pop. You might be getting out of your league, so you need to slow your roll," John replied and the crowd laughed.

The old man just shook his head. "If you like to feel the power and you want something that can really get your adrenaline pumping, come see me sometimes on the west side of the airport on the weekends. I'm usually there all day Saturdays and after 1:00 on Sundays. Ask for Lt. Newman." He stopped the waitress and paid for his breakfast then left. The little crowd sort of broke up after that.

Early that following Saturday morning, Elliott had a class. When he returned back to the room, John was laying on the bed with his helmet in his hand. He jumped up as soon as Elliott entered the room tossing him the other helmet. "Come on man, let's roll."

Tangled Web

"Hold up. Where are we going?" Elliott said organizing his folders on his desk.

"Out to the old airport to find Lt. Newman. I figured we could check out what he's talking about, then I'll bring my ride down in the next couple of weeks so we can drag. Let this old man know who's king of the road."

Elliott had some studying to do but it could wait, they probably wouldn't be out there long. "Alright, let me change my shoes. But man, I'm driving. I can't handle the bike today."

They finally found the spot where the Lieutenant was located. He was standing outside of one of the hangars. Immediately he saw them as they pulled up and he pointed to where they should park.

John hopped out of the car, jacking his slacks like the cocky dude that he was.

"Glad you boys decided to come on out," the Lieutenant said, shaking their hands firmly.

Lt. Newman looked bigger today than he did at the coffee shop. He looked like an ordinary older man at first. But today, he looked taller, his shoulders seemed broader and he was a little more vibrant in his mechanic's jumpsuit.

John was looking around, taking in the scenery, probably wondering which one of the runway strips they would race on. "So where's your car?"

The old man laughed through the cigar he held between his teeth. "Oh, you misunderstood. I never said I had a car. I assured you I had something faster than what you had. You see, I'm an instructor at the aviation school down from the University." He gestured his hand for them to follow him into the garage. "I was really just having a little fun with you guys over at the coffee shop because you reminded me of myself when I was younger," he said turning around to look at them. "I was a speed demon myself back in my day and when I got out of high school and joined the airforce, they taught me to fly." He relit his cigar, enjoying the full flavor of it. "Driving in a car at a hundred miles per hour didn't compare to the rush I felt flying a big plane."

He showed the guys around the hangar then backed his plane out. John and Elliott just stood there. "You're going to try and fly that thing man?" Elliott asked.

"Yeah, if he's going to let me."

Elliott watched John and Lt. Newman taxi down the runway then take off. He had to admit, they had piqued his curiosity. He had been in a plane on only a few emergency occasions when he had to be somewhere quick. But other than that, he sure hadn't thought of flying one. After a short flight which included several rolling loops, they landed and Elliott ran over to where they were.

"WHEW!!!!" John said, as he quickly descended the steps with excitement. "Man you gotta fly. Up there, I am the man! Going as fast as I want. No stop lights. No pedestrians. You gotta try it."

Every weekend, after that, John went out to the old airport. Elliott went too when he could. Lt. Newman eventually taught them how to fly. Two years later, John dropped out of college and joined the airforce to become a pilot. Elliott knew John's parents were a little disappointed, but Elliott was happy for him because he knew his buddy was doing what he really liked.

After Elliott graduated, he still kept in touch with Lt.

Tangled Web

Newman and would go out and fly some weekends, but after he and Savannah got married and moved to Richmond, he didn't get that way very often, and then Savannah hated to fly. She only flew if she had to for business and, even then, she would have a few cocktails to forget about being in the sky. She was never impressed with Elliott's new hobby or his new toy.

Elliott got a fax a few weeks ago from Lt. Newman telling him that he and his wife had moved to Charlottesville, VA and they would love for him to come out on the weekend like old times. He sent a map, as well, with directions to the out of the way airport. This was going to be an up-lifting reunion. Elliott was looking forward to seeing the Lieutenant once again.

As Elliott pulled up, he saw Lt. Newman standing outside the garage talking to another man. When he recognized Elliott, he immediately ran over and gave him a big manly hug. He pumped his hand until they got over to where the other man was standing and he introduced them. "This is Elliott Banks. You remember me telling you about those two boys I taught to fly, Sam," he said to the other man. "You're looking well, Elliott, and I know you're doing well," he said nodding at his Mercedes.

"You look good yourself, Lieutenant. Too bad John couldn't be out here with us. I talked to him about six months ago. He's stationed on the West Coast now, says he's got himself a small plane for a toy." The two men laughed remembering John.

"Well come on, let's get started. We can catch up later."

Elliott was feeling like a very young man again as he

guided the plane high into the sky. He didn't have a care in the world. He thought about when he last spoke to his mother, and she told him he needed to start getting back out and enjoying life again. 'You shouldn't stop your entire life because of Savannah's condition. You're doing all you can for her.' Elliott was starting to think he should take his mothers advice.

"Why the sad look all of a sudden, Elliott?" The Lieutenant asked, then suddenly remembering the condition he told him his wife was in, he changed the subject to some crazy stunt John tried to pull when he was out at the airport once, which made them start to laugh all over again.

The Lieutenant invited Elliott to stay the weekend in his guest-house, so he called to check on Savannah and made a weekend of it.

This was the getaway he had been needing, he thought as Sunday evening came too fast. After an early morning flight and a delicious dinner, Elliott hugged the Newman's goodbye and promised to come back soon.

Tangled Web

"Withhold not correction from the child: for if thou beatest him with the rod, he shall not die."
Pr. 23:13

*P*retty Baby heard the familiar sound of her screen door slamming in the front as she fixed Ashley's bottles. Feeling a bit perturbed, she waited on her eldest to appear in the doorway, his maturity getting more prominent in his features everyday. It seemed like overnight, he had started filling out and getting taller not to mention the facial hair. Everybody said he looked like his daddy but he really looked like his momma. She smiled then suddenly remembering the bone she was about to pick with him she yelled, "Chris, Chris get in here right now."

Chris came dragging in. He knew what his mother was about to say. "I told you to wash these dishes before you left out of this house. So what happened? I'm getting tired of you doing like you want when you want. I run this, you run around in it. Is that clear?"

Chris nodded his head.

"I can't hear you," she said, cocking her head to the side and sounding like a drill sergeant.

"Yes ma'am." He went over to the sink and started running the water.

"Momma, I want to go to the football game at the school and then to the dance afterwards," he said, hesitantly. "That's why I left before I did the dishes. Joe Joe had my ticket to the dance. I had to get it."

"I sure hate you bought a ticket before consulting with me about this." Pretty Baby said with her hands on her hips. "I'm going out this evening and Aunt Becky's coming over here to sit with you guys."

"I don't need no babysitter, Ma," he said defiantly.

"Well she's coming over to babysit your brother and sister and she's going to need your assistance." She said, using a little psychology.

"Aw, Ma, I didn't go to the last dance. I can't miss this one too."

"You missed the last dance because you were grounded. But now that you've pulled your grades up, there'll be other dances. I have plans tonight." She turned away feeling a bit of sympathy for him.

"Where are you going?" he asked, rinsing the last of the dishes and hanging the dishtowel over the faucet. It seemed strange for his mom to go out at night unless they all went together.

Pretty Baby, noticing immediately how fast he was finished replied, "You're not finished, young man. Wipe off the stove, the refrigerator, microwave and table. Then sweep the floor." She went to get the broom out of the pantry. "All of that is part of cleaning the kitchen thoroughly."

"So where are you going, Mother?" he asked again, just as Jason was entering the kitchen.

"Out with a friend," she said mischievously.

"What friend?" Jason asked.

"You guys don't know him."

"We know all of your friends," Jason explained.

"HIM?" Chris said, stopping mid way through his cleaning, as if he were her big brother. "You're going out with a man? What man? I ain't seen no busters creeping 'round here to see you."

Pretty Baby knew she had to nip this in the bud right now. The kids obviously hadn't thought of her dating again. "Don't talk that slang to me, Chris, save it for your friends. I am an adult. A single adult, and sometimes I want the company of another adult. I deserve some fun sometimes too. Now does anybody have a problem with that?"

There was a long silence, then Chris spoke up and Jason followed. "No ma'am," they both agreed.

"Good," she kissed them both on the forehead. She saw a glimmer of a tear in Jason's eyes but she refused to acknowledge it because he was going to have to get use to her having some sort of social life. Pretty Baby ran upstairs to finish putting on her make-up and slip on her black and gold pantsuit.

"Ma," she heard Jason call, "I forgot to tell you, Missy called twice. She wants you to call her right away." Pretty Baby laughed to herself.

"O.K., baby, thank you." Missy just wanted to know who she was going out with. She would keep her in suspense until after the date so she could give her all the details at once. Pretty Baby couldn't keep from giggling thinking about Missy's reaction when she tells her she went out with Larry Thornton.

Pretty Baby was leaving just as Aunt Becky came to the door. "You got everything under control, Aunt Becky? Chris and Jason know how to warm the bottle for Ashley when she wakes up for her next feeding. She may stay up a little while, but then she'll be out for the night."

"I got it, Baby. Just go on now and have a good time. "'Tis kinda cool in here," she said, going into the kitchen and Pretty Baby followed. "I'm gon' turn the oven on and open the door. That'll warm it up...Jason, you not gon' sit here and watch them videos." Aunt Becky yelled into the other room, "It's gotta be something better than that mess on T.V.," she mumbled to herself. "And tell your brother to turn that music down up there," she yelled again, and then mumbling, "I can feel it in my heart."

She smiled and shook her head, Aunt Becky had it all covered.

Pretty Baby pulled up on the theater lot, and was glad she decided to meet Larry there instead of having him come to the house. Her kids really weren't ready for that, and Larry probably wouldn't have been ready for them. Jason whining behind her, Chris sizing the man up referring to him as a buster and then Aunt Becky probably would have wanted to know what church he attended.

Larry was standing in line to get the tickets. The timing was perfect. She didn't want to be caught kicking her way out of the Duce with a screwdriver in hand. She pulled in right beside his two-toned cream and taupe Jaguar. It was definitely a sharp car but Pretty Baby noticed that he had personalized airbrushed license plates that you get at the mall on the front of his car that said "Big Money".

She stared at the plates. Such a nice car didn't need extra visual aids, she thought.

She pulled her belt snug around her waist, lifted her collar to keep out the night air and tipped up to where Larry was standing. He saw her reflection in the glass windows as he was getting the tickets. Larry turned around just as she was approaching. Enough time to get a full glimpse of her from head to toe.

He moistened his lips. Damn, she's sexy, even with her coat on. She gon' be mine.

Pretty Baby could see the eagerness in his eyes. He looked like he could eat her up, which was a total turn off. She hoped her batting lashes and silly grin wasn't giving Larry mixed signals. His sense of style was too overbearing for her taste. Larry's shirt was unbuttoned to his belly displaying a small island of beaded hair between his pecs, his slacks showed his bulge in the front and in the back, and to top it off he had snake skin boots with the snake's head still on them. The outfit was worse than his hungry look. Maybe Chris was right; he was a buster. Whatever that was. He was losing major cool points. This was not the Larry Missy introduced her to, or the one who sounded so intelligent on the phone. Sensing there would not be a 'love connection' tonight, she lowered her expectations because she really wanted to see 'Soul Food'. Pretty Baby decided to have fun and make the best of it.

"Hey Larry," she said sweetly.

"Hello gorgeous." Larry lead her over to the concession stand to select whatever snack or drink she wanted. Pretty Baby got buttered popcorn and a Pepsi, Larry got nachos with extra peppers. "Got everything you need, baby?" he asked, looking as if he could take a bite out of her at any moment.

They were both enjoying the movie and themselves when all of a sudden Larry started coughing, complaining about the peppers on his nachos being a little too hot and saying he needed something to drink. After repeating this two or three times, a red flag went up immediately for Pretty Baby. Her brow furrowed as she thought, 'I know he doesn't want a sip of my drink. It's not that kind of party.' He finally caught the hint that there would be no sharing and excused himself to go get his own. She sat there laughing at the picture thinking if this movie didn't at least get nominated for an Oscar; she would never watch the Oscars again.

Larry returned, sitting down and placing his hand over Pretty Baby's all in one motion. She pulled away and they sat through the rest of the movie in silence.

Afterwards, Larry offered to take her to a nearby bar for a nightcap, but she declined. They sat in the lobby for a few minutes talking. Larry was trying to get her to commit to another date while she smiled sweetly, but all along she couldn't stop focusing on those big juicy lips of his. Finally, they walked out to their cars and said their good-byes. Larry promised to call soon.

On the way home, Pretty Baby started to stop by Missy's but when she drove down her street she didn't see a light on so she kept going.

She was getting in much earlier than she had expected so she could run Aunt Becky home if she wanted, instead of her spending the night like they had initially planned. When she went in the house, Aunt Becky was dozing on the couch and Jason was on the floor asleep in front of 'Video Soul'. Aunt Becky must have fallen asleep before him. Pretty Baby noticed how warm and cozy the house felt as she went into the kitchen to turn off the oven and the other lights. 'I might as well let Aunt Becky sleep,' she thought.

She woke Jason up to go upstairs to get in his bed. Jason was always crazy when she woke him up so she took off her shoes and unfastened her blazer to get ready for the fight. Coming up the stairs, half dragging Jason, she could see little Ashley resting peacefully in her babybed.

Pretty Baby guided Jason into the room that he shared with his brother, turning on the television so she could see a little better without falling over any of the junk that was in the floor. Getting Jason in the bed was a struggle enough so she didn't bother taking his clothes off. She kissed him goodnight and stood up to peek in the top bunk at Chris and give him a kiss too. He always did like the covers over his head, but Pretty Baby thought she would turn it down just a little. When she pulled the cover back, he was not in his bed. Pretty Baby immediately went to turn on the light then went back and yanked the covers all the way off the bed, revealing two pillows squashed together. She went across the hall to her room. Maybe he had heard Ashley crying and got in his mother's bed. No Chris. She started downstairs and was about to wake Aunt Becky when she heard the back door opening. Pretty Baby did an about face on the steps and went to get the old worn leather belt that was used for special occasions such as this. While she was in her room she decided to take her clothes off and slip on her gown so she could be free to light his tail up.

Chris knew his mom had beat him home because the car was in the driveway but maybe, just maybe, she had gone to bed and nobody had missed him while he was at the dance. He slipped his shoes off and put them in the pantry then he took his clothes off that carried the scent of a good time sweat and a sweet bubble gum cologne and shoved them in the dryer. He went in the refrigerator and poured himself a little Kool-Aid. When he turned around, there stood Pretty Baby, belt in hand.

"I hope you had a good time," she said quietly.

Chris didn't say a word. His mouth was dry and his nervous system had temporarily shut down, disabling him from bringing the glass to his lips.

"I'm glad you took your clothes off, you know I don't like to whip clothes, I like skin," she said wickedly, moving toward him. "I ought to make you take a bath so your skin will be a little moist. Make sure you don't forget or repeat this incident."

Tangled Web

Tears began forming in his eyes. "Just ground me, Momma. Please don't whip me," he started to beg. "You said I was too old for a whipping."

Pretty Baby was silent. She grabbed Chris by the arm and dragged him upstairs "Lay across that bean bag," she ordered. Chris was still begging. "Shut up! And if you jump up, I'm gon' give you five extra licks everytime." She gave him a whipping he would not forget any time soon.

Jason woke up to the howling sounds of his brother, "What's going on, Ma? He quickly realized Chris was getting his butt whipped and that was something worth waking up for.

"Go back to sleep, baby," Pretty Baby said to Jason then turned her attention back to Chris. "I don't like to do you like that, baby, but when you disobey me, you leave me no other choice. I discipline you because I love you, now give me a hug and a kiss."

Chris hated when she did that. He let her hug and kiss him then he laid down wishing he could go and live with his dad. That would fix her and her dumb whippings. His dad would never make him miss a dance or whip him. And he was sick of sharing a room with Jason. Tomorrow he would call his dad at work and see if he could come and get him.

*"Chasten thy son while there is hope, and
let not thy soul spare for his crying."*
Pr. 19:18

Pretty Baby was at a full jog on the track. This was her third lap and she hadn't stopped once, until she heard the engine of an approaching car and then the loud blare of a horn. She slowed herself to a trot when she saw the bright red Celica. The woman put the car in park and popped her head through the sunroof. "Get in this car girl. You've been dodging me."

Pretty Baby stopped abruptly, unable to control her laughter. "No I haven't, Missy."

"You haven't returned my calls and every time I come by your house you're gone. Now what's the deal?"

Tangled Web

They were both laughing. "Get in."

"But I'm not finished with my jog. I have to be at work in another hour and a half." She glanced at her watch breathlessly. "Don't you have to be at work in a little while yourself?"

"I'm working at home today," she said, coming back into the car from the sunroof. Missy opened the passenger side for Pretty Baby. "Come on, girl, let's go around to the Waffle House, it's cold out here anyway. You can tell you ain't got no other business," she said sarcastically, "out here in the cold, running around the track." She laughed to herself.

"I'm keeping my figure together," Pretty Baby said as she plopped down into the passenger seat. "And I got plenty business for your information. That's why you're out here hunting me down on the track."

"You right!" Missy said immediately, "So throw the dirt. And don't miss a detail." Missy sped off and headed to the restaurant.

"Larry Thornton?!? Shit fire and call the police. I should've known." Missy roared as the waitress placed their hot chocolates on the table. "So how was it?'

"The movie was good," Pretty Baby said, blowing into her cup of hot chocolate.

"I don't mean the movie, I seen the damn movie. I told **you** it was good. I'm talkin' 'bout the date." Missy said, getting loud and impatient.

Pretty Baby was tickled at how pissed Missy was getting because of her stalling. "Girl, the whole night was a trip from beginning to end," she confessed. Missy was waiting for every word, cautiously sipping on her hot chocolate. "First of all, I gotta tell you, Larry is not the answer."

"What do you mean? What happened?" she suddenly looked disappointed.

Pretty Baby went on to tell her about her first impression of him and then how he wanted a sip of her drink. "Not with them juicy lips," Missy laughed hysterically. "But you know what they say about those men with juicy lips..." she added mysteriously.

"What? They slob when they kiss?"

"Girl, no. You know what I'm talkin' about."

Catching Missy's drift, Pretty Baby shook her head and said, "Uh-uh, I'm not desperate. You can get dick when you can't get bread."

"Sho' you right. I'm too through with those tacky plates on his Jag. I never noticed them before. I thought he was a much classier guy than that. The way he carries himself at work you would never know he was on the country side. I guess you can take the boy out of the country, but you can't take the country out of the boy."

Pretty Baby glanced down at her watch. "I gotta run," she got her money out for her chocolate. "Take me to my car."

"Come on Rachel, call in sick," Missy pouted.

"I can't do that."

"Aw girl, we can shop while the kids are at school. You know the Christmas party is next weekend and you won't have another chance to shop this week. Not peacefully." Missy was looking like she used to when she would talk Pretty Baby into doing things that were against her better judgment.

Tangled Web

"O.K., today probably is the best day to shop. I gotta get to a phone to call in then I want you to take me home to change."

"Let's roll." She hooked her arm with Pretty Baby's and led her out of the door.

Once they got to the shopping center, they went from one store to the next. "I can't seem to find anything that's really catching my eye. Something really festive but sexy," Pretty Baby said, as she sifted through the racks of dresses.

"How about this?" Missy asked holding up a long red form fitting sweater dress with feathers around the plunging neckline, the wrist and the hemline.

"That's not me." She looked through another rack.

"So what are you going to do about Chris?" Missy asked, as they left one store and entered another.

"Pray for him. That's all I can do, and beat his butt."

"You can't be too strict on him, Pretty Baby. That'll make him real wild."

They sat down by the waterfall to take a break. "Chris has plenty of freedom. But more than anything, I worry about that little girl named Sharon that calls him all the time."

"That's the same girl that use to call him last year. They still hanging?"

"Yeah, and that's what worries me. At first they just went together over the phone and at school, I guess. But now that doesn't seem to be enough for them."

"You think they doing it? " Missy looked at Pretty Baby wide-eyed.

"I don't know. They better not, 'cause I sure don't

133

want to be no grandmomma. I think she's a sweet girl, what I know about her, but she's got more titties and ass than I could wish about and my son has probably noticed that too. And then to really top it off, she's in the eleventh grade, and he is only in the ninth. What could she want with him?"

"You don't know?" Missy said standing up. "Let's go to a couple of more shops and then we'll go by the boutique if we don't see anything."

Pretty Baby slowly realized the outfit for her was not in the mall so they headed over to Exquisite boutique.

Missy looked around the boutique for Pretty Baby. She looked to the front then the other side. Maybe she's over in the shoe section, eyeing some the shoes and accessories. Missy wandered through the aisles until she saw Pretty Baby come out of the dressing room with the most elegant dress on she had ever seen. It was a red form fitting, knee-length dress that hung off the shoulders with a long red chiffon scarf draped around her neck. Missy walked up to her in awe as Pretty Baby examined herself in the three way mirror. "Now that is you! How much is it?"

Pretty Baby turned around to face her and simply said, "I don't even care. I'm buying it."

****

On the way home, Pretty Baby was going off on Missy because she had dragged her out to spend her money and she didn't even buy anything. "Colored folks, I tell you the truth." Pretty Baby complained all the way

Tangled Web

home. "But I'll tell you what, I know who will be the belle of the ball. Turn the music up," she reached for the volume. They both grooved to the hip hop sounds of Master P. Pretty Baby was having a good time until they pulled in front of her house and saw William coming out followed by Chris. Pretty Baby's expression fell immediately. What the hell is going on?

Pretty Baby was opening the car door before the car even stopped. She walked up the driveway in a huff with Missy in tow.

"What's up, Pretty Baby?" William said sounding as if he didn't have much fight left in him.

Pretty Baby, sensing this, decided to spare him a little in front of Chris. "What are you doing here, William?"

"I came to see my son," he said a little too testily. "Is that o.k. with you?"

"It would be if you saw them on a regular basis. But you don't, so what are you doing here?" She shifted her gaze suspiciously to Chris who had come to stand at his father's side as if he were ready to defend him. She looked back to William.

William started slowly, "I got two messages at work today to call Chris, so when I got off I just came by here to see if something was wrong." A bit of courage was building in his voice. "He said you beat him in his underwear because he went to the school dance that he had a ticket to."

Pretty Baby narrowed her eyes looking from William to Chris. William faded to the right just as Chris blocked the blow his mom was trying to deliver. Missy pretended to intervene but she was really waiting to jump in if needed.

135

The rage Pretty Baby felt was to the limit. She glared at him. How could William come here, making accusations, not knowing the situation. Not really caring about what happened. He was just going through the motions of acting the way he thought a father should act. "Get out of my damn yard, NOW!" she stomped her foot as she snatched away from Chris and went into the house.

"You'd better go, William," Missy said before going into the house.

William told Chris he would talk with him soon and then ran out of the yard flagging Crazy Pete for a ride as he drove by. The old car stopped and Chris watched his dad disappear into the distance.

Chris came into the house not knowing if the mood had mellowed or not. More than likely it hadn't, because Pretty Baby always let him know that you never bite the hand that feeds you. She was the momma and the daddy. He knew that he couldn't talk to her right now or today, maybe not even this week, about how he was feeling and how he wanted to be treated. He was a teenager, almost a man, and he should get some respect too. Especially if he did things like watch the kids and clean up all the time. He knew it was true, even his dad said so. And if his mom didn't like it, he could just go and stay over at Ruth's and go to school from there. It was just that simple. He would lay the law down as soon as *she* could talk rationally.

"What are these clothes doing in this dryer?" Chris froze as he heard his mother yell, remembering the clothes he left the other night. "These clothes are not clean. They've been worn. Chris!" He could hear her talking to Missy and moving things around in the kitchen. "And what

Tangled Web

are these tennis shoes doing in this kitchen?" She was going into another rage. She came busting through the swinging door from the kitchen to the living room with the broom in her hand. She collared Chris with one hand and pushed him on the sofa.

"Now, if I beat the hell out of you with this broom are you going to run and tell that?" Before he could answer she said, "'Cause if you do I'm gon' beat you again so you can tell that. You get the picture?" Pretty Baby shoved his head with her palm. "What did you call William over here for and then you lied? Don't you know he can't help you? He can barely help himself. I'm the one that takes care of you. I'm the one who makes sure you have a roof over your head." She waved her hands in the air. She never gave Chris a chance to say a word. "Go to your room and don't get on that phone until I say different." Chris obeyed his mom and decided against confronting her anytime soon about anything.

Missy eased out of the kitchen. There was too much drama going on around here for her, which reminded her that she needed to be on her way to get her own brat from glee club.

"I'll talk to you later, girl," she said going out the door.

137

Pamela Williams-Guinn

"There is gold and a multitude of rubies: but the lips of knowledge are a precious jewel."
Pr. 20:15

"**Y**ou think the kids will be alright at the house by themselves? You got your pager and your cell phone, don't you?" Pretty Baby asked as they were on there way to the party.

"Yes, Mother Goose, now relax and let's have a good time," Missy said, breathing a heavy sigh. "The boys know how to care for Ashley and so does Monique. Between her and the boys, I think they'll be safe. Chris won't be easing out because Monique will page me."

Pretty Baby knew she could bet on that.

"Besides we didn't have any choice since Aunt

138

Tangled Web

Becky's gone to that charity ball." Missy cracked the window as she lit a cigarette. "You want one?" She offered Pretty Baby the pack.

"No thanks, I don't want to smell like smoke. I only want to smell like I just stepped out of the garden of Adrienne Vittidini."

"Girl please, I oughtta fire up this joint on your ass," she said holding up her gold purse.

"Please don't," Pretty Baby said reaching for the automatic window control.

"Ha, I'm just messing with you. I had a glass of wine and got my buzz on before I left the house 'cause I knew you would be tripping." Missy pulled into the entrance of the New Millennium, slowly cruising the aisles for a parking space. "Damn, it's packed. It's some money in here. I can smell it."

Pretty Baby looked as far as her eyes would allow, down the parking lot. "There's one." She pointed to the nearby vacancy.

Missy whipped into the spot. She turned on the inside light so they could freshen lipstick and check their hair even though it was going to blow when they ran to the door. The plan was as usual; run inside and find the nearest ladies room and make a grand entrance from there.

Pretty Baby had heard a lot of talk about the majestic New Millennium but had never been there. She entered the bathroom stall and stood staring up at the beautiful ceiling before she smoothed her body gleamers, under her dress. If the bathroom, with its grand paintings and chandeliers was a taste of what the rest of the building

139

was like, they were in for a royal treat. She came out and walked up to the mirror.

"Girl they got real wash cloths in here to wipe your hands on," Missy said picking up the cloth and fondling it.

"Put that down," Pretty Baby said snatching it away from her. "Now who's country?" They both laughed. "That cream color looks good on you." She commented, admiring Missy's cream sweater dress accented with threads of gold.

"Thanks, I went back to the boutique and got it. I couldn't find anything else, " she said looking closely in the mirror at her eye trying to get a lash out. "I see you found the perfect pumps to go with that dress," she looked at Pretty Baby through the mirror. "Come on, you ready?"

They left the restroom and followed the sounds of the music. Pretty Baby looked around admiring the beautiful Christmas decorations. People were everywhere. Black and white. She thought there would be more whites, but it was an equal mix. She saw the maitre'd with a tray of hors d'oeuvres that looked delicious. She didn't want to come in the door eating but she hadn't had any dinner.

Missy had already seen someone she knew and left Pretty Baby standing. Stand is what she did for a while then eased over to where an enticing spread of food lay. Some stuff she couldn't even identify and wasn't brave enough to sample. She stood in the middle of a group serving themselves and mingled on in.

Missy found her. "I knew when I didn't see you, you were probably over by the food. Look who I found." she said pulling on an arm that didn't have a face for a moment because of the crowd.

Tangled Web

"Nancy! Hey girl." Pretty Baby said and the two hugged.

"I'm glad you let Missy drag you out of the house. I've got to get over and see the baby. I couldn't believe it when Missy said you had the baby the night of the shower. We partied that baby right on out," Nancy said, laughing. They clasped hands. Pretty Baby finished her snack and put her plate in the big gold trash can along the wall. Nancy noticed Missy had disappeared again. "Come over here with us, let me introduce you to some people." Pretty Baby followed obediently, looking around to see if she saw her wild and crazy cousin.

Richard, Nancy's husband, was standing with a group of men in a deep discussion about a new contract, when the women walked up. "Honey, you remember Rachel."

"I sure do. How's that little one?" He asked politely. Nancy introduced her to the other men standing around. Then the D.J. started jamming Coolio. Richard, obviously feeling like he had some rhythm tonight, grabbed Nancy and pulled her on the dance floor. Pretty Baby was left standing there with the men bobbing her head to the music when the man, introduced as Isaac, asked her to dance. He was tall, bald and looked as if he had some smooth moves. He lead her to the dance floor and they partied straight through two songs. Isaac was as smooth as he looked and Pretty Baby stayed in step doing the dances she had seen Chris doing, only it was her own version. Coming off the dance floor she could see Missy flirting with an older, but very handsome, white man. She walked toward them just as the man was walking away.

"I saw you out there getting your groove on cous'," Missy chided Pretty Baby. They stood watching as people came and went and couples slow danced. Nancy came over and joined them. "That's that dude," Missy said in a loud whisper as she peered through the crowd.

"What dude?" Pretty Baby asked as she and Nancy were trying to see who.

The crowd disassembled. Missy made eye contact with the man as the lights went up again and the D.J. started playing another fast song.

"He's heading this way," Missy said under her breath trying to keep her cool.

Finally getting a full view of the man, Nancy said, "Oh, that's Elliott."

"That's him." Missy kept saying. Pretty Baby knew which him she was talking about now.

"Elliott, I'm so glad you came," Nancy said grabbing both of his hands. "It's been too long."

He kissed her on the cheek. "Yeah, it has been too long, that's why I came," he explained.

"Ladies, this is Elliott. Elliott this is..."

Before she could finish he said, "Rachel or should I say Pretty Baby," his eyes danced and he turned to Missy. And..." His eyes were apologetic.

"Melissa." Missy said, filling in the blank, since he had forgotten.

"Of course, Melissa. You ladies look as beautiful as the last time I saw you."

"So you already know the ladies?" Nancy cut her eyes at him. "You're not keeping a low profile after all, huh Elliott?" She teased.

142

Tangled Web

"Well we met through a mutual friend," he said almost bashful. "Excuse me for just one moment," he caught up to one of the guys going out to the atrium.

Smelling the lingering scent of his cologne, Pretty Baby and Missy looked at each other in a dream state. Missy was the first to speak. "Nancy, his business is not in the same complex as yours, is it?"

"It used to be a couple of years ago, but then he moved his headquarters to Richmond. If I'm not mistaken he still has an office in the complex but he doesn't work there," Nancy said, getting another cocktail from the waitress. "He's good lookin', huh?

"Baby, he is fine. Is he married?" Missy wanted to know and Pretty Baby was all ears.

"Yes...no.... " Nancy waved her hand in confusion, the champagne seemed to be taking effect, "Put it this way, he's available."

Missy and Pretty Baby were looking at her for some clarification of the yes/no answer.

"It's a long story, but he's really a great guy, and not a dog," she added reassuringly. "Oh, they're playing our song girls," Nancy said putting her drink on the first tray she saw come by and grabbing both of the ladies by the hand. Pretty Baby shrugged her shoulders at Missy. 'What the heck?'

Pretty Baby beat them to the floor and quickly fell into step with the other Electric Sliders. She was suddenly having the time of her life. Her mind was free from any thoughts of anything except the chorus in the background of the song saying 'It's Electric'. She was the belle of the ball as she did a cha-cha version of the Electric Slide to the front, back and then around Missy, teasing her, with her red chiffon scarf, wrapped around her neck trailing her.

Missy, not one to be shown up, immediately started to cha-cha in step with her. The two of them cha-cha'd all around the dancing crowd then back to their original spaces where Nancy caught on and fell in step strutting her black satin, spaghetti strapped, Yves St. Laurent very mini dress. The three women sashayed their hips with the same moves, Missy sashaying a little more than the others, as a small crowd began to stand back and watch. The song came to an end and all eyes were on them, including Elliott's. He made eye contact with Pretty Baby as he raised his glass in a toasting gesture. She smiled then looked away, coming back to reality and feeling a little bashful, she immediately made an impromptu exit in the opposite direction to the ladies room. Missy followed. She was a little tipsy and needed to take a freshen up break.

"Girl this party is live. I told you, Pretty Baby." Missy said as she went into the opened stall. Pretty Baby put on more lipstick.

"Have the kids paged you?"

"Girl, naw, and yes, Mommie Dearest, my pager's on," she said coming out and washing her hands. "You can't tell me you were thinking about those damn kids, just now, on that dance floor."

Pretty Baby looked at Missy in the mirror and started laughing, "Nope. I just thought about them. I'm having a ball." They went back into the dance and immediately Missy was swept away by an older gentleman onto the dance floor to a slow song. Pretty Baby walked over to where Nancy stood talking to another women about

Tangled Web

her hectic schedule at the bakery and getting the kids from point A to point B, when she was approached by a short plump man who wanted to dance. She declined pleasantly, of course, and went on with the conversation with the other women. When the music stopped, the lights went up and the older gentleman who had swept Missy away earlier was standing on stage with a microphone. He introduced himself as Hershel Dunivan. His thinning silvery hair pulled in a neat ponytail, glistened under the lights just as the diamond button cover and diamond pinky ring he was wearing did.

Missy was at Pretty Baby's side whispering, "He owns the whole damn plaza. Do you hear me?"

Pretty Baby nodded her head as Nancy approached them. Hershel thanked everyone for sharing the Christmas spirit with him and without any further ado he wanted to give bonus checks to all his key employees and top salespeople.

Missy, eyeing the room while the lights were up, saw Elliott standing and talking with a woman. The way the woman leaned into Elliott everytime she laughed, made Missy think they were very acquainted. "That couldn't be his wife or his date," she thought. The woman was short, dark and a little on the heavy side with a gap between her teeth that could be seen a mile away. "Is that his maybe, maybe not, wife?" Missy inquired and Pretty Baby wondered the same thing.

Nancy followed their gaze. "Oh Lord no," she said, shaking her head in distaste. "That's just Clarisse. She's his secretary. She use to work at the Dunivan Plaza office but then she moved to Richmond with him."

145

"I was going to say," Missy said relieved.

"I doubt very seriously if she even came here with him," Nancy remarked.

Pretty Baby eased back over to the dynamic food, loading her plate up and putting a ham and cream cheese swirl in her mouth when she looked up and saw Elliott standing right in front of her. "Could I get you a drink to go with your meal?" He teased, flashing a row of beautiful pearl white teeth.

"Not if it's going to be that champagne," she said swallowing her swirl without really chewing and playing it off, hoping there was no cream cheese on her lips. "I really don't drink," she explained, "and a Pepsi on the rocks would do me just fine right about now." She felt rather relaxed talking to this handsome man.

She smiled. He smiled even wider. "I'll be right back. Don't move."

She blinked. He sure does run off quickly. Pretty Baby took this opportunity to pig out real fast before he returned. She finished half of the plate when she saw him come back toward her, flashing that million dollar smile. He stopped at the bar and returned with a wine goblet filled with ice. Then made his way over to where she stood. He handed her the empty glass as she looked at him curiously. From his side he held up a 20 oz. Pepsi. "Ta-da." he announced sweetly.

"Where'd you get this? Out of your car or the kitchen in the back?" she laughed as he filled her glass.

"Honestly," he said hesitating, "Out of my car. This is what I've been drinking all night. You know, some places don't want you to bring your own bottle in." He gave

Tangled Web

her a mischievous grin.

Pretty Baby discreetly emptied the rest of her plate and enjoyed the strong flavor of the Pepsi. A fast record came on and Elliott asked her to dance. He couldn't remember the last time he danced and was wondering where he even got the nerve to get out on the floor. But he caught the groove quickly as he moved from side to side in time with Pretty Baby's steps. A slow song came on and Pretty Baby couldn't believe it. They were playing 'Betcha by Golly Wow' by Phyllis Hyman. She and Elliott simultaneously moved into each others' arms. Pretty Baby moved her hips with the rhythm of his as they danced silently listening to Phyllis croon about the man she loved being a genie in disguise. The song ended and they walked back to the sidelines. Pretty Baby hadn't danced that close to a man in a long time and she was feeling warm and tingly all over.

She saw Missy coming toward her and she quickly excused herself and went to meet her. "You got a quarter?" She asked. "I'm going to call and check on the kids."

Missy rolled her eyes, "You can use my cellular. Come into the lounge so you can hear." Pretty Baby followed and made her phone call.

"The kids are fine. In fact they were sleep," Pretty Baby said, handing Missy her phone back.

"Did you think the house had burned down? Relax."

Just as they were going back into the party, someone reached out and grabbed Pretty Baby's hand. It was Isaac. "I've been looking for you gorgeous. I hope you have a few more dances left for me."

147

"Of course I do," she said easing her hand away from his and catching up with Missy.

"The party is about to end. A couple of people are going over to the Pink Palace to finish the night off." Missy informed her. "Can you hang or do I need to drop you off."

"You're going to my house too, so you can get your daughter."

"Those children are sleep. Don't make me drag her to the house, Rach," she begged. "I had really planned on crashing at your place myself...after we come back from the Pink Palace." She gave her a sly look.

"Why do I let you talk me into things?"

They stood in the atrium waiting to see if they saw Nancy and Richard to say goodbye, when Elliott walked up. " I was hoping I would see you before I left," he said directly to Pretty Baby. "Here's my business card, call me at any one of those numbers at your earliest convenience. I'd love to take you to lunch."

Pretty Baby looked up at this Adonis of a man thinking, 'For real?' She put the card in her purse and said in a girlish fashion, "That sounds like fun."

Tangled Web

*"Boast not thyself of to morrow; for thou
knowest not what a day may bring forth."*
Pr. 27:1

*P*retty Baby was running late for her lunch with
Missy. She had gotten hung up at the school with a new
parent enrolling two children. She thought she was going
to have to cancel but then the concerned father, whom she
had taken from room to room and had gone over every
aspect of the daycare business, from the day to day
curriculum to potty training arrangements, was satisfied.

Pretty Baby raced into the restaurant trying to get
out of the brisk December wind. As she approached
Missy's table, she could see the back of a man seated with
her. His head looked familiar. As Pretty Baby got a little
closer she saw who it was, and the snake head boots

confirmed it.

Missy saw her approaching, and was giving an apologetic eye to Pretty Baby but laughing at the same time. "Hey, Pretty Baby, glad you finally got away."

"Hello, Pretty Baby," Larry said standing and taking her coat, then adjusting her chair for her.

"Hi Larry, what a surprise seeing you here," she stammered, then gave Missy a questioning look.

"I went on and ordered something for you, Pretty Baby. I ordered us a fried chicken salad to split and a bowl of clam chowder each. Doesn't that sound delicious?" Missy rubbed her hands together, ignoring the look Pretty Baby was giving her.

After getting over the shock of Larry's unexpected presence, Pretty Baby said, "Yeah, that does sound good. Did you get me a Pepsi?"

"Yeah," Missy said, then trying to make small talk, "I was telling Larry how much fun we had at the Dunivan Plaza Christmas party the other night."

"We sure did," Pretty Baby smiled, remembering Elliott and how she and Missy partied at the Pink Palace until the last call for alcohol.

"Pretty Baby, you're coming to our Company party this weekend aren't you?" Larry finally joined in, unable to take his eyes off of her.

"I don't think so Larry. I have another engagement that same night." She lied.

"Excuse me ladies." Larry got up and went toward the restrooms.

Pretty Baby immediately moved in on Missy. "I know you didn't bring him here for me. Is this some kind of

Tangled Web

a joke?" she hissed, pinching Missy's hand extra hard. "And then he's got on those damn boots."

Missy couldn't help laughing, "Girl, no. You know I wouldn't do that. I knew that's what you would think. He was in my office when we were on the phone this morning and he invited himself. You know I had planned on talking some girl talk." Missy gave Pretty Baby a knowing look. "Did you call him?"

"No, not yet." Pretty Baby sank back in her chair, thinking about how many times she had played 'Betcha by Golly Wow,' and remembering each time it seemed as if she could still smell the scent of Elliotts' cologne right under her nose. "I didn't want to seem too anxious," she confessed.

"Uh-huh, Pretty Baby, now you're messing up by trying to wait it out. He doesn't strike me as the type to say, call me at your earliest convenience, if he didn't mean just that. No, I think he would take it as a compliment, having an immediate reply from you. Like Nancy said, he really is a nice guy. Then he'll know if you're interested or not." Missy said with her hands folded in an arch under her chin, giving her best Doctor Ruth advice. "I think you should call him...soon." She saw Larry flirting with the waitress before he headed back to the table. "I went over to Hershels' place last night." Missy added quickly before Larry was in ear shot.

Pretty Baby gasped at that piece of information. She couldn't wait to hear the rest about Missy and Mr. Dunivan. Why did Larry have to come? He sat down just as the waitress brought their food.

Pretty Baby asked for more dressing as she tossed

her salad on her plate and poured it on thick like she liked it.

Just as she was taking a bite she caught Larry looking at her, "You've got dressing on your pinky finger," he said in a slick way, not able to concentrate on his own meal. "You want me to lick it off."

Missy nearly choked on her drink but she knew she had to come to her cousin's rescue. She knew Pretty Baby was not impressed with Larry's advances and didn't think it was cute. Missy's biggest fear was that Pretty Baby would go all the way off and say something pertaining to the man's big lips and the fact still remained that she had to work with this guy. Just as she was about to interrupt, she heard Pretty Baby say. "Missy, what are you bringing over to Lula's for Christmas Eve dinner?" Just like she didn't even hear Larry.

Missy sat back relieved. "I don't know. She asked me to bring a honeybaked ham. So I guess I will. I can't handle that salty Virginia cured ham this year. What about you?"

"I think I'll do my usual, lemon chess pies and Macaroni and cheese." Pretty Baby said finishing off her clam chowder.

"And what about you, Larry? What are you doing for the holidays? Missy thought she'd ask since he had been temporarily banned from the conversation.

"Oh, I thought I'd go up to my cabin in Aspen and ski a little then fly down to Vegas and bring in the New Year." He spoke arrogantly, adjusting his cuff links then waiting on a response.

"I didn't know you skied, Larry? A man of many

talents." Missy said, boosting his ego.

He looked over at Pretty Baby, "I'd love to take your cousin on the slopes sometime." He refused to give up.

"I don't know about that." Pretty Baby said finishing her meal, "I'm more of a beach person. I don't particularly care for the cold weather." She responded politely hoping he wouldn't pursue the conversation. "Here, Missy," she handed Missy a ten dollar bill, "take care of my portion of the check. I've got to run." Pretty Baby stood to put her coat on. "Come by my house this evening, Missy."

"Wait a minute, Pretty Baby." Larry said, "I'll walk you to your car."

"No, don't bother, Larry. Finish your meal. I'll see you guys."

"Don't forget to make that phone call," Missy said giving Pretty Baby a wink.

Pretty Baby quickly went into the ladies room then made her exit from there hoping Larry wouldn't see her. He was too much of a creep for her. She ran to the car and climbed in quickly. She sat there for a minute letting the car warm up. Maybe Missy is right. She shouldn't play the waiting game with Elliott. She hated games any way. She shook her head unconsciously. O.k., so I'll call him on my next break. That way, if the conversation isn't going well I can always use the excuse that I'm at work and have to go. Once the car was warm enough, Pretty Baby put-putted off the lot.

****

153

Pretty Baby glanced up at the clock for the third time in thirty minutes as she got the juice and cookies ready for the 3:00 break. It was 2:58. She figured, if she helped out and got everything prepared for the rest of the staff, she'd have a few extra minutes to make her call uninterrupted.

Pretty Baby went into Mrs. Montgomery's office, knowing she would be at another location today. She closed the door and went over and sat in one of the smaller chairs opposite Mrs. Montgomery's. She dialed the number on the card. The line rang once as she fingered the engraving on the rich leathery textured business card. 'Not the kind you throw away,' she thought. She caught the scent of his cologne still lingering on the card, the phone rang a third time. The thought of trying one of the other numbers was her next move when she heard, "Banks Incorporated."

"Elliott Banks, please," Pretty Baby said.

"Please hold." The background music came on and then she heard the phone being transferred.

"Elliott Banks' office, could you be kind enough to hold?" the female voice said pleasantly then waited for a response. It was too late to just hang up since the woman had asked so politely.

"Yes," was all Pretty Baby could manage. She actually had butterflies in her stomach. She couldn't believe this. He probably isn't in, she thought as the jazz music played in the background. I won't leave a message this ti...

"Elliott Banks office, may I help you?" The woman said, interrupting Pretty Baby's thoughts.

"Is Mr. Banks in?" she said building her confidence

Tangled Web

in case he was there.

"Yes, whom shall I say is calling?"

Why did she have to go there? "Rachel Casey," she said trying to make this sound like a business call.

"What company or organization are you with?"

This really caught Pretty Baby off guard. Searching her mind for the right answer, she could only come up with, "This is a personal call." And it was.

"Hold please." The jazz music came on, then in an instant the sound of Elliott's authoritative voice was on the other end.

"Elliott Banks."

"Hello Elliott, this is Rachel," she said with a smile in her voice.

"So formal now, Pretty Baby?" He said teasingly. "I was hoping to hear from you soon." He paused then asked, "So how've you been?"

"I've been doing fine. That was some Christmas party the other night. I really had a good time," she said.

"Yeah, anything Hershel Dunivan does, he goes all out. And then he's a nice guy, too."

"Well, he sure spared no expense for the holidays," Pretty Baby commented, keeping the conversation neutral.

"Oh man, " Elliott said excitedly, "I can remember several times when he sent each employee and their families on weekend cruises to show his appreciation for their loyalty to the company."

"Really? Sounds like I'm employed by the wrong people," she laughed.

"What do you do, Rachel?" he asked, turning away from his work in his swivel chair to stretch his long legs.

"Nothing as exciting as owning my own computer company," she teased. "I'm a daycare teacher. I'm at work now, actually."

"Daycare. That's a good business."

"Yeah, if you own the daycare," she laughed.

"Well it's never too late to have your own. Speaking of owning, Nancy sure is doing a great job with her bakery," he said checking his watch for the time. "I was surprised to find out you two knew each other."

"Nancy and I have been friends forever. We went to high school together," Pretty Baby said, feeling like she was talking to an old friend. "Look, Elliott, I hate to cut this short, but my break is about up..."

"I've got to go too. I'm suppose to be in a meeting in about five minutes, but I'm really glad you called because I'd like to take you to dinner or a movie...soon." Elliott waited nervously for her reply. He felt like he was in junior high again.

Pretty Baby, was feeling more confident than ever. "How about dinner and a movie this weekend? We'll talk before the week is out to discuss the details."

Elliott was a little stunned but delighted by her assertiveness. "I'll call you, Rachel, before then, just to say 'hi', but I don't know your number." They both laughed.

"It's 555-7754. I'll talk to you then. Bye"

"Goodbye, Rachel, and thanks." He hung up.

Pretty Baby was still holding the receiver when one of the teachers stuck her head in to see who was in the office. "I'll be right out," Pretty Baby said. She could've sworn she could smell the scent of his cologne again.

As Elliott gathered his portfolio and the other

Tangled Web

financial reports scattered on his desk, he glanced at the collage of pictures of his family. Savannah with Kaleb and Isaiah after Kalebs' graduation. Another shot of Savannah shaking hands with the governor of the state and accepting an award. She was so happy then. A twinge of guilt started to creep up on Elliott. He opened his side drawer to get out his portable calculator then went down to the third floor.

****

After the big meeting, Elliott was ecstatic knowing that the Langley account had finally gone through and was secure. It was the biggest transaction that had ever been made in the history of Banks Incorporated, and it was all really due to Savannah.

She had been at an environmental research fund raiser where Winthrop Langley was the guest speaker. Mr. Langley was CEO of Techtron, the largest computer information center in the country. Savannah spoke with him and encouraged a business meeting between the two companies. He was immediately impressed with Banks Inc., but did not need the company's service at the time. Savannah kept in touch with him over the years and continued working on a plan to create a merger of the two companies.

Finally the opportunity came when Langley introduced the Envirotech printing machine which enabled computer cartridges to be recycled and reused. Savannah took it upon herself to volunteer Banks Inc. as their first testing laboratory.

She was aware of how conscious Mr. Langley was about the protection of the environment and the monitoring of the ozone layer, so she hired two environmental specialists out of her own budget to handle the assignment. Despite eighteen months of tedious work and various controlled tests, the project was unsuccessful. During that time Savannah was in the accident. The project had been at a standstill until Mr. Langley's secretary contacted Elliott recently. Langley lead a multi-national conglomerate securing several accounts for the Envirotech printing process and wanted Banks Incorporated to be part of the merger. The first joint office would open in Australia. Elliott had thought the Langley deal had come to a stale-mate and since it had been Savannahs' project, he had not pursued it.

Elliott entered his home through the side entrance, as always, and was met by Maria who was preparing a tray to take up to Savannah.

"Good afternoon, Mr. Banks. You're home early," she said, pouring orange juice into a child's safety cup with a lid. Sometimes Savannah knocked over her food or simply threw it. "I was just about to take Mrs. Banks her mid-day meal. She seems to be in a good spirits today."

"Fine Maria, I'll be up in just a minute." he said sorting through the mail. "Where's Mrs. Savage?"

"Oh she just stepped out. She ran to the drug store."

Elliott nodded as Maria disappeared from the kitchen. He couldn't wait to tell Savannah the news. Sometimes he thought she understood everything he said. Recognition shone in her eyes. She would even mumble a

Tangled Web

few words. But other times she would just sit mute, staring out the window, not even looking in his direction. Savannah rarely left her room unless it was for a doctor's appointment.

Elliott remembered a day when Mrs. Savage was off, and he was working at home. He got the idea to bring Savannah out of her room and down to the study. It had always been her favorite room in the house and he thought a change of scenery might do her good. He put her favorite movie, Imitation of life, in the VCR and they watched the entire movie. She sat through the movie quietly and toward the end, during the saddest part, Elliott noticed Savannah had tears in her eyes. To him, this meant she knew and understood everything that was going on in her surroundings. Immediately after the movie was over, Elliott wrapped his arms around Savannah and poured out his heart to her about how lonely he had been and how he wanted her back in his life. He begged her to understand his needs and was close to tears, trying to explain something he didn't understand himself. She just stared at him with a blank expression. He pulled her face close to his and kissed her lips. Then he kissed her again, more passionately. Immediately, she panicked and started to scream and kick her legs frantically. Once Elliott got her calmed down, he carried her upstairs to her room and put her to bed. They had stopped sharing a room when she came from the hospital the last time. The additional space was needed when Elliott hired the live in nurse. That night, Elliott stayed in Savannah's room, sitting in the chair beside her bed crying for the wife he had lost.

The next day he scheduled a meeting with her

doctor. Dr. Kyles was understanding and very sympathetic but he told Elliott that medically speaking, Savannah was progressing fine but mentally, only time could tell. And he thought it was best that Elliott not push her. He also suggested, in a round about way, that Elliott should get out and meet people. It had been three years. He left the doctor's office feeling as empty as he had when he arrived.

Elliott knocked twice then entered the room where Savannah sat by the window eating a sandwich. She never looked up. He walked over to her and kissed her forehead, taking her napkin from her tray and wiping the sides of her mouth. Her eyes smiled as she looked up at him.

"How're you feeling today? You must have been hungry from the looks of your empty plate." Savannah reached for her drink with two hands and drained her glass. She wasn't as steady when she set it back down, and It toppled to the ground. She looked at Elliott like a scared child who had made a mess.

"That's o.k., baby, I got it for you," he said gently. He cleared her tray and set it aside. "I've got wonderful news, Savannah," he said excitedly. He grasped both of her hands as he sat across from her. "We have finally landed the Langley Envirotech account." He waited for a response but there was none. "Do you know how long it's been since we started on that project? Or should I say, you started on it. I had given up on it then, all of a sudden, Langley's setting up meetings and I signed the final contract today. This is our biggest account and it's all because of you," he said, rubbing his hand across her cheek affectionately.

Tangled Web

Savannah looked around as if searching her mind, then slowly she said, "Where are those boys?"

"Boys? What boys?"

He was confused about who she was referring to, then he remembered Kaleb and Isaiah had been home over Thanksgiving. Mrs. Savage had mentioned that Savannah had been asking about them before.

"They've both gone back home to their jobs. I think Kaleb will be back for Christmas. Would you like that?" Savannah shook her head no, but he knew she meant yes. He wanted to tell her more about the new account, but she really wasn't up for that. Knowing he shared this news with her first was satisfying enough. He sat with her while going over some paper work he had in his brief case. Every now and then he would speak out loud to her then answer his own question.

"You like my new shoes?" She asked quietly.

Elliott looked up from his papers and then at her feet. "Yes, those are nice. They're red, just like your bathrobe." He put his papers down. "Red has always been your favorite color. Remember?" He always thought that if he reinforced things to her she would suddenly remember or have some recollection, but she never did. The doctor said it was selective memory. Only things she wanted to remember stayed with her.

Mrs. Savage came in with Savannah's medicine. She knew what those small cups were for and immediately went into a tantrum. Elliott helped her to restrain Savannah. He wished she didn't have to take the medicine all day, every day but it was evident that that was the only way they could keep her in a tranquil state.

161

Once they got her calmed down and into bed, Elliott watched her doze off. He explained to her sleeping form that he would be out of town quite a bit in the beginning process of the new merger but he could always be contacted for her. Elliott kissed Savannah on her lips as she slept, then he quietly left the room.

Tangled Web

*"He that walketh uprightly walketh surely: but
he that perverteth his ways shall be known."*
Pr. 10:9

"**N**ow that was a good movie. I haven't laughed so much in I don't know how long. In fact I haven't been to a movie in a long time," Elliott said, sitting across from Pretty Baby at the ever so soulful Chatterbox Restaurant.

"Chris Tucker is one of my favorite comedians. I was hooked on him ever since I saw him in 'Fridays', Pretty Baby said.

"I haven't seen that one either."

"You can get it on video now. I'm going to have to get you out more often, Mr. Banks," Pretty Baby said teasingly.

"It's funny, I invited you out but you selected the movie and the restaurant." He raised his hands as if to surrender, "Don't get me wrong, I'm not complaining, I'm having a great time. But next time, I'm going to entertain you, I promise." He gave her an assuring smile.

Pretty Baby smiled at the thought of next time. "I know the movie was a hit, but I'm not sure about the restaurant," she said hesitantly. "You don't care for soul food?"

"The food is terrific and I love this setting. I didn't even know this restaurant existed."

"But..."

"It's just that I'm kind of picky about my food intake."

Pretty Baby gave him an odd look.

"O.K., I'm a health nut, some people would say. I just tend to eat more baked and broiled foods. I don't want to eat too much fat or anything too high in cholesterol."

Pretty Baby giggled at Elliott explaining his nutritional intake.

"Why are you laughing?"

"I'm not laughing. I'm taking notes." She narrowed her eyes flirting with him, "Is that how you keep that flawless physique?"

"Yes, I guess so, and I'm going to help you keep yours flawless." They both laughed. "Seriously, all that fat isn't good for anyone and then I try to work out several times a week at the gym. If I don't do that, I go over to the university and run a couple of laps if the weather permits."

"I've seen you out there." Pretty Baby said suddenly. "Do you have a bright orange sweat shirt?"

Elliott looked a little embarrassed. "As a matter of

Tangled Web

fact, I do. That's part of my work out gear." He laughed. "When did you see me? Why didn't you say anything?"

"It's been a while ago but I knew you looked familiar. I go over there myself in the mornings before work."

Pretty Baby and Elliott were having the same thoughts about how comfortable they were feeling with each other. He was flattered at her enthusiasm about his latest conquest with the Langley account and was equally impressed with her questions about his work. It felt good sharing his knowledge with someone who didn't know a lot about his line of work but was truly interested.

The room where they were seated had dimly lit candles sitting in crystal sconces. The flickering flames danced in Elliott's eyes when he spoke of his new business venture.

"I'd say this deal should be sealed with a bottle of wine instead of coke on the rocks," Pretty Baby said stopping the waiter as he went by.

"That sounds good to me. How about White Zinfandel?" Elliott suggested. The waiter was back in an instant with the wine and two wine glasses. "Shall we make a toast?"

"Let me do the honors," Pretty Baby said clearing her throat. She raised her glass. "To you Elliott, congratulations on one of your many successes." They clicked glasses and took a sip simultaneously. They were both quiet for a long moment, enjoying the small jazz quartet that played in the far corner of the room. Pretty Baby was still curious about whether Elliott was married or not, and was thinking of a way to ease it into the conversation.

"Do you have family here, Elliott?" She asked as she watched the candle and then glanced up at him. She thought she saw a little tension appear on his face.

"My mother lives in Dale City which isn't very far. I try to go see her when I can. I have a brother there too," he added.

Pretty Baby thought this was like pulling teeth. "You don't have any children?" Hopefully she could get the information she was looking for with that question.

"I have two adult sons," he said looking directly at her. "Actually they're my wife's boys, but I feel like they're mine. I don't have children of my own."

She tried to seem unmoved by this revelation and tried to keep the conversation light. A married man was the   last thing she needed right now. And having been a wife for many years, she was appalled at people who knowingly stooped that low. Several women she knew had dated married men, they said it was better than having your own man because he was never suppose to tell you no and you could get rid of him whenever you were tired of him. That logic still seemed ruthless in her mind. Elliott hadn't made any romantic moves but why else would a married man ask a woman out, she thought. She would just make sure everything stayed on a platonic level, and that way, no one would get hurt.

"Is your wife out of town or something?" she asked casually taking another sip of her drink not knowing what else to do with her hands as she started to feel a little tipsy.

Elliott shook his head from one side to the other. He didn't know where to start or if he should explain. He just wanted to enjoy the company of someone other than a

Tangled Web

business associate, for a change. He had to admit he was having a great time and considered Rachel a friend. At that point he knew he had to explain.

"My wife," he started slowly, "my wife is at home where she always is because she suffers from a severe mental illness." Pretty Baby was shocked at this announcement, she placed her hand over his as she saw the pain in his eyes. "She was in an automobile accident almost four years ago," he began slowly. "She started to recover but then she had a relapse and has been that way every since."

"Oh, Elliott, that must be very hard on you," Pretty Baby said sympathetically. That explained Nancy's comment at the party. "Who stays with her while you work and travel?"

"I have a full time nurse and a staff of people who see about her. I couldn't stand the thought of committing her to an institution so she has remained at home. I always hoped that she'd suddenly get better but it hasn't happened. Soo.." he took a deep breath, "I spend the majority of my time working and I go out to the old airport and fly twin engine planes when I get the time." They both sat in silence for a moment. "So what about you? Now that you know the story of my life. I can't imagine a woman of your stature not being married or having a significant other," he said smiling again.

Pretty Baby really didn't want to elaborate on the situation she had just come out of. Her so-called marriage. "Well, you know I'm recently divorced and have three children and," she paused looking a bit disgusted, "unlike you, my ex is not a very considerate person. So I'm on my own."

"He doesn't see the children?"

Pretty Baby shook her head.

"Not even the new baby? I'm sure that's a load on you."

"It is," she said suddenly aware that the thought of William hadn't depressed her, "but a girl's gotta do what a girl's gotta do. Elliott, you can fly a plane?" She asked excitedly, changing the mood and the subject.

He laughed at her excitement. "Sure can. I'll have to take you for a ride one day. Do you like to fly?"

"I've only been in a plane twice. It was o.k., but it was a commercial flight. I can't imagine sitting in the front seat, though." She saw Elliott glance at his watch. "What time is it?"

"11:30, time sure flies when you're having fun. We've been in this restaurant almost three hours."

"I hadn't noticed," she said giggling, feeling very young. Pretty Baby had decided Elliott was the kind of friend she needed until someone special did come along. "I have really enjoyed myself tonight, Elliott. It's been a long time for me too. What are you doing for the holidays?" She would have liked to have invited him to their family Christmas eve dinner but decided against it.

"Oh, I don't know. The boys will probably be home. I think I'll go to my mothers' on Christmas day and stay through the weekend. I'm leaving for Australia in a few days and I'll be there a week."

"That sounds exciting."

"If I get some free time, I'm going to try to do a little shopping while I'm there." Elliott stood as he saw the

Tangled Web

maitre'd bring their coats. He helped Pretty Baby with her coat then put his on.

They road in his luxurious car, talking nonstop about everything, from music to strange people in their families. Pretty Baby hated to get out of the warm car as they pulled up to her hooptie that had been left on the theater lot.

"Give me your keys," Elliott said, "I'll start your car and let it warm for a few minutes."

Pretty Baby was pleased at his courtesy and handed him the keys, not even feeling embarrassed about her ride. He unlocked the door, hopped in and started the engine. Pretty Baby was busy changing the CD and hadn't noticed Elliott struggling to get out of the car until she heard the loud horn that startled her. She burst into laughter when she realized Elliott couldn't get out because he had probably knocked the screwdriver out of place. She climbed out in the cold and opened the driver's door from the outside.

Elliott got back in the car trying to shake the chill that had surrounded him and settled in his bones. "What is that, a boobie trap door?"

Pretty Baby was still laughing, "When I realized you were stuck, I started to drive off in this Benz and leave you with the hooptie." She imagined the look that would have been on his face if she had driven off. "You could've climbed out on the passenger side." Elliott had to laugh himself.

Brian McKnight played a sexy love song in the background as Pretty Baby and Elliott talked for well over twenty minutes. "My car should be good and warm by now." She hated to say goodnight. "So I guess I'll talk to you when you get back in town."

"I want to tell you again, I had a really nice time tonight and I hope we can do it again sometime."

Pretty Baby watched his lips as he spoke the words, then she blinked herself back to reality. "Goodnight Elliott," she smiled, unsure of whether it would be wise to make future plans. She got out of his car and into hers.

Shivering cold, she turned the defroster on high and put the car in gear. It sputtered first then jerked and took off. "Come on, Bessie, you've made it through colder times." Pretty Baby said to the car.

Before she could pull on to the main street, she saw Elliott flashing his headlights. He pulled next to her and rolled his window down. "Rachel, I'm going to follow you home to make sure you get in safely. I don't know why I let you talk me into meeting you here, I should've picked you up."

"Really, Elliott, that's not necessary. You already have an hour long drive back to Richmond."

"I insist." He rolled his window up and let Pretty Baby lead the way. He was actually afraid her car may stop on her.

Elliott followed her to her house and watched as she waved goodbye and went in. He pushed his Brian McKnight CD in and headed down I-95 to Richmond making mental notes along the way in preparation for his trip to Australia. Clarisse would handle all the travel arrangements and he would get her to pull all of the necessary files. Hopefully, he wouldn't be gone longer than a week. He glanced at the time on the dashboard, it was almost 2:00 am. Elliott stifled a yawn as he neared his

Tangled Web

exit and thoughts of Rachel sitting across from him, looking beautiful and awestruck as he told her about how he had learned to fly, came to him. She was a great listener and quite intelligent too. Again, he thought it strange that a woman like her didn't have a husband or someone special in her life.

Winding down the dark street in the elite district of Richmond, most of the homes on Elliott's street looked lived in and festive as he admired the brilliant Christmas lights. But as he clicked the automatic garage opener and pulled in the driveway he realized his big luxurious six-bedroom home on the hill looked vacant, even though there was always someone there. He thought about putting some lights up around the house before he left for his trip, then decided against it. He hadn't been in that kind of Christmas spirit for some years now. A wreath on the door and the small tree in the foyer of the house would have to do.

Quietly entering the side entrance, that led into the kitchen, he could see a light on in the hallway. He glanced at the brightly lit digital numbers on the microwave. Surely Ms. Savage wasn't up at this hour. He walked softly toward the front to see if she was sitting in one of the rooms. He opened the door of the study to darkness, then walking further he scanned the great room and dining room sitting on both sides of the hall. Realizing the light was just left on, he went back to the kitchen and poured himself a small glass of Pepsi.

He sat and unbuttoned the first three buttons of his collarless shirt rotating his neck slowly from one side to the other, then kicked off one of his shoes under the table. His dad always used to come home from work and kick off one shoe while he read the paper or watched the news. Elliott and his brother always wondered why he did that and now he had the exact same habit. He sat there for a moment listening to the very quiet hum of the overhead fluorescent light. The silence was overpowering, he then realized that it was just as deafening in the middle of the day when everyone was awake. When the boys lived at home, even late at night, some sounds of life were apparent. Whether it was a television left on or the low thump of a stereo going, there was life behind these walls.

Thoughts of Rachel crept into his mind. He smiled as he imagined her home with her three children, each of them running, yelling and competing for her attention as she had described. He drained his glass, put it in the sink, and turned the light off on his way out then clicked it right back on as he remembered his shoe. Maria often fussed at him when she would find one shoe.

Elliott crept up the stairs turning off any lights along the way when he saw a dim light coming from Savannah's room. The door was ajar. Maybe Ms. Savage was having a bad night with Savannah. He could hear Ms. Savage speaking calmly as he moved closer to the openness. He pushed the door open a little more just in time to realize that Ms. Savage was reading the bible to Savannah as she slept. He watched and listened for a moment as he heard Ms. Savage say, *"And this is the confidence we have in Him, that, if we ask anything according to his will, he heareth us: And if we know that he hear us, whatsoever we ask, we know that we have the petitions that we desired of Him...."* Elliott pulled the door back where it was. He knew

172

Tangled Web

that Ms. Savage was active in her church and listened to gospel music and sermons by different pastors while she took care of Savannah, but he didn't know she read the bible to her through the night. He thought for a moment, glimpsing her sleeping form and was thankful that a God-fearing woman took care of his wife. He went into his room and retired for the night.

Pamela Williams-Guinn

*"A wise son heareth his father's instructions:
but a scorner heareth not rebuke."*
Pr. 13:1

Christmas Eve was wet and nasty. Big white snow flakes were blowing fast and hard, melting immediately as they hit the ground. Pretty Baby covered Ashley's face with her other blanket as she ran to Lula's front door. Chris carried the pies and macaroni and cheese while Jason carried the diaper bag. The house was already filled to capacity. Shouts of Merry Christmas were heard when they came through the door. Hugs and kisses were exchanged as if they were all guests from out of town.

Monique saw Pretty Baby coming through the door and came to take Ashley from her arms. "Where's your momma, Monique?"

Tangled Web

"She's in the kitchen with Aunt Becky, Aunt Lula, Lillie Mae and Hubert Jr.. My momma said she was gonna cut Hubert Jr. before the night is over," she said nonchalantly as she took the baby and Pretty Baby removed her coat.

Pretty Baby took a second look at Monique making sure she'd heard her right. "Girl, you talk too much."

"For real, Pretty Baby. He owes her some money that he said he would pay back last week and come to find out he went to Atlantic City." She paused with the baby on her hip, waiting for Pretty Baby's reaction. "He hit the jackpot then played it all back." she explained with disgust.

Pretty Baby rolled her eyes, hanging her coat on the rack. "He needs to be cut," she agreed. She followed the noise into the kitchen where everyone was dogging Hubert Jr., Missy still threatening to get a knife and cut him because she wanted her sixty bucks.

"Put that macaroni and cheese in the oven a few minutes, Pretty Baby," Aunt Becky said.

"It's still hot," she told her, making room on the counter for her pies.

"Let me cut a piece of that lemon chess pie, Pretty Baby," Missy said reaching for it.

"Go right ahead and cut something so you won't cut Hubert." Pretty Baby laughed while Hubert ducked out of the room.

"Girl, don't start me back up about that loser. Lillie Mae, his own momma, told me that's where he's been. She had to Western Union him bus fare to get back home...pitiful." She shook her head.

"O.K., everybody," Aunt Lula yelled, "grab a dish

and let's take it all to the dining room."

There were about twenty-five relatives packed in the dining room, not including the children. The spread included anything you could think of. Chitterlings, greens, snap beans, corn pudding, turkey, ham with pineapple slices, crowder peas, macaroni and cheese, dressing, spaghetti, and pot roast with potatoes just to name a few. Everyone joined hands for the prayer that was always lead by Aunt Becky. Good thing there were no outsiders present to experience her blessing the table prior to a meal or else they would've gotten a lesson in patience. Aunt Becky, always careful to give God all the praise for the blessings that had resulted in the food which they were about to receive, began: Thank you, Lord for Mr. Rally, who got Samson the special project that allowed him to buy all these groceries and have a home for us to gather and fellowship in, and Mr. Jones for growing and delivering the corn, and Lillie Mae for the fresh crowder peas. Lord, thank you for fertile soil for my garden so that I may add my contribution to our feast. And, lest we forget, the hands and skills of all who worked in the kitchen to prepare the meal. Lord wrap your loving arms around each and everyone around this table calling out a request. Bestow a blessing upon Hubert Jr., Lord, so that there won't be any animosity between him and his cousin...Then she named everybody, one by one, who was present and standing in the need of prayer. Through all of this, somehow, God kept the food warm and everyone's stomachs from talking too loud. "Amen," everyone said simultaneously.

Folks were sitting all over the house, trying to get comfortable while they ate. Pretty Baby looked in on the children sitting in the den. Monique was still holding the baby. Neither one of her brothers volunteered for the chore as Monique weaved in and out of the way of Ashley's busy hands. "Momma, Monique has two plates of food. Look at her!" Jason said.

"I got two plates so my food won't spill, for your stupid information," she protested.

"Give me the baby, Monique." She reached for Ashley out of Monique's lap. "Momma's gonna find that baby something she can eat too." Ashley smiled a big grin as she drooled in anticipation. Monique moved her plate just in time. Chris laughed, assuring Jason she would've eaten it anyway.

Ashley didn't have a problem feasting on the meal her mom had pulled together for her inspite of her two short bottom teeth. Pretty Baby was barely able to keep the child seated in her lap as she grabbed at other morsels of food on her plate.

After going through every compartment of the diaper bag, Pretty Baby got Chris' attention. "What did you do with Ashley's milk and juice bottle? In the refrigerator?"

Chris gave a look of bewilderment then remembered he didn't put them in the bag like his mother told him to do before they left the house. "Oh, Ma...." Was all he could muster apologetically.

Pretty Baby scrambled to her feet from her seat on the floor as she put Ashley in his arms then popped him upside his head. "If you do what I tell you, when I tell you, you won't have these problems," she said for his ears only. "Now I'm going to have to run back to the house. YOU watch your sister. Don't let me come back and Monique is

177

holding her while you're having yourself a ball."

Just as Pretty Baby was about to leave she heard Missy call after her. "Where're you going, Pretty Baby?"

"I need to run to the house for a second. Come on and ride with me."

"Gladly," Missy said. "Let me grab my coat and tell the kids."

Pretty Baby sat in the car with the wipers going and the defroster on high as she saw Missy's bundled up form run out of the house to her car. She jumped in breathlessly. "I had to get something for the road," she said slyly.

"Can you believe Hubert won five thousand dollars and played it all back? What a dumbass...he could have at least set aside my sixty dollars...and bus fare home."

They both laughed as Pretty Baby carefully maneuvered the wet streets. It didn't take them long to get to her house, since most of the family lived in the same vicinity.

"Why can't it just snow for Christmas instead of all of this wet mess?" Missy remarked. "It always tries to snow but never succeeds," she said, getting out of the car and slamming the door when she realized that Pretty Baby was struggling to get out. She went around to the driver's side and let her out. "I know one thing...you need to make it your mission to get some other means of transportation for the New Year."

Pretty Baby opened the door to her home greeted by the twinkling lights of the six-foot tree that stood in the corner. The house smelled of pine, thanks to Chris spraying artificial pine spray to make visitors think the tree was real. "As soon as spring comes," she said

Tangled Web

thoughtfully, "I'm going to try to get a new car. I just hate taking on a car note." She brushed through the swinging door and turned on the light in the kitchen.

Missy plopped down on the sofa picking up a JET magazine with Bobby Brown on the cover. "It was probably his prerogative to wear those too tight leopard pants," she mused, going back to the conversation with Pretty Baby. "I'm so tired of people saying they don't want a car note." She shook the magazine as she spoke then tossed it on the coffee table. "Cars are only built to last long enough for you to get them paid for. And if you're lucky you can ride for a year, maybe two, with no note." She shrugged her shoulders. "Now, in your case, your car is a rarity and it has gone far and beyond the call of duty." Missy doubled over with laughter.

"Don't go there. I can remember several occasions when you, Miss Thang, depended on the Duce," she said opening the door so she could get a full view of Missy. "Rain, snow or shine, she got us where we wanted to go."

"I know, I know...but it's retirement time."

Pretty Baby laughed. "Hey," she said suddenly, "what happened with you and Hershel? Have you seen him again?"

Missy leafed through a COSMO magazine, spying an article entitled 'My Mother Lived Across Town and I Never Knew Her.' Suppressed feelings began to surface as she quickly pushed them aside.

"Of course I've seen him again. Where do you think I got this tennis bracelet," she said, leaving the magazine and going into the kitchen flashing her new jewels. "This ain't costume."

"Oh, it's beautiful." Pretty Baby said, putting the bottles in a paper bag and the formula away. "Chris hadn't even fixed the bottles, that's why he forgot them," she commented with displeasure. Going back to Hershel, "So could he be the new man for the New Year?"

"I doubt it"

"But he's rich, Melissa," Pretty Baby said sarcastically, taking another look at the bracelet and nodding with approval.

"And I love that about him," she pleaded. "But he's old and dull. Hell, he's older than Virgil. And then he's into role playing."

Pretty Baby giggled, "I can't imagine anything dull about playing roles."

"It's not funny," Missy said, trying not to laugh as well. "He likes to play doctor and nurse, Simon says or preacher and the church lady."

"Uh-uh," Pretty Baby, said trying to contain her laughter while turning off the lights and heading to the front. "Girl, you better make sure he isn't a sex offender," she said half seriously, then blundering again, "but don't ever play 'preacher and the church lady'. Where do you get these characters from?"

Their laughter was interrupted by the phone ringing. "Hello," she said hurriedly, as Missy stood in the door way.

"Merry Christmas, did I catch you at a bad time?" The unmistakable sound of Elliott's deep voice pierced her ear and headed straight to her stomach causing it to do a flip flop.

"No, well, you just caught me. I was going back over to my Aunt's for our Christmas Eve dinner." She waved frantically for Missy to sit down and keep quiet. Missy, rolling her eyes, did as she was silently instructed, assuming it was probably him. She picked up the COSMO magazine and flipped back to that article she had just seen.

"Don't let me keep you. I just wanted to wish you a happy holiday tonight because I'm leaving for my mothers' early, tomorrow."

"Same to you. Your mom cooking a big Christmas feast?"

"Oh, I'm sure," he said with a chuckle, "plenty that's not on my food list. But I usually save one holiday out of the year to overindulge because if I don't, it will be an insult to the cook."

There was a brief pause. "Do you and the children have plans for tomorrow?"

"No. I usually stay around the house on Christmas day in case visitors come by and the boys want to have friends over. When will you be returning?"

He took a deep breath. "Probably in a day or two. What are you doing for New Years?" He hoped he wasn't being intrusive, but he just wanted to talk a while longer.

Pretty Baby unbuttoned her coat as she leaned back on the couch. "I like to go to church on New Years' Eve...and on New Years day I'm going to start the year off right with my black-eyed peas for good luck and a pot of greens for prosperity," she laughed, "and I'll probably steam some vegetables and bake some chicken." Missy glanced up at her, motioning for her to hurry up.

"Sounds interesting," Elliott said. Pretty Baby could hear the smile in his voice as her stomach flip-flopped again.

"I'm not going to hold you from your dinner," he said. "I just wanted to wish you seasons greetings and hopefully, I'll see you soon."

"Merry Christmas to you too, Elliott, be careful and call me when you get back in."

"Will do. Bye."

"Bye." Pretty Baby hung up the phone, trying to conceal her smile before Missy noticed.

Missy put the magazine down and stood with her hands on her hips. "Now let's go. You can't fool me, Rachel Casey," she scolded. Pretty Baby laughed as she locked up and followed Missy out to the car. "We're just friends," Missy continued, "His wife is ill and he just needs a friend like I do," Missy mimicked Pretty Baby. "I don't believe you told me everything about that supposed one date." They sat for a minute, waiting for the car to shake the chill off.

"It was only one date and we've talked on the phone a few times. He really is a nice guy, Missy." She said sincerely. "...Who needs a friend," she added with a snicker.

"Alright, friend," she said in disbelief, getting her cigarettes out, "but I've never known you to steam no damn vegetables or bake no chicken. You eat fried everything! You can't fool me. I know the signs, the symptoms, the story," she lectured her cousin lovingly. "I know it must be a trip having an insane wife that's been that way for years." Missy gave a puzzled look, "I wouldn't be surprised if he had several friends. A fine man like that. But I'm happy for you, Cous. You need another interest besides those kids.

Tangled Web

Enjoy while you can."

"Thank you, Missy, but we really are friends and I am enjoying this nice platonic relationship with another adult." She drove the big Duce through the streets, taking the short cut back to Lula's to go down the street where every house was lit up with lights. "I need to be involved with a married man like I need a hole in my head. But you know..." she said thinking before she spoke, "I only know of one male, who I can truly call a friend, that never expects anything from me except friendship, and that's Jesse. So to me, Elliott is like a breath of fresh air. I believe he wants the same thing from me that I want from him. You know what I mean?" She looked over at Missy.

"Yeah, I know exactly what you mean. You should be friends before you give up the panties." Missy laughed.

She pulled back into her same spot and put the car in park. "I give up on you," Pretty Baby said, throwing her arms in the air. "Get out of my car," she teased. "Missy, have you ever been just friends with any man?"

"No." She laughed. "And you're right, that's probably why I'm not friends with anyone now....we were never friends from the beginning. Love 'em and leave 'em Missy. That's me." She pulled her coat up snug around her neck as she waited on Pretty Baby. "I'm going to go to church with you on New Year's Eve. Is that alright?"

Pretty Baby put her arm around Missy as they walked toward the house, surprised at this comment, "Of course it is." Then wondering what could have made Missy decide to give up a typical New Year's party for church service was beyond Pretty Baby, but she was glad. They rejoined the family just as Samson, Hubert Jr. and Robert

Earl were doing their rendition of Silent Night by the Temptations.

Tangled Web

"Train up a child in the way he should go: and when he is old, he will not depart from it."
Pr. 22:6

Pretty Baby stepped her foot into the trashcan trying to compress all the wrapping paper and boxes that had gathered since Christmas, before she set the trash out. All of the hustle and bustle and trash for one brief day was still ludicrous to her but it had made her children happy inspite of the fact that William had not shown up. In fact she only knew of one time that Chris had spoken with him since he had come over that day to try and tell her how to raise her child. Deep inside she hurt for her children who loved a man who obviously did not want to be part of their lives. Even though the children seemed to be genuinely happy on Christmas day, that night she silently shed tears because the person she thought loved them as much as she did, had not even called. She prayed long and hard that the Lord would shield them from William's ignorance.

Once all the cleaning was done Pretty Baby proceeded to make a grocery list for her New Year's dinner. Remembering that she had to pick up a few items for Aunt Becky, reminded her that she needed to tell her she would bring her some dinner for New Year's. Her thoughts were interrupted by a familiar tapping on the door. She yelled, "come on in, it's open." Jesse had a distinct knock when he came to the door.

"Well Merry Christmas," he said happily, giving Pretty Baby a brotherly hug. "I came by here the day after Christmas but you weren't here."

"I know, the boys told me. They loved their gifts, Jesse, especially Chris. Those CD's were right on time with the new CD player I bought him." She motioned for him to have a seat. "Jason loved the game you got him for his Nintendo 64 and I loved the outfit you got Ashley. Boy, I feel a bit slighted that I wasn't on your list." She nudged him playfully.

"I had you in mind while I shopped. I almost bought you a Phyllis Hyman CD," he joked. "Really, though, I figured it would take a little pressure off of you if I got something for the children."

"And you were right of course," she patted his knee as she got up to go to the steps, thinking she had heard Ashley whimper. "I sure got Chris this time with the CD player. He had no idea that's what I had for him. That boy

186

Tangled Web

literally jumped in my arms when he tore the wrapping paper off." She remembered his expression as she walked back to the couch then did an about face realizing she had heard Ashley. "I thought my mother ears were tuned," she said speaking to herself and Jesse. "Wait a second, Jesse." She made a dash up the stairs and returned with Ashley in her arms.

"Hey Baby Girl." Jesse reached for the cute little girl and she grinned at the sight of him. He played with her while Pretty Baby warmed her lunch, then brought her into the kitchen and seated her in the high chair. He was about to go but before he did he handed Pretty Baby a bright red box with a big silver bow on it.

She gasped, "For little ole me?" she said weighing the box in her hands. "Jesse, you didn't have to."

"You know I had to have a little something for you. You work so hard, you deserve a surprise, too. Now hurry and open it before I go."

Pretty Baby did as she was instructed and was pleased when she lifted the lid and saw two large Mulberry candle jars. "Oh, Jesse," she exclaimed giving him a big hug. "You know I love to burn my scented candles."

"Yes, I know, that's why I knew it was perfect when I saw them." Jesse glanced at his watch, "Where're the boys? I wanted to holler at Chris before I left."

"Jason walked over on Aunt Becky's street." Pretty Baby turned to see that Ashley had thrown her Vienna sausage pieces on the floor and smeared her applesauce all over the tray. "And I can't really say where Chris has disappeared to. He better not be over at that girl's house," she said glancing back in Jesse's direction.

"Oh, Pretty Baby," he laughed, "give a brother a break. It's the holidays."

"You just don't know. Would you believe Chris ordered a cubic zirconia ring off of QVC for this young lady?"

"My man Chris," Jesse stated leaning against the wall with his arms folded.

Pretty Baby raised her hand for him not to interrupt. "He decided against giving it to her because he said it didn't look real enough. I asked him what did he expect for $26.95. It was cute enough, I thought."

"I'm out of here, Pretty Baby. You guys are too much for me," he laughed.

"Alright, Jesse, I'll see you at church tomorrow night, right?" She asked, walking him to the door.

"I'll be there."

"Thanks for everything, Jesse," she said out the door. "Missy's coming tomorrow night too."

Jesse turned around once he got to his car and made a cheering motion. "How'd you pull that one off?"

Pretty Baby shrugged, hugging herself as the cold air forced its way into the open door. "It was her idea" she shrugged again. "See you then."

She closed the door tightly and went back into the kitchen where Ashley had poured the remainder of her juice on the high chair top and was stirring it with her hands. "Ashley Lynn..." her mother fussed, "you make so much work for momma." She moved her from her chair to the floor. "Now let me get you cleaned up for your brother before I go to the store," she said hearing the front door open then a loud galloping go up the stairs.

Tangled Web

"Chris? Jason? Who is that?" She finished wiping the baby's face and hands, carrying her to the front on her hip. "Chris?"

"It's me, Momma." Jason galloped back down the stairs.

"Who's up there with you?"

"Nobody."

"Oh, you sounded like a herd stampeding up those steps." She put the child safety gate on the stairs and spread a few toys on the floor in the limited space for Ashley. "Where's Chris? I need to run to the store."

"Go ahead," he said climbing over the gate on the steps. "I can watch Ashley while you're at the store."

She kissed him on the forehead, "I know you can baby but I have to shop for Aunt Becky too, then run another errand and it may take longer than we expect. But thank you, anyway." She looked at her middle child tenderly.

"Speak of the devil," she glanced out of the window, "here he comes now."

Chris entered the house breathlessly bringing the cold air in with him. Ashley, crawled immediately toward him pulling herself up begging for the attention of her oldest brother. "Give me some of that neck," he said grabbing her up nuzzling her neck as she gave a hardy laugh. The boys enjoyed their sister more now that she was getting older and could enjoy their rough housing. Jason joined in on the fun, tickling her stomach as Chris airplaned her through the living room, coming in for a smooth landing on mommy's lap. Realizing the game was over, Ashley reached for Chris, ready to play some more.

He continued to give her quick kisses while she sat in Pretty Baby's lap.

Pretty Baby delighted in the play among her three children, thinking this was definitely a Kodak moment, when she suddenly said, "What's that on your neck, Chris?" She squinted her eyes to get a better look.

"Where?" He put his hand on the exact spot.

"Right where your hand is," Pretty Baby said, narrowing her eyes and becoming immediately agitated. "

Chris took two baby steps backwards, trying to discreetly distance himself from his mother, who was known for having a long reach on a slap.

"You got a passion mark." She sat Ashley on the couch. "That's a hickey on your neck, Chris," she repeated, then stood to get an even better look. "That's where you've been," she accused. Ashley climbed off of the couch and crawled over to Jason as her mother continued to bellow. "Tell that hot tail heifer to keep her mouth off of you! And I mean it. Don't come back in here with another one." She got her coat out of the closet. "I'm going shopping. I'll be back."

Bucking the wind with her head bent, Pretty Baby trotted up to Aunt Becky's door. Shivering, she shifted the bags, using both arms to balance the load and one finger to pull the handle on the screen door, but was saved when Aunt Becky swung the door open. "Come on in here," she said trying to assist Pretty Baby with the bags, but Pretty Baby refused.

Aunt Becky reached out to look in her mailbox, but found only junk mail. She ambled over to the potbelly morning warmer stove, rubbing her hands together to take

Tangled Web

the chill off, then back to the kitchen. "Tis' chilly out there. That temperature sure has dropped since noon, huh?"

"Yeah, and people are packed in the grocery store like a blizzard is coming through," Pretty Baby said, briskly rubbing her hands together in front of the open oven. "I got everything that was on the list."

"You got my Ben Gay rub? This shoulder been acting up something terrible," she asked anxiously.

Pretty Baby let out a deep sigh and slumped her shoulders. "Everything except your Ben Gay rub. I'm sorry Aunt Becky," she said apologetically, removing her coat and hanging it on the back of the chair. "I didn't write that down and it slipped my mind." She started to help put the groceries away.

"Well, I got a little drop left to get me through the night," Aunt Becky said going into the bathroom and coming out with a worn out tube of Ben Gay.

Aunt Becky took the tube back to where she got it and came back to see Pretty Baby staring out into the yard with a deep furrow in her forehead. She studied her for a moment, thinking she was probably still upset with William for not seeing the children over the holidays. "You want to talk about it?" Her voice broke the silence that brought Pretty Baby back.

She hesitated for a moment, then realizing what had been asked, "No, Aunt Becky, it's nothing."

"It must be something, you standing there staring in space, frowning."

Pretty Baby resumed her duties. Putting everything in its' proper place for Aunt Becky. "It's Chris and...Sharon."

Aunt Becky gasped. "She ain't...."

"Pregnant?" Pretty Baby finished. "No. Thank God. But they've got a serious thing going on. A little too serious, and it worries me. I know if I forbid him to see her, it'll just run him to her. But I don't think that Sharon is conducting herself like a young lady should and she's too mature for Chris. I can't figure out what the attraction is."

Hearing the whistle from the tea kettle, Aunt Becky poured herself a cup of tea offering Pretty Baby some. "Chris, is growing into a good looking young man in case you haven't noticed. And as goofy as we may think he is, I bet he doesn't act that way around her."

Pretty Baby sat in a somber state. "Yeah, you're probably right."

"I think you should talk with your eldest about the real facts of life..."

"I already have."

"Then you should talk with her about the way a young lady should conduct herself. It's not like you don't know her well enough. It's hard to believe, but some folks don't know how to act appropriately in the simplest situations....'cause nobody has ever talked to them. So before you lose any sleep over this, try talking to her. As a matter of fact," she continued, "bring her to the church sometimes. We have all kinds of teen awareness groups that speak quite frankly to the young people."

Pretty Baby thought she would start taking Chris to more teen activities and maybe he would meet some other girls. That would get his mind off of Sharon. "Aunt Becky, is this the week we're having the dedication ceremony for the new Family Life Center?"

Tangled Web

"Yes, it's tomorrow night immediately following the New Year's Eve service," she said, sitting at the table excited at the mention of the new building. "I expect to see some faces we haven't seen in a few months for this event. If not tomorrow night, then definitely next Sunday," she said in a knowing way.

"Why do you say that?"

"Well, you know it was a big stink about even purchasing the additional property, not to mention the building. I know I'm old, but a lot of the other older members can't seem to handle change and they prefer to do things by tradition, instead of authority."

"What do you mean?" Pretty Baby asked.

"We've been talking about building this Family Life Center for years. Finally, it was decided then, all of a sudden a lot of people didn't want to make firm commitments to the building fund. I'm not passing judgment, but these very people have been members as long as I have or longer and they should know the meaning of being a good steward. A lot of these people have good jobs, fancy cars and homes," she shook her head in disgust, "but they just can't seem to grasp the idea of Luke 12:48, 'For everyone to whom much is given, from him much will be required'. I think some were offended by the amount of money that was being spent. That wasn't something that was voted on, 'cause voting, in a lot of instances, causes division and we're promoting unity based on God's authority." She went on in her evangelistic way, "Meaning, if you traditionally put a dollar in the collection plate each time you come to church and you earn $500 dollars a week, you are not giving a tenth of your earnings

193

which God has blessed you with. You see where I'm coming from?" Pretty Baby nodded in agreement. "When you give to God first, it'll remind you of where blessing originated from." She got up to poor another cup of tea. "Further more, the church don't run on air. It takes money, and it's gonna be some people who want to see what the money was spent on."

Pretty Baby stood and put her coat on. Bundling herself for the hawk that waited outside the door. She kissed Aunt Becky on the cheek. "I'll see you tomorrow. I can't wait to see the inside of the building." She headed to the door.

"It's beautiful and spacious. And wait until you see the new kitchen. You know they're serving refreshments afterwards." Aunt Becky hugged her bathrobe close to herself as she let Pretty Baby out. "See you tomorrow."

Tangled Web

*"He that getteth wisdom loveth his own soul: he
that keepeth understanding shall find good."*
Pr. 19:8

Pretty Baby pulled her car into the first available spot she saw on the church lot. Just as she was entering the sanctuary, she looked back and saw Missy and Monique approaching. "You guys go ahead and get us a seat," she said to Chris and Jason, "I'm waiting for Missy." She shifted Ashley to her other hip.

They went in and were seated just as the young acolytes were lighting the candles. Pretty Baby could see Aunt Becky sitting on the front row with the other elders of the church in front of the traditional burning can which was symbolic of burning and ridding yourself of old habits and ways. Pretty Baby glanced over at Missy, who looked as

195

pretty as a magazine model, wearing a black and green tweed suit with a pill box hat to match. She held firmly to the same type of envelope Pretty Baby had received days earlier. She glanced down in her purse seeing her envelope lying in the same slot she had placed it.

Last year, at this time, everyone was asked to list their resolutions and goals they would like to fulfill for the new year, put it in an envelope and address it to yourself. It was left on the back of the pews to be collected by the ushers and mailed to members at the end of the year so that they could see if they had gone through with their goals.

Wondering if Missy had fulfilled her resolution, Pretty Baby realized her life had taken a totally different turn from what she was planning the previous year. She had listed two things on her list. First, she would be more active in church and not be just a member. And second, she would make her marriage work no matter what, regardless of the fact that William had gone out that New Years Eve without her, instead of coming to church knowing that she was unexpectedly pregnant with their third child. Who would've guessed she would be divorced and totally on her own? Pretty Baby had decided these tribulations of the past year were only blessings for the future to make her a better person. She had given some thought on what her goals would be for this year on the drive over to the church. Again she would dedicate more time to being more active in church. Her mind was made up that she wanted to buy a home and a car for her and her children and she knew only the Lord could get her through that.

The piano and organ began the familiar introduction

Tangled Web

of 'I Can Go To God In Prayer'. The entire church stood, rocking with the choir and clapping their hands. Ms. Ezra, large and voluptuous under her choir robe, was front and center with her strong alto voice, *'Makes no diff'rence, what the problem,'* she sang.

And the choir confessed in unison, *'I can go to God In Prayer.'*

Pretty Baby sat Ashley in her seat on the pew. The music was stirring her soul. She joined in with the others singing, *'Jesus will work it out. Yes He will! Yes He will! Yes He will! Oh, yes He will.'*

The spirit was running so high that it took a while to get through the devotional part of the service and the minister could start his sermon. His message was entitled, From Bitterness to Blessedness'. Pretty Baby thought it fitting for her at this time as she glanced to look at what she had written on the paper for this year's resolution. She saw Missy silently crying as the preacher spoke. She handed her some of her tissue from her diaper bag then held her hand for comfort, whispering a silent prayer for her cousin who always seemed so together but was obviously going through a private turmoil.

The evening ended with the dedication of the Family Life Center, which was as beautiful as Aunt Becky had said. Everyone greeted one another and ate appetizers served from the new kitchen. Aunt Becky was over joyed at the sight of Missy, who always sent Monique but never came to service herself. Pretty Baby caught a glimpse of Jesse and Charmaine while he talked with Brother Dickson and Aunt Becky but when she looked up again she saw them leaving.

"Where're you going when you leave here?" Pretty Baby asked Missy as they drank the citrus punch that was being served.

"I'm going home to get some rest. It's been a long day," Missy said.

Pretty Baby nodded, understanding just how she felt. "Are you okay?" She asked out of concern.

"Why? Because I'm not hitting the clubs?" She drained her glass. "Some things get old after a while, Rach." Missy stood, smoothing her skirt, "I'm going on home now." She motioned to Monique who sat across the room with the other kids. "I'll talk to you tomorrow," she swung her CoCo Chanel bag over her shoulder. "Are you still baking chicken tomorrow?" She teased, swatting Pretty Baby on the legs.

"I sure am. Baked food is healthier for you," she said, batting her lashes.

"Happy New Year, I love you," Missy bent down to kiss Pretty Baby and then Ashley as she slept. "I'll call you tomorrow."

Pretty Baby and the children waited for Aunt Becky to give her a lift home.

Tangled Web

"In the lips of him that hath understanding wisdom is found:
but a rod is for the back of him that is void of
understanding."
Pr. 10:13

*P*retty Baby eased into the house, hoping the children were sleeping peacefully, the way she had left them two hours ago. The house was still as she glanced at the microwave clock which glowed 10:15 a.m.. Lifting the top to stir the greens that had been picked and washed and cooked slowly through the night, she scooped a fork full onto a saucer to get the first sample of the slick leaved collards. Perfect, she thought picking a small piece of ham hock meat out of the pot and turning the burner off. She started her peas to simmering while she got the ingredients out to bake a lemon chess pie. She wanted everything to be just right in case Elliott came by. Pretty Baby wondered how the day would turn out.

Just as he had said, Elliott called as soon as he returned from his mother's. Pretty Baby extended an invitation for him to come by on New Year's Day but she purposely made it sound like it was an open invite for many guests. Thinking about it now, maybe she should have let him know it was a private invitation for him only. Her thoughts were interrupted by Jason calling her name from the top of the steps. He came down into the kitchen. "Where were you? I got up about an hour ago because Ashley was crying."

"Did you change her for me?"

"Yes, ma'am, and I poured her about four ounces of milk because I didn't know what to feed her and Chris was still asleep. Where'd you go?" he asked again.

"I walked in the mall this morning." She continued to make her pies. "Bring Ashley down stairs."

"We're watching videos," he said going back upstairs. "I've got the gate on in case I fall asleep on her."

"O.k., I'll fix you guys some breakfast in a few minutes. Let me get done with this."

Jason swung the kitchen door back open, "Are we having company? You sure are cooking a lot of stuff."

"Well, we'll have enough in case someone does come by. You know Aunt Becky will want some and probably Missy..."

"Why are you baking the chicken? I like fried better."

Tangled Web

"Jason...go upstairs with your sister," she said annoyed, putting the chicken in the oven. The vegetables could be steamed later, before guests arrived. If they arrived.

Now that dinner was out the way and the kids were fed, Pretty Baby ordered everyone downstairs for a quick clean up before they got their clothes on. Chris in the kitchen, Jason in the bathroom and she would do the living room. Rain clouds had threatened the sky earlier when she went walking but now the sun was out and it looked as if it would be a beautiful day after all.

Pretty Baby sat in the kitchen flipping through a magazine while Ashley took her afternoon nap and Chris bumped his CD player loudly with some of his friends. She realized Ashley was used to the loud noise and didn't ruin their fun. After another hour of viewing the latest fashions and trying to find something on television besides sports she steamed her vegetables. Maybe she should've casually called Elliott to see if he was coming by or not. The doorbell rang just as she walked toward the phone. "Happy New Year!" she heard as Missy walked in.

"Happy New Year to you," she kissed Monique before she could run upstairs to the sound of the music. "Tell Chris to turn that down just a little so he won't wake Ashley," she yelled.

"Too late, Pretty Baby. She's awake. I'll get her for you." she heard Monique say.

Hearing Chris' music go down, Pretty Baby went in the front and clicked on a tape of various jazz artists. Moving to the beat, she went back into the kitchen to see Missy had gotten the scrabble game from under the

201

Christmas tree. Taking everything out, she said, "let's play," then she got her cigarettes out and lit one. "We should've made some daiquiri," she said, inhaling deeply.

Suddenly remembering, Pretty Baby went to the refrigerator and produced a pitcher full of strawberry daiquiris.

Missy took a second glance, "Alright! This is gonna be a party after all." Rocking to the beat of the music, she gave Pretty Baby a sly look, "special company must be coming."

She fixed Missy a glass then sat down to organize her letters for the game. "Well, I told a few people to stop by since I cooked plenty." Knowing Missy was staring at her, Pretty Baby never looked up.

"Uh-huh," she said sipping her drink. Monique came down with Ashley on her hip, looking over her mother's shoulder, coaching her along.

"No fair," Pretty Baby fussed as Missy scored more points.

"Pretty Baby, I want to play that other game, TABOO," Monique said.

"O.k., we'll get to that one next," she said concentrating. "If we can get everyone to participate. That game is a lot of fun the more people you have." Her selection of letters was limited. Missy was killing her.

Jason stormed into the kitchen, "Can I eat now?" he asked lifting each pot to peek at what was inside.

"Wash your hands first."

"I win!" Missy exclaimed. "Beam me up again, Scotty," she gloated, handing Pretty Baby her glass for a refill.

Tangled Web

Adrienne, one of Pretty Baby's co-workers, and her boyfriend came by just as Pretty Baby was fixing another pitcher of daiquiri. They sat around laughing and joking as the phone continuously rang. Each time, Pretty Baby waited for one of the kids to holler for her to pick up, but they never did.

"You ready to eat, Chris?" she asked him as he walked through the living room with the cordless phone stuck between his shoulder and his ear.

"Not right now, Mom."

"I hope you're not tying up the three way." Pretty Baby said, thinking Elliott may have tried to call and the line was busy. "Get off the phone, we're going to play TABOO in a few minutes. Are your friends still upstairs?" He nodded his head yes as he went back up the steps.

Pretty Baby opened her kitchen to everyone who was hungry. She heard them call her name to come play the game as she fixed a nice sized plate and put it to the side, just in case. TABOO was a hilarious game especially when played with some teenagers and a couple of intoxicated adults.

Charmaine and Jesse had come by and joined in on the fun. Poor Charmaine couldn't seem to catch on to what it was she was suppose to do each time it was her turn. Which made it even funnier. Missy made her nervous each time her turn came, laughing and beeping the horn if she made a mistake. Pretty Baby was afraid Jesse would eventually get annoyed but he was a good sport about his girlfriend's lack of understanding. They were all having such a good time that Pretty Baby was surprised when Chris handed her the phone. She didn't even hear it ring.

"Hello."

"Sounds like I'm missing all the fun."

Pretty Baby struggled to her feet to go in the kitchen, away from the laughter and music to hear better. "Hi, Elliott. How are you?" she said with a smile in her voice.

"I'm fine. I'm in my car about fifteen minutes from your place and I was wondering if it was still all right if I came by? That is, if it's not a bad time."

She smacked her lips. What do you mean? I've been waiting on you all day. "No, come on. Have you eaten yet? I've got plenty."

"As a matter of fact, I'm starved. I was thinking I was going to have to go down to the Chatterbox to get my fill of black-eyed peas, greens and neckbones," he laughed.

"Well, I hate to disappoint you but I only have baked chicken and steamed veggies."

"Mmmm, sounds like my kind of dinner. I'll see you in a few minutes. Should I bring anything?"

"No, just yourself."

"Not even a Pepsi?"

"I made lemonade and some daiquiris.....but a Pepsi sounds good."

"O.k., let me stop and I'm on my way."

Pretty Baby hung up, going immediately into the bathroom to make sure her makeup was fresh and the bathroom was presentable, then back into the kitchen to make sure his plate looked inviting. She started to warm it in the microwave then decided to wait until he was actually ready to eat. Her thoughts were interrupted by her team

204

Tangled Web

mates yelling it was her turn.

"I'm ready," she hurried back into the living room, competing against Monique in this round. She began, "I love Victoria Secrets'...."

"Panties," one of her teammates shouted.

Pretty Baby shook her head no. "This moisturizes my skin."

"Oils....Lotion!" another said, which was correct. Pretty Baby explained three more cards before her sixty seconds were up, gaining eight points for her team. She saw Elliott walk past the front window just as Jesse and Missy were up to compete.

"Hi," she said opening the door wide and accepting a surprise peck on the cheek from him. "Come on in. Everybody this is Elliott. Elliott this is Chris, Jason and Ashley, my children," she pointed them out, "and everybody else," she laughed. Elliott was accepted warmly as they made their way through the living room to the kitchen while the game continued.

"Are you ready for me to fix your plate?" She asked, putting the Pepsi in the refrigerator.

"How about a glass of that lemonade first. I can wait on the meal a little longer," he said, not wanting to drag her away from their game. Elliott sat in the kitchen chair admiring how lived-in Pretty Baby's home appeared. He glanced around at her kitchen décor; the plastic fruit in the basket on the table, that reminded him of his mother's home, to the big sign over the sink that said, 'Bless This Mess.'

"Come on," she handed him the glass and he followed her into the front to rejoin the crowd. They were beginning a new round with Adrienne and Joe-Joe, Chris' friend, as contestants.

"Do you know how to play TABOO?" Pretty Baby asked.

Elliott shrugged his shoulders. "I've never played before, but I'll give it a try." They watched a couple of rounds, laughing hysterically at each other's attempts to describe simple words. Elliott was added to Pretty Baby's team, competing against Jason.

"Bravo," Pretty Baby applauded his first try, as she took front and center for her turn, gaining four points for her team. "The word was 'unleaded'!" She scolded her teammates as she plopped on the couch beside Elliott. Ashley immediately crawled into her lap. He readjusted himself to make the three of them comfortable. Sliding his arm along the back of the couch, right behind her neck just as she relaxed her head back to stretch. She lingered a few extra seconds, feeling the warmth of his arm and inhaling his cologne. They continued to play until Aunt Becky and Brother Dickson came to the door.

"Party's over," Missy turned and quietly commented to those close by, just before she eased into the kitchen.

"Don't mind me, I came by to get some of that food you cooked, Pretty Baby," Aunt Becky said after greeting everyone. The two women walked into the kitchen just as Missy was pouring the last of the daiquiris. "Move out the way, gal," Aunt Becky playfully swatted Missy on the butt. "Mm, mm, sure looks good. What made you bake the chicken?" she said scooping plenty on the plate for herself and Brother Dickson. Missy snickered just as Elliott walked in.

Tangled Web

"I was just about to fix your plate, Elliott," Pretty Baby quickly said, noticing Aunt Becky giving him a twice over glance, "Aunt Becky this is Elliott, a friend of mine."

He extended his hand giving her that warm sincere smile he always gave Pretty Baby. "Pleased to meet you, Ma'am."

"Just call me Aunt Becky. Everyone else does."

She went back to fixing her over sized plate while Pretty Baby warmed his meal in the microwave. Realizing Elliott must be a close friend of Pretty Baby's, Aunt Becky asked, "Why didn't you come to our New Years Eve service, Elliott? It was beautiful."

"Well," he hesitated looking up from his meal, "Actually, I knew about it at the last minute but I didn't want to just invite myself." He looked in Pretty Baby's direction, as if he needed her to coach him along.

"You don't have to be invited to the house of the Lord, Son," she said reassuringly as she sealed her plate with the foil Pretty Baby had given her. "All's it takes is an ounce of faith and you're welcome anytime. What church do you belong to? Hand me a bag for these plates, Pretty Baby." She suddenly said, then turning her attention back to Elliott.

"Morning Star Christian Church in Richmond," he said between bites, not wanting to show how hungry he really was.

"Bartholomew Jones is the pastor there. We've fellowshipped with them a few times," she said remembering.

Pretty Baby glanced at Missy, thinking 'what church hasn't she fellowshipped with.' She slid into the seat

207

directly across from Elliott, talking with him as he finished his meal and playfully tapped his foot with hers.

"Kids, I'm gonna leave you now," Aunt Becky said taking in the scene of Pretty Baby and Elliott conversing as if they were the only ones in the room. "Thanks for dinner, Pretty Baby."

"Oh, you're welcome, Aunt Becky," Pretty Baby said, getting up to see them out.

"Nice meeting you, Aunt Becky and Brother Dickson," Elliott called after them.

Aunt Becky looked back into the kitchen, "Hope to see you again soon, baby. Maybe at church." She smiled, pleased that he appeared to be a nice gentleman keeping company with her niece.

Missy slid off the stool she had been perched on and sashayed across the room just as Elliott was getting up to rinse his plate. "Looks like the party's breaking up," she said peaking through the swinging doors then sitting in the seat across from Elliott. "I said it would once Aunt Becky came."

Elliott smiled politely.

"So now we can put the children to bed and let the games begin with the adults," she said dramatically, throwing her head back.

Elliott thought for a second that Missy's body language was suggesting something but before he could start to worry about how to change the subject, he was saved by Pretty Baby and Jason's entrance.

"You guys can come in the front. I'm just trying to clean up a little bit."

"I'm going to get out of here, too, Pretty Baby."

Tangled Web

Missy said, keeping eye contact with Elliott. He couldn't figure out for the life of him what the game was. He was relieved she was leaving. "I'll call you tomorrow."

"O.k.," Pretty Baby said as they all walked to the front to see everyone off.

The crowd had cleared and the children that were left had either gone upstairs or outside.

"You sure know how to have a get together for all ages," Elliott laughed as he followed closely behind Pretty Baby into the kitchen. "Oh, and my compliments to the cook as well. Everything was delicious, baby."

The warmth of his words caressed Pretty Baby as she turned and realized their lips were inches apart and Elliott took this appropriate opportunity to taste the cook's delicious lips. Not knowing that he would not be able to resist a full serving. Immediately going back for a second kiss, he ravished her lips with an urgency that he didn't know existed. Caressing the back of her head with his big hands and letting her feel all of his warmth, he pulled back licking her lips and kissing her tongue. He stared into Pretty Baby's eyes questioningly, hoping he had not crossed an unwanted line with her.

She, in return, gazed into his eyes. She saw no questions, only answers.

*"He shutteth his eyes to devise froward things:
moving his lips he bringeth evil to pass."*
Pr. 16:30

Savannah watched the figure pace back and forth across the room from the corner of her eye as she sat in front of her bedroom window. "I'm tired now," she said slowly.

"This is what I'm telling you. You've gotta pull yourself out of this." The visitor kneeled at her side. "The doctors say that you are physically fine, if you would just motivate yourself a little bit, I know there would be a change."

She was comforted by the hand holding and the sincerity in the visitor's voice, but not moved enough to do anything about it.

"Everybody misses you. I remember when we all agreed that each one of us would do our share of spending time with you. Bringing you back around, even if we only had a few minutes to spare." The visitor walked back to the window staring into the darkness, "Seems like everybody forgot about that agreement except me....and Ms. Savage. You don't need to go to church, 'cause she brings the church to you." The visitor sighed. "I don't know, maybe everybody else has more important stuff on their agendas and someone to do it with," the visitor mumbled. Suddenly lightening the mood, "It's working. You're not as withdrawn as you were." The visitor turned to smile at her just as headlights could be seen slowly approaching the house.

"I'm tired," Savannah said.

The visitor moved swiftly to her side, wanting to leave before Elliott came in. The visitor rubbed her hand soothingly and looked into her weary eyes. How could he be gone all day on a holiday with his wife at home like this? "I know you are sweetheart. Let me help you into bed." The visitor guided her to the bed. "I'll be back in a couple of days." Savannah nodded her head like a hopeful child.

Knowing Elliott had probably not noticed the car parked in front across the street, the visitor said a quick goodnight to Ms. Savage and went out of the front door.

Elliott drove up his street slowly, noticing how some of the neighbors had taken their Christmas lights down already. The street was very dark as he pulled around back into his garage. He sat in the car inside the garage listening to the radio not being able to get the images of

Rachel's face out of his mind.　He could still feel the tenderness of her kiss on his lips.

He was quiet going into the house through the kitchen, trying not to disturb what seemed to be a sleeping house.　Ms. Savage had obviously gone to bed so he looked in on Savannah then retired to his room.

He could feel the fatigue settling in on him as he stood under the steaming shower.　He had an early morning the next day, so a good night's sleep was needed. As he slid between the cool sheets,　adjusting his pillows until they felt comfortable, he started flipping the channels with the remote control only to find nothing on T.V.　He turned it off and as darkness engulfed the room, visions of Rachel started to dance in his head.　Once again, he could feel her lips against his.　The fantasy was so real.　Her tongue exploring his mouth eagerly as he held her head savoring every moment.　Feeling her small mounds of breast rise and fall against his chest as her firm body seemed to rhythmically move against him.　Before he knew what was happening, he had caressed himself to a full climax.　He lay there panting, suddenly feeling guilty as he realized he had never fantasized about another woman in this way.　Only Savannah.　He sighed out loud as he got up and went into the restroom, cleaning himself up and putting on his pajama bottoms.　Sleep was not a problem once he laid down this time.

Tangled Web

"Come let us take our fill of love until the morning: let us solace ourselves with loves.
For the goodman is not at home, he is gone a long journey."
Pr. 7:18-19

"Gosh, I thought you'd never get here," Pretty Baby said, running back up the stairs as Missy followed.

Missy scanned the dresses that Pretty Baby had hung from the baby bed. "I like this one the best," she pointed to the fuschia floral print swing dress with the matching scarf. "With these cinderella pumps right here." She pulled a pair of shoes off of the shoe rack that were in the closet. "I didn't know there were any plays in town right now." Missy said sitting on the end of the bed.

"It's not in town," Pretty Baby said slowly. "It's out of town, and that's why I was asking you to come over early to sit with Ashley until the boys got here. I'll be back later tonight." She moved her hand slowly inside her Berkshire Gleamer hose, checking for runs.

Missy sat for a minute absorbing this information. "You're not the only one who has plans for Valentine's Day, Pretty Baby," Missy said, faking a pout. "That sounds romantic, Cous'. Where, out of town are you going?"

"New York," Pretty Baby said nonchalantly, trying to make sure she had everything in her bag. Elliott told her they had a suite where they could dress later for the play.

"New York City!" Missy got up to follow Pretty Baby into the bathroom. "You guys are flying to New York to see 'Ragtime'? I heard that." She stood with her hand on her hip. "Sounds like my kind of date."

Pretty Baby went back into the bedroom, "Of course we're flying," and then she added casually, "in his plane."

Missy dashed back into the bedroom. "His plane? He has his own plane?"

Pretty Baby gave her a sly giggle.

"Cha-ching!" Missy fell straight back on the bed, on top of clothes and all.

"Girl, get up off of my things," Pretty Baby playfully hit Missy with a baby blanket.

She rolled off the bed and sat upright. "You didn't give me all of those details, Miss Thing. You really did hit the jackpot this time. If you could bump that wife off, you'd have it made in the shade."

"Missy, don't say stuff like that. Anyway, I told you, Elliott and I are just friends."

214

Tangled Web

"Shiiit, tell that to somebody else."   Missy lit a cigarette. "I'm not judging you. In fact, I think you got the perfect set up. His wife will probably never get her mind back. You can be his kept woman forever, with all of the benefits and none of the obligations." She exhaled a big puff of smoke. "He should just put the wife in an institution. Then you and Bae Bae's kids can move in the house." They both laughed.

"I don't know exactly what her condition is," Pretty Baby said suddenly wondering.   She had never given Elliott's wife much thought.   "I imagine a frail old lady, sitting on the floor in a straight jacket. And there are bars on the windows," she added with a laugh.

Missy laughed at the thought, "That's why he should put her ass in an institution."

"Enough about his wife, the thought can get a little depressing. It reminds me of a good man gone to waste." She put the last of her things in her overnight bag.

"You're right, that's why you have to get everything from him now, while you can. As long as he's married, he should never say no to anything that you may want or need," Missy said seriously.

"I hate to think of it in that way. Like he's taking care of me and I'm his hoe. You make everything sound so common."

"I just like to call it like I see it, and to be perfectly honest....the only hoe's that ain't getting paid is broke hoe's and dead hoe's." Pretty Baby had to laugh at that. "I'm just saying, you're not really the kind of woman to date a married man. I know you....from way back. But if you want to be in the big girl league you must use this situation to

215

your advantage."

Pretty Baby toted her things to the top of the stairs. She didn't want to talk anymore about dating a married man. Even though, Missy probably knew all the highs and lows of the game. She came back into the room. "The boys should be here around four and then you're free. What are you doing this Valentine's Day, anyway?"

"I really don't have any plans, to tell the truth. In fact, the kids are welcome to spend the night if you want them to."

"That would be perfect, Missy. Then I won't be worried. I owe you one." They went downstairs to wait for Elliott and to check on Ashley, sleeping in her playpen.

Just like clock-work, Elliott arrived at 10:30a.m, as he said he would. He carried in his hand a long white box, beautifully wrapped in a red bow. "Happy Valentines Day," he said as Pretty Baby opened the door for him.

Pretty Baby lifted the top off of the box to reveal a dozen white roses. "These are beautiful, Elliott. Thank you." She kissed him on the cheek. "Let me get a vase for these. They are simply gorgeous," she said going into the kitchen.

"What did you bring for the babysitter?" Missy asked as soon as Pretty Baby was out of earshot.

Elliott saw her sitting on the couch when he came in but hadn't had a chance to speak. "Hello, Melissa and Happy Valentine's Day to you." He was trying to take a casual approach, so she wouldn't have a chance to get too aggressive as she had done on New Year's Day with her seductive act. "I didn't know you would be here."

She stepped closer, as if to challenge him. "Would

you have brought me roses too?"

"I didn't know there was a fee for the babysitter, but I don't have a problem with that if there is one." Elliott said sarcastically, digging into his pockets.

"Save it," Missy said returning to her seat back on the couch just as Pretty Baby walked in.

"How does this look?" She asked sitting the arrangement on the coffee table.

"Beautiful, Baby, now we've got to run. I told the Lieutenant we'd be there by noon," he said grabbing Pretty Baby's bags.

She slung her purse over her shoulder. "I'll come over to your place in the morning before church....there's food in the refrigerator for the kids...."

Missy waved her off with a magazine. "You kids have fun, don't worry about us," she said closing the door.

Pretty Baby thought they'd never reach their destination to begin their trip to New York. Excitement kept building in her as she realized this was truly a fantasy date that she felt like telling the whole world about. Elliott seemed just as excited. He sang along with Rod Stewart singing, when the one you love's, in love with someone else. She laughed at his pantomime.

At last, she could see aircraft hangars and planes coming into view. "I was wondering where you were taking me," she commented, taking in the scenery. "This is the back side of the airport."

"Uh-huh," he put his hand on top of hers as it rested on the console. "You don't trust me?" His eyes unconsciously traveled the length of her long curvaceous legs. Seeing her in jeans and a t-shirt for the first time confirmed how fine she really was. "Fine time to feel that way, just as we're about to board the plane I'm going to fly," he joked.

She looked at him in wonder. "Of course I trust you," she caressed his cheek then ran her long red nails up the back of his head and down again, stroking him. Looking at him she realized that she always seemed to be attracted to men with block heads. He had taken her subtle hint about his hair being a little outdated and surprised her with a nice low faded cut. He was handsome before....but now he was a knockout!. "I want you to teach me to fly," she said matter of factly.

"Ooh?" Elliott was amused by his feisty companion. The thought flashed in his mind that it was like pulling teeth to get Savannah to ride, not to mention fly a plane. "Sure, but, another weekend. I don't think we ought to start lessons on the way to New York."

"I'm serious, Elliott," she pouted putting her hands in her lap.

"I know you are," he chuckled. He parked next to the Lieutenant's truck as he saw him coming toward the car in the rear view mirror. Elliott got out and the two men embraced.

"I thought you were going to miss take off time," he playfully punched Elliott. "Mr. Punctual."

"I can take part of the blame for that," Pretty Baby said coming around the car. Lt. Newman thought this woman was a business associate of Elliott's, but there was a slightly different air about him as the woman stepped up. His eyes lit up as he spoke her name making the proper introductions.

Tangled Web

"I can forgive the tardiness of a beautiful woman," the Lieutenant said admiring this exuberant lady. They talked briefly as one of the other men rolled the plane out to the runway. "You got a nice clear day to travel so have a good time and be careful," he patted Elliott on the back as they boarded the plane.

Pretty Baby finally relaxed once they got past the turbulence and reached a high enough altitude that they glided smoothly. She glanced back at the blue and gray four-seater passenger section. It had a small table between the chairs, a bar and a small cabinet stocked with chips, nuts and candy. She was impressed.

Elliott spoke another command Pretty Baby didn't understand into the headset to the control tower.

"Is everything alright?" she asked.

"We're right on schedule. We should be landing at approximately 1400 hours.

****

Pretty Baby couldn't conceal her smile as they strategically darted through the busy New York traffic in the sleek black limo that had been waiting at the JFK airport for them. As soon as she descended the steps of the plane, she saw a limo parked to the side and a chauffeur standing there holding a big sign that read PRETTY BABY.

"Your chariot awaits you, Madame." Elliott bowed before picking up her bags.

Pretty Baby, shook her head in disbelief. "What else do you have planned for the day, Mr. Banks?" She asked affectionately, linking her arm in his as he struggled with the bags.

"What do you have in here? We'll be back tonight." Elliott handed the bags to the chauffeur. "Don't strain yourself man," he said sarcastically. Pretty Baby didn't hear a thing he said, as she slid into the plush leather seat feeling as if she were queen for the day.

She sat close to Elliott in the limo. Today he was her man. Her very own Valentine, and she was going to enjoy herself and be his woman.

Pretty Baby admired the classic art deco style of the hotel. She fell in love with the Hollywood celebrity paintings that adorned the wall of the Les Celebrites' restaurant as they walked through.

The Essex House Hotel was every bit as elegant as she had dreamed it would be, she thought, as she hung her dress in the closet of the beautiful suite. She wandered back into the living room, stepping out onto the balcony that overlooked Central Park. She felt Elliott's presence as he stood beside her. The scent of his cologne unmistakable.

"Spectacular view, isn't it?"

"Oh, Elliott, I'm having a wonderful time," she turned to face him looking directly into his eyes. Waves of arousal swept over both of them as he held her hands along her sides, pulling her closer to him. The thought of being completely alone in this hotel suite with Elliott was overwhelming. This is it, she thought. We're going to make love.

He kissed her lightly. "I'm glad you're enjoying yourself because this is only the beginning," he said in a hoarse whisper. "You deserve to be treated special." He brushed his lips across her forehead, then a small kiss to the nose as he tilted her chin up and kissed her deeply. His tongue, explored every area of her mouth. His very being merged through her veins like a bolt of lightening. Pretty Baby responded, wrapping her arms around his neck then caressing his back. He pulled away gently and led her into the living room. Pretty Baby held her hand to her stomach, trying to settle the aching in her groin, not knowing Elliott was going through a private war of his own, between his brain and his body.

"How about a glass of wine?" he asked, popping the cork on the chilled bottle that had been left by room service. Pretty Baby sat leisurely on the couch and he sat beside her clicking their glasses together before they sipped. "I thought you'd like to go to some of the stores...there's Bergdorff Goodman, Tiffany's and that big children's store, F.A.O. Schwartz. You could probably find something to take back for the kids."

Pretty Baby stared at him in wonderment.

"What?" he asked, narrowing his eyes, trying to read her thoughts.

"You are too much," she slipped off her shoe and ran it up and down his leg.

"Well, I aim to please," he said, swishing his wine around in the glass then swallowing the last of his drink, giving her a wink. "I got us another car to drive around the city while we're here. That way, we can be on our own."

"I told you, you were too much. You think of everything. She got up erasing the erotic thoughts that were dancing in her head. Heat suffused her body but she willed herself to ignore it. "Let me change my shoes and I'll be ready."

****

"You *are* a genie in disguise," Pretty Baby said thoughtfully as she and Elliott walked hand in hand from the theater. The cultured pearl bracelet and matching necklace that he surprised her with when they went in the jewelry store earlier, looked elegant in the moonlight. Happy Valentines Day, Baby, his voice resonated in her mind, causing her stomach to flutter.

"I've been called a lot of things," a laugh escaped him, " but never a genie."

Caught up in the thrill of it all as the night air swept through her hair, Pretty Baby began seriously, "This whole day has been magical. A date like this is every girl's dream." The air was brisk but pleasant. She slowed her walking pace as they neared a park bench and sat down. "I guess, what I mean is, you went out of your way to make this day special for me. From the limo ride, shopping, the play and now this fabulous evening." She paused looking down at the beautiful bracelet. "You know, it wasn't that long ago that I was a very sad woman, and I prayed that a special man would come into my life who wanted to make me happy." She stroked the length of his head and neck. A gesture from her, he was becoming very familiar with. "And when I opened my eyes, there you were," she said playfully. "I guess this is the beginning of my prayers being answered, that's why I said you must be a genie in disguise. You made all of this possible."

He lifted her hand in his, kissing first her palm then the back of her hand gently. It felt good to be needed.

222

Tangled Web

Unbeknownst to Pretty Baby, she was the answer to his unspoken prayers. He never prayed that someone would need him, but there was a hidden need to be needed. He admired Savannah's' aggressiveness when she was well but a lot of times he felt that he wasn't needed financially or emotionally. Now, she needed him, but it was a different kind of need.

"I know," he stumbled over his words, "I know what we have is not the perfect situation, but I'd like the chance to give you some of the happiness you deserve at least until someone can come along and treat you as well as I do or better." He pulled her to her feet from the bench. "You've put a new spin on my life as well, whether you know it or not." He kissed her lightly as they walked toward Jezebel's restaurant. Now that this unspoken commitment was made between them, Elliott felt excited. Alive again.

"I think I feel like dancing with the prettiest girl in New York City tonight," He said, giving her a ballerina twirl, taking in the full view as her fuschia dress wrapped the curves of her body. "How does that sound?"

"It sounds like that's how this fantasy date is supposed to end," she replied with a bit of hesitation in her voice.

"But?"

"But, it's already late and you know I'll turn into a pumpkin on you," she laughed, "We've got to get back because..."

He silenced her with his finger, "The kids are safe with Missy. So Cinderella, the deadline has been extended from midnight...to daybreak." She tried to speak again but he stopped her. "This has been granted by your Genie."

Silence for a moment then they both burst into laughter as they went into the restaurant.

Jezebel's was a very romantic place with swings for two hung at the tables. The dim French Provincial lamps gave it a Parisian atmosphere. The restroom, Pretty Baby noticed, with its' fresh cut flowers and dainty what nots on laced tables, had the feel of a woman's bathroom. It was as romantic as the rest of the place.

She rejoined Elliott. They sat closely absorbed in their own thoughts. Elliott spoke first. "I don't mean any harm," he started as they sat at the bar waiting on their table, "but your cousin, Missy, is quite a character."

Pretty Baby didn't know where this was leading but she immediately let out a sigh. "Oh, Missy is harmless."

"Is she?"

"Yes," she said swatting his leg. "She's just been through a lot in her life and I guess that's why she comes out of different bags. She's really a sweet girl once you get to know her."

Elliott raised one eyebrow. He had his doubts. "I've tried to be cordial but she always seems to turn the tables on me and..."

"I know, and you don't know which direction she's coming from." Pretty Baby hesitated to elaborate but then she went on. "I don't agree with a lot of things that she does but she's the kind you have to know to understand. And if you understand her, you can grow to love her."

Elliott nodded.

"Missy and I are actually second cousins. Her grandmother and my mother were sisters. Well, you know my mom died of cancer when I was very young, and Aunt

Tangled Web

Becky raised me. I never knew Missy until we were about twelve and she came to live with Aunt Becky too. Aunt Becky has always been the kind to take people in whether they were relatives or not. We immediately became inseparable because, even though I had gobs of cousins, she was the sister I never had.

"She didn't live in town? What took you so long to meet?"

Pretty Baby took a deep breath as if this was somewhat painful. "Missy's mom, Sylvia, my cousin, was a junkie, a prostitute and a whole bunch of other things. But, before that, she was very beautiful," she shrugged, "a lot of people say I look just like her, she had a promising career as an opera singer. She directed and was one of the lead soloists in her church choir and she sang with the Virginia Mass choir. I mean," she said filled with excitement for her cousins achievements, "by the age of twenty-five, she had sang at Carnegie Hall. Missys' daughter, Monique, sings beautifully too."

Elliott nodded, impressed.

"She also shared her angelic voice with a worldly crowd," she continued, "Not just in the black cafe clubs but, the white country clubs as well. Muddy Waters and Salem Hills on Saturday nights and United Christian Church on Sunday morning." She gave a short laugh then a sigh, "Anyway, I guess Saturday nights won out because she did more of it and was seen less and less on Sunday mornings. Word on the street was that cousin Sylvia had been turned out and would do anything for a drug fix. Aunt Becky says the next thing she hears is that somebody had beat Sylvia up and left her for dead. Aunt Becky had her brought to the house and prayed her back to health. During this time they found out Sylvia was pregnant. She stayed with Aunt Becky during the pregnancy and for a while afterwards, but she never got back involved in church. She was there in body but not in spirit. She did, however, continue to pursue her cafe singing career.

By this time she had moved into an efficiency apartment, so singing was her means of support and she was still clean. Of course, Aunt Becky tried to pull her back into church. Reminding her that sin was pleasurable, but joy was everlasting. Don't die in your sin. This ran Sylvia further and further away. I don't know exactly how it went, but, she was back in the same rut again."

"Word was on the street once more, this time she had sold the baby to somebody for little or nothing. For years Aunt Becky searched for the lost little girl. Some say they had carried the child to D.C.. Aunt Becky never gave up, she always said she was praying for her and one day, sure enough, she found out that she was living not far away with an old couple who were bootleggers and ran numbers out of their house. I can remember so well, riding with Aunt Becky, in her old '65 station wagon that leaned to one side. That was when Becky would drive. We would drive by that big old house on an old woodsy road. She'd park up the street a ways, in different spots and we could see Missy outside playing or doing her chores.

One night we saw her helping an old drunk to his car as he leaned all of his weight on her small frame. Aunt Becky would get her bible out and sit there and silently pray for at least a half an hour. It used to drive me crazy," Pretty Baby laughed. "That particular night, I thought

Tangled Web

Becky was gonna get out of the car and confront somebody. Anybody. But instead, she prayed loud and strong, wringing her hands over and over, asking God for a miracle. I knew, even then, when Becky put a prayer on you.....something was gonna happen. It may be good and it may be a little unpleasant, but as she always would say, if it's the Lord's will, let it be done. We did this, I know, for two years."

"One night, it was said that there was a raid at that house and somebody set a fire. The old woman was killed in the fire and the man went to jail. Missy was taken into foster care and two weeks later Aunt Becky and her attorney went to get her and she came to live with us.

"That's wild," he said, thinking he was understanding Missy's background a little better. "What happened to Sylvia?"

"Sylvia went into seclusion. She moved to Philli with some man from one of the bands. She never tried to reclaim Missy. A few years later she moved back to town but she never tried to see Missy, and Missy knew this. You know how people talk. Anyway, about two years ago she was found dead, in her one-room apartment, of a heroin overdose. I don't think Missy has ever forgiven her for dying without ever reaching out to her. She wouldn't even go to the funeral." They were both silent for a moment. "So, Elliott, you never know who people are unless you know where they've been. It's just past history directing our paths...in a positive or negative way. You can't be so quick to judge a person."

Elliott was stunned by this story, but now he understood. The pager went off that was given to them by the hostess, indicating their table was ready.

They were seated in a quaint booth where the whole room could be viewed. Elliott decided on wine and appetizers since neither were very hungry. He followed her gaze, amused at her excitement. "You see someone you know?"

She nudged his leg under the table, "That's Halle Berry and Tyson over at that table with those people." The woman sitting at the head of the table saw them looking and suddenly waved at Elliott, giving a signal to call her. "She wants you to call her...Do you know Halle Berry and Tyson?" she asked like a little kid.

"No, I just know that woman who waved. She's the VP of marketing for Revlon," he laughed.

Pretty Baby looked around the room to see if she recognized any more faces. She didn't even notice the waiter approaching with their appetizers.

"Could you come back to me long enough to eat?" Elliott teased.

This time, her eyes were fixed on Jackie Collins chatting with a friend near the bar. Pretty Baby laughed realizing she was being ridiculous. They were just regular people with very visible jobs. "O.k., Baby, I'm all yours." She turned her attention to the food. "Mmm, this smells good...what is it?" She laughed.

"Bacon wrapped stuffed shrimp," he said, slicing a piece off feeding it to her.

"This is good," she dabbed her lips with her napkin. "That shrimp is so big I didn't recognize it."

"I knew this sampler platter would be enough for the both of us."

228

Tangled Web

"I know," she said between bites, "I'm going to be sleepy behind this."

"Oh no you don't. We're going to dance this off tonight."

They sat talking after their meal. Somehow the conversation led to dreams and hopes. "That's what I think I like best about you, Rachel, you seem to enjoy and appreciate the simple things in life. All of this extra glamour," he gestured his hand around the room, "is just that, extra, for you."

She nodded her head in agreement. "I didn't have a lot growing up, but I had everything I needed and most of the things I wanted and I'm trying to raise my kids the same way." She declined another glass of wine offered by the waiter. "Sometimes I lie awake at night trying to put together a plan on how to have more and work less. I haven't come up with anything yet, but I'm constantly thinking about it."

"Exactly what is it you're trying to do?" Elliott turned to face her.

Pretty Baby nudged her shoulders. "Well, I want to buy a house for me and my kids and get a decent car." The thought seemed to drain her. She continued, "but before I do any of these things I need to increase my income. I wish I would've gone to college when I had the chance," she stated flatly.

"It's not too late."

"I know. But I need to make this happen in the near future. I can't wait until I've finished college to better my home life."

Elliott placed his hand on hers, "I believe you can do

229

anything you put your mind to." Again he admired her tenacity. He knew in his personal life, a lot of value had been placed on material things for acceptance and approval. But what he really needed in his life was priceless. A wave of emotion passed over him as he realized, not only could he teach this woman something but he could learn as well. "As I said earlier, I want to stay in your life as long as you need me and anything I can do to help you along, I'm going to do." He gave her a wink as he signaled for the check.

"You know what I've always wondered, Elliott?

"What's that?"

"I've always wondered what it would be like to be wealthy." She looked dreamy. "You know, no robbing Peter to pay Paul. Stressing from check to check." She turned to look directly at him. "What's it like to be rich?"

"I have no idea," Elliott denied quickly.

"Oh, you do too," she elbowed him.

It was obvious Pretty Baby was waiting on an answer. He pooched his lips out then drew them back in a straight line, trying to put his feelings into words. "Life has been good to me. God has been good to me. I'm surely not one to complain, but ...I'd have to agree with the old saying, the wealth is nothing if you don't have anyone to share it with." The waiter laid the bill on the table and Elliott looked it over.

Just as he was signing the check, Jackie Collins sauntered over to the table, catching Pretty Baby totally off guard. "Elliott, darling, it's been much too long," she said giving him an air kiss on both cheeks.

"This is...." He started to introduce Rachel.

Tangled Web

"I've got to run but do give my love to Savannah and the boys," she said, running her jeweled hands the length of his arm, holding his hand much too long. "I would love to have you and the family out to the ranch," she said walking away as fast as she came up, not one time acknowledging Pretty Baby, except to remind her, without directly speaking to her, that he had a family.

Elliott felt the blow just as Pretty Baby did. He was truly at a loss for words. "I'm sorry," he started.

"It's alright," she said stirring her fork around in her plate.

He put his arm around the back of the booth. "Jackie and Savannah are old college friends and..."

"It's O.K., Elliott. Really." She drained her nearly empty glass. Tempted to order another under the circumstances. "I think I'm ready to head on to the China Club," she said sliding out of the booth, refusing to lose the magic of the evening.

****

Pretty Baby and Elliott walked straight into the China Club and right on to the dance floor, partying through three songs. The fourth was a slow Maxwell tune. Without taking a break she moved into his arms. The glow from the wine had all of her senses at their peak, as they moved sensuously to the music. Elliott moved his hands in circles on her back then slid them around to her shoulders, their hips swaying to the same beat. He looked deeply into her eyes asking for permission. Pretty Baby felt her body responding before her mind could focus on what to do.

She leaned forward and brushed her lips across his.

****

"No, Elliott, not in here," Pretty Baby said as they rode to the twentieth floor on the elevator. She continued to murmur no as she held on to him with one leg hoisted on his waist. Elliott took this as a yes and consumed her lips with his burning kisses running his tongue the length of her neck as she held her head back, accepting and encouraging it all. Pretty Baby stared up at the mirrored ceiling of the elevator. I won't be going back to Petersburg tonight.

Once inside of the suite, Pretty Baby excused herself to the bathroom as Elliott turned on soft jazz music. "Don't be too long," he said holding her at her fingertips.

She stared at her image in the mirror, breathing deeply with excitement. Good thing I brought that sexy nightie along, she thought, moving in closer to the mirror making sure there were no mascara smears around her eyes. Pretty Baby reached for her perfume that was in her cosmetic bag on the marble counter, dabbing a drop on each wrist, behind the ears and one last dab between her cleavage. Thinking about what lay ahead left her with goose bumps. She freshened her lipstick, rubbing her lips together for evenness as she thought about making love to Elliott. For one quick instant she thought of him being married, but quickly dismissed it because it felt like he was single to her and she was in no position, at this point, to ponder over her morals. She thought of the nightie again. No, that would be a little too aggressive. She would wait

Tangled Web

and see how the night progressed.

The living room was dim with only candlelight as she saw Elliott moving to each sconce, lighting them. The light danced and illuminated his chocolate chest, as he blew out the match and walked toward her. "You are a feast for the eyes," he moaned into her hair then guided her to the sofa. "Would you like another glass of wine?"

Maybe I should've put on the nightie since he's already half undressed. She thought.

"No, thank you. What CD is that?" She asked, leaning back as Elliott removed her pumps.

"Jazzmasters," he said massaging her foot moving up to her calves then back down to the feet putting one of her toes in his mouth sucking tenderly. He wasn't wasting any time picking up where they had left off earlier. A moan escaped her, for this was an erogenous zone she didn't know existed. He planted soft moist kisses on the bottom of her foot, nibbling and making his way up to her thighs. Elliott suddenly stood. His pectoral muscles, lined with beautiful black hair, flexed as he reached for her. She eyed him from the crotch up noticing the bulge in his pants then up to his burgundy nipples that she couldn't wait to suckle. She stood as he swept her off of her feet into his arms carrying her into the bedroom. He kissed her neck as he unzipped her dress and it fell to the floor. The feel of his member was tantalizing against her bare butt. Her thong panties made her feel naked. "I want to love you all over, Rachel." He whispered, cupping both of her breast in his hands, massaging them, paying special attention to her erect nipples. He slid her panties down her legs coming back up massaging her buttocks then moving around to the front, placing his finger on her swollen jeweled spot. He rubbed gently until he heard her breath quickening. Stopping, he laid her on the bed as she watched him remove his pants. His maleness, stood tall and proud as she leaned forward to caress it. "Not yet," he teased, pulling back.

"But I want you, Mr. Banks," she said speaking directly to his penis. He chuckled, aroused by her eagerness.

Elliott, lay raised on one elbow, along side her body. He was seized by her sexiness. He kissed her deeply running his hands as far as they would go down her body. He slid down to the end of the bed. Raising her leg he began to plant moist kisses on her ankles and working his way up her inner thigh.

Pretty Baby thought she must have looked like a satisfied puppy on its' back getting its stomach rubbed and begging for more. She moaned.

Elliott worked his tongue across her stomach then back down. Her woman scent and wetness almost completing him before he could even start. He got on top of her and slowly entered into her warm haven. Pretty Baby cried out with clawed hands, arching her back and gripping his buttocks. "Your dick is everything I expected," she heard herself say.

"Dicks are for little boys," he whispered, raising her bent leg while taking one of her breasts into his mouth. "A woman like you, deserves some cock, and that's what you'll get."

Elliott was showing a side of himself Pretty Baby didn't know about, but she found his lewd words exciting as

Tangled Web

she rose and fell like a tide, coming back for more. They rolled like two twisters becoming one big tornado as he pulsated and she called his name over and over again. Pretty Baby, then, rolled him onto his back straddling him and once again riding the wave. Tasting every chocolate inch of him, circling his nipples with her tongue, she felt his volcano about to erupt. This time he called her name and howled like a wolf.

The morning had come too soon. Pretty Baby stirred as she moved closer to Elliotts' sculpted form. He ran his hands along the curve of her body.

The digital clock showed 6:32am. "Six thirty-two? Oh no, we over slept." She said bolting straight up in the bed.

"Relax, the kids are with Missy, remember? We can be back in town by noon," he said rubbing her back. She looked around the elegant room and lay back in the four-poster bed. As she turned she felt the firmness of Elliott's cock coming to life. She liked the power she felt, controlling his passion this way.

"Why don't we get dressed and go down and have breakfast?" she asked knowing eating was the farthest thing from his mind.

"This is all the breakfast I want," he said lifting her thigh so that he could enter from behind.

So my hair will look like hell for the rest of the day, Pretty Baby thought as the warm shower water trickled all over their hot bodies. One more time Elliott was working his magic on her. Soaping her body from head to toe as she wiggled beneath his touch. She felt like an exotic dancer the way he gazed at her. She helped him to soap his back and chest, reaching her sudsy hands everywhere they could reach then making a nice rich lather on his manhood. She heard a moan escape her as he grew in her hands. Elliott devoured her with kisses clawing through her hair intensely. He feasted on every delicate part of her through the thick steam and the low visibility as the water got warmer and stronger, intensifying the storm that was raging between two bodies. Pretty Baby cried out as Elliott took her to greater heights and back. Panting, they supported each other as they recovered.

****

Pretty Baby sat close to Elliott as they rode back to the airport in the limo. They talked and laughed continuously. "I like you," he said, brushing a frizzy curl out of her face.

"That's because you're a man with impeccable taste," she batted her eyelashes seductively.

He leaned in closer, securing both of her hands under his, trying to resume his seriousness. "I have really enjoyed myself with you."

"Did you expect anything less than a good time?" She laughed a girlish laugh.

"I'm serious, woman," he looked straight into her eyes. "I just want you to know that this is not just a one-time event. There will be many more to follow. Better than a weekend rendezvous."

I can't think of anything better than a weekend getaway. She looked at him lovingly. "Oh, Elliott."

"I'm serious, Rachel. I know my situation..." he

Tangled Web

looked down at her elegant hands in his, searching his mind for the right words to say, then back to her face. "Remember what I told you last night about how long I'd be around?" She nodded. "Don't ever forget it, because I want to make you happy." He kissed the tip of her nose and put his arm around the back of the seat. Pretty Baby leaned in close, as she looked out the window of the limousine, feeling safe and secure as a newborn babe in its' mother's arms.

Pamela Williams-Guinn

*"Whoso diggeth a pit shall fall therein:
and he that rolleth a stone, it will return upon them."
Pr. 26:27*

"*F*irefighters battle blazes at United Christian Church on a early morning call...." The visitor read aloud, sitting next to Savannah.

"Don't tell me they're burning churches again." The visitor flipped through the paper, scanning the pages as Savannah listened attentively.

She was having a pleasant day. In fact it had been a pleasant week and she welcomed the company of her faithful visitor. She sat in her red Oleg Cassini bathrobe with matching slippers, occasionally picking invisible lint

238

Tangled Web

balls off of her robe and rubbing the fabric in admiration. She smiled or nodded from time to time in response to the visitor. A few times she ran her hands over her freshly shampooed and curled hair, bringing the longer strands around to her nose inhaling the fresh scent. She had grayed considerably around the temples over the years since her illness, but it looked nice. On holidays or special occasions, Ms. Savage or Maria would have her old stylist come by and do her hair or one of them would fix her up and get her dressed in something other than night clothes. Just a small gesture to show that she was still a part of the world.

"Listen to this." The visitor started again. "'President denies allegations of affair with College Co-ed'. Humph, I'd deny it too, right along with the other accusations. But I'll tell you what," the visitor said, closing the paper and folding it neatly, "Everybody ain't lying on the old guy. It's some truth somewhere." The visitor got up and walked to the bedroom door closing it slightly so as so not to be overheard. "You'd think he'd have a little tact about his selection of women. A teenager...Give me a break." The visitor peered out the window.

"That's a sign of a man with too much time on his hands." The visitor turned slowly and looked at Savannah. Their eyes met. "Like...Elliott." Savannah didn't bat a lash. "Sometimes I wonder about Mr. Goody Two Shoes." The visitor took a seat across from Savannah again. "What meeting could he have gone to on the weekend? On Valentine's Day?" Savannah looked away. "Did you know yesterday was Valentines Day, Van? The day where people spend time with their sweethearts. I betcha...." The visitor wagged a thoughtful finger and smirked. Then bypassing the thought that was surfacing and letting a smile appear.

"You're looking good, Van." Savannah smiled. "You are getting better." The visitor said as if the power of suggestion would some how, bring Savannah into the present. "I think the rehabilitation center that you're going to soon, is going to be real good for you. You'll be around other people all the time instead of being cooped up in this room." The visitor looked around the expensively decorated living quarters. "Taking your meals alone with only the T.V., radio or me for company. How the hell could anyone even expect you to get better in these isolated surroundings," the visitor said more as a statement than a question. "Maybe that's the plan," the visitor mumbled as an after thought. "Yep, Woodland Hills Rehab Center would definitely be better for you than this." Savannah seemed to suddenly regress at the mention of leaving home. The visitor noticed this reaction, taking this as a positive. Savannah was aware of what went on. Sometimes.

"It'll be nice, Van, and I'll visit you just like I do now." Savannah pouted like a spoiled child but nodded her head in agreement as if to show she was a big girl. The visitor checked the time. "I've got to go now, but I'll be back soon." Savannah never looked up as the visitor quietly left the room.

Tangled Web

"He that tilleth his land shall have plenty of bread:
but he that followeth after vain persons shall have poverty
enough."
Pr. 28:19

*P*retty Baby stood on Missy's front porch, hands on hips and looking from one end of the block to the other, puzzled. Where could they be? she thought as she walked back to the car. She started old Bessie up and headed toward her house. Maybe they went to church. She wrinkled her nose at that thought. No. Missy didn't go to church with those kids.

Pretty Baby reached in the glove compartment and pulled out Phyllis, popping her in and grooving to 'You Know How To Love Me.' She slowed down as she got closer to her house, noticing it looked empty. She realized

Jesse's car was gone too. She looked up and down her street. I know Beckys' at church, so they're not around there. Maybe I'll ride by the church and see if I see Missy's car. She started pass her house slowly. Hell, I should just go in and enjoy the peace. They'll find me. That's for sure. She put the pedal to the metal and drove off.

Pretty Baby ignored the distinct odor of smoke in the air as she drove down Halifax street until she turned on Gilmore and saw the police detouring the traffic. Panic hit her as she could see her church in the distance and she realized that was the source of the smoke in the air.

She rolled down the window frantically. "That's United Christian Church burning?" she said to the officer.

"Yeah. Now make this right and keep moving," he said waving his arm for the thru traffic. "Let's move. Let's move," he said, this time looking directly at her.

Her voice shook. "But that's my church. My family is in there." She started to lose control. "Oh my God. No!"

The officer blew his whistle for all opposing traffic to come to a halt. There were only three or four cars at the intersection but a lot of spectators standing around. He reached his hand in the car lifting Pretty Baby's slumped form off the steering wheel. "Your family is not in there, Ma'am. This fire started in the middle of the night. No one was there and we're just trying to make sure the fire is completely out. The investigator doesn't want any of these rubbernecking spectators coming close."

Pretty Baby looked bewildered but relieved. "They suspect arson?"

"No, it's just standard procedure, Ma'am. Now could you please make this right and keep moving?"

Tangled Web

She drove anxiously over to Aunt Becky's where she found the whole gang. Chris was standing out front with some of his friends, along with Jason and Monique playing a dirty game of 2-square. Jason threw a wild curve, hitting at the tip of the square and bouncing out of bounds and out of Monique's reach. Jason saw the car coming up the street and ran to the curb standing with his thumb out like a hitchhiker until Pretty Baby came to a stop.

"Hey, Momma. I thought you were coming home last night. Where you been?" He rattled off all in one breath before she could get out of the car good.

"Hey, Baby. Can I get a hug?" She put her arm around him walking into the yard.

"Where were you?" he asked again.

"You know I went to New York with some friends. It was getting late so I decided to come back today instead of last night."

"Oh." He looked puzzled at this information.

Monique ran up bouncing the ball off of Jasons' back. "Hey, Pretty Baby. Jason tell you the church burned down?"

"Yeah, Momma, the church caught on fire in the middle of the night." And they all started trying to tell her what happened at once. Including Chris and his friends.

"Where's Aunt Becky and your momma?" She asked Monique.

"They're in the house. Jesse too."

Aunt Becky was in the backyard talking to the neighbor across the fence about what had happened. Jesse and Missy were standing in the doorway listening to the horrible tale once more. They turned as they heard Pretty Baby enter the room.

"Hey girl," Missy said solemnly.

Pretty Baby looked startled as Jesse turned revealing his soot covered clothing. "Oh my God! What...You weren't in the fire...."

"Calm down, Pretty Baby. Naw, I wasn't in the fire. I just came from over there...trying to help salvage what we could."

Aunt Becky came in at the sound of Pretty Baby's voice. The screen door slammed with a loud wack behind her. "Gal...." She rared back, both hands on her hips, "I'm glad you got word to come home. The whole town could've burned down before you knew it," she said sarcastically.

Pretty Baby turned to Jesse and Missy annoyed. "What happened?" She asked, looking from one to the other. "I can't believe this. I rode over there and it looks like half the church is gone."

"Half the church is gone," Jesse confirmed as he sat at the table rubbing his hands up and down his face, smearing the soot even more. He sat there peeking through his fingers in disgust. "The Life Center is totally gone and there's so much smoke and water damage to the sanctuary...it might as well be totaled too."

"Will somebody please tell me what started the fire?" Pretty Baby demanded.

The whole room seemed to be in shock. Finally Missy spoke up. "Poochie came running over to my house about 7:30 this morning talking about the church burned down. I still don't know how she knew. Anyway, I called over here and when Becky didn't answer, I got the kids up and headed this way."

"I didn't hear the phone 'cause I was on the front porch talkin'. Brother Dickson had already called me," Aunt Becky interjected.

"One of the Deacons had called me. When I was getting in the car to go to the church I saw Missy coming down our street," Jesse continued. "I could see the flames several blocks before I even got to Gilmore. The police wouldn't let anybody on the street. So I parked and walked until I saw Elder Mitchell. It took a while before the flames were out and the ashes were cool enough so the investigator could give a report. Finally, we got a chance to talk to the fire marshal and recover what we could. He couldn't tell me a whole lot then except that the call had came from one of the neighbors and the origin of the fire was the storage room."

"Jesse stayed out there with the other brothers until somebody gave them some answers." Aunt Becky looked at Jesse lovingly, "You want a cup of coffee or tea, Baby?"

He declined. "I'm too wired up as it is, Aunt Becky.

"So what did you find out, Jesse?" Pretty Baby asked.

"The fire marshall seems to think...well, he's certain, that the fire started in the storage room on the side of the Life Center. See, the storage room also serves as the utility closet. And I guess since the center was built, nobody really took time to organize the storage room and make sure there weren't any flammable items in there. Evidently there were plenty of flammable liquids, from floor cleaners to a can full of gasoline from the last time someone cut the grass. That room is not ventilated and

245

those fumes started to ease over to the pilot light under the hot water tank and the next thing you know it was on fire."

"I didn't know it blew up." Missy said.

"It didn't blow up. It ignited then smoldered through the night. They suspect it actually started at about 11 or 12 last night. By the time the call came in, early this morning, the fire had caught on to the rest of the center. The firemen tore that place up putting the fire out. It was a mess." He stood slowly, stretching his long firm limbs then looking at his watch. "I'm gonna go on to the house. Get myself cleaned up, relax for a minute then head on back over to the church." Jesse's fatigued movements and tense facial expression showed a man with plenty on his mind. "Pastor Lindley has allowed me to call a meeting with the other men."

"Thank you Jesus, " Aunt Becky whispered. "Lord knows we need our men to pull together and some of ya'll gon' have to be leaders." Aunt Becky rubbed her aged hands across Jesse's back, whispering a silent prayer over him.

"Where's my sweet pea? So much is going on...I knew somebody was missing." Pretty Baby suddenly said, holding her palm to her head.

"Your rotten pea is sleeping. She had a rough night, staying up talking most of it then kicking like a wild mule the rest of the time. I thought you said she was on a schedule." Missy said shaking her head.

"I'll talk to you guys later." Jesse said going out the front.

Aunt Becky called after him.
"Ma'am?"

Tangled Web

"I always knew you was a leader," she said sincerely, "always remember, to whom much is given, much is required."

He smiled a wry smile. "Yes, Ma'am."

Pamela Williams-Guinn

"Whose hatred is covered by deceit, his wickedness shall be shewed before the whole congregation."
Pr. 26:26

Pretty Baby lay on the couch dozing until the loud sound of the Perry Mason theme song bolted her out of her slumber. She opened her eyes wide, looking around wildly and seeing every light downstairs was on. The last thing she remembered was trying to watch the movie of the week with Jason. She reached for the remote control lowering the volume. The kids must have gone to sleep, she thought, resting her head back on the arm of the sofa. The wall clock read a little after twelve. She heard the screen door open just as she was about to turn the volume back up. Her first thought was that Chris had eased out of the house while she slept but then there was a rap at the door. She got up and peeked out the window to see Jesse standing there.

"Hey Jesse," she said going back to the couch falling back into her spot.

"I didn't wake you, did I? I saw the lights on. Thought maybe you were still up."

"Yeah, I'm up. As a matter of fact, I just woke up on this couch. The last thing I remember was watching a movie with Jason." She got up going into the kitchen. "Want something to drink?"

"No thanks."

"Well, where you going or where you been? You and Charmaine hanging out?" She came back into the living room with a glass of Kool-Aid.

"No. Not this time," he said slumping in his chair. "I just came back from her apartment, though, and her roommate says she's still away on her trip."

"Oh, where'd she go?"

"I don't know." He leaned forward with his face in his hands. He saw Pretty Baby's questioning look. "She's a flight attendant."

"I never knew that."

"Yeah, well, she left four days ago and I haven't seen or heard from her. She's usually gone only two to three days."

"Maybe she got stuck somewhere because of bad weather. We don't get much bad weather but other places do this time of year." She paused sipping her drink. "You guys didn't even get to spend Valentine's Day together?" She felt a little flutter in her stomach, thinking of her

249

weekend.

"Yeah, I know. I offered to fly wherever she was scheduled for a layover but she said she didn't have a long layover and we could celebrate when she got back. Something must've come up," he nodded his head assuring himself. "She'll probably call tonight or tomorrow."

"Yeah." They both sat staring at Perry Mason for a while. "What happened at the meeting?"

"Oh, man. You wouldn't believe the mess," he suddenly said. "We're gonna end up rebuilding the center ourselves."

"Why do you say that? What about insurance? Surely we can get that same contracting company to rebuild. They did a beautiful job."

Jesse shook his head in disgust. "We have insurance on the church. But at the time we built the life center, extended coverage was too costly.
You know Mr. and Mrs. Williams that own that car lot downtown?"

Pretty Baby nodded. "I know Mrs. Williams, but she won't let you get but so close to that henpecked husband of hers. I tried to talk to him last year about getting a car and she said they'd get back with me and they never did. Like somebody want her husband," she added.

"They're head of the finance committee and they decided, after they found out the cost of the extended coverage, that we could wait on that until a later date."

"You're kidding? They don't let nobody drive off that car lot without insurance. That was dumb. So now what?"

"We're going to meet again next Saturday in the sanctuary. I'm gonna get busy, starting tomorrow, and try to get some of the local businesses to make contributions in addition to all of us making commitments to the building fund," he paused. "United Christians Church dates back to the early 1900's and a lot of people respect our church and Pastor Lindley for the things we've done in the community, especially with the youth. So I figure it shouldn't be too hard a task." Jesse stood. His cowboy boots made his right leg appear a little more bow than the other one. His starched jean shirt tucked neatly into his jeans fit him perfectly. Pretty Baby thought about how some people look their age and older as years go on but the years were doing Jesse great justice......So why he would have a woman like Charmaine was a mystery.

"I'm gonna call your friend, Elliott," she heard him say. "He was telling me a little about his business. Looks like you might've finally got hold of what you need instead of what you want." He gave her a wink. "Anyway, I got some other ideas I'm knocking around in my head that I want to present at the meeting Saturday." Jesse started for the door. "I gotta be at work early tomorrow, so I guess I'll turn in."

"Me, too." She watched Jesse across the yard, then came in, turned out the lights and retired upstairs.

*"The eye that mocketh at his father, and despiseth to obey
his mother,
the ravens of the valley shall pick it out, and the young
eagles shall eat it."*
Pr.30:17

*T*he clouds were passing over and the sun was coming out as Pretty Baby zoomed down I-95. The old Duce seemed to run smoothly the faster she went or either it was like all sick things that seem to get better right before they die.

Pretty Baby smiled to herself thinking about the seductive message she had left on Elliott's car phone last night.....'Hey Baby. It's been too long.' She purred, 'Miss Kitty needs a little pettin'. Don't make me beg. Call me.'

Tangled Web

She could just picture the expression on Elliotts' face as he checked his messages first thing in the morning, thinking it was a business matter.

When Ms. Montgomery called her to the phone she had almost forgotten about the message until she heard Elliotts' sexy voice on the other end saying, "Miss Kitty will never have to beg me. How about dinner this evening? That's if you can get away." That man is something else she thought. She couldn't wait to show him the surprise she had for him. A little something to hold him until he got back from his trip.

She pulled around the back of Banks Inc., as Elliott had instructed, and parked next to his Benz in front of the sign that read reserved. She would never guess this space hadn't been occupied since Savannah last parked there. Checking her makeup in the rear view mirror, Pretty Baby climbed out of her car and smoothed her dress, feeling quite sexy.

She went into the back entrance and frowned at the thought of climbing the steps to the fourth floor but was then relieved to see an elevator in the far corner. She walked down the long corridor speaking and nodding to the busy employees shuffling through until she came to an opening that was the reception area.

Pretty Baby recognized the young woman at the desk, who sat with a headset on, from the Dunivan Christmas party. She remembered Nancy saying she was Elliott's secretary.

Clarisse stopped pecking at her computer and glanced up. "May I help you?" She thought this woman looked familiar but she couldn't remember what company she was from.

"Yes, I'm here to see Mr. Banks." Yep, that was her. Pretty Baby remembered the big gap in her teeth.

"Can I get you to sign in right here?"

Pretty Baby obliged leaving the space marked nature of business and company, empty. Clarisse rang Mr. Banks on the intercom.

"Mr. Banks, will see you now," she said, just as Prettty Baby was about to thumb through a Black Enterprise magazine. Clarisse stared after the elegantly dressed Ms. Casey as she walked into Elliott's office leaving a trace of her citrus scented perfume behind.

Pretty Baby quietly locked the door behind her. Elliott was on the phone. "I'm leaving out on a 6:30 flight tomorrow morning. I'll come straight there in time for the 10:00 planning meeting." Pause. He motioned for Pretty Baby to sit on the couch. She sat, one leg crossed high. Her side buttoned linen dress exposed the stockinged silhouette of her thigh. "Great. I'll see you then." He hung up.

"Hello gorgeous," he came from around his desk toward her.

"Hey Baby," she said sweetly, standing to greet him with a kiss. He went to the door realizing it was locked. "I already took care of that." She laughed. He went outside the door. She could see him talking to Clarisse as she cleared her desk for the day then walked away with a wave.

Elliott closed the door locking it behind him. He walked toward Pretty Baby with a look of 'I gotcha where I want you'. She laughed at his playfulness as he traced her neck with soft kisses, moving his hands down to her butt, rubbing it sensuously.

"Is everybody gone?" She asked, pulling back a little.

"They should be." He went back to the door, stepping out to look around. When he returned and closed the door, there stood Pretty Baby in her a purple satin bikini thong set. "Whoa." His eyes focused in on her happy tits then down between her legs where a bright yellow banana was stitched on the panties. He stepped closer for a better look. The word 'tasty' was written under it. His eyes twinkled. "Miss Kitty, Ms Kitty," he pulled her close moaning into her hair. "Where have you been all my life?"

He peeked out the door again then guided Pretty Baby into his private restroom. There, they released a lust that had been trapped for what seemed like ages.

****

On her way out, Clarisse saw Gracie in the copy room. "You're still here? I thought this was your early day."

"Yeah, well, I had to get these copies done so I figured I'd finish up today and the remainder of the week should go smoothly. I'm almost done." Gracie took a deep breath, collated another stack of papers then clicked the button. "Mr. Banks really should get us a xerox person. That would take a load off of us."

"That's a good idea." Clarisse stood watching Gracie for a moment then started digging for her keys out

255

of her purse. "Did you see that woman who came up to see him this evening?"

"Uh-uh, what woman?"

"Rachel Casey is what she wrote on the log sheet."

"From what company?" Gracie furrowed her brow, keeping her assembly line going.

"She didn't put down what company," Clarisse said suspiciously.

Gracie caught the tone in her voice. She always thought Clarisse had a little crush on Elliott. "Well, maybe she's just a friend of the family or a business acquaintance, Honey," Gracie shrugged.

The echo of Pretty Baby's laughter could be heard coming down the back steps. Clarisse stepped out of the copy room just as they went out the door. "Look, Gracie. That's her."

Gracie clicked the machine once more before going into the hall just in time to see Pretty Baby hook her arm in Elliotts, giving him a bump with her hip, as they both laughed on their way to the car. Elliott opened her car door for her. Clarisse was surprised that a woman like that was driving such a trashy car and had the nerve to park it in Mrs. Bank's spot. Pretty Baby got something out of her car, then Elliott opened his passenger door and let her in. Gracie narrowed her eyes then turned to Clarisse. "Like I said, maybe she's a family friend."

****

"Elliott, I'm gonna be as fat as a pig foolin' with you," Pretty Baby said, licking the last of the rich cheesecake

Tangled Web

from her fork.

"Don't blame it on me. Blame it on yourself when you can't put on that 'tasty' banana outfit." He laughed at the thought as he pulled his wallet out.

Pretty Baby assumed this was her signal to hurry up. "Let me drink my water and I'll be ready to go."

"No rush," he pulled an American Express card from his stack. "I want you to have this." He handed her the card.

She looked closer, recognizing her name etched on the front. She took a gulp of her water. "It's for me? I've never even had a credit card before."

"Here," he handed her a pen, " sign the back and when you get home, call this number to activate it." Pretty Baby didn't know what to say. "You need this in case of emergency." He paused watching her sign the card. He remembered a few weeks ago her saying she wished she could get a credit card but her ex had ruined her credit. "Now this is the big boy. You could buy a car with this," he saw Pretty Baby's eyes light up, "but don't try it unless you can pay it off next month." They laughed.

"Thanks, Elliott. You are sooo good to me." She kissed him on the cheek. She looked at him for a moment. "You're gonna make me fall in love with you," she said, in mock anger.

He laughed, "We just might do that, but don't purchase nothing you can't pay for." He gave her a wink then looked at his watch. "Why don't you order something to take home for the kids."

"That's a good idea because I need to go to the grocery store bad. Our cupboard is bare." She placed an order with the waiter.

"Come on," he said sliding out of the booth. "I need to make a stop. We'll come back and pick up the food." He told the waiter they would be back in thirty to forty-five minutes.

Elliott drove into a deserted looking car lot. He pulled up to the building where an older, bald-headed gentleman could be seen pacing back and forth talking on the phone. He got out and told her to wait a minute. The man saw Elliott coming, ended his conversation and greeted him at the door. The two men shook hands and hugged as if they hadn't seen each other in a while then went out and disappeared around the building out of Pretty Baby's sight. Ten minutes had gone by that seemed like thirty. Pretty Baby was starting to get impatient. She turned on the CD player. The angelic voice of Aaron Neville filtered through the speakers. It was the CD she had bought him recently knowing he liked the Neville's. She laid her head back on the sandstone leather seat listening. After two songs she looked up and saw Elliott and the man coming back. Finally. He came around to her side and tapped on the window for her to unlock the door.

He opened her door. "Come on, get out. I want you to meet someone." It was obvious Elber appreciated that quick flash of those long sexy legs through the side split, as he stood grinning and she got out of the car. "This is Elber Reid. Elber this is Rachel Casey." They exchanged hello's.

"I need your opinion on something," Pretty Baby hesitantly said okay, wondering what this was about. She followed the men around the building to the preowned vehicles stopping at a red BMW. Pretty Baby felt a tinge of excitement building. 'Maybe he's going to co-sign for this car. Hell, I can't afford this,' she thought.

Elliott opened the driver's door. "Get in," he instructed. She did and he leaned over and put the key in the ignition. "Start her up," he said stepping back, smiling at her expression. She started the car up, speechless. "You like it?"

Pretty Baby eyed the interior of the car, slowly turning to him. "I love it."

"I already test drove it, it runs great. But if you want to take it for a spin, you can."

She got out of the car and walked to the front out of Elbers' earshot. "I love this car, Baby, but how am I gonna afford it?" Pretty Baby asked, searching his smiling eyes.

"Don't worry. Elber owes me a favor from a while back. I figured now would be a great time to collect on it." Pretty Baby smiled. "I'm going to pay cash for all but six payments", he explained quickly. "You can handle that to get you a little credit established."

This was one thing she had come to know and love about Elliott, he always had a plan; He'd think about it, say it, then the next thing she knew...it was done. He lifted her chin up to face him. She was overwhelmed, giving him a big hug.

"Then you can start work on your next project," Elliott said, leaving Pretty Baby in suspense.

She looked at him questioningly. "Which is?"

"A bigger and better home for you and the kids, of course."

Pretty Baby shook her head. "You are too good to

259

me."

"Come on before Reid reneges on the deal." They walked back around to the office to sign the final paperwork. Elliott wrote out a check and Mr. Reid told her to come back tomorrow and she could pick up the car.

Pretty Baby sat in one of the chairs outside of Mr. Reids' office smiling to herself when she heard a woman call her name. "Rachel, is that you?"

"Oh, hi, Ms. Montgomery. What are you doing here?" She was surprised to see her on this side of town.

"My son just got a car from here and I'm picking up the tags for him on account of he's working." She heard Mr. Reids voice and looked around Pretty Baby to see who she might be waiting on. "What about you?" She looked back to Pretty Baby. "You're finally buying a new car?" She said a bit sarcastically.

Pretty Baby, as excited as she was, decided against telling her anything. She'll see. Elliott walked out. "All set?"

Ms. Montgomery stood staring at Elliott even after Mr. Reid had acknowledged her. Finally Pretty Baby introduced them and immediately escaped before Elliott, unknowingly, told her business to the mouth of the south.

Pretty Baby rambled on excitedly while they picked up the food for the kids then went back to Banks, Inc., where her car was. Elliott leaned over in the car, once they parked, to give her a sweet kiss. "Well, my love, this is the last night I will ever have to worry about you riding home in that car."

"Yeah, but you can believe I'm not about to get sentimental about this being our last night together." They

Tangled Web

laughed. "I know now, Elliott," she began seriously, "that you are a genie."

He responded just as serious. "I promise I'm not." Pretty Baby looked at him for a long moment, weighing her words before she let them out. "This is all going so fast," she stammered. "And I want you to know first and foremost that I can't be bought. I'm not that kind of woman." Elliott burst into laughter. "Why are you laughing? I'm serious and I want you to know where I stand. This was your idea not mine."

Elliott got out of the car, recognizing that this was one of those crazy woman moments, and came to her side still laughing. "I never thought the day would come that I would put you out of my car." He ran his hand up her leg, running his fingers the length of Ms. Kitty. "Not that kinda girl, huh?" He gave her a gentle tug pulling her out of his car and pinning her against her car.

Pretty Baby continued to insist that she was letting him know up front, as he restrained her, showering her with kisses between words. He suddenly kissed her firmly. "I have fallen in love with you," he looked into her eyes.

She took a quick breath, not expecting this revelation then melted into his arms. "I don't even know that I can afford you, talk about being bought. But I'm gonna try," he whispered. "You got a house full of children." She pinched him as he joked. "I'm sure I'm biting off more than I can chew." They stood there for a long moment then Elliott opened her car door letting her in. "Don't forget I'll probably be gone until next Sunday. I wish you were going with me," he said through the window.

"Call me. I'll probably be back and forth at the

church.   The big meeting is Saturday."   She explained briefly about the insurance situation, he said he knew because he had spoken with Jesse.

"Speaking of insurance...." he pulled a business card from his breast pocket, "give this guy a call and get a quote before you go and pick the car up."

"O.k."

He reached in his pocket again, this time pulling out a hundred dollar bill. "Get some groceries. Be sure to get some of that teriyaki stir fry stuff. That was delicious." He kissed his fingers Italian style. "I want you to fix it when I get back.   And some strawberries for strawberry shortcake." He leaned his head in the window and gave her a long kiss goodbye. "Be careful and call me as soon as you get in."

She started the engine, revving it a few times then blew him a kiss as she drove off.

****

The next day, Pretty Baby took off early. Elber was standing out on the lot with a customer when she drove up. He quickly pushed them off on the other salesman to help Pretty Baby in hopes of getting another glimpse of those legs. Finally the deal was settled and Pretty Baby got the last of her belongings out of the Duce and transferred them to her new red Beamer. She picked Ashley up first from the babysitters and road over to Missy's where Jason was. Chris was at conditioning training, getting ready for the track season.

"Yeah, Baby. You're riding in style now."   Missy

Tangled Web

shouted her approval as the two women and the children piled in the car and took a ride.

When they returned, Pretty Baby and Missy stood outside the car talking while the kids ran around the yard playing tag. "You're making progress now, cous'."

Pretty Baby gave a sly laugh. "When I first realized that he was really buying me the car all kinds of thoughts were going through my head."

"Good thoughts, I know."

"Well," Pretty Baby hesitated. "I didn't know if he had an ulterior motive or not and I told him I couldn't be bought."

"What? Girl, don't tell that man no mess like that. Oh yes, you can be bought." Missy rolled her eyes. "In fact don't tell nobody else you said that shit. Please." She leaned back against the car with her arms folded.

"I understand his motives now," Pretty Baby said with a far away look.

"Good. So now, keep doing what you're doing and take the money and run. What's love got to do with it any damn way?" She lit a cigarette.

"I think love may have everything to do with it," she mumbled.

Missy didn't hear that. "Come on, Jason," Pretty Baby yelled.

Jason ran across the yard. "Oh, Mom. Come back and get me."

"He can stay," Missy exhaled a big puff of smoke. "I'm getting ready to fix some dinner anyway. Come back and get him or I can drop him off," she was indecisive. "Just call me."

263

"I guess I could go to the grocery store," she said getting in the car. Midway to the store she decided to stop by the house to get a juice bottle for Ashley. The lights were out and the house was quiet but it was evident that Chris had been in the vicinity because his gym bag was in the middle of the floor. She sat Ashley on the floor. "Your brothers' a slob just like your daddy. How many times I got to remind him....." She trailed off into the kitchen coming back with a bottle, sliding it in her purse. "Wait one more minute. Let me run upstairs."

When she got near the top step, Pretty Baby thought she heard a female voice. Three more steps into her room, she was sure she heard a woman's voice. She about -faced and tipped up to Chris' closed door. She stood very still listening. She knocked one time. Suddenly, a lot of scrambling around could be heard. Pretty Baby tried the doorknob but it was locked.

BAM, BAM, BAM! "Open this door before I kick the damn thing in!" She screamed. Pretty Baby waited a second with heat coming from her collar when she realized Ashley was crying. She turned quickly. The gate's not on. She raced down the steps to see Ashley making her way to the third step. Pretty Baby scooped her up being very careful not to startle her. They plopped down in the chair that sat along the side of the steps. 'I can't believe this shit,' was all she could say. Mainly because she had so many mixed emotions about this situation and had never really thought of it happening to her. Her son. The more she thought about it, she realized she was hurt. Why? Who knows.

Ashley climbed out of her lap when she heard her

Tangled Web

brother come down the steps. Pretty Baby never turned to look in the girls' face. She was too pissed.

Once she heard the door shut she jumped up and on Chris' case in the worst way. "You fucked that girl in my house! And you got busted." Chris held his head down. "Look at me!" she yelled. When he did, she smacked him across the face hard. "I can't stop you from becoming a man, but I will stop you from disrespecting me in my home." There were no words, excuses, or lies that could get him out of this, so he said nothing. "I thought you were at track practice. You little liar!" she spat. "Stay your ass in the house, don't get on my phone and tell that hot ass winch, Sharon, don't come this way. And I mean it!" She took Ashley's coat off. "You keep your sister while I go to the store. Do something constructive for a change," she mumbled as she went out the door.

Before she could make it to the car she heard the door open. "Ma, whose car is that?"

She threw him a hateful look. "None of your damn business, now get back in the house." She started to get in the car.

"Is it that dude's car?"

"What dude?" she said out of exasperation. Then thinking of 'what dude', she added, "Don't ask me nothing, I'm grown!"

With that, she slammed the door and drove off.

Pamela Williams-Guinn

*"Commit thy works unto the Lord,
and thy thoughts shall be established."*
Pr.16:3

The members filed into what was left of United Christian's sanctuary. It was a nice sunny day so the absence of electricity wasn't a big bother. The stained glass windows were angled outward for the maximum amount of light and the people sat close together for warmth when a cool breeze whisked in.

Pretty Baby came in just as the meeting was about to start. Taking a seat in the back, she saw old Ms. Williams strolling up to the front pew. She looked just as funny in her Saturday clothes as she did in her Sunday

266

clothes. Her big butt swagging one way and them titties, long enough to throw over her shoulders so she could wear them on her back, swung the other way. She squeezed in next to her dense husband and the other financial officers.

Pastor Lindley opened the meeting with a prayer and thanked the congregation for its support in these trying times. "And without any further ado," he went on, "Everybody knows Jesse from when he was a youngster runnin' round here." He gave a chuckle. "Well he's a man now, making a better way for us all through Christ." Several shouts of Amen could be heard. Pretty Baby could see Aunt Becky nodding her head in approval. "Church please be in prayer as we accept and follow Brother Jesse as our building fund leader."

Jesse stood at the podium, nervous but with a look of determination as he sifted through the notes he had made. He had been up late last night. In addition to working on his notes for church, he was entertaining Charmaine. She had come back from her trip. She explained to Jesse that she had to help some out of town relatives in distress, who didn't have a phone. That's why she couldn't call. He was just glad she was home. Her absence had really made his heart grow fonder.

The applause died as Jesse began, slightly reading from his paper. "Thank you," he said bashfully. "I must say first that I am honored to have been appointed leader of the building fund and I am sure with prayer and all of our ideas we can get through this. The Lord has given me chance after chance after chance and by trusting Him, He has put me in places and positions no man could have told me were possible. I can't help but to remember, to whom much is given; much is required, therefore, I'm committed to seeing this through."

He went on to explain in detail what caused the fire and where the church made an error in judgment about the insurance, for those who didn't know or heard it wrong through the grapevine. "So, Church," he continued, "we don't have any other options but to start all over using our own money. We've already over extended ourselves in credit so a loan is out. I propose...."

One woman stood abruptly. "Why would the finance committee let us be without insurance. They suppose to oversee all that," she blurted and a few people in her cheering squad applauded.

"Out of respect for human error, we're not gonna point any fingers, we're just gonna deal with it." He spoke kindly as beads of sweat were popping across his forehead. He knew there would be some disgruntled members. "As Pastor often says, 'Don't let your location or your situation obscure you from your destination.' This is just a stumbling block the devil has thrown in our way to see who will stumble and fall. He doesn't want us to complete the race together like we started. In the end, he wants us to separate and go against one another. We're vulnerable on our own but there's power in the masses."

Mrs. Williams stood. "I'd like to address any accusations about the finance committee." She sucked her teeth and rolled her eyes in the direction of the woman who had spoken first. "My husband and I have been members of this church for years and we have contributed plenty of money to anything that was asked. I can't handle my personal affairs and the church's too. This is supposed to

Tangled Web

be a committee effort and I really feel like we were let down by Brother Dickson......"

"As I said," Jesse immediately interjected knowing the sparks were about to fly. Brother Dickson sat tight jawed. "It's not important whose fault it is, at this point. Now, I propose...," he tried again.

"Brother Jesse," an elderly man said, as he took the floor up front. "I, too, have been a member of this church all my life. My father was one of the founders and I can handle change....but I can't handle how our funds were mishandled. And now you want us to do this again."

"That's what I'm talkin' 'bout," a woman in the back by Pretty Baby stood and said. "I don't think it's fair to us who was dedicated to the building fund, made pledges and fulfilled them. What about those people who gave only one time, if at all, but they reaped all the benefits. And now they probably laughing 'cause it wasn't their money that went up in smoke. I think you ought to check the books and see who pledged and who did not." She sat down in a huff as the crowd burst into applause and loud chatter.

Jesse knew he had to come strong with this plan or get washed away by these agitated saints. Instead of being tolerant and making proposals he would be firm.

"Can I have your attention please? Can I have your attention?" He spoke loudly. "Now this is what we're going to do," he spoke firmly, going back to his notes. "Several of the local businesses were quite generous and have agreed to contribute to our new building fund based on the history of United Christians. This way we don't have to start at the bottom and with the aid of everyone involved we should see results much faster. At this time, I'd like to acknowledge them. If you know others who would like to contribute see me after this meeting." He looked into the audience at some of the uninterested faces then to the eager familiar faces and continued. "Solomon and Sons' Detail shop-$500. Afternoon Delight Diner-$500. Ms. Betty's Beauty Salon-$350." Two or three people got up and left. Jesse continued, "Virginia Loan and Trust $1500. Futuro Cellular Company $1500. Griffin Auto Sales $3000. Banks, Inc. $5000." Aunt Becky turned to see the look of surprise and the gleam in Pretty Baby's eyes. Several shouts of 'Amen' and 'praise God' echoed. "Al's Tasty Burger $500. Rockman Jewelers $1000 and Pittman Custom Signs $500." He looked into his audience. "Fourteen thousand, three hundred and fifty dollars. Praise God." The members burst into applause. Jesse raised his hands for quiet, regaining control of the crowd. "Praise God for these kind people." He looked out into the audience, unsure of if they really knew what was expected of them at this point. Without his papers, he continued with conviction. "The time is now for us to glory in our tribulations; knowing that tribulations worketh patience. And patience brings experience. And experience brings....hope."

"Amen"

"Everybody's walking around with bracelets, t-shirts and key chains that have "WWJD?" on them. Is it just a fad?"

Several church members start to whisper among themselves.

"Jesus is no fad. Jesus is a never changing, never ending Savior." Jesse walked further into the

Tangled Web

congregation, looking from member to member. "I ask you, Church......What Would Jesus Do....if He was in this predicament?" The crowd grew amazingly quiet.

"Preach, Brother," Brother Dickson suddenly encouraged.

Jesse stood in the middle of the main isle so that his voice could be heard all around. "This whole situation could be so much worse. We could've been here in worship when the fire broke out. But the Lord saw fit to warn us in this way."

"Amen," could be heard from all over the room at this point.

"Psalms 37 says , 'Trust in the Lord and do good and thou shalt be fed. Delight thyself in the Lord and He shall give thee the desires of thine heart. Rest in the Lord and wait patiently for Him. Commit thy way unto the Lord and He shall bring it to pass." Jesse walked back to the front of the sanctuary. "God is saying, 'do what's right and trust Him'. Regardless of how we may seem to be losing, just do His will and leave the outcome to Him."

Pretty Baby, along with everyone else, was hanging on to Jesse's every word. She never knew he could speak this way. She was so engrossed in his words that she didn't see Elliott suddenly slide into the seat next to her. He was back early from his trip. He gave her a wink as they continued to give Jesse their full attention.

Pretty Baby couldn't hold it. "Thank you for that generous contribution," she whispered, giving him a look of admiration. Aunt Becky glanced around to see if everyone was enjoying Jesse the way she was, when she saw Elliott sit next to Pretty Baby.

271

"Keep in mind that God takes ordinary folks like us and does extraordinary things. He'll never put more on us than we can bare." Jesse fell silent for a moment. "Once you get home and have absorbed this information.....ask yourself, What would Jesus do?" The crowd that was left went up with applause and agreement.

"I know everyone is thinking I never talk this much," Jesse said. The audience laughed. "But I want to leave you with a little food for thought I ran across and would like to share." Jesse sifted through his notes that were on the podium until he came to the right one. "This was quoted by a man named Kemmons Wilson. It's his advice for planting a 'garden'. God's garden." He cleared his throat,
"5 rows of 'peas' - prayer, preparedness, promptness, perseverance, politeness.
3 rows of 'squash' - squash gossip, criticism, and indifference.
5 rows of 'lettuce' - let us love one another, let us be faithful, let us be loyal, let us be unselfish, let us be truthful.
3 rows of 'turnips' - turn up for church, turn up with a new idea, turn up with the determination to do a better job today than you did yesterday. Work becomes worship when done for the Lord. Thank you for your time." Everyone applauded loudly as Pastor Lindley got up to hug Jesse and end the meeting.

Jesse was the center of attention. Everyone was amazed with his oratorical abilities and impressed with the job he had done getting contributors. All of the older women loved Jesse but the young women, who had never paid him much attention, were beginning to see him in a different light. Some even stood in the line to greet him

Tangled Web

with their checkbooks in their hands, ready to make new pledges. Pretty Baby and Elliott stood in line talking with others until it was their turn to greet Jesse. A few lingered around wondering who the good looking man was with Pretty Baby.

"Shall we start calling you Pastor Jesse?" Pretty Baby, joked then gave him a hug. "I'm so proud of you Jesse. Let me know what I can do to help." She hugged him again.

He reached for Elliott's hand, giving a firm shake. "I thought you would be out of town, man. But I'm glad you're here...I wanted to thank you myself."

"No problem. Anything I can do to help, just let me know," Elliott said sincerely. Pretty Baby beamed at him with pride. They left the church.

Elliott walked Pretty Baby to her car. "The kids enjoying the car?"

"Of course," she said smiling, "but I can't get over you." She was thinking about the contribution. "That was really sweet."

"It's no big deal, really. I do what I can if I can." He shrugged. "So where are you headed now?" He had that mischievous look in his eye.

Pretty Baby played along. "Home. You want to go?" She got into her car.

"I'd love to, but I can't this time." Elliott looked disappointed. "I haven't been home yet and I need to check on some things." A few people spoke or waved as they passed. "I don't know if I mentioned it or not," he hesitated, "but Savannah has moved to Woodland Hills Rehab Center. The Doctor thought it may be good for her to be in a different environment with other people. He's hoping that this will help her to become more independent because of the surroundings." Elliott saw the look of disappointment in her eyes. "I need to check on her."

"Of course," Pretty Baby said, as she started the engine to her car. "Well, just call me."

"I'm gonna call you when I get home. I just need to see about this first. How about my dinner tomorrow?" He asked, coming back with that million dollar smile.

"O.k., Baby. You're on."

He gave her a wink, wanting to kiss those luscious lips, but he restrained himself because of onlookers. She blew him a kiss and he pretended to watch it soar threw the air, then he snatched it and held it to his heart as she drove away.

****

The warm sun felt good beaming on Pretty Baby through her sun roof as she sped down the winding side street taking a short cut to Miller's Gas and Grocery. She tried to finger her hair in the rearview mirror when she got to the stop sign, but it just flopped its own way. A haircut this week was a must. She would make an appointment at the salon that Missy always goes to. Maybe even get some streaks. Yeah, red highlights to go with her new red BMW! Elliott would probably think it was sexy.

Phyllis sounded just as good in this car, if not better than in the duce. Pretty Baby started feeling sentimental listening to her sing 'The Answer Is You'. She couldn't believe someone as wonderful as Elliott had come into her life. She'd never felt so in tuned with someone on so many levels and there was no doubt he felt the same way. Pretty Baby and Elliott had grown so close in such a short time, exchanging confidences about family and insecurities that they had never shared with anyone else. They enjoyed a lot of the same things, laughed at the same jokes, took long walks, worked in the yard and looked forward to pleasing each other. She had even made up a special strawberry shortcake dessert in his honor and named it after him.

Elliott really got deep the night they talked on the phone for three hours. It all started with him talking about Savannah's accident. Pretty Baby's curiosity was piqued at this time. She treaded ground she had never walked before, wanting to know what his wife and their relationship had been like before the accident. He spoke fondly of the boys and had good memories of her, but he made a comment about them being great together only when it came to taking on the world of business. But not one on one. They didn't seem to have the same leisure interests, whereas he and Pretty Baby both enjoyed museums and having picnics, taking turns reading funny anecdotes or romantic poetry to each other. Elliott said he never thought it would happen, but the age difference between he and Savannah had started to play into the relationship. Savannah didn't know him as a man, only as a business partner or companion. He also said she never thought of wearing sexy negligees for him as Pretty Baby did and she knew he liked that. It seemed as if their sex life was business also.

Then Pretty Baby's mind started thinking about

Savannah going to Woodland Hills rehab. It was actually a housing community for the mentally impaired rich. There, she would somewhat be living on her own. Pretty Baby wondered would she suddenly become well but then she doubted it because Elliott said they had tried every medication, to no avail. The only way she could get better was if she wanted to, but all these years she never has.

She went into Miller's, scanning the shelves then decided to get only a Pepsi and gas.

"That your new car, Pretty Baby?" Miller asked as he rang her up.

"Uh-huh. How you been feeling? I saw your son working and he told me you been under the weather," she said.

"My back was givin' me problems but I'm alright. You the one doin' good." He pointed out to the car. "I love that ride. You look real good in it too."

"Thanks, Miller," she said with a wave out the door. Just as she was pumping the gas, Stank walked up. She thought she smelled a faint trace of him in the store.

"Hey, Pre' Baby."

"Hey, Stank. What's up?" She watched the gallons on the pump add up.

"Nothin'. You got a cigarette?"

"I sure don't." She had given up the cigarettes, which wasn't very hard because Elliott hated them. She looked at Stank then back to the pump. He was drunk in addition to being funky.

"This yo' new ride?"

She nodded, not feeling like dealing with Stank today.

Tangled Web

"This nice, Pretty Baby. This nice." He grinned his rotten tooth grin, peeping in the back window. "Will seen this ride?"

"No," she said in a matter of fact tone.

"Don't let him drive it." He started to snicker.

She cut her eyes at Stank then hung the pump back up. "I'm not married to him anymore. Or have you forgotten?"

He leaned on the car bringing his empty can of beer to his lips. His equilibrium was a bit off. He shook the last two drops out on his tongue then tossed the can in the trash. Pretty Baby left him leaning and got in the car. He slid down to her window and slurred, "Good thang you ain't, cause he'll pawn this car to the man faster than you can say 'come right back'." He laughed flinging spit from his mouth.

She could barely stand his odor. "What man?" She needed to know.

"The dope man," he suddenly got serious, still slurring. Stank's' eyes bucked out of his head and his face looked animated. "I knows from the folks over on the north side, by Lolita's. He go wit' one of them dancers. All them is smokin'." He moved in closer and lowered his voice, "He go wit' Jesse's ol' lady."

Pretty Baby's eyes widened and he gave her a look of solemn confirmation. "Charmaine?" She couldn't believe it.

"Yep, but she don't use, she just deal. She dance," he gyrated his hips, "and she deal. Dance and deal," he chanted then burst out laughing.

Pretty Baby was stunned. She could believe that

277

about William....but Charmaine.   This all explained why William never had anything.   But Charmaine?....She always knew it was something about her.   She wiped her hand across her forehead.   What if Stank was wrong, probably not.   She would have to find a way to tell Jesse. "I gotta go, Stank." She started the car and put it in gear.

"Hold up.   Hold up Pretty Baby," he leaned in the window. "Let me borrow two dollars 'til next week."

She looked at her drunken old friend, knowing he wanted another beer, "I don't have it," she said, pulling off.

Pretty Baby took the long way home circling through the neighborhood a few times.   She couldn't get what Stank said out of her mind.   She hated to believe it but her gut feeling was nagging her.   William and Charmaine going together?   How ironic...and sickening.   A drug dealer, with a junkie boyfriend.   Jesse would be too through with her, putting on this big front as a flight attendant, and really, she sells dope.   Pretty Baby's mood went from agitated to depressed.   She hoped William would get himself together if for nothing else, to keep his job.   She needed that child-support check.

Pretty Baby gave a double beep to Missy and Jesse as she pulled in the driveway.   They were standing in Jesse's yard.   Ashley galloped on Missy's hip when she spotted her mom.   She could tell by Jesse's movements and Missy's reactions that he was telling her about the meeting.   He was standing on top of the world right now and he had every reason to be.   It was true what Aunt Becky would always say about your light shining when you have Christ in your life.   Jesse had a glow all around him that he wasn't even aware of.   The more Pretty Baby

Tangled Web

thought about it, Jesse really was a special man. Kind of different, that's why Charmaine was not the answer. The way he spoke today sounded like greatness in the making. Pretty Baby decided to not tell Jesse about Charmaine right away because she was sure that anything done in the dark, always comes to the light. Maybe Charmaine would play her own self out.

Pretty Baby went over and joined them. Ashley immediately reached for her mom.

"Hey Pretty Baby," Missy said, "Jesse was just telling me about the meeting. I wish I could've been there to see Mrs. Williams' face when she realized her car lot was not the only money in town."

"Is that all Jesse told you about? I thought he was over here telling the real good part." Jesse gave her an uncertain look.

"What else happened?" Missy looked from one to the other.

"Jesse was preachin'."

"What?" Missy kind of laughed and Jesse looked bashful.

"Yes, ma'am. He was up there delivering the word like it has never been delivered before. Quotin' scriptures and stuff." Jesse shook his head in denial and she nudged him playfully.

Missy gave an approving nod. "Preachin', huh? I heard that. I bet them women gon' be all over him now."

"They were today," Pretty Baby said. "Even the ones who weren't before."

They were embarrassing Jesse. "You guys need to quit."

279

"With their checkbooks out," Pretty Baby added.

"I thought about gettin' me a preacher a couple of times," Missy suddenly said, "but I'm afraid he might cleanse my soul and my life would become boring."

"That's about what you need," Jesse said, and they laughed.

Pretty Baby took Ashley into the house for some lunch. Chris had just gone out front and Jason and Monique were upstairs playing video games.

She swung the door open to the kitchen to see Aunt Becky staring out the back door. Four peanut butter and jelly crackers and a cup of juice sat on the high chair. "You scared me, Aunt Becky. I was just coming in here to fix Ashley something to eat."

"What you scared for?" she said lifting the top off the high chair for Ashley.

Pretty Baby sat her in the seat. "I didn't know you were here. So what's going on?" She got the plastic bib that was hooked on the refrigerator and put it on Ashley.

"Nothin'. I rode 'round here with Jesse from the church, thinking you would be here. Guess you run off with your friend though."

"Noo, I didn't run off." She put the dishes in the dishwasher thinking about what did happen when she left the church. "The meeting went well, huh? Jesse is something else."

"I always knew it," Aunt Becky said, then got quiet as she watched over Ashley. "'Twas right nice of your friend donating that kind of money to our fund."

Pretty Baby turned around with a smile. "He's a sweet man, Aunt Becky."

280

Tangled Web

"Hmph, he more than sweet. I s'pose he's responsible for that fancy foreign car you driving."

"Well, he helped. A friend of his gave me a good deal," Pretty Baby assured her. Aunt Becky didn't need to know everything. "Elliott thought I needed something more dependable for me and the kids."

"That's nice." Becky sat wringing her hands the way she did when she was praying. "You need somebody who can do for you and the children. Somebody who can lead and guide you," her voice trailed off. "Yeah, he seems to be a kind man...and I like him." She paused weighing her words. "But I'd like him a whole lot better if he was DIVORCED."

Pretty Baby stood stunned with her mouth open. How did Becky know? "It's not like you think, Aunt Becky," she tried to explain. "His wife has been sick for years."

"I don't care. He's still married. You sure can't plan a future with him no matter how good he is to you." She walked closer to Pretty Baby so the kids wouldn't overhear. "I know people do things for all kinds of reasons but it's not right. And you," she pointed right in her chest, "know better. You gon' miss out on your blessings seeking the lust of the world. You know the lust of the eye, the lust of the flesh and the pride of life," she checked each phrase on her fingers, "are the devices satan uses to distract us. You know this."

Pretty Baby looked away. She couldn't bare to look Becky in the face as she turned the knife that had just been dashed into her heart.

"Nothing good could possibly come of this."

"Aunt Becky," she tried to explain again.

"I'm not gonna say nothing else about this," she cut her off, "I'm just gonna pray that he'll go away." Aunt Becky sat back down in the chair. "You not even the kind of women to go with a married man. You should be ashamed. I didn't raise you like that. 'Tis wrong in front of the children."

"They don't know," she snapped.

"Oh yes they do, 'cause Monique told me."

Pretty Baby nodded her head slowly. So that's how she knew. She always told Missy she shouldn't talk so much in front of that girl

Footsteps from the children could be heard coming down the steps. Chris burst into the kitchen first. "Hey, Momma. I didn't know you were here." He tickled his sister under the chin then walked up to his mom. "You crying, Momma?"

"No, Baby, I got something in my eye." Pretty Baby left the kitchen and went upstairs to her bathroom closing the door tightly with her back. She stood there for a long moment then went and sat on the toilet reaching for the toilet paper to catch the falling tears. She covered her mouth as a sorrowful moan escaped it.

Tangled Web

"For the lips of a strange woman drop as an honeycomb,
and her mouth
is smoother than oil: But her end is bitter as wormwood,
sharp as a twoedged sword."
Pr. 5:3-4

Missy sat at her dining room table downloading a disc that was way over due. Her personal life was becoming so chaotic that she was getting a little behind at work, which was not like her when it came to her job.

Everybody and everything demanded so much of her, she felt like she could just run away. The more she dodged Virgil and put him off, the nicer he was to her. Taking the children (All of the children, including Pretty Baby's) to Fair Day when she couldn't get off from work. Going to get groceries when he noticed the supply was low and making sure everything was in working order. If she mentioned it, it was done. He was always careful to see to her needs before moving on to what she wanted.

On the flip side, Missy dabbled with Rodney's young body for pleasure and play when she felt like taking a walk on the wild side. All along keeping up her extravagant liaison with Hershel, who was becoming a bit possessive at the thought of sharing his woman.

Hershel was four times married and trying to make Missy number five. He was unlike any man she had ever known. Once he captured the object of his affection, he married her until he grew bored. Then he moved on, paying them off if needed. He never had children, and didn't want any. Missy thought he must have been sterile. Hershel only knew her daughter's name and her face from school pictures. It didn't matter that he was not acquainted with the rest of the package that came along with her. Money and power were the answers to all of life's problems and, in his mind, he could conquer anything with those two dynasties. He had it all figured out. They would be married, move into his thirteen acre home, then her daughter could go away to boarding school. He explained it to Missy as if he would be giving the gift of a proper education and culture to a child who wouldn't ordinarily have these opportunities. Missy wanted some of the power and money as well, but not at the expense of her normal life with her child. So she would milk the cow as long as she could.

What Missy didn't foresee was that Hershel knew the game. He had been with and bought many women and he was a master at dirty play.

Tangled Web

Recently he had cocktails on his yacht for some of his perspective clients. He had given Missy his credit card telling her she could spend $5,000 on anything she wanted but be sure to come back with the most exquisite gown she could find for no less than $2500. He was very controlling in that way. She did, however, make good use of what was left of the other half. She made sure to catch every bargain she could find for her and Monique. She happened to run into Rodney while shopping and he talked her into buying him some ostrich print boots. They finished shopping and went for drinks afterwards.

At the cocktail party, Missy was stunning in a blue Versace dress she had express ordered from Saks. It was ornate with baguette rhinestones across the shear bodice, layers of fine fishnet clung to every curve. Missy thought Hershel's guests were boring and too bourgeois. They cruised on the James River for what seemed to be hours before going back to shore to drop the guests off. He insisted she stay, leaving instructions for her to open the box that was left in the sleeping quarters. Missy was disappointed to see the skimpy red g-string and tasseled top along with a long black boa and stiletto heels to match. She was repulsed. They had played this game before. She dressed quickly in the get up then fixed herself a shot of tequila before he returned for the game of strip tease. She began to psyche herself out knowing the more provocatively she danced, the more hundred dollar bills she'd go home with to deposit in her secret account. It took forever for him to come because he was so intoxicated. When he did, he slumped over and fell fast asleep. It was two in the morning. She dressed hurriedly and left trying to think of what explanation she could give Virgil for being out so late at a dinner meeting, she supposedly had to make an appearance at and he was left with Monique. He never questioned her when she came in, but he had began to act distant.

She was just about finished with her last folder when Pretty Baby knocked on the door and let herself in.

"Coming in," Pretty Baby sang, tapping dirt off her pumps before walking on Missy's new Galaxy desert peach carpet. Her feet felt like they were sinking as she tipped into the dining room where Missy was working. "Oooh girl, I love this color. It's so rich looking." She tipped back into the living room gazing around. "It brightens the room and is perfect with your furniture." Pretty Baby sunk into the russet colored leather recliner. Missy had scrupulous taste when it came to home decorating. The room was embellished in unique West Indian Decor. "Wait a minute," Pretty Baby said slowly, pushing the recliner back. "I didn't know you were getting leather furniture. Girl, this is plush. You went all out." Pretty Baby could hear Missy snickering. "This isn't the furniture you told me about originally."

"I know. I went in to get the other furniture. But when I laid eyes on that leather sectional, in that color, I had to have it!" she yelled from the other room. "I couldn't afford it, but you know me. I came up with a plan on how to get Virgil to put a nice down payment on it, then got a chunk of money from Hershel to get the payments on the low low. Make 'em both think they did something grand. Ha! I'm something else." She laughed.

Pretty Baby shook her head. "You sure are."

Tangled Web

"I'm getting ready to have this guy come out and landscape my front and back yard. Line the front with pink azaleas and some tulips around the mailbox."

"Landscapers are expensive. You better get out in that yard yourself."

Missy came in to the living room and sat in the recliner at the other end of the sectional. "I will if I have to, but I'm working on a plan to handle that too." She absently began to flick the channels with the remote control stopping on CNN. The President's photo was plastered on the screen. "Now this is some shit here. He would pick a broad who tells her business to some lonely chick who ain't got nothin' better to do than tape conversations."

Pretty Baby laughed, "Really."

"Shit, if it was me, I'd be sitting real pretty and wouldn't tell a soul. 'Cause he ain't bad lookin'. A sister don't tell her business like that, especially if it could mean a decrease in income."

"That's just it. She ain't in need of money. She got money. She just wanted to kick up some shit. It's almost as if she's seeking immortality."

Missy gave her a side ways glance. "Immortality? What? Is the bitch a witch, too?"

"She's making her mark in history just like any other high profile person, with a scandal. She'll be even more famous than the President down through history"

"You got that right. Next thing you know, her ass will be sittin' up on a postage stamp." Pretty Baby roared at Missy's crazy humor. "But the one who really wants to be on a stamp or immortal, as you say," she went on, "is that damn Prosecuting Attorney. He's trying to compete with Johnny Cochran for the crime of the century."

"See," Pretty Baby squinted her eyes in thought, "a woman like her knows she can't have the most powerful man in the country, so what else is left except controlling his passion? You know how men are, and I bet it ain't turnin' out like she thought."

"Hell naw, 'cause she talk too damn much." Missy matched a jerk of the neck with every word. "And I know she didn't really think that man was gonna leave his wife for her ass." Missy thought for a moment about what was said, " So, the way you see it is the President is just pussy-whipped?"

Pretty Baby laughed, "Exactly. But I wonder about the President's wife. I know she's gotta be sick of his ass right about now. She evidently got her own agenda or she really loves him. How could she stand the humiliation? I feel sorry for her."

"I don't. She ain't just realized he was lickety-slick. She been knowing." Missy reached for a cigarette and lit it. "I feel sorry for that girl who talks too damn much. And I betcha she probably thought he would leave his wife for her. Married men ain't shit. If they have to make a choice between your love and their livelihood, they'll leave your ass high and dry. I don't care how much they claim to love you." She took a long drag on the cigarette, puffing two smoke rings then exhaling a long stream of smoke. Suddenly this conversation wasn't funny any more to Pretty Baby.

They sat in silence for a moment deep in their own thoughts. "I told Monique about her mouth," Missy said.

Pretty Baby waved her hand. "Forget it. You know

Tangled Web

Becky. If she wants to find something out, she will. One way or another. I'm not gonna worry about it because Becky has no idea what it's like to be a single parent of three." She sat upright in the recliner. "I appreciate her advice but I'm running this."

"I know that's right. You'd be a fool to let him go, listening to Aunt Becky."

The phone began to ring. Missy sat her chair up and picked up the antique gold phone that sat on the table beside her. "Hello. Oh, Hey. What's up now? That deadline is this Friday. I can't extend it any longer," Missy said, with the phone between her ear and shoulder.

Pretty Baby got up and went to the restroom then came back and picked up her purse. "I'll talk to you later," she mouthed.

"Don't leave yet, Pretty Baby. What are you getting ready to do?" She whispered. Pretty Baby stood at the door. "Yes, she is," she heard Missy say into the receiver. Then she held the phone out to her.

"Who is it?" She asked taking the phone. "Hello. Oh, hi Larry." She gave Missy the evil eye. "No I didn't know about the Jazz concert." She listened for a long moment. "Well, thanks for the invite, Larry, but I'm gonna have to pass." She listened again, agitated. "I'm sure I won't change my mind. o.k., bye." She hung up. "Whew! Some never give up." She walked back toward the door.

"The jazz concert is sold out. I wonder where Larry got tickets."

"I don't care where he got 'em. I don't want to go with him."

"Girl, it's gonna be the bomb. Don't put all your

eggs in one basket banking on Elliott," she said slyly.

Pretty Baby strutted out the door and called over her shoulder, "I'm going home to cook some dinner for my children and my man."

"Oooh. Doing the family thing, huh? You go girl. She pulled the screen tightly as Pretty Baby got in her car and drove away.

Tangled Web

*"The rod and reproof give wisdom: but a
child left to himself bringeth his mother shame."*
Pr. 29:15

*P*retty Baby picked up Ashley and headed home to find Elliott already there. The yard was half cut and Elliott and Chris were standing by his car talking. She wondered what was going on, knowing Chris' feelings about Elliott. He didn't have a lot to say about him or to him. She sat in the car a few extra seconds, spying in the rear view mirror. It looked like she could see them laughing from time to time but the seriousness could be seen on Elliott's face.

She started having second thoughts about confiding in Elliott about the phone call she received the other day. It was a young lady who identified herself as Celeste. She sounded very mature and wanted to apologize for her behavior in Pretty Baby's home. Pretty Baby was shocked, not only by the phone call but the fact that this was another girl in the picture. She thought that was Sharon in his room. She unloaded all of this on Elliott as well as what she'd heard from Stank about William and Charmaine. He listened and offered to speak with Chris if she wanted him too. If it had been Jason, she would have agreed. They had become good fishing buddies. But Chris was another trip all together. She didn't know if Elliott would have the right approach.

"Hey guys," she said walking up with diaper bag and purse on one shoulder and Ashley on the other hip.

"Hello ladies," Elliott said, pinching Ashley's cheek. She reached for him and he took her, holding her high in the air the way she liked. She gave a deep belly laugh. When he brought her down she reached for his shirt pocket, digging her fat fingers in as deeply as she could get them. "How'd you know about that, Little Bit?" He said shifting her to his other hip then pulling the sucker out of his pocket. They all laughed at Ashley.

Pretty Baby intercepted, taking her from Elliott. "Not until after dinner. You've got her rotten," she said to Elliott, going in the house.

She let out a big breath facing the clutter that was left from the morning chaos. She thought she'd get here before Elliott to clean up a bit. "Jason." she yelled and he came pounding down the steps. "Hey Baby. What are you doing?"

"Hey Mom. Hey Ashley. I was finishing my homework."

Tangled Web

"Come on. Help Mom straighten up a bit. Get these toys up for me."

He tickled his sister and started picking up. "I didn't know Mr. Elliott was here." Jason saw Elliott pass the window and ran to greet him at the door.

"What's up dude?" He slapped him a high five. "Tell your mom to come here." Jason ran off and in a second Pretty Baby was trailing behind him. "Chris and I are gonna go pick up another mower. Yours is messed up and I've got another one in storage at the office not far from here. He can hold on to it for awhile. I'm not using it." He shrugged.

"Well, alright. I'm about to put dinner on."

"Can I go too?" Jason said.

Elliott nodded his head. "You finished your homework? I want to see it after dinner."

"Yes, sir."

"Can you drive?" Elliott asked Chris, as he came through the door.

"Yeah, I can drive."

"Oh no he can't," Pretty Baby said.

"Yes, I can. You just don't let me practice so I can get my permit."

Elliott laughed. Pretty Baby waved a hand and went back into the kitchen. The guys left.

The spaghetti and french bread were ready, the salad tossed and no one was there to eat but Ashley. So Pretty Baby fixed Ashley's plate and straightened up while she ate before giving her daughter a bath.

Pretty Baby and Ashley stepped out on the porch wondering where the boys could be. Jesse was just pulling in. He came over, sort of in a strange mood, and talked for a minute. He said things were going well at church and they were about to start the new building. She thought maybe his mood had something to do with Charmaine, so she didn't ask. Just as he was walking away, Elliott's car pulled up, pulling a riding mower on a small trailer. He pulled up slowly and parked. Pretty Baby and Jesse both looked at each other at the same time when they realized Chris was driving.

Jason bolted from the car first. "Chris can drive, Ma!"

Pretty Baby rolled her eyes at Elliott. "So I see." She turned and went in the house while they unhitched the mower.

The boys came in and ate then went upstairs where she was putting Ashley down for the night. She turned out the light and went in their room.

"Mr. Elliott is hooking me up with a couple of jobs. I'm gonna save up for me a car." Chris said, as he creased his jeans to perfection.

"Oh yeah?" She stood in the doorway with her arms crossed. "What kind of job?"

"Lawn services. Landscaping," he said matter of factly. "He said I could have the mower as long as I took care of it. He knows some people who'll hire me on the weekends to do their yards. And I can get some customers around here too. Watch."

"Oh, I believe you." She looked at her son with a half smile. Elliott must have said something, she thought, because Chris's attitude was 180 degrees from what it had been lately. "Goodnight." She kissed them both.

Tangled Web

"Momma," Jason said getting out of the bed handing her a paper. "Show Mr. Elliott my homework. Tell him to leave it on the table. I'll get it in the morning."

"O.k., Baby."

When she got downstairs, Elliott had fixed his plate and was sitting on the sofa with one shoe off flicking the channels from time to time. "That was delicious, Babe." He sat his plate down and rubbed her back affectionately. She leaned back in his arms. "Did you eat?"

"Yes. I ate with Ashley. You guys took too long."

"I was just spending a little time with the boys. I can always get Jason to hang out with me, but this was a first with Chris." He leaned forward to take a sip of his drink. "He's a good kid. They all are." He kissed her head. She had gotten that haircut and the streaks. Elliott loved it.

"I just want to know how he ended up in the driver's seat?"

Elliott chuckled, "He said he could drive, so I let him. Just through the neighborhood."

"If something happens, it's on you," she warned.

"He's gotta drive that mower if he's gonna pick up some jobs. He did good. As long as the job doesn't interfere with his schooling, I won't repossess the mower. And if you don't object," he cut his eyes at her, "I'll take him to get his permit." She just listened. Maybe this is what Chris needed. He leaned back and propped his shoeless foot on the coffee table. "I told him as long as he was good to you, I'd be good to him. That goes for Jason, too. I'll let you handle Ashley."

"Yeah, 'cause she's got you wrapped around her little fat fingers." Pretty Baby snuggled in closer, putting her arm across his stomach. She couldn't argue with that philosophy. She inhaled the scent of his cologne with a smile on her face. "I love you, Elliott." The words slipped from her mouth before she knew it.

"I been loving you," he said casually. They watched a movie and then he went home.

Tangled Web

"An inheritance may be gotten hastily at the beginning;
but the end thereof shall not be blessed."
Pr. 20:21

*T*he furrows that showed so prominently in Elliott's forehead seemed to have disappeared. He looked younger, more relaxed. He was always a good natured guy, but now his laughter came easily and was sometimes contagious. He worked hard as usual, but he acted as if his load had somehow been lightened.

"That new Public Relations woman seems nice enough," Gracie said to Clarisse and Lisa, one of the other workers, over lunch one day.

"I told you, Gracie, that's the same woman that was here that evening. Remember?" Clarisse asked.

"You sure that was her?"

"Yes. Rachel Casey." She took a bite of her sandwich. "I logged her in."

"Since she's been here, I sure don't have to take as many calls as I had been, and she's got a guy and a girl intern working in the xerox room," Lisa commented.

"Hallelujah!" Gracie raised her hands. "I'll tell you, those proposals are pretty much in tact once they reach me because he has her to edit them. I think they're a great team. Just what he's been needing." They nodded. "Poor man finally realized he couldn't do everything himself."

"Somebody told me," Clarisse looked over both shoulders, "the day that I was off, she came out of his office and he had a sloppy grin on his face and lipstick on his mouth."

Lisa gasped. Gracie raised both of her drawn on eyebrows. "Who said that nonsense?"

"I'm not gonna say," Clarisse smirked.

Gracie started to clean up her area where she was eating. "You girls shouldn't listen to that type of gossip." She threw her trash away. "I worked for Mrs. Banks for years, before she was married to him, and I don't want to be in a position where I'm disloyal to her." She sat back down with her Diet Coke. "Lord knows he's been good to me too, because he didn't have to keep me on after her accident." She circled the rim on her can with her finger and spoke quietly, "It's been so many years. Everybody needs somebody, though, I guess," she said quietly.

"They kind of make a cute couple," Clarisse and Lisa both agreed.

"You girls stop that," Gracie scolded them before she went back to work.

298

Tangled Web

RACHEL CASEY Public Relations Specialist. She handed her card to the woman who had stopped her in the grocery store, she remembered her from the banquet as Director of Administration from the University.

"Ms Casey, I will definitely be contacting you on setting a date for you to come and speak with the freshman class about the internship at Banks, Inc. Elliott is doing such a wonderful job." The large overly perfumed woman went on showering compliments on Elliott.

Pretty Baby smiled politely. "I'll call you soon to set that date." She started to push on.

"Uh, Rachel. May I call you Rachel?"

Rachel nodded.

"Do call me because I'd like to invite you to a ball my husband's fraternity is having. It's gonna be really nice. And," she patted her hand confidentially, "you can bring Elliott."

"Thanks," was all Pretty Baby could say and she strolled off. She hardly knew the woman. It was strange to her how a secret starts out with just a select few knowing. Like family and friends. Then, next thing you know, everyone is in on the secret.

All in all, life couldn't be better for Pretty Baby. Being in the work force in this capacity gave her a chance to do a bit of traveling and a feeling of self worth she hadn't experienced.

When she gave notice to the daycare of her leaving, they got together and gave her a farewell party. Ms.

Montgomery made negative cracks the whole time once she realized Pretty Baby was going to Banks Inc. She claimed her second husband use to work for Elliott. Anyway, the party was nice and Pretty Baby continued to keep in touch with a few of her former co-workers.

Pretty Baby had created and was heading the internship program for College students in their senior year, allowing them to gain work experience with a reputable company as well as a little change in their pockets. She hoped that Chris would want to work some summers there during high school, but he said that was peak season for his business. He had customers Elliott had gotten for him, some from their old neighborhood and a couple in the new one.

They had finally moved into a nice four-bedroom home. It was equipped with a two-car garage, fenced in yard, patio and flower bed already started. The school district was decent and Pretty Baby was pleased with the daycare Ashley attended. It was just what she had always dreamed of. It had just enough space for the kids to move around in without cluttering up so badly and a kitchen big enough to have all her kinfolk's over for Christmas Eve dinner. She and Elliott went all out for the occasion, with a big white fern tree sitting next to the fire place and decorations from the bathroom to the kitchen, right on outside, in unison with the other homes that surrounded the cul-de-sac.

Everyone enjoyed themselves, including Aunt Becky. She only made one snide remark the whole evening. It was when Pretty Baby saw her slip out on the patio in the chilly holiday breeze, peeking around the dimly

Tangled Web

lit yard. Pretty Baby slipped out of the noise and joined her.

"What are you doin' out here, Aunt Becky?" She rubbed her hands briskly up and down her arms.

"I didn't expect for Elliott to be here for the holidays and all. Thought maybe he needed to be elsewhere," Aunt Becky remarked.

"You think too much, Aunt Becky. Even if he wasn't here, it would be o.k. because he has a very demanding job. It would be that way even if we were married," Pretty Baby said sarcastically. Aunt Becky needed to know her predictions weren't always right.

Becky rolled her eyes at her 'too dumb to know it' niece, then started making suggestions on how Pretty Baby should arrange her flower bed around the patio and she showed her the best section in her yard where she could grow some snap beans, corn and maybe some tomatoes.

Missy and the kids visited often and sometimes spent the night. It was Missy's hideaway. When she saw the house for the first time she said, "Ooh girl, I love this place." She walked around peeping out windows and opening closets. "This is what I need, somewhere out of the way, so people won't just drop by. Ain't no tellin' what I might be doing."

No one ever asked about Pretty Baby's professional background at work, they just accepted her as Mr. Banks presented her. Pretty Baby and Elliott conducted their relationship with total professionalism at work. Sometimes they had lunch together or meetings, which often included other people. When he traveled, she took lunch in her

301

office or went to a fast food place alone. One of those times, Clarisse came and knocked on her door and invited her to join her for lunch. Being better acquainted with Clarisse than the other women, she agreed. Soon she became friendly with them all.

They all adored her, especially the interns. Recently she had arranged for a graduation dinner for them. She encouraged the fourth floor execs and their assistants to come and network with the rising stars.

Pretty Baby and Elliott arrived together, hosting and presenting awards to the graduates. Someone commented that each time Pretty Baby got up to speak, Elliott looked at her in awe. He couldn't take his eyes off of her. And when one of the graduates, surprisingly, presented her with a bouquet of roses for her outstanding job. Elliott stood and applauded loudly.

He was leaving the following day to go out of town. He told her later that night to make plans for a babysitter the week of her birthday and be sure to schedule her calendar at work for travel time. When she asked where to, he said, "Make up something, just schedule it." She couldn't imagine what Elliott was up to. Her birthday was almost three months away.

Tangled Web

*"A froward man soweth strife: and
a whisperer separateth chief friends."*
Pr. 16:28

*T*he visitor walked around the small efficiency apartment looking at the necessities that were neatly placed around for Savannah. It was a livable apartment with all the amenities except a stove. Meals had to be taken in the dining area or brought back to the room if she wanted privacy.

Being escorted by the nurse, Savannah shuffled in slowly, wearing a pull over jogging suit. "Alright, Ms. Banks. Looks like you got some company. You feeling up to it?" She spoke loudly as if Savannah was hard of hearing, guiding her to the small sitting area.

She had just come from her daily exercise program; a fifteen minute treadmill walk, at her own pace. Thirty minutes in the whirlpool and a full body massage.

"I'll be back to bring your medicine then take you out on the patio if you like. Ring for me if you need some help in the shower." The nurse left.

"Van, you're looking great." The visitor kissed her on the cheek then stood back to take a look. "I'll have to tell Ms. Savage to send your stylist over for your hair." Savannah ran her hands through her hair that had grown rather long. They both laughed.

Savannah looked around the room as if she had misplaced something. "How long you been here?" She finally asked slowly.

"Not long. I had an appointment this morning so I decided to stop by before I go in to work."

Savannah just sat. The visitor walked around telling her how nice this place was kept up. "I'm sure Elliott is pleased with this." The visitor stood in front of her. "Huh?" Savannah looked down at the new tennis shoes Isaiah had bought her the last time he was home. She didn't respond. The visitor paced back and forth in the small room. "He has time to do everything else. I know he's seeing someone now. That's why he's too busy. It's someone that works for him." The visitor went on. "Her name is Rachel Casey."

The visitor came back and stood directly in front of Savannah waiting on some response. "I told you before, I thought it was her. She has taken your position at the company."

Savannah shook her head, rejecting this

Tangled Web

information.

"She's hobnobbing with the Langleys," the visitor gripped her arms, speaking into her face. "Running your company and sleeping with your husband."

"No," Savannah said weakly dropping her head.

"Yes. This Rachel Casey slut, is fucking Elliott. If you don't snap out of it," the visitor pleaded, "she's gonna take over your life and they'll leave you here forever."

"No more," Savannah started to get up walking toward the bed. She turned slowly. "Don't want to hear no more!" she screamed, knocking a trinket off the bedside table.

The nurse peeked her head in. "Is everything alright. I was walking by and thought I heard loud voices.

The visitor informed her that Savannah was a little upset at some shocking news.

The nurse stepped inside the room looking from one to the other suspiciously. "Maybe you ought to leave now. Ms. Banks has had a busy morning," she said to the visitor who politely obliged.

"Let me get you a pill. Lie down, dear." She tried to swing Savannah's legs onto the bed.

"I don't want a pill," she screamed.

"Oh my," the nurse said picking up the phone dialing for assistance. Immediately two male nurses came. They held Savannah down as she fought not to get a shot.

When she woke up, late in the evening, another nurse was standing over her. She sort of resembled Ms. Savage. "Feeling better?" she asked, smiling. She knew Ms. Banks was one of the more stable tenants. She looked over her chart and couldn't imagine why she had gotten a tranquilizing shot.

Savannah sat up slowly. "Shower," she mumbled.

"Sure, I'll help you into the shower." The nice woman did and then helped her into her night-clothes. She turned on her T.V. "How about some food?" You're gonna need some food with your last pill."

Savannah looked at the woman for a long time. She studied her face wondering if she could trust her. "Just a sandwich and jello," she said. Her voice still gravelly from screaming.

The nurse brought back her request along with her night-time pill. Savannah ate half of the sandwich and some of the jello. When the nurse returned to clear her dishes, she reminded her not to forget her pill.

"Oh, yeah," Savannah said, picking the pill out of the small cup. She examined the small yellow controlling substance.

The nurse dimmed the light and closed the door. Savannah stood, a little off balance at first, then walked to the bathroom. She leaned against the doorway for support and tried to remember what day it was. She tried to decipher thoughts that kept reoccurring while willing her legs to move forward. Leaning on the sink, once again she searched her mind for an answer to when all of the chaos began. Only fragments of screaming, yelling and being strapped down came to the surface. With trepidation, she observed the pill once more then she dropped it in the toilet and flushed it.

Tangled Web

"For the Lord will plead their cause,
and spoil the soul of those that spoiled them."
Pr. 22:23

 *E*lliott admired the waterfall that sat in the middle of the lake as he walked down the long flowered walkway of the Woodland Hills grounds.

 The nurses immediately recognized him, as one of them led him to the patio and the other two giggled behind their backs.

 "I wonder what a good lookin' man like that is doing with that old woman." One nurse commented. "You know that's her husband," she said pointedly to her coworker.

 "She looks good for her age." The other nurse said defensively. "But I bet he's real lonely about now and maybe he wants a little company." Both women laughed.

"You better leave that crazy woman's husband alone."

****

Elliott looked around the patio for Savannah. He saw her sitting up on the deck that overlooked the lake.

"Savannah," he said, stepping up, taking the seat next to her. "Savannah," he said again.

She rocked her body slowly in the chair then stopped to look at him. "Hello, Elliott." She turned back to the lake.

He leaned over and kissed her cheek. "How've you been?" Elliott was pleased at the progress the nurses said Savannah had been suddenly making. She nodded her head and continued to rock. Elliott settled into his seat and looked out at the lake too.

It had been three weeks since he'd come to visit Savannah because of his hectic travel schedule. When he got in last night, Pretty Baby told him about the big garage sale Jesse had organized with another church and all of the proceeds were going to their building fund. She had volunteered herself and the children to help. Elliott thought this would be a good time to check on Savannah and speak with Dr. Kyles.

He glanced at his watch. "You hungry? I thought we could have lunch in the diner."

"Ms. Savage came to see me." She turned to him smiling.

"Oh, that's good. Today?"

Savannah smiled and rocked. "She read to me." She looked puzzled suddenly.   "Who's running the company?"

Elliott looked surprised. "I am."

"Who is Rachel?"

He was baffled at her question. Not because of fear that he was found out, but who would talk with Savannah about the company? Savannah was very well liked, and after all these years, old friends still came to visit occasionally. "Oh, Rachel is one of the ladies who works at Banks in Public Relations and is really doing a fantastic job."

She sat back in her seat. Elliott kept his eyes on her wondering, 'What in the world?'

"Come on, let's get some lunch." He helped her out of her seat and they went to lunch. Afterwards, they walked around the lake. He tried to make small talk. She babbled once or twice about things that didn't mean anything. They went back to her room and Elliott watched T.V. until she fell asleep.

On his way out , he asked the nurse could he see the visitors' log. Elliott scanned the names, surprised at the people from Banks, Inc. that still visited, as well as relatives. The nurse was able to show him a ledger as far back as three months. The holidays had just passed, so maybe that was the reason for so many visitors.

One thing was for certain, Elliott thought, Savannah could have only heard the name Rachel from someone who worked at Banks, Inc.

"He that goeth about as a talebearer revealeth secrets: therefore meddle not with him that flattereth with his lips."
Pr. 20:19

*P*retty Baby was delighted at the plans that Elliott had made for her birthday. She did as he had instructed as far as marking her calendar at work. The other employees assumed she was touring a few of the eastern colleges, telling them about Banks' internship program. But actually, she was meeting Elliott in France on one of his business trips. Missy had agreed to keep the children for the whole week.

At work, Elliott seemed a little agitated and stressed. Pretty Baby thought it might be due to his overload of work and had started sneaking some home cooked meals in at lunch time for him. It didn't stay a secret for long as the aroma of lamb chops, peas, candied yams and blueberry muffins drifted through the break area and out into the hallways.

"Mm, mmm, something sure smells delicious," Clarisse remarked as she peeked over Pretty Baby's shoulder at the large helpings on the plate.

Pretty Baby hoped she had her own lunch because there was only enough for her and Elliott. But Clarisse was always sweet to her, so Pretty Baby was polite, "Have some."

"No thanks. I'm glad somebody came along to make him take a break to eat a real meal." She shuffled four quarters into the drink machine. "You're just what he's been needing."

Pretty Baby smiled, she didn't see any need to try to convince her that all that food was for her alone. She was sure some of her colleagues had noticed how she fussed over Elliott and maybe even saw the looks that passed between them throughout the day. She left the break area taking him his lunch.

****

Elliott had been overloaded with one meeting after the next getting ready for his trip to France. This evening, he had committed to watching Ashley while the boys were out and Pretty Baby was attending a PTA meeting.

Missy was on Pretty Baby's side of town shopping and decided to drop by her house. She rang the doorbell several times and was about to walk away when she heard footsteps. Elliott opened the door.

311

"I was just about to walk away. I knew somebody was here 'cause I saw your car but then I figured ya'll didn't want any company." She raised a brow at Elliott.

"I was back in the back and didn't hear the bell. Rachel's not here. Just me and Ashley," he said, hoping Missy wouldn't stay.

Missy was feeling mischievous so she flounced in past him. He did look at her large butt and tiny waist then shook his head. He was not impressed. By the time he got to the kitchen, she was sitting down chatting with Ashley.

"I see I'm in time for dinner," she said as he walked in the kitchen.

He gave a half laugh, "Have some?"

The baked fish, broccoli and cheese and corn looked inviting. "No thanks.

Elliott moved around the kitchen aimlessly, cleaning up and going on as if she wasn't there. Missy watched him, noticing how handsome he really was in this domestic role. He was still wearing his tailored shirt that defined his upper body and tie that hung loosely around his neck. She always wondered would he play or was he as good as he acted.

"So whatcha know good, Elliott?"

"Not too much, Missy. I'm just trying to get Ashley situated before her mom gets back," he said gruffly. He helped Ashley down from her seat and guided her to the den where he had the Lion King on for her.

"Oh," was all she could say. 'I guess he told me,' she thought. She didn't really want to fool with Elliott 'cause she didn't want to deal with Pretty Baby. Once that

312

girl got angry and crossed somebody out, they were as good as gone. So she decided against testing Elliott.

"Sooo," she walked to where they were, "tell Pretty Baby I came by."

"I'll do that." He said coolly, handing Ashley two cookies for her dessert and immediately walking toward the door to see Missy out.

Ashley climbed on the couch with Elliott, and snuggled her head under his arm, stretching her long thin legs out. By the time the 'Circle of Life' played and the credits rolled, she was fast asleep. He tucked Ashley in her bed and came back, sinking into the recliner.

He turned on the sports highlights channel but couldn't concentrate with all the thoughts going through his head. He couldn't believe that the people he provided jobs for could betray him. He lay his head back, rubbing his hands over his head. Ever since that visit with Savannah he couldn't get it out of his mind. He had to know what person did this. Or what people.

Suddenly it hit him. He knew a way to find out. Just then he heard the garage door opening. He hadn't mentioned this incident to Rachel and hadn't planned to until he had some answers.

****

The following day, Elliott had someone to wire the entire building so that all calls could be tape recorded on a second line in his office.

Every free moment he had, he listened. Catching bits and pieces of business deals, gossip, intimacies and just down right dumb stuff. Elliott even came across an employee calling her mom everyday on the company 800 number to discuss the soaps while they were on. This woman's mom lived in Canada. He decided to deal with that issue at a later date.

After two and a half weeks of listening, he finally heard Savannah's name. He rewound it and played it over and over again.

"Did you visit with Savannah this week?"

"Yeah, Sunday for a little while. I had some other stuff I needed to do," a male voice said. "What about you?"

"I'm going this evening. Seems like she really is getting better. I've been talking to her. Trying to get her to understand, when she doesn't throw a tantrum. I think she's got the part about the other woman," the woman said.

"Huh," the man laughed, "she could care less about the other woman. That woman taking over her company is what's got her attention. You know Van. She lived for that company." They paused. "So what's going on around there?"

"Love is in the air, of course. Listen, I gotta go. I'll be in touch." They hung up.

Elliott was trying to catch the mans' voice. This particular tape had static all the way through. The woman's voice was broken too, but there was no mistaking who it was. It took everything in him not to call her that night. He decided this should be done in person. Instead, he called Rachel and told her. She was outdone.

The next morning, Elliott was exhausted from a

restless night but he was up early and at the office before anyone. He was sure he was not wrong about who the woman on the phone was.

He asked Clarisse to come into his office when she arrived. She brought her note pad in with her and sat down in her usual place to take a dictation or whatever it was he wanted.

"There won't be any need for your pad, Clarisse. I just want you to know that I know you've been going to see Savannah at Woodland Hills and feeding her a bunch of crap.

"No I...." she started to say.

"Don't lie Clarisse. I know you have." He stepped from around his desk. "And I never thought you would betray me. Savannah is a sick woman, why would you do something like this?"

"But I didn't betray you. Savannah has always been a friend of mine," she pleaded. "I've visited her off and on over the years because I cared about her and hoped she would one day get well. At least I did visit her."

Elliott shot her an angry glance. "Pack your things and leave." He walked back around his desk. "Your check will be in the mail."

Clarisse stood smoothing her skirt. "I guess you and Rachel have come to your own conclusions..."

"No, I've come to this conclusion." He picked up a box he had sitting beside his desk then went to her desk. "Put your things in this." He went back into his office to phone for security to walk her out.

Pretty Baby was coming up to the fourth floor when she ran into Gracie who had already heard what was going on. "Did you know Clarisse got fired?"

Pretty Baby shrugged her shoulders. She got back on the elevator and rode back to the second floor to her office, until the fire was out and the smoke was clear.

Tangled Web

*"A false witness shall not be unpunished, and
he that speaketh lies shall not escape."*
Pr. 19:5

Savannah smiled as her faithful visitor entered the room with a fruit basket. Today was a good day and she was hoping for some company. The visitor sat in one of the chairs across from her. They sat through a whole episode of "The Young and the Restless." Savannah had iced tea in her small refrigerator, she offered the visitor some while she fixed her own glass. The midday news came on, then another soap. The visitor sat mute. Savannah eyed the visitor because of her strange mood, then she asked, "What's wrong?"

The visitor turned and looked at her, eyes glazed with tears, "I got fired."

"A fool uttereth all his mind:
but a wise man keepeth it in till afterwards."
Pr. 29:11

*E*lliott rapped at Savannah's door twice. He was just about to turn the knob when he heard the nurse speaking to him.

"She's not in there," she walked quickly to get a chance to speak with Mr. Banks. "How are you today?" She smiled real pretty in his face.

"I'm fine, thank you." He looked down the hall where others could be seen. "Where's Mrs. Banks?"

"Oh, she's on the patio. I'm going that way I'll walk you out." She stepped in stride beside him.

Elliott immediately saw Savannah sitting in a lounge chair. She lay back with her head tilted to the sun. Dark

318

shades on. She was dressed in jeans and a pretty red blouse he recognized as one of the birthday gifts she had gotten recently.

"I'm not disturbing you, am I?" He smiled.

She turned to the sound of his voice. "Hello Elliott."

He sat on the side of the lounger next to her, taking one of her hands. "I'm leaving town going to France in a couple of days and I wanted to come by and see you. You doing alright?"

"I'm fine." She looked out on the grounds.

He finally pulled up a regular chair and they sat for a while. "The weather has been really nice, huh?"

Savannah didn't respond. He looked closer to see if maybe she had dozed off. She hadn't.

"Savannah, I need to get back to the office but I'll be back when I get in town." He looked down rubbing his hands together. "I wanted you to know that I asked Clarisse not to visit you anymore because she upsets you. And you are in no condition to be upset. I think it would be best."

He waited for a response but Savannah never spoke. He'd never know the way she glared at him through the dark glasses as he spoke. She watched him closely. He kissed her on the cheek. "I'll be back soon. Bye."

"Confidence in an unfaithful man in time of trouble
is like a broken tooth, and a foot out of joint."
Pr. 25:19

*T*he large jet made an easy non-stop landing at Charles de Gaulle airport. Exhausted from the nine hour flight, Pretty Baby rotated her neck as she listened to the flight attendant call off connecting flights in French and then in English. She pulled out her compact and mirror and moistened her lips thinking about Elliott. He promised her he would be waiting at the gate with open arms.

Paris was as beautiful as Pretty Baby imagined. She and Elliott stayed in the luxurious LeBristol hotel. It was quite elegant and European, with its Louis XV furnishings and sculptures. Pretty Baby loved the rooftop pool and the courtyard garden below her suite.

Tangled Web

On her first night in Paris, they dined in the hotel restaurant. Elliott, always full of surprises, gave Pretty Baby a card.

"Happy Birthday sweetheart," he raised his glass of wine. "May this be a time in your life you'll always cherish." She opened the card that included 5,000francs. "Surely you can keep yourself busy with this throughout the week while I'm working."

Pretty Baby pulled her napkin from her lap and brought it to her eyes.

Elliott, jokingly, looked confused, "I thought you would be happy."

"I am...it's just..." The words wouldn't come.

"Aww, come here." He held her close, wiping her tears of joy. "Don't go getting soft on me. I should be the one crying, 'cause you're a bad habit I can barely afford, Baby."

The very next morning, Pretty Baby got dressed as soon as Elliott was off to work. She quickly learned how to catch the shuttle. It was a continuous loop that departed every fifteen minutes and it gave her a chance to sight see and shop, browsing through antique shops, bookstores and art galleries of St. Germaine des Paris. She discovered some designer boutiques and that's where she began her shopping. She bought souvenirs and trinkets that she thought would be perfect for different ones on her list.

The third day was her birthday and Elliott worked a half -day so they could take in some sights together. The Eiffel Tower was the first thing she wanted to see. They rode one thousand feet up the elevator to the top of the tower where the view was breathtaking.

On the Left Bank, they found a nice jazz club, a converted bistro called Le Petit Opportun that featured many American soloists. Pretty Baby sat close to Elliott, taking in the artsy scenery and enjoying the familiar music. A man, who sat at a nearby table, nodded to her and she smiled thinking he looked slightly familiar.

Afterwards, lightheaded from all of the wine they had consumed, they hailed a taxi back to the hotel.

Pretty Baby set near the terrace, turning the knob on the radio. "We should've brought the CD player. Do they play any American music?"

"I'm sure they do. I meant to remind you about the music before you left. Keep changing."

Suddenly she heard the beginning chords from Traci Chapman's 'Give Me One Good Reason.' Pretty Baby tuned the station in and got up, moving to the beat. She moved her hips seductively, swaying her hands in the air. Enticing Elliott with a few go-go dancer jerk moves. He joined in, plucking an imaginary guitar as Pretty Baby danced to the cafe beat. By the time the song was over, Pretty Baby had slithered out of her clothes and was ready to party to the next song in just her camisole and high heeled sandals.

"Come down off the Louis XV tabletop, Miss Kitty," Elliott said, turning the radio down and gently pulling her by the hand. She laughed like a schoolgirl as she fell into his arms and he kissed her like a man quenching his thirst in a desert. They caressed and moaned while he tasted the sweetness of her burning desire. They twisted and rolled on the Persian rug, thrusting their pelvises, never breaking the rhythm, as she begged him to take her to greater heights. Elliott shuddered as he buried his head in her firm breast, his tongue licking her erect nipple.

On their last night in France, they took a boat ride down the east canal. As they neared the dock, a heavyset man with a baseball cap and camera equipment slung over his shoulder, was taking pictures. The dockman pulled their boat in and tied it to the dock. The man spoke. "I'm a freelance photographer for a local paper here and I usually target tourists, using natural photos for travel advertisements. May I take your picture?"

Pretty Baby pulled in close to Elliott and smiled big. The man snapped the picture and thanked them graciously as they walked away. She noticed Elliott looked a little tense but knew he was getting tired. They walked hand in hand to the nearest bus stop and waited for the next departure.

Pretty Baby hated to leave France, she thought, as she and Elliott boarded the plane. She smiled at the gentleman she thought she recognized, from the club, as she went to her seat. He looked as if he hated to end his vacation as much as she did.

"That's the same guy who was at the jazz club," she said, settling into her seat.

"What guy?"

"Up a few seats in front of us."

Elliott stood to put his briefcase overhead then walked to the front and spoke with the flight attendant. On the way back, he didn't see the man, in fact there were no men in that aisle.

For the first three and a half hours, Pretty Baby slept reclining in her chair, leaning her head toward Elliott. She stirred, waking with a smile on her face for Elliott who had gotten his laptop down. The expression on his face looked as if he were a million miles away.

"What's the matter, Baby?" Her question broke his train of thought, but he continued to stare at the screen.

"Your mind never stops ticking does it?" She smiled, "I thought you said you got everything accomplished."

"I did," he said sullenly.

"So what's the matter?" She sat up straight and he turned to her with sadness in his eyes. "Come on, Elliott you're scaring me. What is it? Tell me."

"I've got an eerie feeling..."

"About what?" she searched his face.

"I think someone has been following me. Following us," he whispered.

"What? Who?"

He closed his laptop. "You know the man who took our picture? I'm willing to bet he's no freelance photographer. I saw him the other day on our floor at Le Bristol. It seemed like he tried to duck into the shadows, but I saw him. When I saw him at the dock I started wondering."

"But why would someone follow us?"

"I don't know. I've just got a feeling." He shook his head. "After what Clarisse did, I don't trust anyone The more I think about it, I think there was more Savannah wanted to tell me but couldn't express herself. Her mind isn't stable." He unconsciously bit at his thumbnail. "Maybe Clarisse hired someone to get pictures to show her....I don't know."

Tangled Web

Pretty Baby leaned back releasing a sigh. "Well Clarisse is no longer a problem, so I wouldn't worry."

"I don't know, Rachel, I've just been thinking ever since I realized she was responsible for this mess, business has been unusually slow with Langley. I tried to contact him before leaving the States and he never returned my calls. I thought it was just bad timing."

"Surely he doesn't have anything to do with this?"

"No, but everyone doesn't understand what you mean to me. Furthermore, I've always been a very private person and maybe I've gotten a little too open with my life style."

Pretty Baby suddenly felt nervous in her stomach. She didn't like the way this conversation was going. "What are you saying?" She was defensive.

"I'm saying I love you, but I'm still a married man and everyone obviously, is not in our corner. Regardless of the circumstances. I think we need to start being careful. I don't need any bad publicity about Banks or to have my personal life publicized. You see what they're doing to the President."

Yeah, she saw all too clearly and she could hear Missy's voice just as well. 'Married men ain't shit. If they start having to make major choices between your love and their livelihood, they'll leave your ass high and dry. I don't care how much he claims to love you.'

Her thoughts were interrupted by the flight attendant telling everyone to prepare for landing. She couldn't believe her birthday celebration was ending with this. She had never been angry with Elliott before and she was resenting him for spoiling things with his paranoia.

"So what is it you're asking me to do, Elliott?" She asked through teary eyes.

He felt bad. His head was starting to throb from lack of rest and an overload of stress. He took her face in both hands and kissed her teary eyes then her lips. "I want you to let me get off first then I'll meet you in baggage claim."

"I will do no such thing," she spat, feeling as if he was treating her like a back door lover.

"You asked what you could do," he said through clinched teeth, then got up abruptly. He stepped in line with the crowd turning back, speaking more gentler he said, 'baggage claim'. Once out of sight, he reached for his wallet where he had long since tucked his wedding band away. He hadn't worn it since he realized it made Rachel feel uncomfortable. Pulling the gold band out he slipped it on his finger.

Tears streamed down Pretty Baby's face. Elliott's harsh words had hurt so bad. She wasn't used to that tone coming from him. The attendant walked past her twice after everyone was gone. Finally she stopped and asked if she needed help. Pretty Baby said, "No, just some tissue."

She wiped her eyes and got the tears under control, stepped off the plane, through the tunnel and up the walkway to the gate to see Elliott standing to the side with a woman. The woman she recognized immediately as a very stable Savannah.

****

Elliott thought his eyes were playing tricks on him,

326

Tangled Web

as Savannah walked closer to him when he came through the gate. He tried to pull her to the side. "What are you doing away from Woodland Hills? How did you get here? Savannah, you're not well."

"You look like you're not well, Elliott." She stood firm, battling with herself.

A few weeks ago, Savannah had contacted her long time friend and attorney, Max Whartman, who immediately came to visit her. He had visited her off and on through the years but was surprised when his secretary said she had phoned him. When he arrived at Woodland Hills, Savannah's speech was slow but her message was clear. She wanted to start divorce proceedings immediately to secure her assets against Elliott. Revealing her suspicions about him, she asked Max to help her get out of the hospital. She was afraid Elliott would leave her locked in there forever.

"Calm down, Savannah. He can't do that," Max assured her as they sat in her room at Woodland Hills. "Besides, you don't have any proof. You can't go by what someone has told you. You need to get yourself well and get back home." He patted her hand.

"No!" She snatched away. "I know what I'm saying and if you won't help me, I'll find someone who will."

Max had known Savannah for many years. He knew that the accident and the death of her parents had literally taken the life out of her. As much as he hated to see misfortunes of this kind, he realized this trauma was taking a profound effect on her rehabilitation.

"Okay, I'll tell you what," Max ran his hand over his face with a sigh, "You don't have any proof. You must have proof of these things."

"I do have proof!" She argued. "Everyone knows how Elliott has been carrying on with this tramp. She's working at my company, for God's sake!"

"No, I mean proof that will hold up in the court of law. I'm going to give you the number to a friend of mine," he said, going into his briefcase. "He's a private investigator."

****

When Savannah got word when Rachel and Elliott would be arriving back in the States, she convinced a friend to check her out of the hospital for an evening of shopping and then put the duck on the friend at the mall by taking a taxi to the airport.

"Rachel Casey," Savannah said as Pretty Baby walked by, pretending not to see them. "Rachel Casey, come here young lady. I need to speak with you."

Pretty Baby glanced back at Elliott and quickened her pace. She heard Savannah yell, "Let me go!"

Suddenly, she was at Pretty Baby's side. "Whore. Slut. Do you feel like a woman because you've been fucking my husband?" Pretty Baby didn't respond, never looked her way. "Say something bitch!" Savannah stepped back and swung her purse at Pretty Baby, landing it against her head.

Pretty Baby turned, mouth wide, just as Elliott grabbed Savannah's arm and she swung at him wildly. Pretty Baby turned to walk away.

"Tramp. Whore," she yelled. "You'll have to find

Tangled Web

your bastard children a father somewhere else. Too bad they have a whore for a mother," Savannah screamed down the long corridor.

Pretty Baby stopped and turned around. Her ears were ringing and she had had enough of the insults. She walked with clinched fist to where Savannah had slumped in Elliott's arms crying in terrible agony. "You can say what you want about me, but you don't know nothing about my children." Savannah suddenly looked old and worn when Pretty Baby pointed in her face, "The only reason I don't slap the shit out of you is because I know you have a mental problem and you're old enough to be my mother!"

Savannah balled like a baby. "Elliott's a liar. He's wrong! He's trying to ruin my company." She wiped her nose as she freed herself from Elliott, trying to regain her composure. "Did you know he's been coming out to the hospital fucking me?" She said out of desperation.

"Yeah right," Pretty Baby said. She took a step back and glared at Elliott. She knew, at this very moment, she had the power to blow Elliott right out of the water in front of his wife. All of the love and respect she had gained for him in their entire relationship, was nowhere around. "Tell her, Elliott. Tell her," she demanded. Her eyes met Elliotts fiery eyes that were pleading. A long moment of secrecy and harsh realizations passed between them as Savannah stood unknowing of the intricacy of this affair. Pretty Baby walked away from the crowd that was slowing their paces in order to see what was going on and went to the baggage claim.

Elliott came down the escalator with Savannah following closely, hissing in his face. "Get your things!

You're coming with me!"   She walked to the side, away from the crowd of people.

Defeat was all that he felt as he stood among the sea of people waiting for the carousel to bring his luggage around.   At the end of the belt, Elliott could see the tear stained face of Pretty Baby standing alone. He moved discreetly, following his first instinct to be by her side.

Pretty Baby turned just in time to yell, "Look out!"

Elliott wasn't swift enough to avoid the baggage cart full of someone else's luggage that Savannah sent soaring in his direction nearly knocking him off balance. Savannah ran from the building.

Pretty Baby collected her luggage and went out and got on the shuttle bus depressed and wondering why she got on the bus if she wasn't riding back with Elliott.   She looked out of the window and was relieved to see him running with his luggage to get on the crowded shuttle with her.   Pretty Baby broke down crying all the way to the car. Elliott never spoke.

They got off the bus and into his car in silence.   He drove quickly to her home.   Once they were in the driveway he kissed her tear stained face.

"Have you been fucking her at the hospital?" she asked.

"Get real, Rachel."   He got the bags out and took them in the house.   The children were gone.   They stood on the porch in a long embrace.   He kissed her then turned away.

"Where are you going?"   She called after him.   "To be with her?   What about us?"

Elliotts patience was running thin.   "No, I'm going

Tangled Web

home," he turned around. "I had a bad feeling all along, even before our trip, but I didn't want to disappoint you on your birthday," he pointed out. "So don't ask me anything foolish, woman." He started for his car. "No telling what she's done if she's been roaming around like this while I've been gone. I'll call you."

"When?" she sobbed.

"I don't know. Soon. Just go in and get some rest."

"Whoso findeth a wife findeth a good thing, and
obtaineth favour of the Lord."
Pr. 18:22

*E*lliott pulled into his garage, turned off the engine and sat. Immediately the light came on and the kitchen door opened. It was Maria. She ran around to the driver's side opening his door before he could get out.

"Mrs. Banks is here," she whispered loudly. "I was in my room when I heard the doorbell, I looked out and there she was. I don't know how she got here." Elliott got out of the car with the weight of the world on his shoulders. "She told me to leave her alone, she would call me if she needed me. What is going on? I didn't know she was well."

"She's not," he managed to say. "Where is she?"

Tangled Web

"In the study." She stepped aside to let him by.

Elliott walked down the hallway to the study and went in. He could see Savannah's crossed leg swinging as she sat in the high back leather chair.

She heard his footsteps enter. "Not staying with your whore tonight, Elliott?"

"We need to talk, I know," he began as he sat down, "but first I'm concerned about your health. Does Dr. Kyles know you've left the hospital? We need to at least call him."

"Save it!" She yelled, rising from her chair. "As long as I'm tucked away at the nut house everything is okay." Her voice held a harsh edge that didn't sound like her own, as she circled Elliott's chair slowly. "As long as I'm on all of those damn drugs and don't know what the hell is going on, it's okay. But when I'm up, and getting around, you're concerned, 'cause it's a problem." She stepped closer to him giving him a look of contempt.

"How could you? How could you do this to me, Elliott? To us? How could you start fucking that bitch? Treating her like your wife, spending our money...." She walked to the window and looked out into the dark yard. "I know about it all, Elliott. Your lover working at Banks. The house, the car, picking up her kids from daycare. Five thousand dollars contributed to her church." She sat down in the chair next to him. "But you forgot one thing....half of all the money you have is mine. And I'm gonna fix you so that you'll give me half of your half. If I can't do that, I'll tie up everything so you can't make any money. I'll show you who's crazy." She scooted to the edge of her seat looking him directly in the eye. "Half of Banks Inc. is mine," she

333

pounded her chest.

"I know Savannah," he said quietly. He tried to reach out to her. "But please understand, after so many years of your illness, I didn't know if you'd ever get well."

Savannah started to cry. She felt like she was standing outside of herself. "So you go out and get a replacement for me? Just like that? I trusted you. No matter what. I trusted you," she sobbed, her voice rasping with disgust.

"You can still trust me that's why I'm trying to tell the truth." Elliott was at a loss for words. He didn't want to discuss his relationship with Rachel any further because he feared more damage could be done. He didn't want to be forced to admit that deep inside he had found real happiness with another woman for fear of hurting someone he sincerely cared about. After all the years of praying that Savannah would come back to him, he could never admit that he really wanted to spend the rest of his days with Rachel.

"Do you love her?" Savannah searched his face. Elliott couldn't answer. The phone began to ring. "Tell me. Do you love her?"

Maria peeked into the study. "Excuse me Mr. Banks, there's an urgent call for you."

"That bitch has a lot of nerve," Savannah said, trying to grab the phone from Elliott. He restrained her with one hand, motioning for her to keep quiet. He scribbled something on a piece of paper and told the person on the phone he would be on his way. He hung up.

Elliott gathered some things from the desk and put them in his briefcase.

Tangled Web

"Oh no you don't. You're not running back over there to that slut." She tugged fiercely at his briefcase.

"Stop it, Savannah." He was drained and didn't know how or if he should tell her this after past tragedies but he knew he couldn't leave her here. He held her by both shoulders. "There's been an accident. It's Kaleb."

"What?" She gripped Elliott's jacket as his words seemed to shatter her mind. "My baby...what has happened to my baby?" She whined. "It's your fault. Your fault, Elliott."

"Wait a minute," he shook her shoulders. "The details are sketchy, I just know he's up in Massachusetts and we need to get there." He picked up the phone and called his travel agent to secure tickets on the next jet out. "Tell Maria to help you find some clothes to take in case we're there a few days."

"How bad is it? Tell me. Tell me." Her breathing was becoming a pant that concerned Elliott.

"I don't know," he lied. The nurse from the hospital told Elliott he was in critical condition. "Just hurry so we can get to the airport." Savannah did as he instructed.

By the time they arrived at the hospital, Kaleb's condition had stabilized. He had suffered a broken leg and severe internal injuries. After his parents had sat at his side for twenty-four hours, Kaleb opened his eyes groggily. The doctor assured them that he was out of the woods and they should try and get some rest. Elliott agreed.

Before leaving the hospital, Elliott went to a pay phone and called Rachel. He told her he had been called away on emergency business and with everything going on he didn't have a chance to call sooner. She was relieved to hear it was business that pulled him away because her imagination had run wild with her thinking Elliott was with Savannah. She tried to ask him about what happened when he went home but he said they'd talk later. He told her he loved her and promised to be home in a day or two.

Elliott convinced Savannah to leave the hospital and come to the hotel he had gotten for them.

When they got to the hotel, Elliott offered to call Dr. Kyles because he knew Savannah had been missing her medication.

"I don't want the damn pills, Elliott. I'm fine. Just leave me alone," she spoke harshly. She went into the bathroom, showered and came out in her bathrobe, throwing his briefcase on the other double bed. She climbed into the bed and turned her back to him.

Elliott watched her gestures. He couldn't read her mood. He was sure she would start the argument about Rachel up again, but she didn't. "Did you want me to order you something to eat?" He asked.

"No. If I want something, I'll get up and get it," she stated flatly.

The next morning they went to the hospital and Isaiah was there with his brother. They were both happy to see their parents, especially their mother. It was like a miracle. Later Savannah told Elliott he could leave and go home, she was with her sons and she would call him if she needed him. Elliott suddenly felt like an outsider among Savannah and her boys.

He caught an evening flight back to Virginia and drove straight to Rachel's house spending the night and leaving before the children awoke.

Tangled Web

"Can a man take fire into his bosom, and his clothes not be burned?
Can one go upon hot coals, and his feet not be burned?"
Pr. 6:27-28

*P*retty Baby got up early and tipped out onto the balcony in time to see the sun rise above the sea. She watched the waves roll up onto the sand and wash away. The sound of the sea gulls and the whispering of the wind was so tranquil. She leaned her face into the wind and let the tears run freely down her cheeks. Elliott's lovemaking last night was a dialogue of the unspoken. She felt the onset of what was to come.

The work week had been long and strenuous dealing with the whispers and tension that could be felt throughout the building as Pretty Baby and Elliott went about business as usual. Savannah had indeed reappeared at Banks, demanding that Gracie let her into Elliott's office where she and her private investigator went through, and found, several receipts and purchases made by Elliott for Rachel Casey. This was to go along with other personal information the investigator had collected about Pretty Baby, such as to whom she was previously married and that she had recently been employed as a daycare worker, minus a degree of any sort.

Pretty Baby didn't hear Elliott come up behind her, putting his hands on her hips and leaning his chin into her hair.

They stood for a long time with only the sound of the sea and the dance of the waves to entertain them.

"I'm sorry," Elliott finally said. His apology hurt. He turned Pretty Baby to face him. "And I hope that you can find it in your heart to forgive me."

She nodded. "I take a lot of the blame too, Elliott, because I know better. So now what do we do?"

Elliott shook his head, going back into the master bedroom that adjoined the balcony. "There's nothing I can do," he bit at his thumbnail, "what pains me is that I've seen several warning signs of a disaster coming but I chose to ignore them. Yeah, I know better too, but I didn't want to stop doing what I was doing." He took in the full view of the woman he had grown to love so deeply, memorizing every detail about her. "You know, Rachel, you and I have shared everything in the last couple of years, but one thing we have never really discussed is religion and it is very important to me." He looked down then back up at her. "I believe in God, too. And His power. I love Him and I love you, but it's sad to know that I can't bring the three of us together the way I'd like to."

Pretty Baby shook her head unable to speak as the reality of their situation was being spoken.

"Remember when we had that scare with my mom's heart, she had the surgery, and you said, "Pray and give it to the Lord?" When we went to the chapel and you were praying, I wasn't praying. I was just looking down at my shoes thinking how worthless I felt at that very moment because I couldn't pray for my mother." Pretty Baby looked at him questioningly. "I didn't feel worthy enough, because of my lifestyle, to ask for God's help. I was wrong, Rachel. I'm wrong right now, for being here with you. But I love you so much." He hugged her tightly as she sobbed. "I'm not sorry for loving you, and I know I'll never be the same without you," he stifled a sob in his throat. "My biggest mistake was starting a relationship with you when I was already in one. I dragged you into my loneliness for my own selfish reasons."

"Don't say that, Elliott. That's not true." Pretty Baby picked up a tissue and wiped her eyes. "Now that she's better, you can divorce her," she said hopefully. Elliott didn't respond. "All the promises you made me, 'if only you could be free to pursue a life with me and the children'. Were those all lies?" Pretty Baby's hurt was being replaced by anger.

"No, they weren't. You know that." Elliott leaned his head on the wall staring out at the sea. "This is so complicated, I was wrong. I hurt you. I hurt her."

She sobbed harder at his sympathy for Savannah.

It was hard to be sensible at a time like this. All Pretty Baby could think was that he was betraying her in the worst way.

Elliott slipped on his jogging shorts and cut off shirt. "I'm going for a jog on the beach, you want to go?" He asked quietly. She barely heard him. He kissed her on the forehead and went down the balcony steps.

Pretty Baby came out of the shower, securing her bathrobe, she realized Elliott had not come back yet. She couldn't think clearly but it didn't matter because she didn't want to think about this mess as she wandered through the house aimlessly.

She put a couple of strips of turkey bacon in the oven for Elliott, his regular morning meal, and continued to wander around the giant penthouse. She loved coming there with Elliott, it was so peaceful. She ran her fingers across the smooth marble sculpture that sat in front of the fireplace then walked over to the office area and looked at the large golden globe of the world that sat on the cherry oak desk. She glanced at the Langley folder that lay open in Elliott's opened briefcase, then absently plucked the itinerary out of his briefcase from his travel agent and looked at it, wondering if he had a trip coming up he hadn't mentioned. Two old boarding passes lay in the pocket of the envelope.

"Elliott and Savannah Banks?" Pretty Baby read aloud. She recognized the date as being the date they returned from Paris. So he had been away on business alright. With her. She was furious and very intimidated but quickly put the papers back in the same spot when she heard Elliott stomping the sand out of his shoes on the

Tangled Web

balcony.

They made eye contact then he went into shower as she moved stoically around in the kitchen completing his breakfast.

He came into the kitchen wrapped in his velcro towel. The curly hair on his chest glistening with moisture. He sat down.

"How was your run?" she asked casually.

"Fine." He spread jam on his bagel. "You're not eating?"

Pretty Baby sat across from him and shook her head. She flipped through the newspaper as he ate, anxiously waiting on the right moment to ask him about his trip with Savannah.

"You never did say where you were called away to last week on business."

"I did tell you I was in Massachusetts, Babe."

"Oh yeah, that's right." She sat thinking quickly, probing for the truth, waiting for his neck to snap as he hung himself. "What company were you working with up there?"

Elliott looked at her blankly then said, "One of the small companies that's an affiliate of Langley. There was a virus in their main system and some important information was lost."

Pretty Baby held back the tears that were stinging her eyes. "Is that why you took your damn wife?" She jumped from the table. "You are a liar, Elliott. And you don't have to lie to me 'cause I'm the other woman, remember? The more I think about this, the more I realize you have fucked up my life."

"Wait a minute," he said, trying to keep this civil. His shoulders were slumped in giving him an air of defeat. "Yes I lied. Kaleb was involved in a very bad accident. The call came when I got to the house that night we returned from France and Savannah was there. The call came for me, but what was I suppose to do, leave her there while I went to see about her son that could have been dying? I knew it would upset you, there was no time to waste, that's why I lied. You know that woman has been mentally unstable for years. I couldn't leave her to handle something like that alone. And I wasn't going to. I've been wrong enough to her."

This was all repulsive to Pretty Baby. She had sympathy for any mother facing a crisis like that but this situation was taking her to the limit with Elliott. She stomped into the bedroom and started putting her things in her overnight bag.

He walked behind her equally as angry. "You know Rachel, you act as if you're the only victim in this situation. The only one hurt. I hurt too, knowing that I've used such bad judgment. I guess you haven't thought about the fact the I'm taking a risk now by being here with you. But I want to be here. I didn't want to spend these moments bickering about a situation I can't change. I know the pain I've caused you, that's why I never mentioned any of the other things that have been going on."

Pretty Baby turned to him. "Why spare my feelings now? At this rate, nothing surprises me."

"I never mentioned numbers dropping with the Langley account. I thought business was just slow. Now the account has been canceled all together." Pretty Baby

Tangled Web

opened her mouth in surprise. "Yeah, Savannah has spoken with Langley himself and told him about what was going on. Since we were on a five-year test basis, she had the contract broken. An agreement of mutual terms until further notice. That's why he didn't return my calls, he figures we're about to go into a nasty divorce court battle and he didn't want his business tied up in it."

Pretty Baby was aghast. Deep inside she knew how Elliott felt about her and she knew what his business meant to him. A torrent of pain surged through her body as she struggled to maintain control of her voice.

She let out a sigh running her fingers through her hair. She closed her bag and turned to him. "You will straighten things out and get a divorce won't you?"

"I don't know. I mean, I don't know where Savannah's head is. I can't say if she is mentally competent to go through something like that."

"She looked competent enough at the airport. She thought her plan through enough to hire a private eye," Pretty Baby protested. "What about us?"

He observed Pretty Baby for a long moment. "You know, all along while I was helping you to build something for you and the kids, I was tearing down what I have. And what I could gather from what Savannah did say, was that she is going to strip me of everything I have. I know how I feel, but what I feel and what is right are two different things." He spoke morosely from the other side of the room. "Do you think I can just leave her and marry you and we ride off into the sunset? No, there's gonna be a price....and I don't know if I can pay it. Not right now. Not like this."

343

The silence was thick between them as they packed to go back to town. When they got to her house, he didn't go in. Just kissed her goodbye and promised to call later. "Just give me some time, Baby. Please," he pleaded. She slammed the car door.

Missy had promised to drop the kids off after a weekend at her house. When Pretty Baby opened her front door she was assaulted by the loud blare of Chris' rap music. Jason's skates were thrown in the hall leading to the den with a mess of other toys that belonged to Ashley and the cordless phone from Pretty Baby's bedroom. She picked up the phone in disgust, realizing it had been off the hook. Her eyes roamed past the dirty cereal bowls that sat on the kitchen table and she headed straight to Chris' room where she found the children jamming so loud they didn't know she was in the house.

She went over to the stereo and pressed the volume down. Her head was pounding. Ashley jumped up from her play and hugged her mother's legs. "I can't believe you guys could be in the house for a short period of time and tear up like this. I don't like to come home and see my house torn up like this. Get in here right now and start cleaning damnit!" She yelled. "Chris, clean the kitchen. Jason, get all these toys off the floor." She started down the hall to her bedroom as Ashley followed. Pretty Baby turned on her heels. "Get in there with your brothers and clean up," she scolded the little girl.

She closed the door to her bedroom, thankful for the large room where she could hide away. Sitting on her chaise lounge with her legs tucked under, she gazed around the room at the beautiful furnishings Elliott had

344

Tangled Web

splurged for as a house warming gift. Her boudoir was where she kept him captivated with plenty good loving, conversation and even political debates. She felt nauseous as insecurities started to set in and an even worse thought engulfed her mind. My job. I'll have to give up my job. Pretty Baby already knew she wouldn't subject herself to the humiliation of a dismissal and would give a two weeks notice immediately. Two years of experience at Banks, Inc. ought to stand for something, she thought. She'd give up her job, but she wasn't gonna give Elliott up that easily because she knew he didn't want Savannah.

She bent her head low, feeling the strain in her neck and stretching her muscles. Slowly she raised, leaning back on the chaise giving into the relaxation. The phone startled her back to realization. She picked up the phone leaning it on her shoulder. "Hello."

"I'm warning you, Bitch, for the final time," the woman hissed into the receiver. "Stay away from my husband!"

Pretty Baby immediately knew who it was and was armed and ready for battle. "No. You tell your husband to stay away from me," she held an undertone of nervous laughter in her voice. "Yeah, that's it." She laughed, a little more boastfully. "See if you can keep your husband away from me. I was just with him and he's gone home to see if he can straighten out this misunderstanding with the Langley account."

"I'm tired of you knowing every move my husband makes." Savannah narrowed her eyes, realizing what had just been said. "And what would someone like you know about the Langley account?"

Pretty Baby didn't appreciate that someone like you comment, but it was imperative that she keep her cool and the upper hand in this confrontation, she just calmly replied, "Actually, I don't know a thing about the Langley account." She caught a glimpse of herself in her bedroom mirror. Her usually cool exterior not looking so cool. In fact, it was startling to know how evilness and hell-raising came so easily. She hadn't forgotten about Savannah's scene at the airport and she owed her one good lick, regardless of how it had to be delivered. "All I know is where he's going, what he's doing and where he's headed afterwards!" She yelled in a take that manner. "Yes, girlfriend, I know what you do know and **everything** you don't know. I even know what kind of underwear you wear and he doesn't like it." She was on a roll now. "Always shopping for comfort, never to please. You'd think an old broad like yourself would know better." This was becoming humorous to Pretty Baby, knowing she could get under this bats' skin.

"You're nothing but a whore. A slut who can't get her own man," Savannah yelled.

"And maybe if you knew how to please your man you wouldn't have these problems," she retaliated. The confrontation excelerated until the two women couldn't hear each other. "Listen! I did not set out to steal your husband, but he has feelings too. And all during your illness...."

"My illness?" She interrupted. "So that's it, you try to build something for yourself out of someone else's misfortune?"

"Of course not," Pretty Baby shook her head

Tangled Web

profusely, feeling maybe this would be her only chance to explain. "All during your illness, that man stuck by you. Not just for a little while, but for years." She ran her fingers through her hair as her head started to feel like a giant weight on her shoulders that her neck could barely support. "As time went on, he met me...and we fell in love." She let out a breath, "I guess I was what brought him back around. And at the time I needed someone." That victorious feeling was fading fast and a tinge of insecurity came rushing back. "There was a strain on your relationship before your accident, but to show you how dedicated he was, he stayed by your side. You've never stopped to think about the length of time he's been alone."

"You don't know what I thought about or what went on at my house," Savannah screamed. "You are just a low-life whore."

"No, no, no, Honey, you've got me and the situation all wrong," she said wickedly, "because, you see, he's not the kind of man that has an affair or just sleeps around for the hell of it. He's the kind of man that falls in love, and probably any problems you have now didn't start with me and they won't end with me." Pretty Baby's temper was rising again and the vindictiveness reappearing. "I won't take your husband from you," she paused, searching for the right words to make it count, "because, no matter what happens, my presence will always remain and you can believe he'll always be thinking of me. So I don't have to *take* him."

"I'm warning you," Savannah's voice cracked with tears, "he doesn't want you."

"You wish he didn't. Let me tell you something.

Keep your tired ass warnings for him and your private investigator. It's you that he doesn't want but he's willing to put his happiness to the side because I guess he feels that he owes you that much. Plus they always say, 'It's cheaper to keep her'." She laughed a sarcastic laugh.

Savannah slowly tried to pull all the strength she could find to fight this woman who, to some degree, spoke the truth about her personal life. There was a long silence on the phone. All she could think was that she was about to slip over the edge.....again. Her shoulders heaved uncontrollably because everything was out of her control, including her husband's love.

Finally Savannah spoke, "I didn't come this far in life to let someone like you tear me down. I pray," she said between mournful sobs, "that all this pain that you two have put on me will come back on you. You may not feel it now, but God will whip you in the worst kind of way, when you least expect it. Take heed to my warnings," she said in a barely audible whisper.

Her words were chilling. They pierced Pretty Baby's ears, through her heart, straight to her stomach. She slammed the phone down. "She is one sick woman!" she said out loud, looking around the room wildly. Her hands were still trembling. Pretty Baby sat in disbelief as thoughts ran back and forth through her mind. She had been threatened with a lot of things, but never with God. This brought on a reality check, and a lot of the truth was starting to hurt. She stood, her face streaked with tears, and looked out her bedroom window. Something so right was turning out to be so wrong.

Out of the corner of her eye she could see a spider

Tangled Web

crawling to the far end of the window. She despised creepy crawly things with their antennas and unknowing rapid movements. Carefully, she watched as it made its way to the web that had been spun in the corner. Pretty Baby peered closer at the well-crafted silken strings, as she could see another species of a bug fighting for his life in the tangled web. She could suddenly see herself in that same predicament. It reminded her of the old Shakespearean quote: "Oh, what a tangled web we weave, when first we practice to deceive." Sobs racked her body as she destroyed the web with her slipper in order to save the bug from its' predator. Slinging the shoe across the room, she lay on the bed and cried. This didn't feel like the victory she had anticipated after all.

"An hypocrite with his mouth destroyeth his neighbor:
but through knowledge shall the just be delivered."
Pr. 11:9

"*I* can't leave town tomorrow without my own stash," Missy thought.

She drove down Shay Shay's street slowly, realizing she wasn't home. Missy looked to see if she saw anyone who looked kind of familiar, but no one was out. Their hook up on the dead end street got busted, not too long ago. Some people say that the old lady, who use to sit on the porch, snitched. The only other place she could think of was up on the hill and she didn't know those people. It was more of a crack house and she didn't deal like that. Being a product of the late 70's, she was a pot

Tangled Web

smoker only.

She was giving up her search for now as she came around the side street that ran along the hill. Missy stopped at the stop sign, seeing little children running around the bald yards of the rundown duplex apartments, as their smoked up looking caretakers looked on. Some sat and drank. On the other porch, a card game was going on.

Missy came to an abrupt stop at the sign then made a quick right winding down Crater Road. She was just heading back to her side of town, when she saw Stank and knew he could tell her where to get some smoke.

She made a wild u-turn and blew her horn driving up beside him. He turned looking like she caught him in the midst of a withdrawal attack. Beads of sweat glistened across his face.

"You could give me a ride?" He asked in his wine-slurred voice, as soon as Missy rolled the window down and his funk drifted in.

"I want you to get some smoke for me, Stank. Where you trying to get to?"

He looked toward where he wanted to go. "I just want to go over by, uh, by Pearl Street."

"Where's that?" Her eyes clouded. "Oh, you mean by the hill."

"Uh-huh," he came around the other side and got in. "I could pro'bly get you some good weed, too."

They pulled up the steep driveway and parked. Stank got out and Missy followed. They were greeted at the door by a petite, chocolate, well groomed man. His relaxed hair was cut with precision and swung to the side.

He wore tight slacks with a silky blouse that had puffed sleeves. He was adorned with gold, laying on his hairy chest, across his fingers where he had long manicured nails and along his nice straight teeth. He wore a hat half cocked with a feather in the side. Rudy was his name.

"What's up, Stank?" he said slapping him five and pulling him in the house, never taking his eyes off of Missy. "Ya'll come on in here."

Missy could see other activity going on in the house. There were people in different rooms. Music blared loudly from speakers hung in the corners of the ceiling. They sat in a den area outside the kitchen where a loud dice game was going on. It sounded like a woman was in there winning, and boasting loudly.

Rudy looked over at Missy with a smile as he methodically chopped the cocaine on the mirror, lining it up perfectly. "You know, Baby, you look like you could be one of my girls."

Missy gave him a rejected look then turned her attention to the bag of marijuana. "The only thing you can do for me is continue to have some good smoke and I'll come back." She looked at the bag she was about to purchase, smelling it as her test of its quality.

"You probably got a little freak in you," Rudy mumbled to himself. He did a dip as a new rap song came on then he did a James Brown shuffle and rolled his pelvis suggestively at Missy.

Missy rolled her eyes at him as she sat off to the side in the noisy house with a magazine, rolling a joint for the road when she noticed Rudy started going off on Stank. Stank apparently owed money and was trying to lie

Tangled Web

his way out of it to get a hit for today. Rudy thumped Stank upside his head causing him to slump over in the chair.

"All that ain't called for," Missy jumped to Stank's rescue.

"Sit your freaky ass down and stay in your place," Rudy snapped at her.

Missy came over to where Stank sat, picking up her keys that were on the couch. She accidentally bumped the wobbly service table, spilling a baggie of the white powder onto the floor.

"Aw, Hoe, you gone pay for this." Rudy yelled.

"Who you callin' hoe? Superfly wanna-be pimp motherfucker," Missy yelled as she backed out toward the door. Stank was ahead of her. Missy's voice could be heard all through the house as a few of the 'house on the hill' junkies came from there hiding places being led by Charmaine to see what the commotion was. William followed close behind. Missy stopped not believing her eyes, as Rudy continued to curse her about the cocaine and calling her hoe. She glared at Charmaine then at William, who ducked back into the kitchen.

"Get your stupid ass out of here, Bitch. Before I pimp slap you." The little chocolate Prince ranted and raved. Missy backed out the driveway, racing out of the neighborhood when she realized she still had the weed and hadn't paid for it. She laughed nonstop, dropping Stank off at Miller's Gas and Grocery.

Later that night, without any hesitation she went over to Jesse's and told him what she knew about Charmaine along with what she heard from Pretty Baby. He seemed a little pissed at first, then he admitted that he had gradually realized Charmaine lived another life, but he didn't know it was that bad.

Missy left his house feeling depressed, like maybe she shouldn't have been so eager to tell Jesse. She could've left well enough alone.

Tangled Web

"Therefore shall his calamity come suddenly;
suddenly shall he be broken without remedy."
Pr. 6:15

Elliott massaged his temples forward, clasping his hands over his face then running his hands over his head. He couldn't concentrate on the work in front of him, trying to figure out how he could work this all out. He pulled the papers out of his briefcase and stared at them.

Savannah was back in town and was released from the hospital over the weekend. Yesterday he was served with a divorce petition. Savannah wanted him to get out of the house and the matter of the company would be settled in court. Her grounds for divorcement were adultery and mental cruelty. Those words made Elliott nauseous, he wish it were that simple. To just divorce without losing most of what he had worked so hard for. Then to top the day off, Rachel had given him a two week's notice that she would be resigning. He tried to talk her out of it, knowing what she said made since, but he was worried about what she and the children would do. In the end he told her he would continue her salary for six months, even if he had to pay it out of his pocket.

He was brought back to reality by the ringing of his private line. He had instructed Gracie to hold all of his calls on the main line. He picked up. "Elliott Banks."

"Hello, Son," the voice said.

"Hello, Mother. How are you?" He felt a tad lighter as he heard the familiar voice.

"I do just fine.   But you don't sound too good. What's the matter, dear? Working too much probably."

"Same work load as usual, Mom. So what's been going on around there?" He tried to sound a little more upbeat. "I was thinking about flying up there, probably, next month. I'll let you know exactly when I get a date."

"That sounds good. I'll be sure to make strawberry shortcake and fix a rice pudding, just for you. It'll give us a chance to talk some." She started to sound a little hesitant. "Why don't you plan to come this weekend. That'll be perfect."

"No, Mom. I can't come this weekend. I'll let you know when. There's nothing wrong is there? You sound kind of funny."

"I just want to talk to you."

Elliott rested his head in his hand. He remembered when he was young and he was in trouble, his mom would say, I just want to talk to you. He always got that same

Tangled Web

nervous feeling in his stomach he was feeling now. "If you need to talk to me, mom, you need to tell me now because I can't come this weekend."

There was a long pause then she started right in. "As long as you and your brother been on your own, I stay out of your personal business. You boys have made me very proud of you, becoming successful in your own rights and just being good men. Ain't that many good men," she reminded him. "But you're never too old to learn or listen. You hear me?"

"Yes, ma'am." Elliott leaned back on his leather chair with his eyes closed.

"Savannah was here this weekend." Elliott squeezed his eyes tighter. "I 'clare, Elliott, I thought I was seeing a ghost. Why didn't you tell me she had made this miraculous recovery?"

"I was just as surprised as you." He said sullenly.

"I'm happy that she's better but I'm concerned about her state of mind."

"What did she say?"

"What didn't she say, humph. I thought she was talkin' some crazy talk but I quickly realized she knew exactly what she was talkin' about."

"What did she say, mother." Elliott wanted her to get to the point.

"She said she was divorcing you because you had some other woman you been carrying on with for the last couple of years and the two of you were planning to take over the company while she rotted away in the hospital." Elliott let out a big sigh. "I didn't want to believe it to be true until I talked to you first. But I know you're only human with Savannah being sick all these years..." her voice trailed off.

"Thanks for letting me know, Mother, and please try not to worry. I'll take care of it."

"Lord, son, I'm afraid for you because she is so bitter. People like that get desperate and do desperate things. It's not worth all that. She was rantin' and ravin' about how she was gonna see to it that you pay for what you've done. Publicly humiliating her and all. She said you had been taking care of this woman and her kids then you turned around and gave this woman a job."

Elliott couldn't say anything. He just sat with his head bent low. He didn't want to admit to the affair over the phone, but the one thing that gave him comfort was that, when the time was right, he could confide in his mother about his true feelings and she wouldn't try to judge him. "Mom, do me a favor and don't worry. I'll call you in a couple of days. O.k.?"

"O.k., but you listen to me." She waited until she felt he was listening closely. "I know you needed someone in your life after all this time. And I'm sure any woman that you picked is probably a very nice person, but you have to do the right thing. See if you can salvage your marriage before you move on, and you need to pray. Ask for forgiveness then guidance. I'll do anything I can to help you, no matter what the outcome of this may be. But you got to go to God for yourself."

Elliott felt choked up at his mothers' truthful words then he felt angry that Savannah would worry his mother with her vendetta against him.

"I'm gonna be waiting to hear from you in a few

358

days. Bye-now."

"Mom," he spoke quickly before she could hang up, "I love you."

"I'll be praying for you, Son." She hung up.

Elliott held the receiver in his hand while his mothers' words played back in his head. You got to go to God for yourself.

Gracie knocked on the door and came in before Elliott could speak.

"Excuse me Mr. Banks," she spoke in a whisper, closing the door behind her. "But I thought you might want to know that Mrs. Banks is here and she's in Ms. Casey's office."

Elliott came from around his desk quickly. "Rachel hasn't come in yet, has she?"

"No, sir," she said, following him to the elevator.

Elliott turned on his heels. "I can handle this, Gracie."

When Elliott turned the corner he heard a loud crashing noise. He swung the door open to see Savannah destroying some of Pretty Baby's belongings. Elliott stepped across the shattered remains of the family portrait of Rachel and the kids as he tried to restrain her.

"Let me go," she jerked away. "That bitch is still here? What nerve!" She yelled, opening drawers and file cabinets. "Do I need to fire her myself?" She came around the desk looking at him. "This whore has really got you going. The two of you can do what you want," she walked toward the door and snatched it open, "but you won't be doing it here. You must have forgotten who is half owner of this company." She stormed down the hall to the elevator. Elliott stood numbly looking at the mess. He picked up what could be salvaged and put them in place. He closed the drawers then glanced out the window to see Savannah getting in her Lexus, driven by her old driver.

When Elliott walked out to get a broom from the storage closet, eavesdropping employees scattered like roaches just exposed to the light.

He returned to the office and stared a long time at the picture without a frame of Pretty Baby, Chris, Jason and Ashley. "I'm sorry," he whispered into the silence. He didn't hear Pretty Baby come in the door.

"Hey Baby," she said casually giving him a quick peck he didn't respond to. She stepped back. "What's wrong now?"

Elliott showed a look of dread but he knew he couldn't put this off. He was starting to be afraid for her not knowing how far Savannah would go. "Could you take some of your things home...now?"

Pretty Baby looked at him confused at first, then glancing around the room she realized her things were not as she had left them. The picture in his hands looked crumpled. She quickly understood what was going on. "NO!" She shouted. "I gave two week's notice and now you're firing me?"

"Listen to me," he pleaded. "Savannah was here earlier and she is pissed that you are still working here after what's happened."

"Oh, so now you're letting her fire me?"

"You just said yesterday that it would be best if you left."

"I had planned on resigning, not getting fired," she

360

Tangled Web

spat, feeling close to crying but she refused. Pretty Baby dumped the computer paper out of the box and started throwing her personal belongings in.

Elliott felt useless. "I can get these things together for you and bring them to your house."

His words stung like a smack in the face. She turned and glared at him, grabbing her purse and rushing out.

On the far side of the lot she could see Savannah sitting, poised as a hawk, in the Lexus.

Pretty Baby's stomach trembled when she pulled out and realized the Lexus was coming her way. She hoped they wouldn't try to follow her and run her off the road. Elliott stared from the window in horror, thinking those same thoughts. The automobile glided into the reserved spot that Pretty Baby had pulled out of, next to Elliott's Mercedes.

****

Pretty Baby drove toward home, tears stinging her eyes. Humiliation rocking her to the core. She found herself driving up in front of Aunt Becky's house. She sat there for ten minutes or more before she saw Becky standing in the door way. She got out the car slowly coming up on the porch as the stench of steamed cabbage hit her nose.

"Now this is a pleasant surprise," she said closing the door behind Pretty Baby, following her into the kitchen. "I'm just puttin' a little supper on. Guess I'll freeze some of this since I can't eat it all myself, 'less you want to take

361

some home for the children." Aunt Becky got an onion out of the refrigerator and sifted a few pots around on the stove, realizing Pretty Baby hadn't heard a word she said. "What's troublin' you, girl? Pretty Baby?"

She turned around slowly shaking her head then took a seat at the table.

"What's goin' on now, Rachel? Look like you lost your best friend."

How ironic for Aunt Becky to say that, she had lost her best friend, as far as she was concerned. And for all the times that she had alienated Aunt Becky because she felt she was too nosey and she didn't want her advice, she needed her now. She knew, eventually, it would become apparent that she wasn't working. "Oh, Aunt Becky, everything is a mess..." she shook her head in disbelief.

Aunt Becky sat at the table beside Pretty Baby, seeing the pain in her eyes. "What's going on?" she searched her niece's face.

Pretty Baby took a deep breath and told her everything, starting with the incident with Clarisse all the way to the private investigator.

"Private investigator?" Becky yelped. "Lawd, have mercy. If that woman'll hire a private eye, she'll hire a hit-man. And she's fresh out of a mental institution, too?"

Then Pretty Baby told her about what happened today at work as she cried in Becky's arms.

Aunt Becky didn't say I told you so, she just held Pretty Baby, telling her, 'And this, too, shall pass'.You live and you learn, baby, just make sure you learn while you're still living. You were playing a dangerous game." She rocked her back and forth. Rubbing, massaging and

Tangled Web

kneading a prayer into her soul.

"Tis' a funny thing about life," she began, with a faraway look. "You know when a man is no good, from the beginning. You know if he *is* a good man, and we sometimes tend to take that for granted. But deep down inside we know all along; we just can't accept it." Aunt Becky rocked Pretty Baby in silence. "I think Elliott's a fine man. I'm sorry for his situation. Nobody deserves a tragedy like that. But you knew all along you couldn't have a future with him...but you couldn't accept it." She held Pretty Baby's face in her hands. "I think you have now."

"I love him so much, Aunt Becky. I feel like I've been betrayed." She wiped her eyes with the tissue Becky handed her.

"I know you love him. And there's no doubt in my mind that his love isn't genuine for you and the children. Don't look at it as betrayal, honey. Look at it as a lesson for living. Times like this, you continue to praise the Lord." She got up and fixed Pretty Baby a tall glass of iced tea with a mint leaf floating on top. "Sometimes you have to have darkness to appreciate the light. God reveals things to us about ourselves in the dark. You know that don't you?" Aunt Becky gave Pretty Baby a warm smile. "Give us a chance to work things out in that busy mind of ours He's blessed us with, before things are exposed in the light." Tears streamed down Pretty Baby's face as she reached for more tissue. "You look like you come out ahead in this deal, anyway." Pretty Baby looked doubtful. "Oh, yeah. Elliott made some things possible for you that might not have been so at this point in your life. So get it all out your system, ask for forgiveness and let one good cry do, then give it to the Lord. If that man is for you, you'll have him. And if not...." she shrugged her shoulders, "that too shall pass. If any situation seems too bad to take it to the Lord, you really ain't got no business doin' it. You want His blessings in all you do."

Pretty Baby went into the bathroom and looked at her puffy face in the mirror. She heaved a sigh as she went back into the kitchen.

Aunt Becky held her hands in a moment of prayer then warned her to stay out of that crazy woman's way before she left.

****

Pretty Baby got home with two hours to spare before the children were out of school. She went straight into her bedroom noticing there were three messages left by Elliott. She listened to the sadness in his voice begging her to call him immediately. He said he was worried about her.

"Fuck Elliott," she said out loud, removing her suit then going into the bathroom running a tub full of water.

She stepped up then down into the round jacuzzi tub, letting her feet take the heat first. She then eased down and leaned her head back on her bath pillow. Her very first thought was of all the time she and Elliott had spent pampering each other in here. The candle that she had lit in the dim bathroom flickered, dancing to its own beat, releasing an aroma of mulberry in the luxurious bathroom.

The sob came all of a sudden from deep down

364

Tangled Web

inside of her. She cried, cried and cried. Tears seemed to flow through her pores. She mourned for the love she mistook for her own until her hair started to frizz. Grieving until her skin was pruned. Pretty Baby whimpered while going through the motions of washing her body in the cooled water. Exhausted, she stood and turned on the shower letting the warm water rinse away the tears. She prayed, then decided that this was the last cry and it would have to do.

"Things hateful to God: "A proud look, a lying tongue,
And hands that shed innocent blood."
Pr. 6:17

Missy was excited about the all expense paid trip the company was sending her on to Charlotte, N.C. where the headquarters for Simmons & Burns Advertising was located. There, she would be attending seminars by day and partying by night.

She had been looking forward to it all month long, squeezing Hershel for as much money as she could. He obliged, giving her his credit card and one thousand dollars for spending money. Virgil helped as much as he could but all she really needed him to do was get Monique from school or Becky's, and take her out to Pretty Baby's house.

Tangled Web

Hershel never minded doing things for Missy. In fact, he told her he thought he would fly to North Carolina and join her. The countryside was spectacular and he knew a lot of nice places he would like to take her in Charlotte. The last thing Missy wanted was Hershel along, so she waited a few days before her trip and told him she had it all wrong. She was going to South Carolina. Not North Carolina.

Hershel thought for a minute, then said, "I guess that's just as good, all though I don't know much about that area."

"It'll probably be boring and we'll be working non-stop. We can take a little weekend vacation when I get back," she smiled stroking his silver hair, which aroused him, and he agreed.

Missy had been acting sweet toward Hershel ever since her car was in the shop with over two thousand dollars worth of work. Hershel offered to let her drive the old Cadillac he had in his garage. Once he had her car repaired, he didn't ask for his car back right away. So it just sat in her yard. She told Virgil a girlfriend from work let her use it. He knew better, but he never said a word.

One day Rodney came by. He wanted Missy to take him on a job interview in Richmond. Missy was excited for him but she didn't have time to take him. Against her better judgment, she let Rodney take the Cadillac. He didn't come back for a whole week. She cussed him from here to Spain when he pulled up in front of the house the following week. A few days after that, Missy was working at home and happened to look out the window to see a tow truck pulling the Caddy away. She

367

immediately called Hershel. He informed her he had sent the truck because someone told him they saw that thug she used to hang with driving his car. She assured him it wasn't true. "That car has been parked ever since I got my car back," she said innocently.

"Don't play games with me, Melissa. You'll be sorry," Hershel warned.

She knew she would want money for her trip so she lured him back in. That's when he came up with the idea of meeting her on her business trip but she talked him out of it by tricking him, or so she thought.

In Charlotte, Missy worked all day and partied every night just as she had planned, meeting some interesting men and a couple of cool women. On her third night there, Rodney arrived right on schedule. They had so much fun, they stayed an extra night after the seminar was over.

She and Rodney flew back together, arriving at the Richmond airport. He took a cab, saying he was going over to his cousin's house in case someone called him for a job. She didn't really believe that but she let it slide and caught the shuttle to the parking lot. She got in her car and drove off the lot dialing home on her cellular. She told Monique to tell Virgil she was on her way. The next number she dialed was Hershel's. He had been paging her the whole time she was gone. Her lie would be as usual, when she didn't want to answer a page, "My pager didn't go off once. I was wondering why no one tried to contact me." Missy laughed at her own mischief, dialing Hershel's house where there was no answer. She tried his cell phone again then the car phone. Still no answer. She turned her cell phone off and reached for a cigarette.

Tangled Web

Missy lit it, looking in her rear view mirror and she noticed a car following close behind her. She regretted taking that last flight as she quickly but carefully drove around the road that led to the expressway.

The radio seemed to distract her as she tried to concentrate on all of the construction signs on the road and the car that was following so closely behind her. Finally, the sign that read, '95 end of detour, one and a half miles,' was in sight. No sooner than she passed it, the car behind her rammed in back of her throwing her car out of control and running it in a ditch. The last thing Missy remembered seeing was a dark haired guy, she couldn't tell if he was black or white, run down into the ditch, open her car door, pull her out and land a vicious blow against her skull.

"My son, eat thou honey, because it is good;
and the Honeycomb, which is sweet to thy taste:
So shall the knowledge of wisdom be unto thy soul:
When thou hast found it, then there shall be
A reward, and thy expectation shall not be cut off."
Pr. 24:13-14

PRETTY BABY

I couldn't believe how all of our lives suddenly took a twist for the worst and eventually turned out for the best. I know now, that they really were lessons for living.

Missy wasn't found until the next morning after that horrible incident. Monique and Virgil assumed she had made a detour on the way home, which wasn't unusual for her, until the hospital called. Some construction workers

370

had found her. She was fortunate to have only a mild concussion, but a terrible gash lined her face from her hairline to underneath her eye. When she woke up in the hospital, Virgil was at her side and Becky was sitting at the foot of the bed with her Bible.

Missy only went to work and family functions in the subsequent months. Hershel never called her again, and she was glad. She was afraid he could have been behind the assault, because of his silence. She clung to Virgil and he loved every minute of it.

As always, the town junkie is somewhat like the roving reporter of the neighborhood. Stank heard, from somebody on the other side of town, that Charmaine was behind Missy getting jumped because she told Jesse about her. We were never certain. We just wanted to pray those evil spirits away.

Poor Jesse was hurt over Charmaine. He tried to pretend it didn't bother him but I knew him so well. Lord knows, I've cried on his shoulders enough times about Elliott. Jesse was always encouraging, never judgmental and he never once said anything bad about Elliott.

That last day at Banks, Inc. was the straw that broke the camel's back, for me. Elliott and I did continue to try to make our love work discreetly, but it was a strain because Savannah had her foot on his neck so tightly, he could never go back to being the Elliott I once knew.

I kept feeling like we still loved each other when we were together. Mostly, because he always treated me like a queen. Elliott always gloated on how smart I was and his confidence in me was like an aphrodisiac. But then I would begin to feel the pain, and I would love and hate him at the same time. When I realized he couldn't stand up for what he really wanted for fear of losing his empire, I knew he'd fall for anything, including a loveless relationship of convenience with Savannah. Nonetheless, I remained on the sidelines continuing to know what she did and everything she didn't know about her husband. It wasn't enough for me. Daily rations, as if I were a prisoner. I needed more. I deserved more.

Savannah never did go through with the divorce. She continued to hold the affair over his head as a punishment. Probably afraid he would come running back to me. Or maybe she didn't want to give up her security. So we all suffered. I don't know. Who cares? So I distance myself without him realizing. Sort of like easing your hand from the lion's mouth so you don't get bit.

One of the things about the whole situation, I think will always baffle me, is what was the motive behind Clarisse's betrayal. She didn't stand to gain a thing. Does jealousy and envy really drive people to that sort of destruction?

Every time I talk to Elliott, he is becoming more active in his church. Recently he started a workshop on entrepreneurship and computer basics that he leads after Wednesday prayer meeting. I'm happy for him. I was always afraid the competition would forever be Savannah and it turns out she's the least of my worries now that she's living in Australia, running the Langley-Banks Center. She's lucky God has filled the void in his life or else she'd be paying another private eye.

It's hard to come across a good man who can love a woman the way she wants to be loved in the mental sense as well as physical. I keep thinking, maybe Elliott loved so deeply and loved so well because he knew he could never really have me.

From time to time I felt the need to talk and express myself. I went to Aunt Becky trying to explain how I felt and what I was thinking. The mental relationship that Elliott and I shared.

She suddenly snapped, "Don't even speak about that. It was just a bunch of...mess!" She turned up her nose as if the subject was do-do. I was defensive explaining the friendship that Elliott and I still had.

She turned and looked at me and said, "Good for you. Now, you need to hush up and be still...."

Aunt Becky still got on my nerves telling me what to do and I still continued my platonic affair with Elliott. He always gave subtle insinuations about how much he missed me and he knew his relationship with Savannah could never be like ours but he was trying to do the right thing. Before, those comments made me feel as if we were still connected, but then I realized they had become insults and a smack in the face I didn't want. I decided to take Aunt Becky's advice.

True to his word, Elliott continued my salary and some, even though we had broken up. I couldn't believe it, but I really couldn't find a decent job. I did a little temp work to make ends meet and volunteered my other time at church. The sanctuary and Life Center were finally complete after two years of hard work.

Just like Jesse said at the first rally: The devil wants us to separate and go against one another. Some members did become rebellious and leave United

Christians. But the ones who stood the test of time reaped the benefits abundantly. It went so well that the finance committee decided to add a daycare. Jesse and Pastor Lindley wanted my input on every detail of the building. What started out as volunteer work, turned into a full- time position as Director of Education for United Christians pre-school. Through some of my contacts with Banks, Inc., I was able to get the school accredited by the state.

That blessing put me back above water. When the hard times passed and I could finally exhale, I realized it was because I had become focused again and my faith was no longer in a man but in God. It felt good to have survived on my own, like I used to.

Missy didn't party at all now, and I never had anybody to do anything with except walking. She had started walking with me on the weekends. I finally graduated to the steps and I'm looking damn good because of it.

I found myself part of the singles committee at church, planning a Christmas party. It was a big turn out like all of the singles activities. A thousand women, two or three gay men, a few young bucks and Jesse.

He saw me standing to the side while the band played and the gay guys danced with all the women at once. "You look like you're having a good time," he joked.

"I am having a good time. I just get tired of the slim to none selection of men."

"Well, thanks a lot," he said, in a hurt tone of voice.

"Not including you, Jesse," I said, "You know I'm fickle sometimes. Hard to please."

"Fickle is right. But let's not waste this song

standing around talking about your fickleness."

It was a slow song and Jesse was leading me to the dance floor before I could resist. I looked at him, noticing the silky gray around his temples that made him look distinguished, just as his eyes sparkled at me. Out of all the years I had known Jesse, I had never slow danced with him, but it somehow felt very natural. The jazz band sounded good playing Chaka Khans' "Sweet Thing", so I relaxed and nestled my head on his chest.

Before the song ended, Jesse said something that shocked and disappointed me at the same time. "Pretty Baby, If you're looking for a guy like Elliott, I don't know too many good thing men like that. Not only was he good to you, but I always admired the way he took up with your kids."

Jesse told me later, he didn't know why he said that. Must've been blind.

One thing was for certain, I was at peace with myself and I had a joy that couldn't be snatched away this time.

EPILOGUE-seventeen months later

*A*ll the CME members (Christmas, Mother's Day and Easter) squeezed into the church, forcing the ushers to put seats in the aisle. The occasion for this gathering was Mother's Day and oh, what a day it was.

Aunt Becky sat proud on the front row as the youngest of the oldest mothers of the church. She glanced around from time to time spying one family member or another as she rocked and fanned herself, praising the Lord.

Chris was seated in the balcony with a young lady friend of his he had recently met at a youth shut in. He had grown into a very handsome and mature young man, mostly due to his growing landscaping business and the fact that he had saved twenty five hundred dollars and was planning to buy a car. Pretty Baby would never forget the positive impact Elliott left on Chris' life. Elliott's relationship continued with the boys even though he didn't see them as much.

It seems that Jason had taken Chris' place in the puberty crossfire. He always sat in the highest pew of the balcony with his friends. Like today, they laughed and joked until Pretty Baby glanced up from her floor seat and saw one of the ushers scolding them. This usher was known for being very strict, so Pretty Baby knew she didn't have to intervene. She'd get him later.

Dressed in pink lace, Ashley sat next to her mother, digging in her patent leather purse for her pad and pencil to draw pictures while the minister preached.

Missy had started coming to church often after her

Tangled Web

accident. But Becky continued to say she was praying for her, because she was there in body but not in spirit.

The only person missing from this joyous Mother's Day was Pastor Lindley. He had been called away on a family emergency and a visiting Pastor stepped in for him.

He said he was from Memphis and the Pastor of a church with over eight thousand members. He was a dynamic speaker, keeping everyone hanging on his every word. He spoke from the book of Genesis, which told the story of a woman named Tamar, who seduced her father-in-law, resulting in the birth of twins, who were ancestors of Jesus Christ. He called this 'a mess turned into a miracle', which seemed to give the whole church hope and they stood to their feet cheering the Pastor on as he talked about God being a God of restoration.

He ended his sermon by saying, "If a little voice deep down inside of you is asking, 'what must I do to be saved?' Then come. The doors of the church are open."

Jesse and all the other deacons stood with out stretched arms, beckoning any lost souls to come forward while Monique's beautiful voice rang out. Dipping and diving in an operatic overture of 'His Eye Is On The Sparrow'. She had grown into a beautiful young woman. Her teenage years had rid her of some of the baby fat, placing it more in proportion and giving her the glamorous look she had always strived for.

"Don't be intimidated by the crowd," the visiting pastor said as he came into the audience. "Praise God."

No sooner than he said that, the audience applauded the person coming down the aisle. The woman looked elegant in her periwinkle Chanel suit with a matching saucer hat that adorned her head. Tears flooded Pretty Baby's eyes as she raised her hand in praise when she saw it was Missy coming to the altar. She looked back to where she knew she was seated and saw Virgil sitting there crying tears of joy which made Pretty Baby cry harder knowing how much Virgil had always loved Missy, no matter what. The spirit was moving so high as Monique continued to sing, that others came up to join or rededicate their lives.

Aunt Becky stood next to Missy, supporting her every step of the way. Raising her hands to the sky, giving thanks for the child she never gave up on.

Jesse, Brother Dickson and the visiting Pastor broke bread with the congregation in remembrance of Jesus Christ.

Afterwards, before the service was over, Brother Dickson asked to say a few words to the members. He cleared his throat and began, "Members, I know you would all agree with me that it only seems right that we give recognition to one of our own who has been a mother to many of our children." He paused, smiling at the whole church then reached behind the podium and came out with a large bouquet of roses. He handed them to Jesse, catching him by surprise. "Deacon Jesse, I think it only appropriate that you do the honors and present these to your new bride.

Jesse walked down the main aisle to the fourth row and Pretty Baby stood. The church applauded as she accepted the roses from her husband giving him a shy kiss.